I0597976

BLACK DUNGEON MASTERS

Edited By

MARCUS ANTHONY

Herndon, VA

Published in the United States by STARbooks Press

PO Box 711612, Herndon, VA 20171

Many thanks to graphic artist Emma Aldous:
www.arthousepublishing.co.uk

Printed in the United States

Herndon, VA

CONTENTS

AFRAID, WHITE BOY
By Diesel King

You just didn't know, did you white boy? I betcha your punk-ass knows now, huh? Look at me. Look at me, you punk motherfucker! You no good piece of cunt. You fairy-ass cock sucking motherfucker! Do I really look like I give a damn about those crocodile tears streaming down your sweet-looking white boy face? Shed them for all I care. Bawl out, boy! Ain't nobody going to hear you all the way down here anyway! Even if somebody did, nobody in their right mind is going to do shit about it! All they got to do is see me down here with you tied up to know what time it is. Let me make it real simple for you, so there's no misunderstanding whatsoever, cunt. This here is my fucking house! My house, my fucking rules! Okay. Everything I say goes. Is that clear enough for you? I know you are a lot of things, faggot, but being a stupid ass bitch ain't one of them. So I shouldn't have to waste my time or my breath breaking down this elementary shit to your dumb ass. Mr. College-Educated Man. I guess graduate school doesn't prepare you for everything, huh? It sure as hell didn't prepare you for how to survive in the real world. 'Cause I bet in a thousand years the last place you ever expected to live was with your black brother-in-law in his fine-ass house out here in the suburbs. But let me tell you something that you're overpriced education failed to tell you, boy. Real men have to work to get theirs. Got it? They don't get it sitting pretty hoping that the highest paid job will fall into their laps. Maybe if your stank-pussy mama wasn't whoring it up with every hard dick in town, maybe she could've kept your daddy around long enough to teach you a thing or two about manhood. Don't worry, though, boy. Your new Big Black Daddy's here to teach you a few things! First lesson, you unemployed MFA cunt is to write this!

1

Ha, ha, ha! I see you like that lesson, huh? My spit flying right into your mouth!

I won't even lie. It's a beautiful thing to see. It can heal race relations long term.

A black man's hot spit in a white man's mouth. Wow! We've come a long way!

I can't even lie. You look so fucking pretty like that; tied down to the table with that spider gag holding your sweet mouth open like that. It's like your mouth and ass got that 'Come Fuck Me' look. And the way your asshole sinks into the crack like some deep dug out crater, it looks like it has given that look to a few hard dicks over the years 'cause that shit ain't normal wear and tear.

I don't know why the fuck you're tensing up like that. A good experienced white boy bottom like yourself should know that it'll hurt like hell if you fight it. I'm really surprised at you. You're a smart fuck, you know. Even the slowest of fucks can see what's about to go down! Shit, with as much as I'm working with, I know that's the last thing in the world that you'd want to be doing. I know you don't want to be up in some emergency room ass up explaining to a roomful of doctors and nurses that you weren't sent in from state prison as a gang rape victim, but as a common civilian that was working on one big juicy-ass dick to get into your hungry butthole like that. And all I want to do is do the gentlemanly thing and make a new honest woman out of both of your sweet cream-hungry openings.

I mean, just look at it. Just look at it! Thirteen inches! Thirteen inches of rock hard dick for both of your sweet holes! I know, I know. If you were a man, it wouldn't be fair to you. Especially with that little thing you're working with. But lucky for you, you're just a piece of cunt with an enlarged clit that's both doable and fuckable.

What? You think this ain't right? You think this ain't fair? This ain't slavery either, cunt. Your ass ain't gonna just sit up in my house and eat my food while I'm handling my business making this paper without your sweet ass giving me a little something-something in return.

Your sister? What the hell she got to do with this here? Cornbread, please! Fifty-fifty, my ass! That dumb blonde bimbo knows where her bread and butter is, and knowing the bitch like I do, she ain't about let her simple twin brother ruin that for her either! That bitch never had it so good before I came along. The insatiable slut was bouncing from small dick to small dick trying to find her insatiable way home. Then I came along and put her on all this good black dick, and she's been riding it out ever since. Shit yeah, it left those white boys that was used to getting at her with a cheeseburger wanting to form a lynch mob around my black ass. But I can't help that it turned her out, made her a whore for this good black dick. I don't know what I was thinking when I got her ass out of that trailer park, though. It must've been some good liquor and the pussy was twerping just right that night because I damn sure wouldn't have been dumb enough to marry her sober. But I did. I don't regret it, though. She works the dick out like a champ, and in return I showed her ass what running water looks like from indoors. What an electric bill in our name looks like. Shit, I taught her what going to grocery story without food stamps look like. Do you honestly think that bitch wants to go back to the way it was? No cable TV. No central heating and air. Sheet, she'd probably pimp her baby sister out to me to keep it moving. I guess Dear Abigail hadn't gotten around to telling big sis that I'm popping that coochie, too. And that baby growing inside of her womb might've been put up in there by this grand old thirteen-incher.

I don't know why you look so surprise? Do you honestly think that blonde bitch thinks I keep my pants up when I'm out there on the road? I can't pull over to take a leak without finding some cocksucker on my dick. That ain't to say that the blonde bitch don't get mad about it, boy. But all is forgiven when I come home and drop my drawers, and beat this big dick right up in her. It quiets the rumblings. I bet you didn't know that your sis was a pro at giving out brains. She drinks ball juice like those college boys down a keg! The bitch doesn't feel like cooking some times after I feed her. And sometimes I hold back from getting off for a couple of days just to bust a nutt right in her mouth just to clog up her throat. It keeps her quiet for a few minutes longer before she wants to talk about her feelings and shit.

I listen as I wait to reload. When I get tired of that mouth of hers, I just beat the pussy up. Take a little break and then hit it from the back. I don't have to tell you this shit. I know you can hear her from your bedroom down the hall. I make sure that it goes down that way every time I'm up in it. I want to make sure the neighbors know when I'm back at home. Even the folks on the other street know my name the way your sister hollers it out so loudly. You can hear it, can't you? I bet when I'm up in your sister your faggot-ass fingers are up your pussy wishing it was me ripping you open a new one, huh? You probably got a pervert's collection of fake dicks in your room pretend that its black brother-in-law in your bed, huh? Huh! Well, consider this a late birthday gift, then! Hah!

I got a little secret for you, white boy. Of all the freaky positions that I like to get my big dick off in, I love missionary the most. It's simple I know. Not as primal as doggie-style. But it's something about looking down at a piece of fluffy ass that I'm fucking that just does it for me, me watching them take the dick I'm pumping into them take them from extreme pain to guilty pleasure with plenty of priceless expressions in between.

Oh! Oh my! Oh fuck!

I'm telling you all this shit just in case you were wondering why I got you tied down to the table on your back. Why I got your legs bent double. Why I got your knees pointing the rafters with your big toes roped to your inner thighs. I tied down your hands because while I love my back being clawed, I couldn't risk a smart faggot like you trying to escape. You wouldn't have anywhere to run, given that you live upstairs. It just takes the hassle of chasing you around the house for no apparent reason.

Just as I've been gracious enough to open up my home to your broke ass, I've also been gracious enough to put these tit clamps on you. I found them in your bedroom next to the stack of colorful fag comics. You sure got a hard-on for white boys being tied up by big black men, doncha little fella? Shit, it ain't nothing to be ashamed of. It's nice to know that I got more than one option in the house. I can fuck her pretty little mouth and then fuck your pretty little ass whenever I want and don't have to worry about getting another one of your family members knocked up.

How the fuck I know if I pulled on this tit chain like this that you'd get so excited? I've fucked enough fags to know that all of you hate having your clitties touched, but having your titties tugged on is like a direct pipeline to getting your pussies soaking wet. Is yours wet, white boy? I don't mean fucking hungry! I mean whet wet. Whet wet whet wet. Soaking through your pink panties wet. Damn, you just amazingly peed out of your butt hole wet! Wet as in your sweet pussy is shaking and drooling at the thought of this big black man sinking his thirteen inches of meat into it!

I can see the nervousness in your eyes, in your sweet innocent face, boy. Don't be scared. Judging by your hole, you've had your fair share of dick over the years; some big ones, some small ones, some round ones, some square ones, some black ones, some brown ones. I don't have to tell you what kind of slut you've been. You know that better than I ever could. Even with all that experience between your crack, you've never fucked a dick this big. And it's uncut just like you like 'em, with plenty of hanging foreskin. And he's black and he's built like a bulldog and he's a motherfucker cross-country trucker driver on top of that eighteen-wheeler. Oh, shit! I know what your little pussy is trembling about. Will this big dick ruin you for other dicks for the rest of your life? Will it be like one of those cheesy interracial cartoons where after the black man resized your pussy will fucking other white boys still be enjoyable? It didn't bode well for the blonde bimbo. She used to fuck every Confederate flag waving white dick in town, and now her pussy knows the strength of One Black Power. She never thought once of looking back. She now looks at those other white boys as her pussy-bumping equals.

Nah, I can see you don't give a shit about being scared of this dick. You practically welcome the new challenge. If the dick is that good to you, then it'll be well worth it! Sore asshole and all! You're a smart little faggot. You know how to take dick. You're a pro at it just like your sisters and your mama and here mama before her. You've been tied to a bed and been forced to take dick by some of your frat brothers that struck out on date night. Shit, they put a pair of pink stocking on you and you served them up like the frat house cumdump. You were so busy being a ho that you had to take appointments between classes and study hall. No. That ain't what got you scared. Nah, I see it now. I see it clearly now. You're afraid that every dick you've ever taken has brought you to this point. You're afraid that you might do too good of a job with that incredible butt hole. Riding a bunch of regular-sized dicks at once is one thing, but taking one super-sized dick up the butt chute speaks to the sluttishness of your asshole. As you can see I got plenty of inches to satisfy that insatiable hole of yours and then some for the rest of your family. But you're afraid that just like them that you might not ever get enough of this big dick once you get some. Unfortunately, we both know what that means. In plain English, it means that you'll have to compete with your sister and the rest of the world for a place in line for this pipe. You shouldn't be worried about this. You got this! You know how to throw it back! But still, though, you scared.

You're thinking about the next fuck before we even get the first one started. You want to do a good enough job that one day you're hoping that brother-in-law may throw you over his shoulder and put you in the back of his sleeper. You most definitely going to get this dick again, but you want him to take you across the country with him. You'll be his little white cocksucker. You'll be his little white booty boy. Hell, you'll let him pimp you out for pocket change just for the hell of it! You'll do anything he wants you to do, and to show his appreciation you'll stay between his legs while he drive his big rig and let him fill you up with the black man's piss!

Oh, shit! Look at that little pussy twitch that clear water! I've seen fags cum out of their assholes before, but never like this! Damn! There's a fucking famine in Somalia that could used the flow from this water to end it! Man!

I should just run my dick up in there and end your torment right now! But watching the water just flow down your crack is a sight in itself. I don't think a porno has ever shot a shot like this! I've never seen a butt hole come harder than a well-stroked dick! You sure your ass wasn't born with a twofer? Two for one — an asshole that doubles as a proper pussy. I'm just saying. I've gotten ass like you've probably gotten dick, and this is like the new ninth wonder of the world to me.

Man! I can't even lie. I want to ram that pussy so fucking bad! Habit, my man, my bad! Oh, damn! It is really like that! Like that, white boy? It even feels like pussy on my finger … fingers … three fingers … four. Now, ain't this some shit! I got four fucking fingers up in you just like that! Like it ain't nothing. You must be a soaking wet hungry ho. Noooo! Don't take that as a bad thing. Not at all! That's a great thing for a man packing as much meat as I am. I usually got to put in a lot of prep time for somebody to take this big fat dick with some kind of ease. I don't even have to suck your toes or eat you out or fuck you down to get you open like that. I don't even feel any walls in this bitch. It's just a soft wet pillow ready to bring comfort to anyone ready to venture on inside. And it's still pouring wet. Shit! Remind me to get you a bottle of water after were done because I don't want you dehydrated for Round Two. Oh, yeah! There's going to be a Round Two!

Let me pump your hole with these fingers a bit. Let me see what happens. I got an idea. Oh, you like that? I bet you'll get bored before I do. Oh, yeah. I got that stamina, baby! You know that! Yeah, just let it on out. Big Daddy got you covered! Just let Big Daddy know how good his fingers up in your snatch feel to a pussy boy like you. I hadn't forgotten. I'm still going to fuck your sweet little ass after this. I just want to see how much over the edge I can bring you with just my fingers. Just consider it the finger food before the main course.

Oh, yeah. I see you're getting the hang of it, white boy. Just ride those big meaty black fingers to kingdom come! Just think of it as being magically quad-fucked by those small dick frat boys. Oh, you want to think about the boys in the locker room back in high school? No. The coaches? Really? Fine. It's cool. Just ride my fingers like you're getting regular double-fucked by the two coaches. Oh, you can't, huh? My fingers are too big for that? Oh, c'mon now. Consider it a do-over from the first time you got your cherry popped by those two. There you go! Now you know how to ride dick you wished you would've thrown it back harder, huh? Throw it back, sweet cunt, throw it back! Ride those fingers for Big Daddy. Ride like you need Big Daddy up in that sweet pussy like yesterday. There you go. There you go! I knew you serious about riding dick. Keep this up and I'm going to make you shoot with my fingers in your ass. Nah, baby, I'm not talking about those pussy juices that are pruning up my fingers. I'm talking about making your clit come. You don't think I can do it, huh? I ain't got these big hands just because they go well with my big feet. Just throw it on back, white boy. Feel those fingers hit your spot. Bounce that sweet ass back and let it just hit that spot. It's like you got dick up in that hole!

Yeah, you didn't believe me, huh? I can feel your spot tensing up on my fingers because I'm breaking it off so hard. You just like your sisters. Holes wet, hungry for dick. It hurts. Two imaginary dicks ramming your hole hurts, baby? I imagine it would. But think of the real one waiting for a crack at your asshole after you finish up with my fingers.

Go ahead, yell it out!

Not for nothing. I wasn't lying about nobody giving a shit up there. Your sister understands she gets dick down on the regular. She knows you're a fag. She knows that your asshole doubles as pussy. Cunt! Slut! Ho!

There you go! Let that nutt pop, motherfucker!

Damn! That shit shot up like a cannon! Got up about a foot or so and then came back down on you like water ride roller coaster. You caught some in your open mouth? I ain't surprised. You ain't never shot a like a geyser before? If that excites you, then we're going to have some fun. I see that you're going to have a lot of firsts with me, if I got you going with that.

You tired now? What do you mean that was fun? It ain't over! Shit, no! It's just gotten started. I haven't even got my nutt yet. There's something about our little arrangement that I got to get you straight on from here on out. I don't just work a bitch to make her cum. I work a bitch to get my nutt — even if I don't ever let you bust another nutt another day in your natural born life!

But while I got it out of you, let me scoop the remaining nutt off of your white boy body. I'm not normally in the business of playing with another man's busted nutt, but I got some wonderful ideas for it. See, I knew you were a smart little fag! I got some for your mouth and some for that juicy wet asshole, something for you to eat and something to make taking this dick a little bit easier on your backside. Oh, yeah, you're asshole is still flooding with juices, but I pack dick in more ways than one, though.

You're hole is still stretched wide open from my fingers and you still fell that? Damn, baby. Breath, bitch! It's just the tip of my dick playing with the outside of your hole. You don't think you can take it? Too bad, so sad! 'cause it is going in. I worked to damn hard to get this cunt just right for me not to fuck it. It should be an honor to you that I'm going to fuck you raw in your own juices. I got to, white boy. I got to push this dick in.

Just breathe and push out. There you go. You got about an inch of it in you. Now you just got twelve more to go!

Ohhh!

You feel like your asshole is being ripped open, white boy? I only got five inches up in you and I feel them walls player hating like crazy. I thought I got rid of them with all that finger-fucking. I guess my dick is where it at, huh? Oh, shit. I forgot, man. I spent all that time talking about my length that I forgot to mention my width. My length is about thirteen inch, but my width is about eight and a half. Not beer-can thick, but far thicker than your average man!

See, this exactly what I'm talking about! Fucking folks in this missionary position! I can look down at your sweet, sweaty beet red face and see how you truly feel about being posted up on this big dick. You ain't got to open your mouth. Your face says it all! You taking dick is like trying to watch a really soft dude with a tight dry asshole shit out a brick. When I roll through and pop open that sweet second ring up inside of you, it looks like you were trying to pass a kidney stone. And with me popping through that third ring, I can see that is beginning to feel a lot like date rape! The way you kept on losing consciousness and shit. You were out for a minute or so from the immeasurable pain. Don't feel bad, though! Ain't no dick like my dick, partner! I just kept on fucking. And that's just getting into that sweet little pussy hole. You should see the relief written across your pretty little mug when I pulled out just enough to keep the head in. I could feel those walls close around the head my dick. I thought you were going to piss on yourself! That little bitty dribble doesn't really count, though. That post-nutt piss still got to be up in you. I expect that much out of this bladder thumper I got.

Oh, you like me calling it that? You like having this bladder thumper digging you out, huh? Roaming your guts with this big bad bladder thumper? Making sweet love to your intestines with this big-ass bladder thumper? Alright, then! Yeah! Yeah!! Yeah!!! That's what I thought! I know you love this bladder thumper up in you. You want it in you forever don't you? Oh, man! That what I like to hear! Call me Big Daddy! I know with all that metal in your mouth you can't say it right, but I love it just the same. Oh, yeah. You're putting your ass into it. Oh, man. Watch this! See! See! You got that guilty look in your eyes! You know you're supposed to be a man about yours, but you like getting dicked down by another man, a real man to your pussy ass.

Man, I want to bust this nutt right up in your pussy so bad! I want to put these babies up in you and coat your sweet womb. I can't, man. I can't. I need you to drink this fresh baby batter I'm making! I want you to taste your wet-wet on my dick. I want to see you drink Big Daddy's cream straight from the faucet for me. It's got all the protein you need for a well-rounded meal.

Oh, see. You thought I was going to go in for the kill. I know when to pull out. I had to tag that hole long enough to let your ass know that I own it now. I got you so open now you'll be on Jerry Springer in a wig and some fishnets fighting that blonde bitch and Dear Abigail for rights to the dick.

Ah, thank goodness for the spider gag. I want you to stick out your tongue and start tonguing my balls first. I don't want to milk your throat just yet. I want you to suck on those balls like they're your personal pacifiers. Give me a reason to put you on my truck for a run. Suck that ball sac man. Yeah. Sniff them. Lick them. Taste them.

Now open your mouth and shine that pretty big black dick for me good. You like shiny black dick, huh? Ah, thank goodness for that spider gag! You know what you got in your mouth, doncha white boy? You got the taste of your cunt juices on your tongue. That's the funk of your ass right there! Behind that shit is the taste of a dick of a man who works hard for a living. Big black dick that makes sure you got enough to eat when I'm gone. All thirteen inches of it. Suck it! Suck it! Suck it like I know you know you like a big dick in your mouth. Yeah, I know you like it cocksucker. It's what you cock sucking faggots live for! Yeah! Yeah!! Yeah!!! Oh, yeah!!!!

You're doing a good job, white boy, real good job. You're really good at what you do. It's that I got break this nutt straight off in you and I just want to fuck your throat, man. You know how it is, cunt, just another hard dick that just wants to get off. Just relax your throat, boy. Relax your throat. Relax your throat! Lay your tongue flat now, you got it? Just let the dick go in and out of your mouth. Fight the gag reflexes, it is what it is. It's a big dick up in your mouth. I can't help that. Big Daddy is going to feed you that sweet jizz real soon. I'm about to bust this nutt, man! Milk this bull! Spray this cum! Open up that mouth, faggot, and don't spill a motherfucking drop!

Aw, shit! I'm going to nutt off in your faggot ass mouth! Drink my babies, bitch! Take my gotdamn nutt! Drink it! Drink it! Oh, motherfucker, drink it! Oh, yeah! Oh, fuck! Oh, oh, ohhhhhh, fuckkkkkkkk, yeeeaaahHHHHHHHhhhh!!! DRINK IT, YOU COCKSUCKING MOTHERFUCKER!!!

# # # # #

The black man makes eyes with his white brother-in-law from across the table, staring at him like he is some alien from another planet. He can obviously see that he got something on his mind but is afraid to speak up.

The black man was already agitated that after breaking his neck to get home to his sweet young, wife she had to run off this morning to her appointment with the gynecologist, meaning no pussy for him before she left. His only reward for making it home early was to catch his highly educated, unemployed brother-in-law roll out of bed just in time to pour them a bowl of cereal.

The black man could understand if his brother-in-law was striking out in looking for a job, but his wife was on the brink of throwing him out because she suspected that her twin brother was inviting guys over to have sex in their basement. That came as no surprise to the big black man, of course. He's always had a strong feel that his weak-in-the-knees brother-in-law was nothing more than a filthy cocksucker, probably a skilled one at that. Just like some of those that he's come across servicing the glory holes at those dingy truck stops. He didn't mind his brother-in-law being a fag. He was just offended that he could offer strangers online the courtesy he should've been offering him in the first place. He was the one working six to seven days a week to put a roof over his sorry head, too. The least his brother-in-law could've done was part his lips and serviced his dick every now and again, as a way of saying thanks.

The black man eyes his brother-in-law. He likes to watch him tremble thinking that the big black man is about to get him.

"Still can't find a job?" The black man asks as his brother-in-law fumbles with the classifieds.

"No," the white boy sighs.

The black man pauses. "I was thinking. With you not working and me having an extra seat by my side in my truck, maybe a ride out on the open road might be all that you need to clear your head, so you can regroup or refocus or whatever fancy jargon you college boys use. The sleeping arrangement might be tight, but I think we can work something out that could work well for the both of us."

The black man wasn't sure, but he figured that his brother-in-law was one of those white fags that didn't like black dick, but he was going to try to convince him otherwise. And if not, he could think of a few ways to make back his money for all the free room and board he's given his wife's brother over the past nine months.

There was no need to worry about that, the way the white boy had a shit-eating grin, especially about the sleeping arrangements.

"I'm cool with that."

The black man smiles back with his big black thirteen inch dick twitching in his corduroys, just thinking about having that scared white boy tied up with him.

LET THE CHURCH SAY AMEN
By Diesel King

"We church boys got a little freak in us, too, Brother Hercules," preached Brother Willie C. Ammons sternly, between deep intakes of foot funk from out of one of my size thirteen Stacy Adams dress shoes.

I still can't wrap my big head around it, nor can I stress it out even more:

Church was the last place on earth I ever suspected a grown-ass man like me to be snatched up from.

It wasn't being taken like some weak little punk that got my goat, because good logic dictates that the best way to capture your prey is to get them when they're least guarded. But the mere fact that church boys pulled that shit off? Christian goody two-shoes who fall to their knees for Christ? Really?!?!

There I was minding my own freakin' business and standing on my own two big black feet with my wife and kids by mind's side after another long-ass Wednesday night Bible Study when a couple of the brothers skillful separated me from my family with a generous invitation to dinner. I was hesitant to go, but my new bride insisted on it, telling me that I needed to stop being a loner caught between two worlds and walk with the brothers that walk with God.

I was new to this whole church thing after spending the first thirty-eight years of my life dancing to my heathenism. Old habits die hard. I started out way back in my late teens living off of gorgeous women with low self-esteem and for kicks prowled the streets taking the plump asses of some poor queer just because I could. And who in the hell was going to complain looking as phyne as I do? See, I don't think I'm a big sexy motherfucker. It's a fact, standing at six-three, two hundred and thirty pounds of rock-solid muscle with a shiny coal black dome and a menacing scowl across an otherwise strikingly handsome face.

It was only within the last year after the mother of three of my kids threatened to go after me for child support did I decide to get right. I may have married the girl for all the wrong reasons, but I quickly grew fond of being her husband and a real father to my kids, and, in the meanwhile, tried to heed some wisdom by trying to stay on the straight and narrow by going to church with my family.

I already knew going in that they weren't the kind of people that I was used to associating with anyway. I had already accepted and embraced the reality that I was going to be the oddball out of this small tight-knit group of eight or so members. But I was blown out of the water to find out that practically every man in the congregation over the age of twenty-eight was a professional of some sort. Doctors, lawyers, accountants, bankers, policemen, firemen, teachers, athletes, retired athletes turned successful entrepreneurs, etc. It went the gamut of successful career-oriented men. And here I was, a man that spent the better part of my life coasting off of my good looks, now getting my balls sweaty and scratchy as a shade-tree mechanic that hauls junk on the side trying to make a decent living for my family.

So I took one look at these straight-laced churchgoers and knew that they secretly thought that they were better than me with their big fine houses and fancy cars. So I said forget it. I needed to work on getting this family thing right.

But you know how the missus is, a wayward glance at one fine booty walking down the aisle, and she's trying to keep her man in line. And because my wife wasn't stupid enough to believe that she was going to always keep me at home, she was sneaky enough to try and steer me toward a new brand of associates.

"We can't be that bad for a modest guy like you not to want to hang out with a bunch of boring Christian brothers like us, can we Brother Hercules?" asked Brother James Stallworth, a man of medium height with these formidable jaws, after peeling me away from my beautiful wife taking off with my kids in our broke down pickup truck.

I didn't appreciate him putting his arms around my shoulders, but let it go for the sake of argument, seeing that he was my ride to this late night feast and my ride back home after the fact.

The last thing I remember wholly before my evening took its "interesting" turn was getting in the passenger seat of his car. Before I could even make myself comfortable, this mysterious hand appeared reaching around my head and held a faintly damp cloth across my face.

"He's coming to," another voice stated over my shoulder to someone else behind me out my sight, followed by another hard familiar sniff of shoe in the dark room lit by a single bulb over my head. "Man, do you know you got some sweet-smelling feet!"

"Um-hmm," Brother Willie hummed out-sniffing the other man. "Just the right blends of genuine leather and foot funk. It should be bottled up and made into some kind of cologne."

Even though I was wide awake and free to move my mouth, I just couldn't respond. I was too busy biting my bottom lip trying to make sense of the inconceivable sensation getting at the bottom of my feet. It was ticklish yes, but it was something else behind it, too. Something much more salacious as the spot behind my ball sac and in front of my asshole speckled quietly with this ecstatic energy that I never felt before.

I wanted to ride this new feeling, give into it and see what became of it. But I quickly found my senses to overcome it by looking down at my right leg. It was stretched out under this man in a fedora with his arm around my knee slow-stroking his long skinny dick while his other hand made nice with my foot at the bottom of my thin black church socks. I wanted to do everything in my power to tell him to stop but found that the bottom of my other foot was also victim to a similar assault. Except this other guy, who was also in a fedora, was leaning back with his squat dick in hand smothering his face against the arch of my foot.

I went to go swat both of them off just to find that my wrists were bound to the ceiling above by this thick white waxy rope. I was free to kick from my seat on the rocking stool, but with one man having my leg on lock and another having such a sturdy grip on the back of my heel, it proved not to do much good.

"You're not enjoying the pleasures of our company, Brother Hercules?" My ride, Brother James asked timidly, turning his head to show his face behind the hat down my right leg.

I stopped shy of bursting with laughter and mumbling a groan as he steadily worked on my foot even more, and found the even keel to ask, "What the fuck kind of freakin' freak show is this?!"

"Now, now, Brother Hercules," the shoe-sniffing voice from over my shoulder spoke again. "There's absolutely no need to use that kind of language in the House of the Lord."

I was about to say more than that when I felt his strong, well-worked hand come over the collar of my unbuttoned dress shirt and undone tie to my exposed wife beater. He then stopped to make a grab for my beefy left pec before moving his hand further over to my nipple.

With the flurry of sensitive nerves surging through my body with these bags of sensual feelings to boot, my breathing grew shallower knowing that one hard tug of my tit tips could send me over the edge. I was just about cool in playing into their little game when I felt his hard dick charge against my back.

"Get your fucking hands off of me!" I screamed involuntarily.

The guy working on my left foot with his face swiftly mashed the back of my Achilles tendon to the point that a small yelp escaped through my lips.

"What did the brother just finish telling you about using that bad language up in here, Brother Hercules?" The brother barked annoyed.

"I just wanted him to get off of me." I gritted through my teeth.

He let go of the back of my ankle barely accepting that as my apology as he then decided to nibble at the sole of my foot nearest the toes.

The man behind me with his hand over my left pec quickly moved his fingers to play over my left nipple and squeezed it to the point that it felt like a bead of cum escaped out of the head.

"Ohhhhhhrrrrrrrrrr, you shit!" I screamed venomously after the man twisted my nipple even harder.

The man on my left foot was ready to get on me about my cussing again before the man torturing me from behind spoke up.

"Don't worry about Brother Hercules here, Brother George. Back in my playing days, I dealt with a number of nonbelievers that needed the Devil cast out of them. This young buck ain't much different."

Young buck, I thought. The men scattered around me were roughly my age give or take a few years, so it would've been a stretch for any of them to call me a young buck at thirty-nine without some significant age on me.

"That doesn't mean I like it too much, Brother Lee." Brother George voiced angrily.

Brother Lee? Of course, it would be Brother Lee. I shook with both comfort and fear.

Behind being a legendary baseball player from back in the '60s and '70s turned community business leader with his fleet of car dealerships today, the upstanding sixty-two-year-old father and grandfather was the wingman next to Brother James in encouraging my wife to let me run off with them that evening.

In fact, I was almost certain that he was the one that sealed the deal for my naïve bride. And why wouldn't he? He, too, was a hard-ass back in his heyday, with his exploits of multiple orgies and drug binges making the paper before the days of the looming paparazzi. He turned his life around after turning it over to God. As a reward, he looked better than ever in his muscled-out frame donned in crashing waves of black and silver hairs.

He wasn't going to risk his good fortune on a runt like me, was something to the effect that my wife was thinking when she let me go off with these freaks. And with him vowing to keep me out of trouble and onto the straight and narrow was all the assurance she needed not to send her and my kids off to bed.

"Just think about the bigger picture here, Brother George," Brother Lee said, giving another jolting turn to my nipples that almost made me cry out again. "We're here to convert this nonbeliever."

Ultimately, Brother George got back to his nibbling duties on my left foot while his podiatry pal Brother James never missed a beat finding one ticklish spot after another on the bottom of my foot.

Oh, how I fought the urge to give in for about another twenty minutes. But it was hard not to crumble underneath the increased tickling and the extraordinary fingers of Brother Lee going back and forth twisting and pulling on both my poor nipples.

"Yeah, just let it out, son," Brother Lee commented after some time against my moaning like a little bitch. "It's no shame in giving yourself to your fellow brothers of the church."

I didn't know what to make of that last statement. I just went with it.

Like I said before, it was hard not to give in, especially with everybody so highly content with what they were doing that I thought it was just hot having them tie me down and take pleasure in the pleasure they were handing out to me.

"Ohhhh, m-m-man, w-w-hat're-re f-f-f-fff you-u-u do-ing-g-g-g to me? You-r-r drivin-g me crazy-y-y with this sh-sh-sh ... OHHHH!!!" I shuddered between euphoric heaves and raining with sweat fifteen minutes later, once again riding this budding ecstatic energy now throbbing in the inners between my legs.

"I see it took a little less than an hour to break down our newest brother." An anonymous voice lured from the dark corner with heavy footsteps.

In my heavenly bliss, I wrestled with the fact that there had to be at least six other men around me: Brother James and Brother George working on my feet. Brother Willie singing sweet melody snorting the funk out of one shoe while Brother Lee pulled double duty shoe-sniffing the other Stacy Adams and tweaking my nipples with abandon with two other brothers behind him also sniffing shoes and socks like crack heads sniffing lines.

Where exactly this other man come into play or even enter the room completely baffled me. I wasn't too worried, though, assuming that he was a foot freak, too. And with one or the other bound to bust a nutt playing with my feet, I just assumed that he was going to take over where the other one left off.

The mysterious man kept on fooling around behind the shadows before I saw the head of his dick jut into the light. For some odd reason, looking at another dick look at me made me pay attention to my own. Because my hands were bound to the ceiling above and my head was lost in this tailspin of these foot fetish freaks and this weird thing going at the seat of my pants, it didn't even occur to me to look down, where I found my own vein-popping dick straining out of my opened fly with dribbles of nutt juice making its way down to my balls.

I knew this because once I was made aware that my dick was out in the open, I felt the coolness of the room and saw the cinderblocks that made the basement with crosses and church junk scattered about the darkness.

These freaks got me in the basement of the church!

I wasn't so much alarmed by that as I soon was pushed over the edge that one of those married down low freaks unzipped me. When did they do this? What did they do after that? Was that why I had these sensations with my prostate?

I was more than ready to go off on this motherfucker before me, knowing that everyone else was content with my size thirteen feet in one form or another. Even without seeing his face, I knew he was the oddball out, wanting a bit more from me than anything else.

"Who are you?" I asked angrily with his angry dick staring back at me.

The man slowly emerged from the dark shirtless with his dick hanging out of his dress pants. Even with his dress shoes on, he appeared much shorter than I expected with a goatee hanging long off of his chin. Minus the short-trimmed beard, he looked mildly familiar. Not like from the congregation familiar, but like from-time-gone-by familiar.

"Why Brother Hercules, I'm glad you've decided to join us tonight." He said, with his elephant hung and bass voice failing to match his sinewy redbone body.

"It wasn't like I had much of a choice, now did I?" I said.

"Don't you now, Brother Hercules?" He said playing tongue-and-cheek.

"Very funny, what the hell do you want?" I asked, and after I got the words out, I saw that it was the choir director, Brother Quentin Stevens.

I had never seen the man up close before, only just behind the pulpit in his robe with his back turned to the audience directing the wannabe singers.

"Why in the hell you and your dick looking at me like that?"

"Brother Hercules, you know that a phyne brotha like you, have always excited me."

For about a brief second, something clicked in my head that I had dealt with Brother Quentin before this moment. I just couldn't think of where or when or why.

"Always?"

"Don't tell me you've poked around so much with that big ol' thing that you can't remember where you've poked it before."

I looked Brother Stevens over again, coming out of his shoes with someone else coming out of the corner to retrieve them to start inhaling them as well.

"Let me give you a hint: Think back ten years ago to that house on the lake, under the deck."

I thought, but nothing was coming to me. Then, as I was about to ask him to be more specific, old memories came flooding back.

I remembered him well, sweet piece of ass.

He was the first and last piece of ass I ever really spent money on for the purposes of sex. Of course, that was after I tagged that ass a couple of times and he fattened my pockets greatly in return.

I got my hands on him just before his nineteenth birthday off of the chat line. He was one of those frustrated virgins that was desperate for his first sip of dick. So I gave it to him with the mistake of giving him my cell phone number whenever he was in need of a sexual fix. Like most young bucks with their noses wide open, he took that to mean that I was now the new man in his life. Maintaining my cool through his incessant calling, I thought I would push the envelope by soliciting him as the star bottom for a couple of threesomes and foursomes. In which he did.

With my then-girlfriend away on a long business trip, I got a hold of her credit card, took out a cash advance and transferred the money over to my account, and went on an online shopping spree at this local leather store where I bought these matching sets of hand and ankle restraints. I honestly had no particular deviants in mind when I ordered, other than I thought they looked cool. However, one lonely weekend at the lake house with a then-short and stout nineteen-year-old that didn't know how to take a hint, I got him in the restrains and hung him upside down under the deck. And with the help of a few paying "friends" and a few jars of Vaseline, we just decided to have a little fun that last a bit shy of seventy-two hours.

The hungry bitch acted like he didn't want it at first, squealing and crying. But he definitely got into it after I opened him up real good. He loved getting his ass plowed so much that he had the time of his life holding back all of the nutt draining out of his gapping little butt hole.

I almost forgot about the spider gag we slapped in his mouth and started face-fucking the poor sap like it was before we got the brilliant idea of using his mouth like a urinal, so we didn't have to miss our turn using his ass.

"You know why you're here, right?" Brother Quentin asked, much more muscular and leaner than the plump teenager I fucked all those years ago.

"I guess it's my turn, huh?" I asked more like a man, more than ready to repent for my sins as I tried to suppress this need to laugh.

I wasn't in the business of getting my shit pushed back in, but quickly understood that this wasn't my revenge, and I wasn't about to offer any apologies for helping him find his way to these freaks around me.

"No, my brother, I've turned the other cheek because you and I have found our path to this place. Even though, I still have to live with the remnants of that weekend."

He stepped out of his pants to reveal a harness in the place where his underwear should've been, and when he went to take it off, a long slender butt plug with about five different ridges was exposed.

"Damn," I mouthed through the need to laugh with my feet become the most sensitive with every touch through the socks.

"You see, Brother Hercules," Brother Quentin said approaching me. "You're right what you said to me about our first night together."

I wanted to ask what that was, but I was sure that he was going to tell me.

"Once a boy like me gets a taste of some good hard dick and cum," he said, taking his finger against my runny dick and putting its gooey contents in his mouth. "We'll come back for it again and again."

"If you wanted some dick all you had to do was ask for it."

"And what, let you invite your so-called friends over when I can easily have the backs of my brothers here that are equally as fond of you as I am?"

I have to give Brother Quentin some credit, he was right. The "friends" I got to fuck him were just anonymous bums that I picked off of the chat line whereas his brothers were crème de la crème of the community.

"Well, then, I know you see a hard dick in front of you, so why don't you get on your knees to it?"

"Oh, Brother Hercules," he smiled after he kissed me on the side of my lips. "I see you're still trying to run this show."

I must say that I was still a hair confused. I didn't have time to form a question before Brother James stopped with my right foot, reached over to my chest and snatched the tie from around my collar.

25

"Oh, yeah," he huffed. "I'm about to blow this nutt!"

A few seconds later, Brother James gave out this loud grunted and shot this super sperm that leapt in the air and over to where his bare feet were tucked nearby. He then proceeded to use my tie to wipe away the nutt dripping onto his hand and the bit that got on his feet and dress pants.

"That's a tie from the Donald Trump Collection!" I said a bit teed, with a nice little payday going down the drain.

"I'll get you a new one, you crybaby," he said, discarding my tie and my foot and the leg it was attached to like a used toilet tissue and got up from his seat on the floor. "I'll be upstairs, if you need me."

With my ride making his exit, Brother George over there nibbling on my left foot, stopped with the foot play, too. He reached up for my calf, pulled off my sock, and with his firm grip steady on my foot decided that his hand wasn't enough and decided to put his dick between my big toe and second toe and started fucking the opening like it was pussy.

"Don't you dare, fuck," I said, listening to him grunt like he was about to come.

"What I tell you about that cussing up in here, Brother Hercules?" He asked going for the back of my heel again.

My toes were getting sore the way he was forcing them apart with his stubby little monster. I was just used to his velvety skin against my sandpaper feet when Brother Lee tossed Brother Willie my other shoe and started twirling both nipples simultaneously.

"Oh, what the hell are you trying to do to me?" I asked of Brother Lee looking Brother Quentin in the eyes, leaking with more nutt.

"Don't you know by now, Brother Hercules? Brother Lee said it best earlier. We're making sure that you give of yourself to your fellow brothers."

I still wasn't quite following, and then I felt the swelling of a dick between my toes and heard the gripe of a mad man before I felt a hot cream stingingly soak the front of my leg and the top of my foot.

"Oh, that's just disgusting!" I mouthed, feeling like some used piece of foot-ass left to do the walk of shame.

I had just barely a second to sulk in my revulsion before Brother Quentin grabbed my pants leg and shucked them off me.

"What?" I said, believing Brother Quentin when he said he had turned the other cheek.

Brother Lee worked on my nipples again, causing another surge of pleasurable jolts, and when I came back to I found a warm mouth working on my dick.

Brother Quentin teased me playfully by running his long tongue and full lips up and down the length of my shaft, and soon hungrily went for it. He proved himself a little too eager in the beginning, trying to take down the entire length with no thoughts to his gag reflexes. He had to keep them in check a few times over. Overall, however, he turned out to be a great cocksucker. No teeth whatsoever, scraping the sides of my fat dick along with the rare ability to breathe through his nose with no need to disengage. I felt my balls working overtime aching to unleash, but I wasn't ready. Not ready. Not yet.

As I thought my evening couldn't take any more of an unusual turn, Brother Willie still sniffing my shoe came to the side of me and decided that my pubes was the best place to squirt his load. It burned hot like hell, and I was getting ready to cuss him out when he quickly did the oddest thing. Instead of getting his gunk off of me, he got some kind of cloth and wiped down my foot from where Brother George had come and decided to put back on my sock and shoes, telling me to keep on making that sweet foot funk. All the while he was doing this the other two came simultaneously.

"Leave me be with the young brother." Brother Lee warned those three, leaving Brother Quentin working on my dick.

They went upstairs, and probably no later than five seconds later, I felt the hard dick charging against my back make its way over to my side before I saw it jutting out underneath my arm. For the first time since everything got started I got scared, even more when Brother Lee decided to climb up on the rungs of my stool to present his foreskin dick in my face. It didn't take a rocket scientist to know what he wanted, and to that I called it "blasphemous" citing that we were in the "House of the Lord" where he wanted me to perform a vile act.

"I don't know about you, Brother Hercules, but I like to freak my woman in a bed, and we ain't lying down." Brother Lee growled, slapping my face with his hefty dick underneath his big belly. "It's called respecting your elder brother ... just like I'm respectin' you." He said taking a hard sniff of my shoe again and then shoving it under my nose.

I was reluctant to do such a thing, but I was desperate to breath. Even though it smelt like leather and feet to me, my foot funk wasn't so bad. It wasn't all that good either, but it wasn't all that bad either.

"Inhale deep," Brother Lee mouthed jerking his dick. And after I obliged him, he took the shoe back under his nose.

He switched from me to him to me again before he put it back under his nose, rubbing his precummy dick on my lips and then spewed like a deluge on the side of my neck.

It burned hot like fuck, which sent a major jolt down my spine to my penis engulfed in the warm mouth taking care of it.

"Ohhh, you Bible-thumpin' mofos! I hate you! I-I hate you!! I-I-I h-h-h-hate all of yyyoooouuuuuuu no good mmmoooffffooosss!!! Ahhhh!!!!" I moaned sucking my teeth and then grunted fervently as I felt this heavenly experience wash over me with all my demons leaving my body as a boatload of cum shooting into Brother Quentin's ready mouth, soulfully swallowing every drop.

I passed out immediately thereafter, drained of all of my common and uncommon senses.

When I came back to, I was laid out on the swing cleaned and dressed under the porch light in front of my house. As I made it over to the front door, I found myself quite excited about the Sunday coming up because I was ready to let the church say amen!

ETHIOPIAN ADVENTURE
By Jay Starre

Sweat poured from Max Downing's brow as the rope fastened around his chest and under his butt tugged in a jerking rise against the steep wall of the cliff in front of him. He dared not look down. The dizzying height of the mountain citadel was daunting enough when viewed from below. He didn't want to think about how far it was to the ground where his friend and expeditionary partner, Donald Grant, watched and waited for his turn to ascend the sheer cliffs.

Their expedition into the remoteness of Africa's eastern highlands into the mysterious land called Ethiopia had taken two brutal months in late 1885 to culminate in this discovery. Their guide, the young Somali Tata had led them here with the promise they would meet a prince of the land, Melchior.

The pair of American adventurers were best of friends but hardly two of a kind. Max was sandy-haired, hazel-eyed and boasted a peachy-smooth complexion. Slender and rather short, he looked younger than his twenty-five years. Donald was a massive man, with broad shoulders and beefy arms and thighs. His dark hair was thick and unruly, while his trimmed beard surrounded a pouting mouth that often was set in a smirk. He was sometimes arrogant. His blue eyes were quite striking against his deep tan. He was only a year older than his partner but looked much more mature.

In the end though, it was the arrogant and husky Donald who whimpered and begged, not Max. It was Donald's big beefy ass that suffered the most punishment, the deepest probing and the most gut-churning stretch. When the laughing Ethiopian Prince who at first feasted them, turned to more lusty pursuits with the

Americans as his prey, it was Max who was first to submit, and readily so. It took Donald longer to surrender.

Max exhaled a gasp of relief as he arrived at the lip of the mountain top and was pulled up and over to lie flat on his belly on solid ground. There to raise him to his feet was none other than Prince Melchior himself.

The Ethiopian was a giant. When he lifted the young American up, it was as if he was light as a feather in the grip of the mightily-muscled nobleman. He laughed, a booming rumble that set Max's entire body vibrating as the Prince hugged him tight.

Tata, the first to ascend, stood at the side and translated as the giant babbled in his native tongue. "Prince Melchior bids you and your handsome friend a hearty welcome to his humble abode. He has a feast prepared."

Releasing Max, the Prince beamed down at him with the most amazing smile. A truly enormous mouth gaped open. Plump lips surrounded the whitest teeth. Amidst those white teeth, a pair of gold ones glittered on either edge of the top row.

Gold! It was rumored gold could be found in these remote highlands, and perhaps this was a sign it was true. On closer inspection, Max noted more evidence of the precious metal about the Prince's body. Dressed in a shimmering gown of multi-colored wool that fell to just above his knees, his obsidian limbs were bare in all their spectacular muscularity. Glittering at each wrist were at least a dozen bracelets of more gold! More of the precious metal adorned his ankles, while a pair of incredibly thick bands even encased his upper arm above the bulging biceps.

While Max gazed in awe at the man, his partner was raised up by rope to join him. According to Tata, this was the only way to reach the isolated mountain castle. Donald arrived breathless and flushed, but also with a bright grin plastered over his face. He was certainly the most adventurous of the pair, and usually the one to lead them into the most exciting, and often most dangerous situations.

He, too, suffered that mighty bear hug, and he, too, noted with greedy eyes the gold that adorned the black prince. But they had little time to stand and gawk as Melchior immediately ushered them into his mountain citadel.

It was a remarkable structure. Seemingly carved right out of the mountainside, it reared up under the eaves of an even higher cliff. On the plateau at its feet, lush gardens of fruit and vegetables were being tended by dozens of black attendants. All men, and all naked!

They paused as the group passed and bowed deferentially to the Prince, but also smiled and waved while jabbering and gesturing at the pale strangers.

"They look well-fed and fit. This Prince doesn't seem a mean-spirited man," Max whispered to Donald at his side.

"And rich as Croesus, I'll wager. I intend on doing my damndest to leave with some of his riches in my pouch!"

Max felt the first inkling of trouble ahead on hearing those words. Donald was rarely patient enough to allow events to unfold. More likely, he'd jump the gun in every circumstance.

His misgivings were only increased as he noted the hand Prince Melchior used to caress their guide's short nap of dark curls as they walked ahead side-by-side into the citadel. It was both affectionate and seemingly familiar. How could that be? Tata had claimed he was leading them to this isolated location not from personal knowledge, but from information provided by others.

Perhaps the Prince was merely an affectionate person, he reasoned. As they were led into a broad hall, it did appear this might be the case when a number of other servants scurried up to him and were equally caressed and some even embraced.

"Naked as the day they were born, every damn one," Donald whispered to Max.

It was true. It appeared of the dozens of denizens they had so far confronted, all but Prince Melchior chose to wear no clothing. It was a hot and humid environment, so perhaps there was good reason behind the oddity.

A low wooden table, made of a single enormous slab of some exotic tree, graced the center of the chamber. On it, a feast was piled high. Brightly-colored cushions surrounded the low table, and they were seated across from the Prince himself while Tata faced them at his side, serving as translator.

The food was delicious, though some of it was strange to their palate. Fruits they had never seen or heard of were offered up, while vegetables cooked in exotic spices were an adventure to sample. The meats were familiar; fish from the stream below, fowl they recognized for the most part, and goat and antelope roasted to crispy tenderness.

The honey-sweetened fruit drink was spicy and proved to be slightly intoxicating. Donald suffered the effects almost immediately and began to pepper their host with a barrage of questions.

Max sat silent as he listened with keen ears and gazed about with keen eyes. The room was large but sparely furnished. The walls were all of a grey granite and obviously carved right from the mountain itself. A work of incredible will and patience, it seemed to him.

There were a few woolen hangings scattered here and there, all splashed with glorious color. A few wooden chests were placed in the corners, and a pair of large pots contained flowering herbs. Notably, the chests were hinged and banded with bright gold, while the pots were trimmed with broad strips of the same.

And every plate and platter, every knife and spoon, every cup and bowl, all were made of gold!

Donald had to be aware of all that gold himself, but at first didn't mention it as he asked his bold questions and Tata translated.

"There are only men here in the citadel because this is a holy site, and only men may enter. Everyone here is a priest serving the Prince, who himself is also a priest," Tata explained

The slender guide continued to translate Melchior's replies as the Prince emitted a lusty roar of a belly laugh after every question and offered up his toothy grin. It was easy to tell this priestly prince enjoyed life and all its pleasures.

"The Prince rarely allows visitors to ascend to his palace, but in your case, he recognized men who might share common interests. Perhaps they could exchange knowledge, or other more tangible gifts."

Donald seized on the opportunity provided by Melchior's words to mention the gold.

"And what could we offer in exchange for some of this?"

The half-drunk American raised a golden bowl he'd just licked clean.

The Prince raised a dark brow and offered a radiant smile as he replied. Tata translated.

"Come, White Adventurers. I will give you the gold you crave, after you give me what I crave."

He rose on the instant and beckoned for the pair to follow. Donald leapt to his feet with a smile and tugged on Max's arm to lift him up. The sandy-haired American was more reluctant than his partner to accept the Prince's offer at face value. He guessed that behind the big smile and hearty laugh beat a shrewd and lusty heart. He recognized these deeper, hidden lusts because he knew someone who shared an identical greed for life — and that was his friend and fellow adventurer, Donald.

But it was too late to back out, he believed. As well, he found himself intrigued by the Prince's rather vague offer. As they followed the giant black, he also found himself experiencing a sensual stirring in his loins. The regal stride, both confident and jaunty, was exceedingly masculine and potent. The man was exotically gorgeous. Max found himself imagining what lay beneath that colorful robe. The ass globes outlined by the clinging garment rolled along with powerful purpose. Max felt certain that between those globes, a pair of balls swung free, no doubt full to bursting with juicy seed. And a man of that tremendous size must also sport a prick to match!

Even fantasizing about the naked charms of their host, Max was able to note their surroundings as they passed through a number of rooms on their way to what Donald whispered must be the Prince's treasure chamber. All the apartments were lightly furnished, although the tables, chests, pots and benches were all of great yet simple beauty. Gold adorned every piece.

They eventually came to a room barred by a massive door. Gold padlocks barred entrance, and Donald at his side let out a huge gasp of anticipation as he squeezed his partner's arm with a shaking hand.

A servant unlocked the door and pushed it open, grinning up at the Prince as he led them inside.

What awaited them was indeed a treasure trove of gold. But not in the form of coin or ingot, or even of cup or other bauble. In fact the gold that glittered in that room was fashioned into what seemed at first to be objects of puzzling purpose. There were just two of these odd furnishings. One perhaps might be described as a chair, and the other a bench, both adorned liberally with glittering gold.

The chair was a rather simple piece of furniture once Max looked at it carefully. A smooth piece of thick animal hide which had been dyed brilliant yellow was suspended by chains from the ceiling. It was a kind of sling, which one might lie back on, he guessed. The chains themselves appeared to be of pure gold. Peering closer, he gasped as he noted the four chains suspending the sling each boasted a golden shackle! He shuddered as his imagination offered up a grim picture of how those shackles might be employed upon the occupant of that chair.

In a bid to rid his mind of that daunting vision, he turned his attention to second piece of furniture. The bench was fashioned into an exquisite semblance of a horse. Four legs carved of a golden-hued jungle wood held up a cylindrical body covered in a smooth animal hide dyed in the same yellow color as the sling. A horse's head was carved in the front, but it was lowered down between the fore-legs in a gesture of submission. The bench sat upon a low, wheeled platform. Gold gleamed everywhere on the bench, from the wheels of the platform to its flat surface, while gold bands encircled all four legs and the neck of the bowed head.

Each of the horse's legs included a golden shackle.

"Prince Melchior offers you gold in exchange for submission."

Tata's translation of the black prince's booming words snapped Max's attention back to their host. He mouth dropped open at what he saw.

The giant had discarded his robe. Other than his golden jewelry, he was naked.

Not only was he naked and grinning lustily, one of his big hands rubbed an erect prick that was truly monstrous in size. Max had never seen the like. The size itself was practically inhuman in its dimensions. It reached upward in a wicked curve to his navel, while the girth of the shaft had to be thrice a normal man's. But it was the gold adorning it that had Max shuddering in shock.

A huge gold ring was embedded in the black crown!

"What damned foolishness is this? We refuse! Let us the hell out of here!" Donald, as quick-tempered as ever and more than a little inebriated, had shouted that defiant reply.

The Prince continued beaming and pumping his enormous prick with one hand as he gestured at his servants with the other. Two of the naked blacks ran forward toward the opposite wall.

A floor-length curtain ran all along it. Jade-green wool glittered with gold thread. In itself the curtain had to be worth a fortune just because of all that gold thread. The pair tore back the curtains to reveal a bright blue sky.

Max felt certain he knew what lay beyond that opening. Fearfully, he stepped forward to peer out over the edge.

Plunging cliffs and the sparkling stream where their porters camped lay far below — that exit was certain death! Donald was at his side gasping as he shared that gut-churning view. Behind them. Melchior spoke and Tata translated.

"You want your freedom? There is your freedom. Go."

Quailing at the prospect, the pair turned to face their host. Max dared look into the giant Ethiopian's eyes. The dark pools gleamed with dangerous lust, no question about that. But the young American detected no cruelty in those eyes, nor in the broad smile and regal stance.

As well, there were four quite strong-looking servants besides the gigantic prince to contend with if they dared engage in a fight. They'd been told to leave behind their weapons when they made the ascent to the citadel, but neither had obeyed completely. Each had a sharp dagger sequestered in one of their boots.

Max dropped his eyes to the Prince's crotch once more. He shuddered as he stared at that monster pole jutting upwards. Even so, he made up his mind.

"We'll take your gold then. Do what you damn well please with us in the meantime."

He stepped forward, kicking off his boots and tearing off his shirt. His hat, suspenders and trousers followed as Donald stood speechless beside him. He slipped off his under drawers and was now as naked as the Prince and his servants.

His pink cock betrayed him. It leaped to attention, bobbing and beginning to drip. He didn't care. He was ready for whatever happened — at least he hoped so!

With a pleased smile, Melchior nodded and gestured toward the sling. Max understood. He stepped up to it, very conscious of his bouncing prick and bare ass, and climbed up onto it. Two servants moved in to help him.

He was turned onto his back immediately and spread-eagled. His ankles and wrists were raised up and locked within the golden cuffs. Before he could even take a breath and assess his new situation, another servant scurried in to stand between his splayed thighs and secure a lewd cup over his crotch. It was solid gold and fit over his cock and balls to trap them against his body. Straps of yellow leather fastened it around his waist and ass-cheeks.

Staring down at his belly, he could no longer see his own privates. In their place remained only that gleaming gold cup. He gasped and shuddered. It seemed he was effectively emasculated!

Arms and legs high in the air, his pale ass gaped apart, leaving his tender asshole on display, and totally vulnerable. He dared a glance at his friend.

Donald was fuming. That was no surprise — but he was also stripping! What else could he do? His cohort had already capitulated to the mad prince's demands. He had to go along now, but he was also snatching furtive looks at all that glittering gold. His greed most likely matched or exceeded his chagrin.

The minute he was naked, equally naked servants took him by the arms and led him toward the other lewd furnishing the room contained. The horse bench.

Max noted that his friend's fat cock had swollen slightly as it swayed between his hefty thighs on his march toward that bench and his fate. It didn't rear and dribble like Max's had, or like the rest of the room's occupants. Even Tata stroked an erect prick, having apparently been ordered by Melchior to remove his own drawers.

Donald offered one final gesture of defiance just before he was placed face down over that bench. He threw off the servants' hands and glared at the black prince. "Damn you to hell," he blustered.

Tata kept his mouth shut, not daring to translate. The dark-haired American knelt over the bench with a scowl but otherwise allowed the naked servants to quickly seize his hands and feet and shackle them to the horse's hoofed feet. Then, instead of cupping Donald's privates as they'd done to his slim partner's, they bolted on a lewd kind of golden tube at the base of his cock which served to stretch downward on his ball-sack. The heavy gold ball-stretcher looked altogether ludicrous as it caused his cock and balls to dangle downward between his beefy ass-cheeks along the rear of the horse.

Max flushed as he experienced a debased sensual thrill to see his powerful friend so bound and helpless. His own position, just as helpless and vulnerable, elicited a matching thrill. Now that he had the Americans at his mercy, what would the leering prince do with them?

First, it seemed it would be Max's duty to watch his friend's degradation. Melchior moved in behind Donald and seized his burly ass-cheeks. The massive black hands gripped those pale mounds and used them to swivel the horse around so that its backside now faced Max in his sling. The sandy-haired American was offered a perfect view of his partner's ass.

With that mighty prick rearing up between his thighs, Max fully expected to see his friend gored on the instant and shuddered at the thought. But that was not what the Prince planned. Instead he fell to his knees, hands still spread across the white adventurer's large buttocks, and buried his face in the parted crack.

Max gasped in disbelief. The handsome black face crammed between his friend's rearing white butt mounds. That enormous mouth opened wide to attach itself to the puckered pink hole between them.

"Stop! Get your big damned tongue out of my ass! Stop, I say! What are you doing to me? Damn it all! Stop! Oh God ... please stop!"

Donald's shouted demands degenerated almost instantly into a whimpering plea. His ass quivered and squirmed, but there was no way he could escape that mouth and the tongue apparently twirling deep into his snug anus. The lewd sounds of Melchior's smacking lips and licking tongue only added to the depravity of the moment, and Max felt his own asshole quake and pout in empathy.

He didn't expect at all what Melchior next did. Maneuvering the wheeled bench by his hands planted firmly on Donald's chunky white butt, he spun it around and shoved it forward. Right between Max's legs!

The dark mouth rose from its wet feast and grinned up into the young American's startled hazel eyes. Those plump lips glistened with spittle. The big tongue wagged as it flicked out before he spoke.

Tata translated the lewd remark. "We shall ensure your friend cannot continue with his unmanly protests. He shall feast on your delicious ass as I feast on his!"

With that, the bench was shoved farther forward as two obedient servants stepped in to seize Donald about the head and force his face into Max's splayed ass. His mouth, open wide as he offered a blubbering protest, was pressed directly against his partner's pink pucker.

Max gasped aloud. Donald's lips continued to move around as he fought to speak, which only caused them to caress and tickle his friend's vulnerable ass-lips. At the same time, the giant prince winked one big brown eye, licked his plump lips, and descended back into Donald's ass for more lusty slurping.

41

The shackled American gawked in awe as he witnessed the depraved scene. The mighty prince was on his knees with his dark face buried in that husky white ass, his dark pate shaved to a gleaming smoothness, his loud smacks both lewd and thrilling.

Two naked servants held Donald's head against Max's own trembling ass. Their black pricks reared up on either side of his dark locks and dribbled precum all over his bull neck. His powerful body was draped over that horse and shackled helplessly. His eyes were closed, as if in denial of the experience.

It was altogether unbelievable. But it only got more incredible. Of course he himself was shackled in place but could move somewhat if he tried. The lips of his partner on his tender asshole were driving him crazy, and almost without thought, he began to rear into that mouth, straining against his ankle shackles and pushing his ass forward.

It must have all proved too much for Donald. All at once, his beefy ass began to wriggle and rear. Then, he began to lick at Max's hole, then he even began to dig into it with a probing tongue!

The change did not go unnoticed by the Prince. He responded to the wriggling ass in his hands by rearing up out of that pale crack and grinning before diving back in with big tongue out. He stabbed at the wet hole, sucked loudly on it, pulled out and spit on it, then attacked it again with loud slurps. He even raised a palm and smacked that beefy butt as he ate out the American's defenseless anus.

The loud smacking of black palm on white ass resounded in the chamber along with the nasty slurps of both Ethiopian and adventurer. Max squirmed himself as lips and tongue assaulted his own asshole, and he watched the black prince root in his friend's wriggling butt.

With a final smack to those jerking buttocks, Melchior all at once stood up. Coming to his full regal height, he towered over the bound Americans. Max's eyes dropped to the black's crotch, where that mighty prick reared.

The crown glistened with a sheen of gooey precum. The gold ring embedded in it also shimmered with slippery ooze. The curved tool bobbed eagerly and dribbled out more juicy seed. It was a fascinating and daunting sight.

The servants apparently knew their master's mind. Two scurried over to present him with a golden bowl he immediately dipped his fingers into and scooped out some kind of white paste. He used the stuff to lubricate his rearing prick as he stared directly at Max and grinned wickedly.

Max shuddered from head to toe. Tongue still twirled into his asshole as his partner continued to obey the prince's command while unaware of what threat reared above his well-eaten ass.

The black pole was completely coated with the slippery paste. One of the servants took hold of the thick base and pulled it downward so the curved tip now aimed directly at Donald's vulnerable asshole.

Max trembled and bit his lip in fascinated anticipation as the flared crown settled against that hole, golden ring and all. It was now that Donald felt what was coming for the first time. What would he do? What could he do?

Again the Prince and the American locked eyes. With his mighty prick poised to do its worst, there passed between the pair a moment of intense understanding. The Prince did not employ sword nor gun to insure his power over others. It was this prick, in all its glory, that was his weapon of domination.

He grinned and licked his fat lips as he began to dominate Max's bound partner with that very weapon. Of course the dark-haired American's powerful body was shackled in place and there was no possibility of resistance. But there was still a choice to be made.

Would he fight against the savage intrusion? That course would be futile, and even though he gurgled loudly against Max's hole as the black servants held his face there, it was immediately apparent what path he chose to take.

His husky buttocks all at once reared upward. His straining pink ass-lips blossomed outward in a sudden gulping. The massive black knob, including the glittering gold ring, were swallowed whole.

Max found himself fighting back hysterical laughter. His greedy partner now had the gold he craved — up his ass!

Melchior may have thought the same. He threw back his head and laughed. The lusty boom echoed up into the ceiling and out the open wall into the African skies. Perhaps they even heard it below in the Americans' camp — and wondered.

The Prince, Max believed, was not interested in pain. He was interested in submission. And now that his prey had indeed submitted, his gaping asshole obscene proof of this, he immediately yanked back control.

He began to fuck the hapless American.

Max was spell-bound. The dark prince towered over his captives. His obsidian flesh gleamed, set off by the bands of yellow gold at wrist, ankle and biceps. His gigantic black paws squeezed and kneaded the plump white ass at his mercy. His prick's lengthy curve slithered in and out in a rapid pummeling as he planted it deeper with every brutal thrust.

In his sling with his feet in the air and his own ass as vulnerable as his partner's, Max could only imagine how it felt to be gored so relentlessly and profoundly by that monstrous prick. His asshole pouted outward in empathy while Donald seemed to have only one outlet for his own aggression. He stabbed at his friend's pink hole with a long tongue, twisting inside and probing for his prostate. He sucked the tender ass-lips inside out, then stabbed even deeper with his tongue.

Meanwhile that curved black scimitar ravaged Donald's hole. The gooey paste shone over the dark prick as it slammed in and out, but that was not enough for the Prince. He nodded to his servants who stepped in to apply more of the paste.

Donald's entire heaving buttocks were now coated with the white stuff.

The Prince ran his giant hands all over that ass, sliding in the paste, rubbing it into the parted crack and even lower down over the gold-strapped cock and balls dangling below. He maintained the vigorous pace of his rear-plowing, but then all at once used those big hands to swivel the horse around.

Donald's mouth was pulled out of Max's ass. In its place, a big black hand settled over his spit-wet crack. The Prince's greasy fingers found his tender asshole and began to fondle it!

Gasping at the feel of those slippery digits toying with his puckered ass-lips, his eyes dropped down to gaze at the new view of Donald's butt now suddenly offered. He could see it from the side, and the oozing hole was clearly visible. The black prick sliding in and out was perfectly on view as well. Out came the slippery head, massive and blunt, along with that huge gold ring embedded in it. Although not in the fashion he'd hoped for, Donald was getting the gold he craved — stuffed up his ass with every plunge of that curved black tool.

Below that squishing stab of prick in hole, Donald's own cock and balls were visible.

The ball stretcher pulled his sack away from the base of his prick and had caused them to swell into large pink orbs. That was a lewd enough sight, but what surprised Max the most, was the state of his friend's pink cock. It was swollen, too, so stiff it looked twice its normal size. It leaked against the yellow wood of the horse's behind.

More surprising yet, were the words that came out of his friend's mouth now that he could finally speak.

"Oh please! Fuck my poor ass! Fuck it hard! Fuck it deep! Drive it into me! Please. Ohhhhh, please!"

Shocked to the core, Max was not prepared for the next sensation he experienced. A finger slid past his quivering ass-lips and thrust deep inside. He groaned and reared as that finger began to twist and dig.

Looking down at his own pale belly, he couldn't see his cock and balls, trapped within the golden jock-strap, nor could he touch or feel them. With his feet high in the air, his ass was wide open and his hole gaping between his raised thighs. A dark finger was buried inside, coated with slippery paste.

Without any ability to see or touch or feel his cock and balls, Max was left with only the sensations of his asshole to occupy and thrill his tumultuous thoughts. As he gazed downward and watched his friend's heaving ass take the vigorous ass-pounding from that obsidian prick, another finger slid into him.

The pair of fingers together created a huge and insistent column of gut-probing heat. They wriggled and stabbed. They found his prostate and massaged it relentlessly. They pulled out and rubbed all over his distended, pasty ass-lips. They drove him wild.

He realized he was blubbering along with his partner. The Americans had fallen totally into the Prince's dark thrall, whining, whimpering, and pleading for his attentions.

It seemed it was enough for Melchior. With a booming laugh, he pulled out his massive prick and sprayed. Aiming first at Donald's heaving ass, he splattered it with gooey jets, then turning to the side, he sprayed Max's splayed pink ass-cheeks.

Still laughing, he crammed not two, but four huge fingers into Donald's battered asshole while he continued to root deeply into Max's with his other two.

Max nearly swooned as he felt orgasm seize him. His cock, trapped inside that golden cup, spurted. And Donald's cock also spewed, a stream of gooey juice spraying down the legs of the golden horse he straddled.

Melchior's laughter followed him out of the chamber as he abandoned his prey, holes gaping and cocks dripping.

"Wait! Our gold! Release us Prince Melchior," Donald cried after him.

The door slammed shut, and they were left alone, not even Tata remaining behind.

Max had to wonder what part their guide played in all this. He seemed altogether too willing to go along with Prince Melchior's instructions, no matter what they entailed.

Even as he wondered, the door that had slammed shut with such finality was again opened. Tata!

"Help us, damn you! This depraved prince intends on abusing us again if my guess is correct. And he won't be parting with any of his damn gold either!"

As he ranted, Donald remained shackled on his belly over the horse. Between his hefty buttocks, his hole was rosy pink from its recent use, swollen open and oozing paste. It was almost laughable to hear him complaining about being cheated out of his gold.

Tata put his fingers to his lips to indicate silence, then swiftly unlocked the cuffs around Donald's ankles and wrists. He speedily performed the same service for Max. The sandy-haired American was quick to snatch up his discarded clothing and dress, but Donald paused long enough to unfasten all four golden cuffs at the horse's feet and stash them in his pockets.

"Hurry," Tata urged in a loud whisper.

Donald threw on his clothing as the other two waited by the door. Stealthily, they exited then immediately entered a chamber across the hall through another locked door Tata had the key to. It was a dark stairwell that led downward. Tata lit a torch and they scurried down winding steps behind him.

He explained in a rush as they descended. "I have been one of Prince Melchior's priests since I was very young. Last year he dispatched me on an errand to find white men and bring them here. He told me he was interested in learning from outsiders. I believed him, even though I knew of his lusts from personal experience. I thought he would let you go once he got what he wanted, but now he boasts that he would keep you both for months, perhaps years to satisfy his cravings. I'm sorry."

It was all water under the bridge as far as Max was considered, although Donald fumed and blustered and had to be rebuked by his younger partner.

"He's making up for it now by leading us to freedom, man! Be thankful for that at least. And for the gold in your pockets."

Donald ceased his complaining, most probably at the reminder of their haul of gold. Not only did they have the four heavy cuffs to take away with them, each of the two Americans had a more intimate treasure they had managed to steal away from the Prince.

Max hadn't removed the gold jockstrap when he dressed and Donald hadn't removed the gold ball-stretcher either!

It was dusk when they exited the base of the mountain. Tata led them to their camp where they immediately organized a hasty retreat into the darkness. Fortunately, the former priest and their present guide knew the environs like the back of his hand.

For the last time, Max looked back at the mountain they fled from. He gazed up at the high citadel and mused on the fate he might have expected there. Life under the thrall of the giant prince and his equally gigantic black prick — would that have been so bad?

He would never know.

DESCENT TO THE DOCKS
By Jay Starre

As they ate, Frank Sanchez found himself staring at Lee Smith's hands. He couldn't seem to take his eyes off them, the long dark fingers with the opaque neatly-trimmed nails. Something about those large yet elegant hands fascinated him. He glanced up into the dreamy golden eyes and was transfixed. Those big orbs hovered beneath ink-black brows and above a long broad nose, small but full-lipped mouth, and a bold chin. He was a gorgeous man.

After spending the morning at Lee's downtown office, the local San Franciscan had offered to show Frank around the metropolis. He'd gladly accepted. This was his first visit to the city by the bay. From Chicago, he'd been more inclined to head out to the East Coast than the West Coast.

They took a short jaunt to Golden Gate Park, headed up Market Street on a cable car, and finally ended up on Nob Hill to dine in one of the finest restaurants in town. It had been a real pleasure, especially since Lee was such an easy-going host.

That relaxed attitude was not at all typical for an investment banker. Frank himself was wired on coffee from dawn to dusk and frantic most days with his driving need to keep ahead of the market and the competition.

"There's one seedier side of the city you might enjoy. The docks. You never know what you can find down there."

Lee's smile almost looked wicked. The glint in his soft golden eyes might be described in the same way. It had been established over coffee in the morning that they were both gay, and Frank assumed this was why Lee had offered to be his tour guide for the day. Not necessarily for sex, but out of camaraderie for a fellow gay boy.

Frank had naturally heard of The Castro, the gay district of San Francisco and would have expected Lee to suggest going there after dinner. This notion of exploring the docks came entirely out of the blue.

Now he wondered if there was something else up. He hoped so!

Not given to shyness, he asked outright, "What kind of fun and games are we talking about?"

Lee laughed, a soft chuckle, before he gave his reply. Frank practically fell out of his chair at that answer.

"Ever heard of bondage and domination? A no-nonsense ball-breaking stud like yourself might just enjoy a little submission on the side."

"Uh ... sure ... ummm ... sounds like a hell of a good idea. Lead the way," he managed to sputter out.

"In that case, dinner's on me."

The easy-going grin remained in place, and Frank just had to trust he'd understood correctly. The handsome businessman wasn't joking, at least he didn't think so.

Lee continued his guide duty as if nothing out of the ordinary was planned for the evening ahead. "The Port of San Francisco is no longer the real player in the Bay. Oakland and Richmond have taken over with their extensive container docks. San Francisco's dock district has transformed into a touristy and trendy area like Fisherman's Wharf or The Embarcadero. But there are still a few places where real dock work goes on. Like here. My buddies let me use the place. I have a key."

Frank could only assume Lee put the place to use doing what he'd promised. Bondage and domination — fuck!

They'd eaten late, and it was now after 11:00 pm, so the area was pretty quiet with the work force pared down to the odd night shift employee or security guard wandering about. The nondescript warehouse they entered was dead silent and cavernous. Lee flipped on a light switch and a bank of overheads flickered on. They illuminated an area in the center of the room where a forklift squatted on the cement floor. They headed for it.

Frank stood in front of it and tried to make sense of what he saw. The forks of the lift were raised to just about their highest extent, maybe eight or nine feet off the floor. A sturdy table sat under them. A metal bar dangled from chains attached to the forks themselves.

It hit him with full force. This was for real! He shuddered and then realized his cock was rising and stiffening under his slacks. He wanted it. He wanted whatever it was that bar and chains and table and the dark-skinned mild-mannered investment banker had in mind for him.

Fuck yeah, he wanted to submit!

"I see my pals have set everything up for us. Sweet. Strip, then get up on that table and kneel on it."

Lee spoke in a matter-of-fact tone, with no bark or demand to it. Frank wondered if the relaxed banker had it in him to really put him in his place — or if it was just wishful thinking on his own part.

He found out.

He wasn't really nervous as he stripped, not quite yet. Although the place was dingy and dirty, the table was clean, and the top was actually covered in a kind of leather mat. Of course above it hung that bar and chains, which obviously would play an important role in what was coming.

Once naked and kneeling on the table, he did feel vulnerable, especially since the place was so big. With those dark corners, he couldn't actually be sure no one was lurking around to see him like that, with a huge boner jutting up between his thighs.

"Nice," Lee murmured as he looked Frank over with the appraising eye of a practiced broker.

Frank wasn't ashamed of his body. He worked out regularly. Not a big man, but with muscles in the right places and a strong lower body from a lot of squat work, he also played tennis fanatically when the Chicago winter didn't prevent it. With a fair-haired Irish mother and a Chicago Hispanic dad, he was auburn-haired and had a dusky complexion with broad features and grey eyes. Soft swirls of auburn hair coated his chest and trailed down his flat belly to a nest at his crotch. Otherwise he was fairly smooth.

Still, he couldn't help feeling somewhat pale and inadequate in comparison to the gorgeous black man looking him over so calmly — and so intimately.

"For now, hold your hands behind your back and grab your wrists. Don't move them."

The cool command was followed by an easy smile as Lee leaned in, then to Frank's surprise, kissed him. Gentle hands cupped his face as tongue slid into him and the kiss became more intimate. Then those large hands slid down over his neck, then his chest, lightly still, tracing their way lower and lower, until finally they slid between his thighs and surrounded his cock and balls. They held him there, one hand slowly rubbing up and down the stiff length of his cock, the other gently massaging his balls.

Even though it was done with subdued calm, it was so intimate it felt like he was already being controlled — and dominated. Just not exactly how he'd anticipated. When the hands on his cock and balls slid out of his crotch then around his waist and over his ass-cheeks, he shuddered slightly. Slowly still, but inexorably, both those hands trailed over the round globes then into the crack.

Sitting back on his knees, his open ass made his hole an easy target. The fingers didn't hesitate as they slid into the crack and then along it. They found that hole and immediately began to stroke it.

He groaned around the tongue in his mouth. The fingers didn't let up. His heart pounded, and he began to breathe very fast. It was maddening, those strumming fingers tapping at his sphincter and then rubbing the inner flesh as it began to pout open.

He couldn't help himself — he began to writhe into those fingers, his ass-lips gaping apart as if with a will of their own. It was absolutely amazing how Lee had managed it. He moaned and writhed like a bitch in heat, and it had all been practically effortless on the dark-skinned banker's part.

"Raise your arms. Reach up and grab hold of the bar."

He obeyed instantly, his mind set already framed around the need to follow commands mindlessly. Once his hands gripped the cold metal bar, he shuddered from head to toe, merely at the sensation of having his armpits now as vulnerable as his crotch and ass.

Lee's hands abandoned him temporarily, leaving his strummed asshole quaking and his hard cock leaking. The broker moved around to the open door of the fork lift and reached inside. He returned a moment later with a couple of items in his hands.

With a quiet smile on his gorgeous face, he set down an open can of lubricant, right between Frank's spread knees. Then, with an agile leap, he stepped up onto the table to stand in front of him. In his hands, he held two long strips of black leather.

Obviously experienced at what he did, it took only moments for Lee to wrap both of Frank's wrists and then secure them to the bar.

It was for real — he couldn't get out of those leather bonds until Lee untied him! He was at the mild-mannered broker's mercy.

"Fuck! What are you going to do to me?"

It came out almost like a whimper. Hearing that tone in his own voice, his cock lurched and his asshole quivered. What the fuck was happening to him?

"We'll see. I like to be spontaneous. Play you like a fine instrument, sort of tune you up if you get what I mean."

The smile didn't falter as the black stud descended from the table and began to strip. Fascinated, Frank watched as the suit and tie and dress shoes came off and fell to the floor alongside his own discarded business uniform.

It was immediately apparent Lee was proud of his body — and why not? His skin was a rich chocolate, and he was entirely smooth, without a hint of hair anywhere. He shaved his head, something Frank had noted of course even before he'd stripped, but now it looked as if he shaved his body, too. Sleek muscle rippled from neck to ankle and in absolute symmetry. It was quickly obvious he was also proud of his cock and balls, and his tits and ass and hole.

He strutted in front of the bound broker, grinning as he played with his own nipples, pinching them and twirling them with his thumb and forefinger. He dropped his hand to his cock, a heavily-veined tube of blunt proportions that seemed almost too large for his taut body. He pumped it slowly and winked as he also cupped his enormous balls and lightly squeezed.

Now Frank did feel inadequate. His own cock was long and good-sized, and his balls were also fair-sized. But faced with that club of a cock and those grapefruit nuts, he had nothing to boast about.

Lee quickly proved he was not only cock-proud, but ass-proud, too. He turned around and bent half-over. Both big hands came back to settle on his butt-cheeks. The twin globes were high and firm and the crack between deep. He spread them and revealed his perfect pucker. Dark, snug and smooth. He ran a fingertip over the hole and teased it.

Frank heard a loud moan and realized it was coming from him. He was totally under the man's thrall!

Lee turned around and came forward. That easy grin never faltered as he stared directly into Frank's eyes. The banker quaked at the look of sheer self-assurance he showed. He was acutely aware of his own posture. He was naked, and trussed up like a slab of pork, defenseless!

Effortlessly, the black broker sprang up onto the table, directly in front of him. All at once, that club of a dick was right in his face.

He snorted in air and the ripe stench of male crotch. It was a heady aphrodisiac, and he couldn't help himself as he lunged for that bobbing hard-on.

Lee chuckled as he placed his big hands on his own hips and thrust them forward. His rearing cock slapped against Frank's face as he batted it back and forth with a swing of his hips.

Unable to grab hold of the bouncing boner with his hands bound above his head, he attempted to capture it with his lips, but Lee evaded the trap by twisting and writhing and slapping the fleshy meat against his fellow broker's gaping lips, chin and dilated nostrils. A smear of precum began to leak from the plum head, and Frank got a good whiff of that, multiplying his excitement.

"You want to use your mouth on something? Here you go."

The black broker whirled around, and instead of cock in Frank's face, that taut round butt hovered before his mouth and nose. Just like that, Lee sat back on his face. All at once, he was buried in black butt. He snorted for air, inhaling masculine ass. The firm cheeks pressed against him, forcing his head back as Lee straddled him and began to rub his sleek butt-crack all over his face.

He mewled against that dark flesh, opening wide and sticking out his tongue. The skin was warm and so smooth, a sheen of salty sweat tingling over his lapping tongue and pursed lips. He probed, finding the dark hole and attempting to lick at it as that rock-solid butt rubbed up and down over his mouth.

Once he'd targeted the black pucker with his stabbing tongue, Lee apparently decided that's what he wanted. He squatted right down over Frank's face, forcing it back and causing his arms to strain against the leather strips binding them to the bar above. The chains rattled, sweat broke out all over his body, and Lee even grunted a little himself as Frank's tongue began to push beyond the snug ass-lips.

"Eat it, Lee. Go ahead. Eat my black hole out."

The sultry command encouraged him to slurping effort. The asshole quivered and then opened, and he dove in as far as he could. Lee's deep sigh only made him more frantic to please the hot stud. He clamped his lips over the wet hole and sucked.

Wallowing in the smell and taste of that dark hole, he would have been content to lap and suck for hours, but Lee was in control, and he had other plans. He pulled away slightly, then pushed back and down on his fat cock. The gooey head slipped between Frank's gaping lips.

"Yeah. Now you can eat black dick."

The quiet murmur was followed by a deep pump downward. Frank gurgled loudly as that blunt knob slithered past his tonsils and into his throat. The huge thing pulsed and leaked as the broker held it there.

He pulled slowly out, and Frank snorted for air. Asshole replaced the cock, and he was eagerly lapping at pouting hole again. Then, those enormous nuts settled over his mouth. He sucked one in, then the other. Then both, which proved a real mouthful.

"It think it's time to fuck you."

The kneeling banker shivered and mewled as he slurped up Lee's giant black cock one final time before it was pulled away. The thought of that huge slab sliding up his ass had him twitching all over. He hoped the sexy stud planned on using lots of that lube he'd brought out!

The broker did plan on using lots of lube, but Frank was surprised when the slippery gel was suddenly applied to his own cock. Lee turned around to face him and squatted over his knees, one hand behind him as he rubbed a handful of the lube all along the length of the auburn-haired banker's stiff rod.

"I'm going to fuck your cock with my ass," he murmured just before his mouth came down and covered Frank's. One of Lee's big hands aimed that cock at his own spit-wet asshole and held it as the dark pucker began to swallow it.

It was tight! Even though he'd just sucked it open, the sphincter still clamped and seized as it gulped up first the head of his dick then the shaft. He sat right down on it, his firm hamstrings pressing down over Frank's thighs.

But that wasn't all. A big tongue roamed deep in his mouth, while two big hands found his armpits and began to stroke them. It was incredible! That tight asshole encased the entire length of his cock with slippery heat. It pulsed around his stiff meat like a quivering vice. The tongue filled his mouth. Those hands stroked his vulnerable pits with tantalizing fingertips.

He squirmed and bucked, but he couldn't escape that tongue, those hands, or that ass. He was trapped in and under lean black body. No escape, even if he'd wanted it!

The fingers in his pits trailed downward, relieving some of the ticklish sensations that had set him jerking. But it wasn't more than a moment before they found another sensitive area of his body. Down they slid until they rounded his hips and began to cup and squeeze his ass-cheeks.

At the same time, Lee started rising and falling over his trapped cock. The tight ass channel constricted around his aching hard-on, although thankfully it was well-coated with slippery lube.

The hands on his ass squeezed gently at first, massaging the full mounds while pulling them apart. Frank felt his asshole pucker outward as his knees slid farther apart, and Lee bounced up and down over his lap. Those hands moved into his open crack.

The fingers of both hands trailed all along it, stroking the tender area just like they'd stroked his armpits. They wandered over his pouting asshole, fingertips rubbing the lips and the pouting center. They tapped at it, rubbed it, and massaged it.

He groaned around the tongue buried in his mouth. It was driving him mad! But it got worse, or better depending on how you looked at it. While continuing to rise and fall over his squeezed cock, Lee pulled one hand out of his ass-crack and reached back to scoop up a handful of that gooey gel from the can on the table behind him.

The hand returned to Frank's crack, this time liberally coated with lube. Now fingers slid along his crack in a slippery glide. They settled on his hole again to tease it. They coated it with the lube and rubbed all over it. The sensation had him wriggling his ass and gasping. But he was buried under Lee's powerful body and his ability to move was limited.

Lee scooped out more lube with his other hand while fingers rubbed in the stuff already there, now beginning to lightly press between the distended lips. He grunted and jerked as one finger finally pushed past his sphincter and slowly into his gut.

That finger took its time, sliding deeper and deeper as the other fingers tickled and stroked his crack and his butt-lips. The finger burrowed home and began to twist, exerting pressure against his ass rim while asshole continued to ride his cock in a steadily increasing pace.

That finger up his ass slid out, leaving his hole oozing and gaping. But a pair of fingers from the other hand immediately replaced them. Both slowly pushed inside. He arched his back and grunted as the larger intrusion strained his ass-lips. But there was nothing he could do except take it. Shortly those two black fingers were buried to the hilt and slowly twisting around inside him.

His prostate ached as they found and rubbed it. They hooked inside him and pulled outward on his ass-rim from the inside. They pulled out half-way, then pushed all the way in again.

They slithered out, only to be replaced by a trio of fingers from the other hand. He couldn't see what was going on, but could feel the powerful stretch as those big digits dug into him.

He grunted and squirmed as three fingers burrowed deep, twisting as they explored his fuck channel. He tried to relax his convulsing hole, but that only served to allow those three fingers to twist and stretch him even wider.

They came out with a slurp. Fingers from both hands tickled the gaping flesh left behind before pushing back into him. Three fingers again pumped his aching hole.

His entire body thrashed. He hung from the bar and jerked all over, the rattling of the chains echoing in the tomb-like warehouse. The squish of Lee's humping ass blended with the gooey slurps of the fingers he used to probe Frank's hole.

Three fingers from each hand took turns probing him. They never forced their way in, nor did they ram in and out at a hurried pace. But they stuffed him thoroughly and with inexorable totality. They filled him, then slowly twisted in circles to stretch his aching hole in a gut-churning pressure that only increased the pleasure in his cock as that snug asshole rode it just as thoroughly.

Finally, Lee broke their kiss and stared down into his eyes. "Time to give my cock what it needs."

And what was that, Frank wondered? He found out as the black broker rose off the cock up his snug hole and removed the three fingers up his victim's aching hole. He scooped out more lube from the can on the table and slapped it over his rearing black bone. Frank bit his lip and moaned as he gazed down at the huge tool. It twitched and bobbed, glistening with goo.

Chuckling, the lean banker crawled around behind Frank and shoved his knees up tight between his dangling victim's thighs. He felt that rearing club slide against his open ass-crack. One black hand came down to seize the fat shaft and aim it between those spread cheeks and the other hand came around and took hold of the glistening cock that had just been up his ass.

He began a slow pump along Frank's shaft with his fingers while he pushed upward and inward against the bound broker's asshole with the blunt head of his own cock. Frank grunted and jerked as the huge crown slid past his gaping, stretched ass-lips.

"Now you're going to get fucked."

It was no idle promise. Before then, all Lee's actions had been restrained, deliberate and thorough but steadily-paced and performed without any rush. That suddenly changed.

"Take my big black dick up your ass!"

Cock rammed home. He squealed like a stuck pig, even though it didn't really hurt. By this time, he was so completely under the black banker's control, and so opened up, his asshole took the wild plunge with relative ease.

Not that he didn't feel it. He did! And he definitely felt the series of gut-punches his assailant punished him with immediately afterwards. The fingers on his own cock squeezed tighter as they pumped up and down in a rapid slide. The prick up his ass slammed balls-deep, yanked all the way out, then drove home again. And again. And again.

He was fucked and fucked good. But in the end that wasn't how he got off. Lee planned it differently, and Frank could only go along.

It was those big black hands that eventually drove him over the edge. The cock up his ass pummeled him relentlessly for a good long time before suddenly it was yanked out and Lee slapped his sweaty butt with the flat of one hand and whispered huskily in his ear.

"Get up one foot. Spread your ass for my hand."

Frank grunted with battered excitement. That fierce ass-pounding had him shaking all over. He obeyed, pulling one foot out from under him and planting it on the mat. Half his body came up in the air and his ass-crack was wider open than ever.

Lee reached around him and dug into the open can of lube to scoop out more of the stuff.

His fingers returned to Frank's open crack and zeroed in on his gooey hole. This time they didn't merely push inside and slowly stretch him out. No, they thrust up into him and twisted. Four fingers began to rub and shove and yank as they worked around relentlessly to stretch out the groaning broker's hole.

By this time his ass had been transformed into a gaping cavern seemingly able to take anything. Lee knew what he was doing, now truthfully playing Frank like a fine instrument, as he probed and dug in that well-lubed slot. At the same time, he slid his other hand up and down Frank's stiff cock in a merciless pump that had him writhing back and forth between the twin pleasures.

He felt orgasm rising as those fingers yanked out and then shoved back in. His cock was on fire and so stiff he thought it might burst. He cried out as cum shot up his shaft and rocketed out of his piss slit.

"Sweet! Shoot a load for your black buddy! Here's mine!"

Lee's fat tube erupted behind him to splatter his heaving butt as those fingers continued to root in his gut and force every drop of jizz from his roiling nuts.

Frank hung from the bar in Lee's arms as the two caught their breath and came down from their wild release. He felt suddenly relaxed and almost limp, leaning back into that firm body and feeling his neck nuzzled by soft lips.

"Nice. I love how it feels after the first blow. Now that we're relaxed, we can take our time and get real nasty."

Frank could hardly believe what he'd heard. Fuck! What else did Lee have in mind? There was nothing he could do but wait to find out. Lips traveled down his neck. Fingers trailed over his flat stomach. Where were they headed?

THE VAMPIRE'S CHALICE
By Donald Webb

I'm cruising down the Extraterrestrial Highway. I'm close to Groom Lake and Area 51, a super-sensitive military airfield that — according to the U.S. Government, doesn't exist, but I've viewed it on Google earth, so I know it's out there. Go figure. I smile when I catch myself checking the sky for UFOs. The smile quickly fades when I glance down at the fuel gauge and see the needle pointing to empty. My pulse rate immediately increases when I realize I'm going to be stuck out in the middle of the desert.

I ease up on the accelerator and keep a sharp lookout for signs of civilization. Relief floods through my body when I see a building on the horizon. I'm even happier when I draw near and see it's an old service station. Normally I don't stop at such dilapidated places — who knows what they'll put in my tank, but I have no other option.

The car's running on fumes when I park next to the rust covered no-name gas pump. When I step out of my car, the only thing I hear is the ticking of cooling metal. The place appears deserted, and the empty service bay is open to the elements.

A sudden fierce eddy stirs up sand and debris enveloping everything around me. I jump when a young African-American, who appears to be in his early twenties, suddenly materializes. He's about five-eight, and probably weighs 150 pounds. He's barefoot and is wearing coveralls. Dark hair glistens in his armpits when he lifts his straw hat and runs his hand over his shaved head.

"Fill 'er up, mister?" he asks.

"Please," I say.

When he bends over the hood to clean the windshield I get a tantalizing glimpse of a smooth hipbone and a hairless six-pack abdomen through his gaping coveralls.

"Check under the hood, mister?" he asks.

I shake my head. "You have a restroom?"

He indicates with a thumb. "Round back."

The restroom's in no better shape than the rest of the place. The door squeals on its hinges when I push it open. Two stalls without doors fill one side of the room. A mirror and sink are attached to the opposite wall.

The entrance door blocks the first stall, so I walk into the second stall, push my jeans and briefs down to my knees, and let my piss stream into the stagnant toilet water. A huge glory hole between the two stalls looks promising. I can't get the sexy young guy out of my mind. I close my eyes and picture him whimpering with lust as I slide my naked dick into his tight hole. I'm tugging on my nuts and stroking my erection when the entrance door squeals.

Two coverall clad knees hit the floor in the next stall and a dark brown eye peers at me through the glory hole. I lean against the far wall, push my pelvis out in his direction, and milk my dick. His eye opens wide when a long thread of precum sags to the floor. His mouth appears at the hole, and his tongue wiggles at me.

I step toward him and rub the head of my dick over his moist tongue. He licks my dickhead for a few moments. When he opens wide, I push my dick all the way into his velvety throat. Most guys have trouble deep throating my big dick, but he's not bothered by the size. He must get plenty of practice at the hole crosses my mind.

He grabs my nuts and plunges his lips down my shaft not stopping until they press against my short and curlies. With a twirling motion he backs off until just the head is in his mouth. He gets into a rhythm, but holds his mouth in place when I grab the top of the partition and fuck his wide open throat. I can't hold back, he's too good. I can hear him gulping down my jism when I unload.

The door squeals, and he's gone. I'm disappointed. Even though I'm strictly trade, I'm so excited I would do him if he asked. I lean back against the wall and take a few deep breaths. My dick's squeaky clean. Not a drop of cum left.

When I get back to the car, he's leaning against the hood. I can see a wet spot over the bulge at his groin. I'm tempted to ask if he wants me to blow him, but I'm already late for an appointment.

"That'll be fifty bucks, mister," he says.

He smiles when he sees the shocked look on my face.

"It be for the gas," he says.

I take eighty bucks out of my wallet and place it in his hand. He's worth every cent.

"You be back here sometime?" he asks.

"Yeah," I say. "I'm coming back this way in a few days."

"Come back on the ninth," he says.

"On the ninth?"

"Yeah, on the ninth. But you come after dark. I be here then."

Two days later, I'm back at the gas station. This time it's dark. The only light showing is an oil lamp which casts a dim glow over a black vintage hearse parked in the service bay. The gas-jockey must work for a funeral parlor during the day, I'm thinking, or maybe it's the wheels for an avant-garde rock band.

He once again materializes when I step out of the car. "You wan' gas?" he asks.

"No, I just need to use the restroom."

"There ain't no lights back there, so watch how you go."

I stumble around the building. The door squeals when I enter the impenetrably dark restroom. I feel my way into the furthest stall. This time I push my jeans and shorts down to my boot tops. I'm stroking my dick when the door squeals. I wait for a few seconds and then push my dick through the hole. His hot mouth engulfs me. I'm really getting into the blowjob when the door squeals. I try to pull away but he's got my nuts in a vise grip, and he continues sucking like he's starved for dick.

I shiver when the restroom temperature suddenly plummets. I can feel a presence behind me. I'm stunned when my T-shirt is suddenly ripped off my body and my boots, jeans, and briefs are removed. I want to object, but I can't, it's like I'm in some kind of hypnotic trance, and I'm stuck to the wall like a bug on a windshield.

I shudder when something cold, wet, and slimy, slides down my spine. My cheeks are roughly parted and the slimy object presses against my asshole. My immediate thought is that an extraterrestrial has escaped from Area 51 and is trying to impregnate me. I try to scream and get away from the alien form, but I can't. I'm mute and paralyzed.

The slimy entity probes my hole and then slips into my chute. I've always resisted anal sex, but tonight something is telling me to try it. I can't resist the alien's advances. The slimy thing withdraws, and some type of lube is applied to my hole. Next two items — which feel suspiciously like fingers, slide in and probe around in my chute. I'm in heaven. I never thought it would feel so good. I want more. I'm craving something bigger ... I want him to fuck me with his alien cock.

A raucous laugh emanates from the alien. "You want me to fuck you," it says in a disembodied voice, as if it's reading my mind.

The probes pop out of my anus, and the cold slimy object slithers up my back. The alien holds my chin, tilts my head back, and the slimy thing — which I now realize is a tongue, licks my throat. I can feel the alien's big dick stretching my anal tissues to the tearing point, but I'm enjoying the pain. I gasp when I feel the thick protuberance glide into my channel, touching areas that have never felt anything alien. I'm pinned against the wall by a power greater than I've ever felt, and the gas-jockey's hanging onto my nuts while he keeps sucking. The alien bites my neck. It's no love hickey he's making, it's a sharp penetrating gouge that makes me shriek in silent agony. I feel as though all the energy is being drained from my body when my cock erupts in the gas-jockey's mouth.

Four hands pry me away from the wall and lay me on the filthy floor. They pull my legs up to my chest, and a huge object is shoved into my dilated chute. I move my hand down to my ass and feel a thick, very human, cock sliding in and out of me.

"Fuck me," I say. "Fuck me with that big cock."

"Oh, mister," the gas-jockey says. "You got a tight ass."

A hard cock brushes against my lips. I open my mouth and let it slide down my throat. I can taste my juices on it, but I don't care. I'm flying like I've overdosed on poppers, and I'm sucking cock like I've never sucked before. I'm disappointed when his pubic bone grinds against my lips ... I want more. My throat feels bottomless. I place my hands on the alien's humanoid butt and finger his hairy cleft. I pull him to me and work his shaft with my throat muscles. I'm startled when chilled cum fills my mouth and throat.

He pulls his dick out of my mouth and says, "Move," to the gas-jockey, and then he's back between my legs. The head of his dick grinds against my prostate when he lifts my ass from the floor.

The gas-jockey covers my mouth with his hot pucker. I'm really getting into rimming him when he suddenly lifts up and covers my face with warm cum. I scoop it up with my hand, suck my fingers clean, and then I pull him to me and deep-throat his still erect dick.

I don't know how long they use me because at some point I sink into unconsciousness.

When I awake, I'm naked and lying supine on a four-poster bed. A dull light on the bedside table fails to penetrate the periphery of the vast room. I'm disoriented and petrified as I struggle to my feet. A plethora of questions fill my mind. Where am I? What's happened to me? Am I dreaming? I'm covered in dried cum. Two streaks of dried blood stain my chest. Both sides of my neck are tender to touch. I remember the one bite, but the other must've occurred while I was unconscious.

My ass is on fire. I spread my legs and push two fingers into my chute to see if I've been injured. Cum oozes down my thighs when I pull my fingers from my hole. With that amount of cum, I'm thinking, there must've been more than two people in the restroom. I've been gangbanged, but I don't care, if I have the chance I'll do it again.

A familiar raucous laugh emanates from a corner of the room. I walk in the direction of the sound. A muscular looking man — with mocha colored skin and the pink eyes of an Albino — dressed in a black leather vest and black leather chaps, relaxes in a wingchair. Black leather straps encircle his pumped up biceps. His muscular thighs are draped over the arms of the chair. A steel cock-ring gleams in the dim light. His hypnotic stare freezes my movement. Now I know how a deer feels when it's caught in a car's headlights.

He's communicating telepathically, as if my brain's plugged into the internet. He's telling me I've been genetically transformed and I've joined the ranks of the living dead.

"You are Abarran ... my master?" I ask when the transfer of data is complete.

"I am the Regent, father of multitudes."

"You drank my blood?" I ask in a tremulous voice.

"Yes."

"How come I'm still alive?"

"I wished it so," he says.

It's incredible. I can't believe it.

"On the ninth day, of the ninth month, of the ninth year," he explains, "we admit new members to our Coven. This year, I chose you."

I shake my head. "If I hadn't stopped at the gas station you wouldn't have seen me."

He smiles. "That place does not exist."

"You mean you arranged for me to stop there ... but how?"

"You have much to learn, Lalit ... but not tonight."

"Lalit?"

"I have named you Lalit because of your beauty."

I'm confused and disoriented. He reads my mind.

"You are mine now," he says. "You will forever be subservient to me."

I'm not sure if that's what I want — but if life is going to be a continual orgy, then I'm all for it. "Am I a vampire?" I ask.

"No, you are my spare chalice and daytime protector." He points to the door. The gas-jockey, still in his incongruous outfit, stands in the doorway. "Salman is my primary chalice and protector. You will both provide me with sustenance."

Neat, flashes through my mind, his own blood bank.

"You will also provide sexual relief to the Coven. They've been wanting a white boy for some time."

My dick starts to harden when I think about the previous night. I'm hoping the Coven will use me in the same way.

White teeth sparkle in the gloom when the vampire smiles. He has once again read my mind. "The Coven will arrive later tonight. But I am in immediate need of relief," he says as he shakes his enormous black dick.

I walk over to my master and drop to my knees in front of him. I open my mouth and sink his shaft down my throat.

And so my life as the vampire's chalice begins.

BOY MEETS MAN
By Thoby Musgrave

Arms raised high and with his head thrown back, Max squinted, seeing the twinkling colors of the disco-lights through closed eyelids. The music sizzled with cheap, sing-songy melodies that hashed-up the chemical filled air. Around him he felt — sensed — the swirling, sweating bodies. The other boy was on his knees, down on the dance-floor, nuzzling the front of Max's loaded shorts with a wiggling nose. Max wiggled in return, squirming forward with his hips in time with the beat and shoving his packet into the consenting face. The boy licked him through the stretched Lycra.

The inside of Star-Q was a packed ocean of limbs and flailing bodies, as usual, with shimmering sequins and half-dressed, fake-tanned gym-twinks. The rough, slurping tongue moved up to Max's bare midriff, licking his sweat and twiddling his belly-button.

"Hmm … Hmm … Hmm …" Max hummed to himself and to the orchestral stabs of the witless remix playing from the DJ booth. "Woo … Woo … Woo … It's Friiii-day!" He swung his head from side to side, apparently in some kind of far-gone ecstasy, but thinking really of approaching necessities. Where might he choose to be pierced on Saturday?

Georgi had given him a voucher for his twentieth birthday — for a free chrome ring at Shield's Boutique.

Peter had said, "Get your navel done! That'll be so cute!"

Roberto said, "Do your nipple."

Marky suggested the next organ on the list. Oh no! Not there!

Max considered these questions under the impressive lighting-rig of Star-Q as he shimmied to the music. The kneeling

71

boy's hands were now sliding at his waist, the fingers curling into the rim of his little, little shorts, when ... Pow!

Fuck!

A hoarse, strained voice spoke to him, just audible in one ear over the pulsating screeches of the nightclub.

'You're a lying little whore-bag!' Max thought he heard. *'You two-timing, shrimp!'*

Oh shit. It was Dora, and Max had been whacked in the back of the head with a fake-pearl studded handbag. "Yeow! Shit! That fucking hurt!" He rubbed his skull and scrunched his face in displeasure.

His mind passed back over the last twenty minutes. Dora had been promised a peanut-butter martini, but once Dora had passed from the realm of Max's consideration in the crowded bar, other enticements had beckoned him to the dance-floor, and his wallet had been shoved into his sock — there being no pockets or room in his tight shorts. The boy with the big blue eyes had occupied him with tongue and tickling fingers for the last four songs and ... Oh, these damn drag-queens were so bitchy sometimes!

Dora flounced away toward the bar on crazy heels, the pearl handbag swinging. Then, with an elbow on the counter, she turned a seductive eye back to Max. Through the colored strobes and smoke, he saw a pencil-arched eyebrow rise and painted nails planted on a jutting hip.

As if in a movie — and that's exactly what Max was thinking — he ran at her, planning in those moments to land in her arms like a Hollywood starlet about to be carried down a sweeping staircase by Clark Gable, a bare, slender arm draped around her neck and the rest of his body sagging delicately in the cradle of her grasp. Except, the articulately planned maneuver didn't work out like that at all. Max, drag-queen, handbag, and some glasses from the bar, all went crashing to the floor in a momentous collapse and terrible tangle. It was loud enough over the music to make heads turn with indistinct expressions of curiosity and annoyance. On the floor with his shoulders and torso propped-up on his arms, Max peered aloft in bewilderment at the assembling security-guards, their black T-shirts and earpieces, their stern faces, boding a displeasing result from his flying, athletic endeavor.

Ejected to the street with a civilized but firm little toss and with the rubber soles of his chunky, designer running-shoes pattering on the sidewalk, Max began to make an inspection of his heavily bumped backside, but Dora was on a mad warpath. She flew at him from the dark glass doors of Star-Q, handbag flying and heels clattering. The damage to her person was considerable. Max's little stunt had cost her an expensively styled hairdo as well some other rips and breakages which she shrieked about as she gave chase. Bounding in long, light strides in his bouncy running-shoes, Max first laughed, and then as he ran, he gave some consideration to the surprising speed of an angry queen, heels and all.

'Shit! What an embarrassment!' he thought. An easy lope kept him well ahead of his screeching pursuer, but Dora voiced no intention of breaking away from her attack, and a handy little alleyway presented a useful means of final escape.

Pitter-pattering on the dirty roadway with elevated breath, Max noticed that his glo-green shorts and too-small T-shirt were the brightest things to be seen in the dark, smoky lane. The clamor of the main street receded and a steady, heavy thumping came from the shadows ahead. Max knew of a nightclub down here in the narrows of trash-cans and rising steam, but he and his friends had always found little need to venture beyond the places for popular people, such as Star-Q and similar show-off venues.

There was a heavy door of buttoned, hammered stainless-steel. With nowhere else to go, he pushed it. The thumping became suddenly louder, and thickly laden air pulsated with the hard-cranking music as he descended cement stairs.

At first, Max was hardly to be noticed. The place was crushed full of ... men. Hairy bodies, slick bodies — big bodies, and leather jackets pushed, jostled, and pressed. He slipped between them, feeling his chest against someone's shoulder-blades, his backside against a large, firm lump. A rippled haze of smoke was near the ceiling, and there was the smell of sweat and cigar.

'*Yikes!*' he thought. '*I must bring Roberto here!*'

His hand went to his crotch where a stiffening exerted itself, unfolding and pushing against the fabric of his shorts. The cotton G-string underneath zipped tautly in his crack. He saw a weathered pool-table through the throng and a small dance-floor. There were chains strung in a spider-web pattern between two metal poles. Max breathed harder, feeling the punch of the music in his guts and the sticky, moist atmosphere prickling his bare limbs.

A low doorway was spied. '*Good,*' Max thought. '*That must be the bathroom. I need to wee.*' A bit of ducking and squeezing took him to the low, darkened orifice, and by now, there were a few heads turning across shoulders to grimace with disapproval at the Lycra-wearing boy pushing through. Some were bald. Some wore peaked leather caps. Some wore earrings suited to pirates and some wore bushy moustaches. Most of them snorted in derision and surprise.

The bathroom was a white-tiled cavity, low-lit with ultra-violet. But the weird, slightly-blue tone made Max's little green shorts and T-shirt glow like a firefly in a jar. Elsewhere in the gloom, dark shapes moved. He heard the soft creak of leather. He hummed self-consciously as his piss streamed against the stainless-steel, and just as he popped his cock back into his shorts with a snap of the waistband, there was a hand on his shoulder. A big hand. It was heavy, and gripped hard. Another hoisted him suddenly and shockingly by the small Lycra pants from behind, hefting and handling him like a piece of beef on a hook.

"Hey ...!"

As he was propelled toward an opposite wall on tippy-toes with his shorts wrenched into his crack, a deep, controlling voice whispered into his right ear — so close he could feel the cool lips.

"You look like a handy little cocksucker, boy. That's a pretty mouth you got!"

He went hard into the wall. Not slammed, but firmly enough to make his head turn sideways and his cheek press on the tiles. Wetness soaked through the front of his T-shirt as he was pushed from behind. He heard someone laugh. For a few seconds, he was held with his shorts in his ass-crack and a powerful, steady hand between his shoulders. Then he was let go.

"Turn around," came the voice. It was low, filled with resonance and command, its acoustic clarity formed with masculine control and the hard echo of the tiled surfaces. Max's eyes flicked around the weirdly-lit room as he pushed his back up against the wall. Some darkened outlines faced him. Boots scraped as five or six big men edged toward him, one step each. But a single impressive figure seemed to eclipse everything in the ultra-violet chamber. Towering before Max stood a figure of sinister midnight. The door was blocked from view. Max knew not to say anything, but he breathed sharply as his maleness throbbed painfully at his loins. He was glad he'd had that piss.

"That's a sweet little you outfit you got on, twink-boy. You lookin' for a job as a go-go dancer?"

Max could barely make out the face. A lustrous, shaved dome of a skull formed-up with a solid neck, which flared outwards with wings of muscle onto wide, wide shoulders. There were mountains and ridges of shining bare black skin. The massive torso bore a ringed, four-way harness of heavy belts going under and over, crossways. The getups and swaggering imagery of the hidden, San Francisco style bars had been something Max had sometimes giggled at, but now, he just swallowed and thought nothing but to do as he was told.

"Strip."

The command was as casual as anyone would like, but delivered with an enunciated directness, which barred any question of disobedience. Max's T-shirt came first, and with an instant flick at the waist and an overhead pull, it was tossed to the floor. His clunky running-shoes clattered softly on the tiles as they were kicked away. The surface was cold at his bare feet. With a wiggle and two hooked thumbs, his shorts were gone, too, but the tiny G-string was wrung from him by an impatient hand. It snapped loudly as it was pulled away by a strong fist, and there were muffled sniggers as the broken little cotton thing landed in a wet pool on the floor. Bared and with his skin tingling in the moist air, Max felt the cold wall with his rump-cheeks, fingertips, and sharp shoulder-blades. His straining penis bent upwards and pressed into his belly.

"Ooo hoo!" said a voice in the background. "Slim little greyhound, ain't he? Look at that boner!"

"Tsst!" said the mountain standing before Max, commanding silence. Max shivered, and gingerly brought a hand to cover his immodestly upstanding organ.

"Leave your crank alone, twink-boy!" was the sharp directive, and Max instantly whipped his arm away. His hard, curving meat continued pulsing and aching, its sensitive underside feeling the brush of cool air.

Now, the singular authority in the room stepped back. Smooth muscles moved like a sea of oil, shining with polished gloss and authentic blackness even under the abnormal light. Guys came in, looked, used the urinals with hard, drumming streams, and looked again at the naked young man against the wall before passing back into the smoky, noisy nightclub. Max's heart beat to his throat, and he felt his stomach, his legs, and his backside tightening. Hard against the wall, he realized he was standing on his toes.

An arm like a tree-branch was held out, and a slithering network of black leather straps was dropped to the floor with a clink of steel buckles.

"Get your tackle into that harness, twink-boy. You're on a leash tonight."

The circlets, rings, and hoops of the small man-harness Max was to wear lay on the white tiles, forming and uncoiling. He blinked, and his eyes darted to the smooth-edged face of his master. Shining white teeth and fulsome lips snarled.

"Get it on, punk! Move!"

It was the kind of thing Max and his pals had laughed at in the windows of the crazy boutiques, strapped onto Perspex mannequins. Now, he felt the firm leather against his own skin. He stepped into it, his bare feet and toes curling on the cold, tiled floor.

"Can you figure it out, twink-boy?" said the rising black tower of the man who had deigned to command him. Impatient hands moved in. They were strong and dexterous, with dusky smooth skin and powerful fingers working quickly. A tall, black leather collar was buckled around his neck, raising his chin high.

"That's a cute little pucker-face you're makin', pretty-boy. Don't be so gloomy!" His chin was held hard between thumb and forefinger. He could smell that luminous skin.

Another piece of the harness went straight down the front, all the way to his blonde nether-region where a chrome ring was worked onto the base of his genitals. Max gasped as the steel hoop was first passed down over his bar-hard upright shaft. The metallic coldness of it and the disparate warmth of those authoritative, quick-moving fingers made his cock surge and beat upwards with yet more urgency. Max whimpered as one testicle was passed through, then the other. He was a harnessed mammal, stirruped by the balls at the hands of an unquestioning and dominant creature — and the experience of it was a crisp, new thing which made the blood thump in his ears and his Adam's-apple pulse against his collar.

Two horizontal belts encircled him, one just below the nipple-line and near his armpits, and another at the waist, pulled, cinched, and buckled tight. At the rear, another vertical strap passed down the center of his back from the collar to a hard rubber thong, which pressed firmly into his crack and connected underneath with the cock-shackle. He breathed sharply when he felt it there. Arms of shining black muscle gave a solid wrench, lifting him onto his toes with a yelp, and Max heard the 'click' of the tightest possible notch.

"You're a shapely little whippet, boy. If you're a decent cocksucker, you'll stay mine."

Max wiggled in the harness, feeling the cool buckles on his bare skin and the pressure at his anus. The words spoken by his imposing new dominator were like a slow, chanting hymn vibrating in his being. Their meaning washed onto him in measured deliberation. He was owned — hitched like a prize animal in a yard. The ring at his nuts bit hard, but still, his stretched organ curved and reached in its male fullness.

A thick, meaty fist was at the collar. It moved with firm steadiness, directing and turning him. He moved with it, fastened bodily into the leather rig and following its inflexible control. Slowly — slowly — he was pushed down, bending with his legs but stiff at the waist where his shackled cock and tautly-fixed under-support kept him straightened. On his knees and with toes curled, Max braced his upright torso and looked straight in front.

"Spread." That deep voice was casual and easy, but impossible to disobey. He shuffled his knees wide. A bulging pack of leather was at his face, almost touching his nose. Now, it was as if he'd changed places with the blue-eyed boy in Star-Q, kneeling with his own face attending a generously endowed crotch — but this wasn't the pink-marble bathroom of Star-Q, and these guys weren't dancing. He blinked at the prominent, leather-sheathed package at his face. Long fingers — sturdy and robust but somehow delicately tactile — flicked at the big metal tag of the heavy-duty zip. With a long, steady 'zzzzzzzz,' it came down, the teeth separating and parting — releasing. Up-close, Max saw the leather shifting as it unloaded its burden. A lavishly rounded snake of black meat uncoiled and slumped forward with a hefty weight. Max's eyes widened.

It rose slowly like a waking reptile, nosing the open air and swaying gently with curiosity. The enclosed head of it was dark purple and the rest was glistening black, long and visibly thickening, and textured with a wriggling network of veins. It rose some more.

"Not many punk-asses can get puckered-down on that, twink-boy. See how your pretty mouth does. Go on. Taste it."

The sharp tang was of unfamiliar sweat. Max extended his tongue, reaching forwards. He lifted it, feeling the weight. Then suddenly, it was at full hardness, its underside presenting a ridged surface of shining beef.

Max formed his lips into a wide aperture and worked down on it diligently, but it was massive, and the steely hardness of it propped his jaw wide open. Above him, the big-chested man was silent but for deep, regular breaths made through his nose. Max heard it. The inhalations became harder and deeper as the giant flesh-prong in his mouth pulsed, and the swinging balls jerked heavily against his chin. His cheeks were full, and the solid node of meat pushed to his tonsils. His tongue was pressed flat by the volume inside his oral cavity, but he worked as best he could with his mouth utterly full and his cheeks and lips stretched.

He moved slowly and rhythmically, lubricating carefully and kneading the moveable skin of the mouth-filling cock with his tongue. No one spoke, but Max felt a number of eyes on him as he worked, sliding, up and down, up and down. He used his knees and thighs to raise and lower, his harness biting tightly and moving in his ass.

The black master's breathing was harder now — pointed sniffs — and the rock-solid pole began to throb. After some time, Max sensed the approaching climax and sucked in hard through his nose. In his mouth, there was a mighty heave, and a hot, gushing explosion. The thick cream tasted strongly of salt, and jetted in flooding streams. Max swallowed desperately, gulping and slugging it down with eyes closed. The leather of the guy's pants felt slick and oily as Max gripped them, pressing with his palm at the formidable hips and wrinkling the stretched rawhide with his fingers. He swallowed and swallowed, fighting off the reflexes of his tonsils and listing with the pumping rhythm. As the quick-coming shots receded and the powerful emissions shallowed, he breathed again. Slowly, his aching jaw drew back and released the thick, slippery meat. It glided from his mouth with a slurp and dangled before him, wet and gleaming.

"You been watered, fed, and nourished now, boy. Get to your fucking feet!" The voice vibrated deeply and musically as before, but now with sharper authority. An iron-grip fist was at the collar-link, raising him.

On his feet, Max was spun, and his ankles kicked apart. Behind him, his wrists were grasped in those enormous meaty hands. He felt steel. Handcuffs made a metallic snick in the small of his back, and his hands were locked together, palms outwards. The collar was handled roughly, and the enveloping harness lifted him, the hard rubber loop at his ass boosting him to his tippy toes again.

He saw a parade of wicked grins as he skipped toward the door, driven from behind, and as the beating music thudded in the swing-opening, he was twirled forcefully, and a thick leash was attached. Max resisted briefly, feeling the pull of the tether clipped to his collar before it drew him into the pulsing crowd and veering lights. The noise — dulled in the bathroom — was now constant and strident in his ears. He kept looking straight ahead, peripherally aware of the many eyes lifted from their discussions and drinks. Hands were on him, too, tweaking a nipple and sliding in his hoisted ass-crack, and he detected a rise in the babble of conversation under the music as he was hauled — harnessed and cuffed — through the press of the crowd. He licked his lips, still tasting the thick, salted juices he'd swallowed.

At the bar, his master pulled on fingerless leather gloves and held the loop-end of the leash, handling and feeling it sensuously. The shaved, gleaming skull shone in all the colors of the overhead lights. Deep-set, dark-brown eyes were warm in hue but fiercely imposing in their forceful scrutiny. A black boot was placed on the bar's brass footrest.

"Get down, twink-boy. Lick."

Max knelt. Again with his knees spread wide on the rough floor and his stiffened man-prong projecting upwards from its encircling shackle, he leant forward. The tight harness creaked and his fingertips waved in the air behind him where his wrists were locked. He tasted leather, boot-polish, and dust.

"Beer," the towering figure said to the barman, simply.

# # # # #

The place was empty except for a cleaner with a mop, the barman stacking glasses, and Max. The leash was secured to one of the posts holding the web-formation chains, and Max remained kneeling. Under normal lighting, the hard interior looked dirty and the concrete floor was streaked with stale spillages. Max shifted in the harness and wiggled his fingers behind him. As a dribble of oily fluid squeezed from the slit of his aching cock, he groaned. How he longed to touch it! It begged mercilessly for attention.

What time must it be? The steel bucket was pushed noisily across the floor and the swilling mop sluiced the cement between his parted knees. "Pretty boys like you don't normally come in here," the guy said. Max looked up.

"An' when they do, they get taken care of. Usually by Lem. Yeah, you met Lem. Guess Lem's got himself a nice little pet for the weekend, huh?"

The barman behind the counter laughed.

BOUND TO PLEASE
By A.J. Damian

By day I'm a top lawyer, all suited and booted. I look snappy and have a ninety-nine percent success rate in winning cases, but to be honest, once the day is over, I like to get that suit right off and take a shower — it drains the sweat of the day from my body, so I feel renewed and ready for what comes next — as at night I'm my own man, I work for no one, others work for me. Well, they work their asses off for me at my own private dungeon; Sado's where the cream of the submissive crop comes to be my slaves for the night. My bondage name has got around you see, and with a name like Ballbreaker, it can bring along quite a crowd to this venue.

It sounds awful, but I've broken many hearts in my time and have come to realize I'm not cut out for having a regular boyfriend. For one thing, I don't have the time, and I don't understand the meaning of relationships, what they're meant to achieve. It's funny, but for all my intelligence, I can't even keep down a proper relationship — there's always someone better around the corner, someone better until that night, the night I met him.

Sado's staff only let in the best-looking guys then closes their coffin black doors to the world. We only cater exclusively for submissives that need the feel of leather being tightened over their bodies, being shackled to a wall and teased until they can take the torture no more. That meant the men who had the patience of saints would soon be bound and subjected to all forms of erotic torture. For some from the looks on their faces, they had never been subs before, not when they saw the chains and other equipment lining the black walls. I thought it might look too heavy for them, but the other Doms and I got them into the whole bondage thing, and if they wanted to use a safe word, then they could go right ahead and tell me, and I would spread it to the others. Not many were prepared to allow the doms to do whatever they wanted — everyone had limits.

I got thrills from plenty of guys who came through those doors. Some were eager to please; I liked that, the feeling of control over another person who equally enjoyed what I did to him. I wasn't a sadist though, not unless the guy who was strapped to the wall happened to want that doing to him. I didn't draw blood, cut or maim anyone. I teased and tempted their senses keeping all the excitement and sexual gratification right up until the end.

When I saw him, I recognized him straight away. His slender, muscular body had a cat like sleekness to it even though he hardly wore much of an outfit at all. Rumor has it he was supposed to be happy with his current guy. He can't have been that happy when he had come in here, but I knew it was Liu from a few years ago. He was one of the sexiest men I had ever met, but couldn't have. It burned, and hurt me before, and I thought I had accepted it, but I suppose a man can convince himself anything if he tries hard enough. He looked young then, but somehow a few years on him looked good, and he had grown out of that late teenage youthful angst I remembered him for. To have him at my mercy would make my day, and then I thought about it — I owned the fucking place, so yeah, he'd be mine alright, but it would still be anonymous thrills and sex afterward, and I wondered if it would ever be enough.

Tonight was different. Tonight I didn't get the chance to have Liu, but one day I would — I felt certain of that.

The Doms got to choose whom they wanted as their subs for the night, and we all had different levels of dominance. Nearly all the men who came in had bags with them that had extra gear they needed for the full effect; ball gags, hoods, rubber phalluses in case they wanted a three-way with some other guy. It happened, and I encouraged originality in such a dark setting as this one.

The guy I chose was lean, and had a cock that was long and thick and hidden inside a thong. His dark eyes and full lips enticed me to him. I yearned to have him as my slave, but also my companion for the night should he prove to be the slave I hoped he would be. The thrill of hearing him moan at what I did to him is what would make me relish this moment. I stroked my hand down his cheek, then his neck, down slowly to his pecs, the criss-cross of black leather straps enhancing his naked frame, and ringed nipple piercings sent a surge of pleasure through my veins and caught in my throat. I tweaked one nipple, squeezing its nub between my thumb and forefinger. He took it well and never gasped or flinched. He accepted it as normal, and as a master, that impressed me. I slapped him across the face — he took that well, too, like a submissive should, his chin rigid showing defiance, I can sense that, but I don't care as long as they are quiet. I slapped him again, and he acted the same. He licked the sweat from his upper lip, it was humid in Sado's tonight. The kind of balmy heat that makes one man submit to another.

"You like this, don't you?" I've had submissives before, slaves too. The ones I take and around town on a leather lead sometimes — we're both anonymous, but feel liberated, especially around the Castro district among many places, but when the slave says he wants something tasty from the shopping aisles, I do what any self-respecting Dom would and slap him right then and there. It's a good thing he enjoys it.

"Yes, master, I love it when you treat me bad." I went into the full scenario now, and he went along with it. He knew he'd been bad and for that he must be punished. I used the best form of punishment ever, I teased him without mercy. He deserved it.

"You've been a bad slave haven't you?" I got the first stirrings of an erection in my leather thong as I picked the riding crop from the wall. I know I wanted to use the cat o' nine tails at some point, but that was for later. I glanced down. He had kept his cock from getting erect, let it lay coiled in his thong like a python waiting to rear. I refrained from stroking him there; I would make him wait for those kind of touches.

He didn't look me in the eyes, they remained downward; like all subs, this one had the same respect for his betters. I liked that. The feel of true dominance over others, yet I am a benevolent Dom, and this master also knew how to please. Stroking him with the riding crop for a while, I took a look over his physique. His body seemed just right, not too muscular, not too skinny, his flesh covered strong muscles, and from what I saw, he looked like he spent some time in the gym. He had toned his body enough to have those muscles show he had respect for his body as well and looked after it.

Raising my arm, I let the crop fall over his fine chest, not hearing a single moan. Then again, this time much harder. I struck his muscles another time, then changed areas, his side being a prime place to whip him next. All I saw throughout this were his nipples staying erect and the sweat running from his near naked body in rivulets. I found that to be sensual enough, stroking my own cock encased in rubber. I knew he would like nothing more than to see me take it out, and stroke it right in front of him, maybe slap his naked cock with it, too, but that, I thought would only be fantasy, and I dealt in reality for fantasy. This was my fantasy. My Sub opened his legs wider. I supposed he wanted me to touch him there, or beneath them, but I never do what others want. Not when I operate using my rules.

Drawing the crop over his abdomen, I saw a slight flinch; it wouldn't have been noticeable if I wasn't looking for it. But there it was. He had flinched, and his cock was starting to show signs of arousal. Even the word brought out my erotic side.

"Naughty slave, you flinched. I will have to whip you properly this time." I stroked his body with the crop a few more times to get his senses used to my touch, then putting it back on the wall my eyes scanned for the next tool to use, when I noticed he, like the others, had brought a bag full of the most essential and erotic contents. I felt him draw breath in through his teeth, preparing for his punishment. I stared at the other men hung on the walls beside me, they were covered in sweat, and oil from what I had noticed, but that night I didn't have the best looking one there. Someone else had that pleasure. I could have shown my dominance, but why should I. It's not like Liu hasn't been fucked by other guys before. If I looked to the left, I could see him, the third one there, his eyes closed, a smile as secretive as the Mona Lisa's on his lips. He kept me there for a moment. I couldn't help it; I just stared, and had to pull myself away.

"I know I'm bad, master ..." he paused, his voice dark and sultry. "And I'd like to make it up to you." What a sweet promise. I wasn't one for torture, but I found his pierced nipples arousing, they stood on end and dreaded me picking another instrument of torture. Why do that when you can go straight to the source.

"Yes, you are," I purred back, like a panther whose right it is to be entertained. Grasping both pecs in my hands I licked each nipple, the hardness a prize in itself. I felt the sweat, smelled it, and the heat he gave off. He didn't need to wear cologne; his sweat gave me enough reason to keep torturing him. When he didn't expect it, I bit down on one, feeling him jerk. "Naughty boy, you reacted," I said. He saw my smile, cruel and wanton. "You know what that means." Judging from his face, he did.

"Do what you want, master? My body's yours." I knew it was from the moment he'd been chained to the wall.

Liu came back to Sado's a month later. I didn't think he would, considering I was the place's owner, but at least he hadn't left for good. The pain of rejection can hurt, even for a Dom. And Doms also recognize their regulars. Liu became a regular and tried not to notice me. I noticed him though and made sure he was mine this time. I hung around while other guys were being chosen and I left him no choice but to accept me as his master. Even if he had tried to say no, he'd have had a hard time with the staff — they'd have still chained him up, even if it meant hog-tying him while he struggled.

"You know you don't want anyone else," I boasted, but it got Liu's attention. His eyes met mine, and I could feel the attraction between us.

"I kind of like the look of him." Liu pointed to the buff guy with the short cropped hair and the ball gag. I saw by the look of him he was just teasing me.

"I'm better than all of them; they might go easy on you as you're a regular. Me, I'll show you a good time; keep you hard right up until ... the end." I kept his gaze; he stood still, and then leaned over, whispering.

"I noticed who you were by your tattoo, Darren, so that kind of bullshit doesn't work on me." I laughed, while he waited for my response.

"Touché Liu, you're tat stood out real nice, too." He held his hand up ready to hit me, but I caught it in my gloved hand. "Since when have you acted the Dom? It doesn't suit you." I nodded to one of my guys, Trevor, to come over.

"Bind him while I get some torture devices sorted out." I could see my dominance took him by surprise. While I rummaged for some tools in the bag he'd brought, I could hear a whispered, "Bastard!" come from his lips from above. I picked out a few — these would certainly get a reaction out of him.

"You didn't bring much with you, so I thought I'd bring out the best stuff to make you moan, Liu." Now I'd had him right where I wanted him, I wasn't about to let him go or create a poor show either. I slipped on a metal glove with sharp talons at the end. He must have had them based on some martial arts weapon I'd seen before, or he had a Freddy Krueger fetish. When I held the glove up for him to see, he got wide eyes and a slightly open mouth. Oh well, I suppose it gets that kind of response all the time.

Being the sort of person I thought he was, he had it decorated, so it's not just functional, it's attractive, too, like Liu could be if he stopped pouting.

"I could do anything to you, Liu," I went along with how I felt, how my cock felt at seeing him again. Drawing one talon down his cheek, I heard him hiss out at its sharpness. As I continued to scratch it over his flesh, I made sure I didn't hurt him; his skin was my canvas. I could attach a collar to his neck with a chain lead, or use a restraint on his legs. You never knew with Liu whether he would knee you in the balls. "Anything at all, there's a myriad ways to satisfy myself, and you if you will let me."

I came closer, used the same talon to push his chin up. He'd shaved that same night, smooth and slick, I licked my way up it and along the cheek. He didn't say a word, but I looked down and his cock stood out hard as rock, and I noticed through his black rubber pants, it had wept. He needed me to stroke it. Inside I enjoyed myself playing the Dom with someone like him, someone I had history with.

I took him from the wall; his wrists still cuffed and attached a leather collar around his neck, pushing him onto his knees. "Lick my boots, slave." I ordered, and reluctantly he did. His tongue snaked up the shiny PVC fabric from the toe; his obedience made me love him even more. He held onto my boot for stability at first, but once he got into it, he started to stroke my leg with the other hand. In mock anger, I slapped his hand away.

"Naughty, you're not supposed to do that. I didn't say you could," That way he knew to do as instructed. "Now lick my other boot and use longer licks," I pulled him up with the chain, and kissed him, then pushed him back to my boot. "Now you'll have enough saliva to do it." I watched each lick he slithered up my boot, savoring the control I had over him. Poor thing, he'd enjoy it soon, if not already, and once I'd got tired of his boot worship, I yanked him up again.

"You performed well, slave," He looked good there, defenseless, handsome and mine. "If you do this next task right, I will reward you, but if not — you shall be punished ... harshly."

Kissing him once more, I pushed him to the floor. "Lick my cock slave ... every inch of it. I want to be pleased ... I demand it." This time his gaze never met mine, I don't know if it was out of embarrassment or reverence. I hoped it was the latter.

From the moment I felt his tongue stroke up my length, I remembered the first time I met Liu, on campus. He resembled a fresh-faced teen with a rich Chinese heritage. He got his eyes I expect from his mother's side, and I liked my men on the effeminate side. Secretly, we had dated, but it didn't work out. I had issues, he said but he never told me what they were. Liu was the one man who triggered the apathy in me to find boyfriends and stay with them. What was the point of the heartache? I still wondered why he came in here to be punished night after night. Did he come to see me, or any man? Did he care which one fucked him. I guess not. He licked much longer now, at ease with how I liked his movements. I could feel my cock spring to life after the fourth lick, and when I looked down this time, he glanced up at me.

"Is this to your liking master?" His obedience just made me harder, and with one movement of my talon, I pushed the thick material to the side, watching his expression when my cock fell out, long and thick, an ebony rite of passage.

I ignored his inquiry, with only one statement in mind. "Suck my cock — that would please me, slave."

"But, master. It's so big!"

"You've sucked big cock before, slave. It never bothered you then. You should be used to it by now," Then it dawned on me. He never sucked my cock when we dated; it was all about the fucking. Maybe he couldn't take my size. "Suck it, slave." I demanded, and Liu fell silent, licking his full lips and pressing them to my cock head, opening wider and plunging down the thickly veined shaft, and then coming up for air. With my other hand I push his mouth over my cock, forcing him an inch deeper until I let him breathe again. We were like that for minutes, me demanding more from him; him giving me an endless supply of his patience.

"That's good, yes." I let him up again seeing him gasp, chest heaving from the strain. "Good slave, you've earned your reward." I dragged him up by his chains and bound him to the wall, fastening a blindfold over his eyes. Crouching down so my own ass stuck out, I freed his cock from his thong, stroking and slapping it around like it meant nothing to me. With each slap, I made sure they grew harder, as did his cock. It seemed he liked a good amount of pain after all. Writhing in his bonds, his hips swaying with my slaps, I threw him when I took the whole of his length down in one go — hearing his gasp. I let it fall, licking the length from tip to base now, holding the shaft, licking around the tip I waited for him to calm down, then plunged all the way down. He tried to stifle a moan, but I knew he couldn't hide his enjoyment. I did this several times until his tip was engorged with blood, the skin tight, and his shaft as rigid as it could get. It jerked in my hand desperate for release, but I wanted to hear him beg first.

"I need to come ..." He whispered while everyone else was already engaged in fucking and discipline.

"You need to beg me, slave, before I even allow it." I pulled the skin down so his cock head stood proud, needing the rush of orgasm through his body. In another movement, I teased him, stroking his cock, letting him think I would encourage his balls to release their juice, then stopping. I let his cock twitch, the sight of it keeping me happy. I'm bad when I get into the bondage zone.

I still hear nothing, so I rub the bulbous tip, circling it with his precum juice, and from the rigidity of this body he needs to come, but he does not ask now, as in asking, he is surrendering completely to me. He's mad at me, but I don't know what for. I suppose at some point I will find out, but it won't be pretty.

"Please master, will you let me come?" There it was what I wanted to hear. It sounded so genuine coming from his lips. I sensed his need, his lust all flowing through to one organ, the one I moved in rhythm with my sucking it in fast and hard strokes until I heard his cries, and felt his seed hit my throat. I swallowed it like this was the only time I got anything from him, feeling his cock still hard even after I let go.

Later on in the night, clients were already packing up and ready to leave. Liu had headed for the door along with the staff; I locked the back door, turned to get to my car when he stood there. I nearly told him he made a good slave, but it wasn't the best time.

"Why have you stayed behind? I thought we weren't going anywhere."

He didn't breathe a word, just stared into the sky, the moon huge and looming over us, its silvery light made him look ethereal. "I wanted to torment you by being nice." I listened to him. I couldn't do anything else. For all my nights fucking other guys, I realized I'd missed him, missed his touch and him being there.

"You did ... torment me I mean. I couldn't bear the thought of other guys fucking you, not when it should be me. I thought you liked my touch, the way I fucked." Just to get things straight, I don't get all sentimental with men. It's not me and I've never been emotional, but Liu, well, he brings all those emotions out in me.

"What makes you think you know me?" Liu's eyes flared with anger I had only seen when he was younger and more reckless. "I've already got a man who's treating me like a kid, I don't need another one. And, anyway, aren't you too caring for a Dom?" That stung.

"What am I supposed to be, a complete bastard 'cause I like to be someone else at the weekend?" That's all I desired to be another person than me in a suit day in day out. I could see Liu had something else to say, and inside he was seething with already built up rage.

"When we were going out, you always took the lead whether you did stuff at college, or when we were alone at your place. When have you ever let anyone dominate you?" He had a point. I've been a top since I knew what sex was at aged eighteen; I never knew any other way to have sex. I kissed, caressed, and fucked. That's all I knew.

"If I was that bad as a boyfriend, I'm open to suggestions." He thought I was joking, but the shocked look told him otherwise now.

"Okay, here's the deal. If you let me dominate you and you can't deal with it − I leave and you never see me again. If you succeed, I'll let you have me, and we'll continue as before." Tempting it was, but how did I feel about opening myself to him? He had hurt me with what he said, but I knew why he felt that way about me. If my dominant attitude was the thing that ended our relationship, I had to think long and hard. Did my love for him, my longing to have him by my side outweigh my need to dominate him?

I had thought about this enough, we ended up going to my car, really slow and deliberate. "You want to do it in here?" I asked him. "It's roomy enough to take us both in the back." He nodded; I got inside and lay back ready for him, kicking off my clothes while he did the same. I felt him straddle me, his cock hardening near my groin.

"Put your arms behind the seat." He ordered. Liu pulled a black bandana from his belt, tying my wrists with it. A nice touch, I had never been defenseless like this before. I didn't know what being a captive felt like. No time like the present.

"You wouldn't believe how many times I dreamed of your dark skin on mine, holding me close. I've missed you for ages."

Oh, I could. I thought trying to relax as his hands caressed my upper torso; his fingers pinched my nipple nubs while he ground his cock into my groin, feeling my need. I hadn't come even if he had, but I got the idea he had more cum to get out of those balls. He changed the pace by slapping my face, and then leaned over, taking my lips in a selfish kiss, then another, his passion exuding from those lips.

"Good, you passed the first part." Pushing up my legs, he reached around grasping my hard cock, liking what he felt no doubt. I felt excited as a stag in spring and when I started to moan, Liu stuffed another bandana in my mouth. "You're being too loud, Darren." I didn't complain when my moans were stifled, tears streaming down my cheeks from how fast he pulled my cock. "Be prepared for the next part."

Pulling the bandana from my mouth, he thrust his cock deep inside, bucking into my throat with an energy that only knew domination. I wondered where he had learned all this, and thought maybe he was pissed at me that all this built up anger was saved up just for me. Just for this night. His cock grew harder in my mouth, fucking it, drawing my head deeper. I imagined he had his head thrown back in pure ecstasy.

"Yes, that's good. You've done very well, and ... If you pass the third level, you might get me permanently." As he thrust for the last time, he made it count, his thickness gagging my throat. Liu pushed the bandana back in my mouth, his attention going to my ass, feeling the coolness of a gel lube being smoothed over the puckered surface. I didn't even feel the press of his fingers priming my ass hole for entry. I wanted to scream out so loud. I'd never been fucked before, I was an anal virgin, but I whispered instead hoping he didn't hear me.

"You're pretty tight down there. Either it's been a while since someone fucked you, or ... ohh, my," He purred. I felt his tip forcing inside my body, it hurt at first, and I needed to clamp down on it, but I held back my instinct or it would have hurt much more. He drove it in to my ass by this time. "Yeah, you're so tight. I like that. It's one of those things I didn't know about you I just ticked on a sheet in my mind." *Bitch!* I thought, *sometimes what you do in life comes back to bite you in the ass.* Liu rocked back and forth, I heard his breathing deep and labored, liking the way he rode me. I felt him pulse under my body, shivering, sucking in air though his teeth. He felt so big, his shaft filling my hole, and just when I thought he couldn't go any further, he did. Talk about pushing the envelope. I gritted my teeth against the movements, and felt his last desperate thrusts as he groaned, guttural, shooting jets of cum inside, filling me up until I moaned greedily into the bandana as he brought me to full orgasm. Glad I didn't miss one.

"There," he said, pulling out the bandana. "That wasn't too bad, was it?"

"I never thought getting fucked felt so darn good. No wonder you loved it so much," He lay on me, spent and hot, sweat mingled with my own as we made contact. He kissed my cheek, then my lips. I missed him, too; him being so close made everything in my life complete, all this for the man who is crap at relationships.

"Yeah, but I like variety, Darren. It's the thrill of sex being different every time. No one has to be the Dom, we can both play at being the Dom and the sub each time."

"And if you lived with me, you know, to test it out ... see what I was like."

"Then I don't know, with you being around I guess one minute I'd be tied to the wall, the next the kitchen sink." he said, his voice indicating that he had a beaming smile, it was good to hear the joy in him again.

"I'd never do that to you. We'll get a bondage maid in who's got a bubble-butt you'll want to spank all the time."

"Like that would ever happen." I heard him get out, the back door slam shut, and then the sound of the engine humming. Bastard must have taken my keys. "Hey, untie me!"

"Well," he laughed. "I thought I'd drive for a change. You just relax a bit."

"Hey, wait up!" I shouted, but it was too late, Liu had taken off with me in the back, and there was nothing I could do about it.

CONTROL POINTS
By Mark Apoapsis

I was startled at how big and imposing my new roommate was. The University didn't allow freshmen to choose their roommates, but we did get a certain amount of input, in the form of a long questionnaire that their automated systems used as fodder to find a good match. When I filled out the form, I figured it was going to be stressful enough making the transition to college life, away from my family, having to do everything for myself for the first time, with the academic pressures of a good school, without also winding up with some huge homophobic jock to deal with. If I could have specified that I wanted a short, scrawny geek just like myself, and one who had no problem sharing a room with a gay roommate, I would have listed those as my top priorities. Even if the University had been willing to admit that anyone might care about a potential roommate's sexual orientation, and ask them that question on its web form, no one would have checked a box admitting they were homophobic. Nor was I allowed to specify a height or weight requirement; discrimination based on build was illegal. They did let me specify my roommate's intended major, so I put down theater, figuring that was as close as I could come to ensuring a gay or gay-friendly roommate and avoiding someone who got in on a football scholarship and would use me as a tackle dummy.

They'd found me a future theater major, and in our brief email interchange Jim struck me as a well-read, intellectually passionate kind of guy, so I figured we'd get along fine and didn't consider using my one veto to roll the dice again.

At first I thought there'd been some computer glitch because the man who strode in while I was unpacking, carrying two heavy duffle bags and a backpack with much less effort than I had, was built more like a boxer, or a lean football player, or a husky basketball player, than someone whose main interests supposedly were theater, genetics, and American history. The stranger looked at least as surprised as I felt, supporting my suspicion of a screw-up.

"Uh, hey," he said uncertainly. "Are you Wally, by any chance? Or do I have the wrong room? I'm Jim."

"Nice to meet you in person," I said, rising to shake his hand. That forced him to find a place to set his bags down, but I tend to shake hands when I'm introduced; it's a reflex.

"Yeah, nice to meet you ..." he said distractedly.

"Something the matter?"

"Sorry. It's just ... You didn't mention that you were white."

"Oh. Sorry, was I supposed to? Is that surprising? A lot of students are white."

"Uh, yeah, I know. One of the largest groups. Almost 40 percent. Significantly higher than the general population of the state. Which I find — well, don't get me started on that."

"For that matter, you didn't tell me you were African American."

He looked offended. "We prefer to be called Amerafrican."

"Oh, sorry. I didn't mean anything by it. My parents use that term. They don't mean anything by it either, they're just a little old-fashioned. Did I say something in my email to lead you to believe I was Amerafrican myself?"

"No, no, it's not your fault. There must have been a mix-up." He gave me a friendly grin. "By the way, 'black' is fine if 'Amerafrican' is too much of a mouthful."

"Did you ask them for a black roommate? I didn't know they allowed you to."

"They don't. But there was a choice on the form to ask them to try to match me with the closest distant relative they could find."

"Based on our DNA profiles?"

"Right. That was the closest I could come to a racial preference. And they claimed they found a tenth cousin, give or take a generation. Guess they were wrong. But I don't want you to think I'm some kind of reverse racist. It's just that I went to a small, mostly Latino, Asian and white high school that had like five other black students, and it happened that I was the only one in my honors classes who was black. I didn't have much in common with any of the other five and didn't really hang out with them. So I saw college as my chance to connect with my Amerafrican heritage for the first time. I thought, in a good school like this, I'd be able to find friends who were worth talking to and black."

"I'm sure you will. They must have screwed up the DNA match, though. I don't have any black ancestors as far as I know. It would be interesting to find out I did, but I doubt it. Two pairs of great grandparents were Swedish immigrants, one English. The fourth were born in Virginia, I think. I have pictures of their wedding that I could find if I dug around. The colors faded a little before they were digitized, but they definitely looked white."

"I'm planning to look into what happened. I'll let you know what I find out. But I'm sure we'll get along fine; sorry for being startled. I'll find other ways to get back to my roots. Which closet do you want? And are you going to use any of these built-in shelves?"

"I can't even imagine why they thought a student would need more shelves than an old lady with knickknacks."

"They're called 'bookshelves.' This building dates back to the turn of the twenty-first century."

# # # # #

At least his imposing build settled one thing that I'd been wondering about, a little apprehensively, since first arriving: who would be on top and who was be on bottom, and how we'd fight it out if we both had the same preference. One look at tall, muscular Jim convinced me he should be on top. And he immediately agreed. All I had to do, when he asked my preference, was meekly admit that it would be a struggle for me to climb into the top bunk every night, and he instantly offered to let me have the bottom bunk. I don't think he minded being on top at all. With pecs and abs like his, as became even more obvious the first time he took off his shirt for the night, it was no surprise how athletically he was able to swing himself into his bunk.

By the time we were getting ready for bed our first night together, we'd dropped the initial wary politeness of two guys trying to make a good first impression on each other — especially after the initial confusion — and we'd started to relax, thanks to a bottle of rum that we obtained with the help of an upperclassman neighbor to celebrate our first night of total freedom, living on our own out from under our parents' thumbs, making our recently-minted adulthood feel much less theoretical. It was the first time I'd gotten even slightly drunk. College was going to be great, I thought. And the booze helped give me the courage to do something for the first time that I was obviously going to have to do a lot, living with Jim, whether I liked it or not: take off my shirt in front of him, exposing my comparatively pathetic physique, as the penultimate step for getting ready for bed. Leering down at me from his bunk, his beefy, dark shoulders and upper chest visible over the edge, he said, "We had private showers in the gym in my high school. So I've never seen a white ass before."

"And you're not gonna," I shot back. "I sleep in my boxers." And the dorm had private showers with changing areas, too, which was where I planned to change my underwear each day.

# # # # #

We did get along great, once I got used to the looming presence of someone who looked as if he could break me over one knee if I so much as left the cap off the toothpaste. It did take me several days to get accustomed to seeing his sculpted dark-chocolate-colored body set off by his tighty whities enough for me to find the right compromise between averting my eyes or staring at his magnificent physique every morning and evening.

We helped each other with our homework, although for a theater major he had a pretty good grasp of math and science and needed less of my help in his physics for poets class than I needed his insight in my required humanities and social sciences classes. Jim knew more than me about history and had some well-thought-out and provocative opinions, although to me he seemed almost obsessed with certain aspects of the past, like the racial tensions before and after the civil rights movement of the middle of the last century, and the legacy of slavery in the centuries before that. He claimed we still lived in a far from race-blind society, no matter what anyone said. None of my black friends in high school had seemed so concerned about that, but maybe it was just because it was only in college that I had a chance to have deep philosophical discussions about the world's problems late into the night. On the other hand, when I casually brought up the analogy of homophobia, he seemed to buy into the party line that that really had disappeared sometime in the Nameless Decades. I still hadn't told him I was gay.

We had different viewpoints on a lot of things and enjoyed arguing about them. Whenever we disagreed about a factual point, Jim was almost always right; he had an amazing number of facts in his head, and what he didn't know off the top of his head, he could look them up about ten times as fast as I could have, and almost always proved himself right.

Not that we argued over anything personal. We shared the space in the room without resorting to drawing a strict imaginary line down the middle as some guys in our dorm did, although we didn't become close buddies who shared everything, either. Since he'd been so nice about the bunk, I gave him his choice of desk, closet, and everything else.

But we loved debating just about everything else on the planet, and he was a formidable opponent. We'd known each other almost a week before I caught him in a key factual error he'd used to support his argument. When I called him on it, he looked it up, stared at his computer in disbelief, spent a few seconds double-checking it with another source, and then said, "Looks like the facts aren't on my side on this one. So I guess there's only one way I can win this argument."

"What's that?" I asked unsuspectingly.

He lunged from his desk chair over to where I was sitting on my bunk, and next thing I knew, I was on my back with him on top of me, with one hand pinned over my head and the other trapped between our bodies.

"Expose your soft white underbelly," he replied, pushing my T-shirt up to my ribcage with his free hand, "and tickle you until you concede my point."

I couldn't believe he was doing this. I struggled in vain, laughing helplessly. I managed to hold out for several minutes before gasping out, "You win!"

After that, I started trying really hard to catch him in a mistake. I even did research in advance, so I could start an argument on that subject. It took me a week, but finally I hit on the idea of searching an urban legend fact-checking site, looking for myths I'd have sworn were true. Sure enough, I found one he'd bought into also, and once I proved him wrong, he pinned my head under his arm and held me there, bent over, while his free hand reached under my shirt and mercilessly attacked my belly and ribs.

A few days later, in another discussion, I pointed out that he was using circular logic. He thought it through, then pulled my shirt off and tickled my armpits as well as my belly and ribs. It became clear that every time I pinned him down with in an error, he would literally pin me down, and I'd get tickled within an inch of my life for my trouble. He didn't do it in response to my merely disagreeing with him; if I was wrong he'd win the argument by reason, and if it was a matter of opinion, he was happy to agree to disagree. He would only grab me and tickle me when I was right and he knew it.

So I really started working at it. He knew enough now to check urban legend sites when in doubt, but I found it worked well to bring up one of the topics he was emotionally wrapped up in, in hopes he'd overstep his knowledge without stopping to check his facts. For example, he believed that people have to be taught in school to speak their native language with the "correct" grammar, and therefore, what he called "ghetto talk" was proof of continuing inequities in public education funding. When I showed him reliable sources — I was getting quicker at finding them — proving that the consensus among linguists was that the quaintly-named "African American Vernacular English" was a dialect with its own grammar rules every bit as self-consistent as Standard American or British English, and argued that it was more a case of one culture looking down on another's dialect, he gave me that long steady look that meant that in sixty seconds I was going to be stripped to the waist, eagerly agreeing with whatever he said while I still had breath to do it.

I found that it was less work to trap him in logical arguments, since I was at least as good at logic as he was, whereas I couldn't match his Web search skills. Besides, with no fact-checking needed, I could spring my trap after our computers were shut down and charging and we were both getting undressed. It would reduce the risk of getting my shirt ripped in the struggle, if he didn't have to pull it off me. One night I trapped him in a corner like that when he had just taken off his shirt and I had already stripped down to my boxers and about to turn off the light. He grappled with me, skin to skin for the first time, and pinned me to my mattress. Even with my entire torso and my legs at his disposal, he didn't stop at tickling my already voluntarily-bared skin, but eventually pushed my boxers down a couple of inches until my pubes curled over it. This was a whole new level of humiliating defeat.

He stopped tickling me for a moment to comment, "You're even whiter than I thought, under that tan."

"I spent a lot of time at the beach over the summer," I said breathlessly. "I used sunscreen, but I still slowly got tan."

"Is your ass as white as this?"

"I haven't seen it lately. And neither will you." I made an attempt to break loose, but failed.

"I'll bet you're extra ticklish here," he said, lightly stroking the tender white skin above my pubes with his fingertips.

I was.

# # # # #

As we got to know each other better, we remained very accommodating to each other. For example, when he asked me the third week if I'd mind if he used the room for a video project he had to do for a class, I readily agreed. And the night when we were getting ready to go to our first big dorm party, he said, "Maybe we should arrange a signal if one of us gets lucky and needs the room for awhile. If you leave something tied to the doorknob, I'll assume you've got a girl or a guy here and I'll stay away."

"Sounds good," I said, feeling very relieved. Not because I realistically expected to get lucky that night, but because he was so casual about saying "a girl or a guy."

"And I'll do the same. I don't want you to have to stay out all night; I promise to make sure he doesn't fall asleep afterwards, and I'll take the thing off the doorknob as soon as he's gone."

Wow. That was a surprise. "Sounds good," I said, trying to sound like I hadn't just heard a momentous revelation.

# # # # #

I came home from class one afternoon, and Jim gave me a smugly self-righteous look. "I found out what happened with our DNA comparison. We really do have several segments in common, like I mentioned." He'd discovered that surprising fact the first week and had been trying to account for it ever since. "Well, I started by searching for geographical locations where other people related to each of us might live. I already knew mine show up in four or five different tribes in Africa, because the slave owners bred my ancestors like cattle."

What I thought, but didn't dare say, was that I could well believe that he was the product of generations of selectively breeding strong powerful male slaves to work in the field. There are some things you just don't say, even to your roommate.

Instead, I said, "As opposed to castrating them and buying a freshly captured batch from the slave traders." I was hoping to bait him into one of those arguments where he'd get too worked up to check his facts, so I might catch him in a rare mistake.

He didn't argue the point; apparently this was just an aside for a more important revelation. "We can't directly look at our ancestor's genomes, of course. Most of them were dead and buried before the technology became practical. Some of our grandparents were genotyped with primitive technology before they died, but any further back we have to do detective work. But people didn't use to move so much, so if you find a large concentration of relatives in one area, that's probably where one of your ancestors lived. Those would be the ones who never moved and lived their wholes lives where their great grandparents did. And here's what I found by searching for one place that has both our relatives." He showed me a map on his computer he had marked with scattered white and black dots. "They're concentrated between Petersburg and Tuckahoe, Virginia. I correlated the Virginia Historical Society's online slave database with some family trees that were put together by some of my distant cousins who are genealogy buffs, and I'm pretty sure I found a particular slave woman on a particular plantation in Chesterfield County who's my great-to-the-tenth grandmother. And some of your cousins trace their descent from the owner of that same plantation."

"What are you saying?"

He glowered at me, triumphantly outraged. "Your ancestor raped my ancestress."

"Wow. Uh ... sorry?"

# # # # #

I didn't see a lot of him the next day, and I thought he must be mad at me for the sins of my multiple-great grandfather, which seemed a little unfair. But it turned out he was just busy. He was in an excited mood a couple of days later and eager to share his news with me. "I finally figured out what I'm doing for my video project. You know, the one I should have been planning instead of spending time on extracurricular ancestry research to answer that question that was bugging me. I was looking for a topic that would make a strong artistic statement and also be an opportunity to connect with my Amerafrican heritage. Then I realized I could leverage the ancestry research as an inspiration for my script. Did you ever hear of the miniseries last century called *Roots*?

"No," I admitted. "I don't know as much about film history as you."

"It was groundbreaking. It won nine Emmy awards. The author traced one of the branches of his family tree and told the story of his African ancestor who was captured as a teenager and reduced from a proud young warrior to a helpless slave. Here, let me show you the trailer for the 50th-anniversary edition." He struck a few keys and played a short video.

"That looks like a big undertaking for an undergraduate project due at the end of the semester, especially your freshman year."

"Oh, I won't attempt anything nearly that large-scale, of course. I'll leave out all the African cultural stuff and the Civil War and the family relations, and just focus on one theme, 'The Evils of Slavery.' And I'll limit the scope to just one ancestor when he's first sold at auction, and then one or two whipping scenes. To me, the whippings were the most memorable part of the mini-series. Now I just have to find a cast. Hey, now that I know I'll need some white characters, are you interested? You'd get academic credit."

"Much as I'd love to get one of my humanities requirements out of the way without actually taking a class, I'm no actor. Besides, I have a pretty good idea what you're going to write for the white characters, and I can't see myself holding a whip and acting like I enjoy using it."

"Too bad. You could play your own ancestor. Are you sure you didn't inherit a sadistic streak from him that you could tap into if you tried?"

"You're joking, right? Especially since I can't have inherited more than a tiny fraction of his genes after all those generations. Anyway, everyone owned slaves then, even the Founding Fathers. How do you even know my ancestor was any worse than all his neighbors? He could have just been a man of his time. If he'd been born today, he might have been a perfectly reasonable guy."

"Well, maybe."

"Besides, I've been thinking. If you found traces of him in your DNA because he raped your ancestress, doesn't that make him just as much your ancestor as mine?"

For the first time I'd known him, he looked as if he wanted to slug me. "That's different!" he snapped.

But the next morning, as I was pulling my shirt on, he grabbed me without warning and threw me onto my bunk, with my shirt covering my face and my torso bare, and began one of his merciless tickling attacks as I desperately sucked air through the fabric of my shirt.

"You win!" I finally gasped. "Whatever I said, I was wrong!"

# # # # #

"I found someone for the part of Overseer," Jim told me a couple of days later. He was in a good mood, possibly because he'd been relieving his tension more often than usual in the way that healthy young guys are wont to, at least if I'd correctly interpreted the squeaking springs and heavy breathing coming from above me the past two nights. And mornings. And once in the afternoon.

"He's perfect: big and beefy, and wants to be an actor. He's actually a pretty good actor. Manages to look cruel, even though he's really a nice guy. But I've had no luck at all casting the other main character."

"Your ancestress?"

"Actually, I decided to make it a male character. Male whippings play better, and are also more dramatic since you can show a man stripped to the waist without tagging it adults-only. They won't grade an adult video. This is America, though; I can make it as violent as I want."

"So you're having trouble finding guys who'll sign up to be filmed shirtless getting whipped?"

"Only pretending to get whipped, of course. I'll add the bloody stripes with CGI later. I can do that in my sleep. Yeah, I've been auditioning guys for two days. I didn't get that many, even though I posted in all the Amerafrican student communities and even physically approached every good-looking black guy I spotted at the student union. Turns out very few black men in this school want to play a slave getting whipped."

"Imagine that."

"I had hopes for this one guy in particular: really nailed the reading, darker than me, seemed to be well-built. But when I showed him the prop and asked him to audition that scene, he said, 'My mothers didn't raise me to star in some S&M flick.' I told him to quit being such a mammas' boy and take off his shirt, and he threatened to file a Hate Speech complaint with the University. Actually brought up the app and started filling in the form on the spot, until I apologized."

"That sucks. Did you get anyone to through with it at all?"

"Oh, yeah. A few. I only wish just one of them were a decent actor. The only guy with any acting talent at all who was willing to audition for the whipping scene was this Latino." He clicked the mouse on his desk a few times and showed a hunky Latino with his arms raised out of frame and his armpit hairs, handsome face, and muscular chest visible down to his navel. He unfroze it and showed the guy pretending to moan in pain as a black arm I assumed was Jim's pretended to flay his back with a bull whip I assumed was a prop. There were empty bookshelves and an unmade bunk bed in the background, so I assumed this was shot in the privacy of the guy's room.

"He doesn't look African at all," Jim said, licking his lips as he watched the light-brown chest twisting this way and that. "Of course, I can easily darken his skin with CGI. Actually, I should probably do that with whoever I cast because Africans are a lot darker than any Amerafrican. But it would take more work to change his features. I could do it if I had to. Last century there was a reaction against actors crossing racial lines — minstrel singers played by white men in blackface, Asian villains played by white actors — but it's getting to be acceptable again because the actor isn't playing the character so much as the character's computer-generated almost from scratch, using a mix of one man's skin mapped onto another man's motions. But it's a lot of work, and frankly, this guy's not enough better than the others to be worth it. None of them convince me they really feel humiliated." He flipped through a few clips of shirtless black men of various shapes, sizes, and colors pretending to be whipped. He was right; it was obvious they were acting, and badly.

"So what are you going to do?"

"I've got some acting experience myself from high school plays, although it's hard to direct and act at the same time. But if it comes to that, I'll play the part myself before I pick one of these hams. Meanwhile, I'm going to audition every guy I can find in the next day or so. But right now, I feel like, uh, stretching out in my bunk and relaxing." He then stripped to his briefs, placed his computer on his bunk, and swung himself up after it.

I put on my earphones, brought up a textbook, and started studying. The privacy signal on the doorknob was for when one of us had company, if we ever got lucky. Otherwise, our tacit agreement was to just pretend we didn't notice what the other guy was doing.

# # # # #

It was the middle of the next afternoon, and there was nothing tied to the doorknob, when I walked in the room and found Jim tied up, bare-chested, with a guy roughly as big as him and maybe a couple of years older standing behind him holding a whip.

"Oh! Sorry!" I stammered. "I didn't realize — I'll just go."

"No, it's all right, Wally. It's not what it looks like. Owen, this is my roommate Wally. Wally, Owen is playing my overseer. We're filming. What do you think the green sheets are for?" I saw that he'd pinned bright green sheeting over the foot of the bunk he was tied to, and over the bookshelves that we'd never figured out a good use for. He'd cut windows in the ones over the bookshelves, and I thought I saw a camera behind each one.

Awkwardly, I reached past my roommate's bare flank to offer Owen my hand. He had a nice firm grip.

"You're welcome to come in and watch, or study," Jim said. "It's your room, too. Just be very quiet, please."

Owen was clad in one of those linen shirts that had been popular around the time I'd entered high school. Now I realized it could pass for 17th-century homespun, at least by student-production standards. He might have dug it out of his closet to use as a costume.

I left my earphones off but tried to study, being careful not to create any noise in the background underneath my roommate's moans and screams, but really, his were only slightly more convincing than the ones I'd heard coming from the audition recordings, and his facial expressions looked fake, too.

Jim seemed to realize this himself. "This isn't working, is it? I just can't get into the part. Let's face it, I've led a pampered life and have no idea what it was like for a slave to face pain and humiliation. Maybe it would help if you actually hit me with that thing."

"You're kidding," Owen said. "I'm not going to hit you for real."

"It's just a prop. It's not going to take my skin off even if you put all your strength into it. It'll just hurt. The pain might get some genuine reactions out of me."

"Are you sure, man?"

"Yes. Do it."

The fake whip slapped audibly across his dark, muscular back. "I hardly felt that. You can do better than that."

"I don't know, man. Acting is one thing, but actually hurting you? On purpose?"

"Look, do you want this part, or not? I'm the director. Do as I say."

"OK, man. Let me know if it's too much."

"I'll call out 'cut' if it's too much, of course."

Owen wound up and slapped the whip really hard against my roommate's bare back. This time, I heard a good solid thwack.

"Ow! Shit!" Struggling free of the loosely tied bonds on his wrist in seconds, Jim whirred around and grabbed the student actor, who was just starting to apologize, by his shirtfront, almost lifting the big man off his feet. I heard fabric ripping. Then he came to his senses.

"Sorry, man. I did ask for that. Guess we know now how I react to pain. I suck at this." Releasing him, he said, "Hey, did I rip your shirt? Sorry about that. I'll pay for it."

"Don't worry about it, man. I've got like five of these, and they were out of style by the end of my freshman year. I never wear them anymore."

Toying with the torn edges, Jim said thoughtfully, "We should film you this way; it actually looks good." Owen had a hairy, muscular chest, now partially exposed under the ripped shirt. "It'll screw up the continuity, but I'm not sure we got any usable footage yet anyway. OK, let's try this one more time. Tie me up again."

For the first two lashes, Owen must have lost his nerve, because Jim said, "Harder, damn it!"

The third and fourth ones smacked loudly enough to hear. I could see Jim cursing and gritting his teeth, looking angry. After the fifth one, he said, "Cut! Sorry, man, I don't think I can take much more of this. Let's look at the playback."

He viewed it on the large screen on his desk, scowling. "What do you think?" he asked Owen.

"Well ... I've seen worse acting," he said diplomatically.

"Wally, would you come here and take a look?"

I wasn't getting any studying done anyway. He played it back for me. I asked, "You want my honest opinion? I think it looks like you're putting up with some minor pain because you know you've got to get through it. And look, right there, for a second, it looks like you want to turn around and sock Owen in the mouth. That isn't in character, is it?"

"I hate it when you're right," he said. Then he grinned. "You know what happens to you when you're right, don't you?"

I felt that now-familiar thrill of excitement pass through me that I felt whenever I knew he was about to pin me down and tickle me. Was he at least going to wait until we were alone, or would he actually humiliate me in front of this stranger, I wondered.

"There!" Owen said excitedly, pointing at me. "That's the expression you should be going for. That's very close to what humiliation looks like, or the anticipation of it. I don't know what the little runt thinks you're going to do to him, but ..."

"You're right!" Jim said. "Man, if only I could fake that expression. Seeing it isn't enough to let me copy it."

"Maybe if Owen held you down while I tickled you," I suggested, "you'd get the hang of it."

"Nice try, buddy. Anyway, I doubt it. But you, you're a natural. Maybe I should offer you the part." I laughed, and he said, "No, seriously."

"But ... where do I even start? First of all, I'm no actor."

"The character has like three minutes of dialog, and if it doesn't come out good enough, I can dub my voice in, or someone else's. The important thing is you know how to look utterly humiliated. I've seen it. All you have to do is get in that frame of mind. It's called Method acting."

"How about the little detail that I'm white, and the character's black?" I said.

"The character's African. A full-blooded African. I'd need to darken my skin anyway, and reshape my features to look more African. I told you, I know how to do that with CGI. To really do it right, I can computer-generate the character from your motions and expressions, and map my skin and face onto you, only darker and more African. They do that all the time in movies these days. What I can't do is turn my 'let's get this over with' expression into fear and or my 'touch me one more time and I'll beat the shit out of you' expression into humiliation. Even Hollywood animators can't do that convincingly, or movies wouldn't use actors at all anymore."

"It would take more than darker skin to make my body look anything like yours."

"Actually, you're perfect as you are. People were shorter back then, and in the scene when you're on the auction block, you've just spent months chained up on a ship on bread and water. When it was me, I was going to have to make myself scrawnier in post production. As for the whipping scene, if I want to make you look like you've been working in the field for a few months, I can just beef you up in the computer."

"Well ... I'd like to help you. You're a great roommate. You've done me plenty of favors these past few weeks."

"This could make the difference between my acing the class or flunking an important prerequisite. I'd owe you big-time. Will you take the part?"

"OK. Sure. I'll give it a try."

"Great!" He clapped me on the shoulder, grinning.

"Thanks, man," Owen said, putting his hand on my other shoulder. "And sorry about the 'runt' remark. It just slipped out."

"Actually, we in the little-runt community prefer the term 'wimp.'"

Both men laughed, and Owen joggled my shoulder in a playfully friendly way. Then Jim said, "OK, man, ready? Take off your shirt."

I hesitated, glancing at Owen, then at the cameras. I think I was blushing.

"OK, so what part of 'take the part' did you not understand?" Jim said. "Look, no one's going to recognize you when I get through with you. And it's just me and Owen here. As your roommate, I see you bare-chested every night and morning, so what's the problem? Is it that you don't want to take off your shirt in front of Owen?"

Owen said, "He's getting that look again. Maybe I should take his shirt off for him, to get him in the right frame of mind."

"Great idea, Owen. Maybe I'll even be able to use it, if I post-process the shirt to make it look like homespun."

I reluctantly allowed the hunky white actor to strip me to the waist as my roommate filmed us from all angles with a hand-held camera to supplement the ones on the bookshelves. I felt pathetic next to these two powerfully built men.

Then Jim took out a pen and said, "Hold still. This will save me a lot of processing power and tedious work later. Don't worry, it's invisible to the human eye."

"What's it do?" I asked as he touched the pen to my forehead, cheeks, chin, and throat.

"These marks will help me track the movement of your body parts later, when I map another man's skin and muscles onto you." He began to draw on strategic points on my bare chest, outlining my muscles, such as they were. "When I get done with you, your chest and arms will look like you've been doing heavy work in the fields for six solid months. In the video, of course." He moved down to my belly, drawing in imaginary abs.

"Using invisible ink to outline my almost invisible muscles."

"You said it, I didn't."

"Do you really need so many marks?"

"The more control points I have, the more realistically I can make you move. Make the character move. With just a few points, I could map new skin over you, but your body would come off as wooden as my acting. More control points let me make each of your muscles move independently. For instance, pretend your nipples are control points."

I didn't have to pretend, I thought. He had already pressed the pen against each of my nipples.

"Right now they're this far apart." He held his hands with palms facing each other and with the edge of each hand pressed against one of my nipples. "But they don't stay that distance when your muscles slide around underneath. Owen, pin his arms behind his back as if you're about to tie him up. No, further, so his shoulder blades are forced almost together."

Owen obeyed, and my nipples slid slightly outward from under the edges of Jim's hands.

"See how they move a little further apart? Your serratus muscles are pushing your scapulas closer and pulling your pectorals toward you sides. Let him go, Owen. Now, bring your hands together in front, as if someone just stripped you naked and you're covering your crotch."

As I did, my nipples brushed past the edges of his hands and wound up a little closer than they'd been with my hands at my sides.

"And if your hands are over your head, like we're going to have them for this scene, your pecs stretch out and your nipples move further away from your navel. Owen?"

Owen grabbed my forearms and pulled them over my head, almost lifting me off my feet. I wasn't paying attention to my nipples this time, I was thinking about how my armpits were now completely exposed and in easy reach of Jim. He didn't take advantage of it, though, although he did add some invisible dots down each of my exposed flanks, and even that tickled enough that my arms would have reflexively jerked down to protect my sides if they hadn't been held in Owen's strong grip. Finally putting the cap back on the pen, he brushed the hair out of my eyes in what might have been either a tender gesture or a way of emphasizing that I couldn't stop him. Later I realized he was probably just making his image-processing job easier, since the character wouldn't have the kind of hair that could fall over his eyes.

"OK, Owen, he's ready. Tie his wrists to the top of our bunk bed post, there. Oh, that's great, Wally! I'm totally using this footage, even if I have to spend an hour masking out the background. Just let your shame and humiliation show. Don't fake it, but don't hold back at all." More gently, he added, "Hey, man, if it gets to be too much, you're allowed to yell 'cut,' too. OK, Owen, get the whip. Start out light. Let's see if we can get ten lashes in one continuous take. And, action."

Owen gave every appearance of enjoying himself. I could hear his convincing maniacal laugh, and whenever I glanced over my shoulder, his eyes were full of glee. The fake whip, in his skillful hands, barely stung, but the humiliation of being tied up helpless, waiting for the touch of the lash, was even more intense than being held down and tickled. By the time Jim called "cut" after eight lashes, I was whimpering, practically on the verge of tears.

Instantly breaking character, Owen came around to face me. "Are you okay, man?" he asked in concern. He gave my upraised, fettered arm a friendly squeeze, just above the armpit. "You were great!"

"Thanks," I said weakly.

"Yeah!" Jim agreed. "This is going to work! Ready for another take?"

After three takes, Jim had Owen untie me and ordered me to strip down to my boxers. After drawing invisible marks on my newly exposed skin, he instructed Owen to lie on his belly in the top bunk and help me hoist myself off the floor, so he could get pictures of my bare feet dangling just above a green sheet he'd spread on the floor. He'd edit it to make it look like the character was suspended by his arms the whole scene, he explained.

I was sure if it had been either of these guys playing the character, he could have held himself off the floor for as long as needed by the strength of his own muscles, but I could never have done it without Owen's strong hands under my armpits. Having hands other than Jim's invading that sensitive part of my body was a strange experience, but at least he wasn't tickling me.

We got a couple of longer shots of my whole body, wearing nothing but a torn-up pair of homespun-looking pantaloons that barely covered up my boxers even after Jim had pushed the boxers down to my hips. Then I needed to take a leak. Jim made me go down the hall in that costume, explaining that he was worried about smearing the invisible ink. At least it was an all-male floor, but the stares were almost as humiliating as the fake whipping.

"Let's get some shots of you guys sweating," Jim said after I got back, and we'd done one more take of the whipping, this time with me in full costume, in case Jim wanted to show some of my lower body. "I'll use that at the end of montage, to show the whipping has been going on for around an hour." Without asking permission, he unbuttoned the torn shirt of the unresisting Owen about halfway down, revealing more chest hair, which Jim slicked down with his fingers after wetting the shirt and chest with something from a spray bottle. "Close your eyes," he advised, "although it's just water and glycerin." He sprayed his face and hair, artistically matting the hair on his forehead.

He approached me as though intending to spray every inch of my chest and back with the stuff. I wondered if it was cold. At least Owen had had a choice about standing still and putting up with it. I was still tied up.

"Won't this smear the invisible ink?" I objected. "You didn't let me put any clothes on when I went to pee."

Jim said, "I'm not going to spray you. I have an easier way to make you sweat. I'll add the sweat when I add the blood. I already have to completely change around this skin of yours; a black guy's muscles are defined mostly by the light gleaming off the sweat, and a white guy's muscles, what little you've got, are defined more by the shadows they cast. What, did you really think I was going to spray you down? That wouldn't save me any work at all." And he stuck his fingers into my helplessly exposed armpits and began to playfully tickle me, which is how I knew I hadn't mistaken about what he'd been about to do. I couldn't see Owen's reaction, but I knew he was watching, which only increased the humiliation.

# # # # #

118

"The auction scene we're shooting today," Jim told me after Owen met us in our room the next day, "is the other key scene in the video. If this comes out half as good as I think the whipping scene will, the rest will fall into place. All I'll need after today is a few quick shots for a montage where you'll pretend to be planting and picking and hoeing, and some footage of you standing around shirtless reading lines off a computer screen. I'm not worried about how you deliver that dialog; I've already got some preliminary audio with a sophomore who puts James Earl Jones to shame."

"Who?" He kept forgetting that not everyone was a classic film buff.

This second time around, it wasn't quite so weird to be greeting Owen in my boxers or to having my roommate mark me up like a butcher labeling the prime cuts of beef as he talked. That sense of comfort might not be a good thing, I realized, since my only job today was to look as if I was feeling humiliated and trapped, and I had no acting skill at all, unless it was Method acting.

When I was thoroughly but invisibly marked up for later processing, Jim said, "Since I know you're shy about this kind of thing, Owen and I will step out into the hall while you change into your costume.

"That's okay," I said. "You already made me strip to my boxers, so I might as well just put it on. Where is it?"

He handed me a ragged cloth that looked as if it had been ripped from a sheet. In fact, I recognized the color as matching the sheets he'd had on his bunk when we'd first moved in. "I sacrificed one of my bed sheets for his project," he confirmed. "Take off your boxers and knot this around your loins. Open the door when you're ready."

"How about if I knock when I'm ready?" I suggested.

# # # # #

If Owen had radiated ruthless glee when he'd been whipping me — I'd seen the playback by now, to my mortification — today he radiated businesslike indifference, treating me like a piece of meat he was haggling over with the butcher. My only instructions today were to stand there looking defeated and humiliated, as he gave me a thorough inspection. That was easy, especially now that my wrists were actually bound behind my back. We'd tried having me just hold them behind my back out of sight, but I kept reflexively trying to protect myself every time he touched my belly or even my chest, and Jim had resorted to having Owen actually tie me up.

While I had been working up the courage to put on my own costume, Owen had changed out in the hall. It was more elaborate and formal than the simple linen shirt he'd worn while whipping me: a hat like George Washington's, a vest, an old-fashioned tie, a coat short in front and long in back, and what I guess they call breeches. In character, he squeezed my skinny arms appraisingly, ran his hands around my chest, and said in a passable Southern accent, presumably speaking to some off-screen slave merchant character whose scenes would be filmed later elsewhere, "He's quite scrawny. Almost no meat on his bones."

"Some good Southern cooking and honest hard work in the fields will fix that right up," Jim recited from memory as if was his own script, apparently acting as a stand-in as well as handheld camera operator. "You can see he had plenty of muscle once."

"And yet, some never recover from the voyage. I have to take care with my boss's money. I dare not squander it on a slave who will prove useless."

I wasn't convinced the stilted dialog was historically accurate for the period, but for once, resolved not to research it, for fear of catching my roommate in a rare mistake. I'd been humiliated enough this week as it was and didn't care to be tickled again.

"If nothing else, he'll make excellent breeding stock," Jim said.

"Will he?" With that, Owen grabbed my loincloth and whipped it off, moving so smoothly and confidently that I later wondered if he'd been practicing at home, maybe with his own roommate. All I knew in that instant was that I was suddenly standing, utterly naked, in front of two big strapping guys, and that I was the center of their attention. This was even worse than yesterday.

"Yes, I suppose he'll do," Owen said.

"And cut. Great job, guys! Don't worry, Wally. Your dick wasn't even in frame; I was focusing on your head and shoulders to get a close-up of that wonderful expression. And I promise I'll crop it out of any long shots I use from the other cameras, or introduce some object in the foreground that conveniently blocks it. No one outside this room is going to see the raw footage. Besides, don't forget, no one will even know it's you unless they read the credits."

"I trust you," I said faintly. "Hey, where are you going?" He was circling around behind me.

"I knew I'd get to see your lily-white ass before the year was out. Again, great job!" He slapped me on my white ass.

"So that's it?" I asked, stepping down from the auction block. With my hands still bound behind me, I lost my balance and stumbled into Owen's sturdy chest.

He caught me and set me on my feet. "There you go, buddy. Can I untie him now, Jim?"

"No, I want to do a few more takes just in case, so let's get one more in, and then we can take a beer break. You got that six-pack I asked for? Thanks, man. Put it in the mini-fridge there so it'll stay cold. Remind me to pay you back."

"Will I get some?" I asked wistfully.

"Of course," Jim said. "You're not really a slave." He paused, then added, "But remember the rule. If you need to go to the bathroom before we wrap, you do it in your loincloth. OK, Owen, get him back up on the block and wrap the sheet around his loins again."

By the fourth and final take, the subjugation of being repeatedly stripped and inspected was getting to me, and I actually started tearing up a little. Crying in front of other guys made me feel even more ashamed than I already was, and soon I couldn't stop.

"Get him down on his knees," Jim directed, and Owen grabbed my arm firmly, pulled me off the block, and eased me gently to my knees. Jim filmed me weeping naked on my knees with my hands bound behind my back for a good two minutes, then said, "Perfect! I'll cut that in after the branding scene."

"Branding?" I asked.

"Look behind you," he said, still shooting.

Owen, obviously back in character, was approaching me with a branding iron. I cringed, even knowing it was a prop and seeing that it was obviously not glowing. When it touched my chest, I screamed, because it actually did burn. It left my skin unmarked, and I realized the thing had been ice cold, probably chilling in the mini-fridge all this time.

# # # # #

"For the auction scene, the first take is definitely the best, Jim said, turning away from the screen on his desk to look at us as I put my boxers back on and Owen changed into his street clothes behind me. "You looked increasingly humiliated every time he did it, but nothing can match the raw shock that crosses your face, then the horror a split second later as you realize you're standing there naked and helpless. There's a flash of betrayal for a few frames, but I'll edit that out since it isn't in character. It'll be perfect if I do a prequel someday and write a script where one of your tribe mates sells you into slavery. But hey, sorry to spring that on you, man. It was the only way to get that reaction out of you."

"So it was all for art, huh? Just purely for the utilitarian goal of getting a good shot? You didn't actually enjoy playing those little pranks?"

He gave me that steady, silent look I've come to recognize meant that I was right and he knew it. "Don't bother putting your shirt back on," he said. "The only question now is whether I'll take pity on you and wait until our guest leaves."

# # # # #

A few days later, I walked in to find three bare-chested black strangers in our room. One of them, the beefiest one, was clad in nothing but boxer shorts, and Jim was kneeling at his feet. I wasn't sure what to make of it. We hadn't bothered to take down the green sheets, since there was nothing we needed on the bookcases behind them, so that didn't mean anything one way or the other. Nothing on the doorknob.

Jim looked up. "Oh. Hey, Wally. Still not what it looks like." He flashed me a grin.

Now I noticed he was holding his special pen and using it to draw invisible marks on the guy's bare legs.

Standing up, he put his hand on the shoulder of the brawny guy he'd been marking, slightly shorter than he, with slightly lighter skin, the color of milk chocolate. "Behold the only man with a greater body than myself," he said, squeezing his shoulder muscles. "For the whipping scene, I'm going to slap his muscles onto your scrawny frame to make the character look like he's been working in the field. Or maybe a composite of his body and mine."

The guy grinned at me, obviously embarrassed. "Hi, I'm Duane."

I stuck out my hand, as I reflexively do when introduced. I'm normally a little shy, but this was my own turf, and after all, this time I was the one who was dressed. So I said gamely, "Hi, Duane. I'll be proud to wear that body of yours for my big scene."

I watched as Jim shot footage of Duane's legs and bare feet, then the chests of the other two. He instructed them to turn around, and when they obeyed, he shot footage of their backs. Then he ordered the other guys to take off their shoes, socks, and pants, and repeated what he'd done to Duane. The thinnest guy wore briefs, the pudgy ebony-skinned guy, boxer shorts.

"All of you, raise your arms over your heads, wrists together," he ordered, looking at tiny the camera display. "Hold it. Beautiful. Now turn around slowly."

He took his time. I guess he needed a lot of footage to work with. Finally, he said, "OK, guys, drop your shorts and turn around."

They hesitated, but first the skinny guy and then the pudgy one turned around and dropped their shorts. Not the order he'd specified, I noticed. After hesitating slightly, the brawny one, Duane, followed suit.

Jim knelt, getting video footage of their behinds from all angles. "I'm trying to decide which of these guys to put on top of your ass — if you know what I mean. Damn. Forgot the control points." He found where he'd set down his invisible-ink pen, and knelt down again.

# # # # #

He spent endless hours in post-production the next several days, right through the weekend, staying up long after I'd gone to bed. The first time I got a good look at the nearly-finished product, I was blown away. The character in the whipping scene had Duane's or Jim's muscles, just about the darkest skin I'd ever seen, and my submissive body language. He'd replaced my hair, of course, even remembered to go into my armpits and do his magic on the hair visible there. The character's pronounced African features were movie-star handsome, and while he was no taller than me, his shirtless torso was model-perfect.

"Did you really use me to make that hunk?"

"Sure did. You, me, and three other guys."

"He's almost inhumanly good-looking."

"Yeah, researchers have known for a long time that people find composites more attractive than the real people that were added together to make them."

"Should make the film popular."

"That's not what I'm going for. I'm trying to make a serious point, that a lot of good genetic qualities were wiped out due slave-owners breeding for good slave qualities. Or when they forcibly interbred with them themselves, like your ancestor eventually did with this character's future daughter."

"Our ancestor," I corrected him. "Cousin."

He grabbed me and yanked up my shirt.

"OK! OK! My ancestor," I conceded.

"As I was saying, our friend here is my reconstruction of how the pure Africans they imported would have looked. There were no cameras in those days, so we'll never know for sure."

Later I looked up pictures of twentieth and twenty-first century African villagers on a National Geographic site. Maybe it was just what I was used to, but to my taste, they were no more attractive than Amerafricans; if anything, there was something to be said for hybrid vigor. Certainly they didn't look movie-star handsome like the artificial construct Jim had redecorated my bones with.

I showed him my screen. "These are the descendants of your character's brother who evaded capture by the slavers and stayed in Africa," I said, letting him judge for himself. He looked at the photos, looked at his masterpiece, and stared at me for a long time.

"What do you think?" I said.

"I think you might as well take your shirt off now, unless you want me to do it for you."

# # # # #

"Are you still filming?" I asked, after coming home and walking in on Jim and Owen unexpectedly in the final week of the semester. "I thought you turned that in weeks ago."

"Oh. Hey, Wally. I did. This time it is what it looks like. I forgot to tie something to the doorknob."

Owen was kneeling naked at my roommate's feet. Jim was still fully clothed, except for his belt, which he was holding folded into a loop.

"Sorry. I'll go to the student union."

"No, no," Jim said. "Not on my account. Stay if you want to. On your feet, slave," Jim said. Owen rose reluctantly to his full, normally imposing height, bashfully shielding his privates with his hands. His thick chest hair, I now saw, covered most of his muscular chest and spilled down his belly in a narrow stream that continued past his belly button and merged with his pubes. His legs were hairy, his arms smooth and bulging with muscles.

I had developed complex feelings — a mix of fear, camaraderie, and adoration — for the big friendly guy who'd so skillfully humiliated me for the camera. Now, witnessing him humbled and naked, reduced to my roommate's plaything, sent an exquisite thrill through my body, even more than the first-hand subjugation I'd experienced the first time Jim had pinned me down and tickled me.

"You remember Owen, Wally."

"Of course." Out of habit, I stuck out my hand to Owen, who didn't see it, since he was staring fixedly down at his huge bare feet.

"Where are your manners, slave? When a man offers you his hand, you shake it."

Looking mortified, Owen reluctantly shook my hand. I noticed that his handshake was firm and so was his dick, still at half mast, although it didn't look as impressive as the rest of him.

"I don't mind you sticking around at all," Jim said. "I don't think Owen likes it, though, do you slave?"

"No, master," Owen said, his eyes back on the ground and his hands back in front of his crotch.

"That's exactly why I'm inviting Wally to stay. Because what a slave wants doesn't count for anything, does it, slave?"

"No, master."

"Owen got an audition for a major role in the spring play based on his work in my film, and he just found out he landed the part. So he was very grateful. Isn't that right?"

"Yes, master."

"He bought me a bottle of rum to celebrate, and we shared it. But he must have had a few too many because he started mouthing off, accusing me of having kinky sexual desires. He claims I wrote and directed the video the way I did because I actually enjoy seeing guys tied up and humiliated, not for purely artistic and political expression. That I get some kind of sexual charge out of that. No one has ever suggested such a thing to me before! And after I gave him his big break! I decided to teach him a lesson." He swatted the upperclassman's bare ass with his hand. "You're sorry, now, aren't you, slave?"

"Yes, master."

Jim looked at me. "You know, he owes you some thanks, too, man. It would have been a disaster without you stepping up at the last minute. In fact, I think you should get down on your knees and thank Wally, slave."

"As you say, master." He crawled to me on all fours and rose to his knees right in front of me. "I'm very grateful to you, sir," he said, looking up at me diffidently.

"And while you're at it, you should beg him for forgiveness for calling him a runt."

"Sorry, man," he mumbled, hanging his head.

"You can do better than that. In fact, I think Wally deserves a blow job."

"But master," Owen objected, alarmed, "I thought you were going to let me give you ..."

Jim cracked his belt in the air in Owen's direction. "Are you arguing, slave?"

"No, master," he said meekly.

"Wally, you obviously haven't spent the night with anyone all semester, or I'd know. When's the last time you at least had a quick blow job?"

"That would be never," I admitted. "But I don't think Owen really wants ..."

"As long as he's in this room, it doesn't matter what he wants. He's mine to do with as I please." He walked over to us and rubbed the loop of his belt against the submissive, muscular student actor's nipple. "And you know, just because the cameras aren't running doesn't mean he couldn't have used the magic word to stop things cold if he really wanted to. You want to be here, don't you, slave?"

"Yes, master."

"I can tell." He dangled the belt and placed it around his half-erect cock like a hangman throwing the noose around a bound prisoner's neck, and lifted it for my inspection. It had already started lifting on its own. "And I say my roommate gets a blow job. If you do a really good job on him, then I'll think about letting you pleasure me." He slapped the upperclassman's muscular back very lightly with the belt and turned to me. "Owen here is a willing slave. You, on the other hand, are a free man. And I don't just mean that we're finished filming you in the role of an unwilling slave, I mean you're eighteen, and it's time you start enjoying your newfound freedom as much as I am. You're not under your parents' roof anymore; you've got a room hundreds of miles away from them in building they don't even have a key to. So you can have sex in the privacy of your own room without worrying that anyone will see. Except, of course, for me."

He walked to the bunks, leaving the submissive upperclassman kneeling at my feet. "So I'm going to give you three choices. Well, four, counting the student union. You can unzip and I can watch you get a blow job the easy way, with you standing on your own two feet and Owen kneeling in front, with your hands on his head to control what he does. You can come over here and I can watch you get a blow job the hard way, with you tied spread-eagle and buck-naked on your own bed while I control where Owen puts his mouth and when." He slapped one of the posts that supported his own bunk, and I realized that those four posts at the corners of my bunk were perfectly positioned to tie my wrists and ankles to. "Or, if you really truly object to a blow job today, you and I can just jerk off together, like the roommates and cousins we are. All over Owen's chest."

I gulped. Owen still had his eyes downcast, but I could see his muscles trembling with anticipation of whatever fate was chosen for him. I knew how he felt.

COPPING A FEEL
By Landon Dixon

I punched in the number, waited.

Lenny finally picked up his cell, squealed, "Yeah? What the fuck?"

"Get your ass down to the stationhouse! Now! We've got some questions."

My voice could've been any cop, but me. With Lenny, it didn't matter; it only mattered that it was a cop on the end of the line. He didn't know what it was about, either, but when you're a paid snitch, it could be about anything. And you'd better answer the bell — quick.

The light stayed on in the basement apartment. Lenny slipped out the front door of the crumbling, five-storey brick building. He glanced right, left, hustled his skinny black ass down the darkened sidewalk. It was a twelve-block hike to the stationhouse, and Lenny couldn't make bus fare.

I got out of the car and hoofed it down the sidewalk. Lenny heard the heavy clomp of my shoes. He swiveled his neck, stared, almost took off running down the sidewalk ahead of me. He couldn't make out my face in the night, just a big, dark, menacing body that was bearing down on him in long, hard strides. Lenny had a lot of enemies. I could've been any one of them.

I caught up with him as he was scampering across the street against the Don't Walk sign. "You just broke the law, Lenny," I growled, clamping a big hand down on a skinny shoulder.

His close-set, brown eyes just about bugged out of his bony face. He recognized me now. "Hey-hey, I gotta get down to the station! I just got a phone call!"

"Let it wait. I got business of my own with you, Lenny — personal business." I half-carried the frightened little guy across the street, down the sidewalk and into an alley.

"W-what gives?" he jabbered. "If I had any tips, I'd tell 'em to you."

"You're talking too much — when you should be sucking."

His eyes darted down to the crotch of my pants. He stared at the bulge swelling up there. The guy had a big mouth, and he knew how to use it. For good and bad.

"What's the pay-off?" he grated now, eyes gone shrewd, face hard.

He was only twenty-three, still had some of the bloom of youth left on him, despite his years on the street. His lips were blue-black, plush and sensual, his tongue a neon-pink snake of impressive length and agility, his red, depthless mouth and throat elastic.

"This one's on the house, Lenny."

His avarice grin faded. "What!? Why the fuck should I ..."

"Because you like it. Because you like big, black cock stuffing your mouth and clogging your throat! That's why!" I slammed both hands onto his shoulders, nailed him down to his knees in the garbage. He was in his element.

He opened his mouth to say something else, thought better of it, placed a hand on my hard-on and rubbed.

I grunted, heat shimmering up from my dick and through my groin and body. The guy's small, dark hands gleamed in the cloud-shrouded moonlight. They were dirty, fingernails chewed to the bone, but they were knowing, caressing and rubbing. Lenny hooked the skinny fingers of his right hand around my outlined dong and shifted his palm up and down, using the fingers of his other hand to latch onto my balls in my pants, squeeze and twist.

I gazed down at the punk's wild, three-inch Afro, at his upturned, grinning face, at those hands of his at play on my pipe and sack, building a fire in my loins. He had me pumped up full-length in seconds, my balls tight and boiling.

"Take it out. Suck on it."

He could take orders, was used to it. He slowly unzipped my fly, running the zipper over the massive, throbbing hump of blood-engorged flesh beneath. Then he slid his hand in, both hands. He pulled my dong out into the open night air, out there in that stinking alley.

My cock shone black and lethal, pulsating in Lenny's palms. He breathed over it, stuck out his tongue and licked the vein-ribboned length of it, from bloated cap to pube-pebbled base. I shuddered, shifted, my cock jumping in the punk's hands, up against his lips.

He gripped my bare balls and shaft, swirled his hand up and down my prick, milking my sack. His one little hand moved faster, really polishing my dong, his other hand gripping harder, really pulling on my bag. I whipped handcuffs out of my pocket and spun Lenny around on his knees, cuffed his skinny wrists together behind his back.

He wasn't going to jack me to joy. He wasn't getting off that easy.

I walked around in front of him, cock bobbing, pointing, huge and threatening at his face. He opened his mouth in surrender, and I shot my cap home.

"Fuck!" I groaned, the guy's soft, wet lips sealing around my knob, sucking like it was second nature.

His eyes shone up at me, his lips working, cheeks billowing in and out. I felt the tip of his tongue press against my slit, warm and wet and writhing. Then I felt the sharp points of his teeth, as he bit into my hood.

Lenny was having some fun. I was having none of it. I slapped his face, smacked it the other way, my cock springing out of his mouth in a spray of saliva.

He instinctively strained against the handcuffs. But there was nothing he could do, but suck. He opened his mouth up wider, and I rammed my dong into the red velvet cavern.

My dick glided over his tongue and bent down his throat, filling his mouth. He didn't bat an eye, gag a bit. His lips closed over my shaft, his mouth encasing my cock, throat stuffed with the swollen member.

His face beat with my meat. Lenny could deep-throat, it was one of his few talents.

I shot my thick fingers into his bushy hair, grabbing hold. My cock was locked up solid in his face, submerged in wet, heated satin, every pulsing inch of it up to the balls. I shook, shaking Lenny, the sexual pressure intense.

Then I pumped my hips, his face, thrusting back and forth. Spit drooled out of the corners of his crammed mouth, and his flared nostrils sucked for air, his eyes watering only a little. I slammed into his mouth and down his throat, hard-fucking the punk's face.

He was hot and moist and tight as any hole on a man or woman, his cushioning tongue and gripping lips and clasping throat heightening the sordid sensations. I had to pull all the way back, pop out twitching and dripping, before I blew a load down Lenny's throat.

He licked his lips and grinned up at me, mouth hanging open. I fed him my balls, pinching the pair at the top and dropping the tightened sack into his mouth. He sealed his lips around it and sucked, tea-bagging with as much talent and appetite as he deep-throated.

I pinched his nose, smacked his cheek. He sucked even harder, really vaccing my nuts, slapping them around with his tongue. My cock stretched out over his face, looming molten as a rod of steel. Sweat beaded my forehead and ran down into my glaring eyes.

I pulled my balls out of Lenny's mouth, plugged my cock back in. Gripping his small ears, I really fucked his face, pounding my dong into his mouth and throat. Snot bubbled out of his nose and rolled down onto my churning, shining shaft. Sweat poured off my face and down onto his.

His throat constricted around my plunging cap, lips riding shaft, tongue bathing. I lost control, fucking Lenny's face in a frenzy. Then I bucked, howled, blasted, ramming my lust home as deep and hot and heavy as it would go.

Jolt after jolt of blistering joy made me jump, cock bursting ecstasy into Lenny's mouth and throat. He swallowed hard and fast, taking every drop of my sizzling cum. Then licking his lips with satisfaction in the dismal moonlight on the floor of that dirty alley, when I flopped out of his mouth, spent, for now.

He laughed and nodded his head when I uncuffed one of his wrists — frowned and cursed, and when I locked the bracelet ring onto a metal rung in the wall of one of the buildings.

I was out of the alley and striding back the way I'd come before the punk could cry me a river.

# # # # #

I pushed my way inside the dilapidated building. Lenny's subterranean apartment was two flights down. The battered grey door was locked. I picked it open and went inside, down the pitch-black hallway to the strip of light cracking out the bottom of the bedroom door. I shoved it open.

A huge, naked black man was leather cuffed by the wrists to a steel chain that ran up to an iron eyehook embedded in the ceiling. He was stretched out up on his toes, muscular arms pulled taut over his head. His ebony body gleamed under the single overhead bulb, horse cock jutting out from his groin shiny with spit.

"Hiya, Clarence," I said. But he couldn't respond, what with the ball gag in his mouth. His large, brown eyes stared into mine.

There were various sexual torture devices mounted up on the walls and strewn about on the floor of the small bedroom/dungeon. The window high up in a corner was rendered opaque with dirt. I picked up a pair of nipple clamps and walked up to the cuffed and chained giant, fastened them onto his thick, licorice nipples.

His eyes rolled back in his head, his body jerking, as I twisted the clamps — painfully, pleasurably. Then I stepped back and stripped off my own clothes. My cock stretched out hard and black as the man in front of me.

I popped off the clamps and applied my mouth, tonguing and sucking on one fiercely erect nipple, the other. Clarence shivered. I swirled my wet, pink mouth-organ all around the rubbery buds, painting them harder and higher still. Until they shone like his dick. I bit into them.

There was a studded leather cock-choker lying on the floor. I reapplied the nipple clamps, picked up the cock-choker, wrapped it around the base of Clarence's nightstick. I pulled it tight, tighter.

The big guy groaned from around his gag, sweat trickling from his shaven pits down the sides of his barrel-staved upper body. His straining dong engorged even more, the choker bloating it out huger.

I dropped to my knees at his club, slapped the purpled appendage one way, the other. He jerked, rattling his chain. I sucked his blue-black cap into my mouth and sunk my teeth into his shaft.

Clarence spasmed, thick lips writhing around the orange ball in his mouth, eyes glaring down at me. His squeezed slab of dark meat wasn't numb enough not to feel the pressure of my teeth, the wet warmth of my mouth. I inched my lips down his pipe, started sucking on it.

I gripped his bulging, shaved sack and tugged on it, twisted it, as I pushed my head back and forth, glided my mouth up and down his dong. Until I tasted salty tears of precum leaking out of his slit.

Then I lashed his balls tight together with a strip of cord I found on the floor, and got to my feet. I moved around in behind. The view from the backside was just as spectacular, Clarence's buttocks twin molded mounds of thick, plush, black-velvet flesh.

I gripped the pair, squeezed, plied. I smacked them with my open hands, hard. Clarence jumped forward, his bound prong spearing up into the air.

I grabbed onto the guy's prick to hold him steady. Then I fashioned my big hand into a hard, flat blade and slashed it across his rump. His cry of passion broke through the ball gag. I whacked his humped rear-end again and again and again, savagely spanking him. He shuddered with every brutal hand-blast, his cheeks rippling, his cock surging in my other hand.

Only when the gunshot-cracks of skin against skin became one continuous sound, the man's whaled buttocks burning hot to the touch, did I stop the one frenzy. And start the other.

I lubed my cock, his crack. I thrust in between his beaten cheeks. His butt cleavage was deep and hot and smooth, heavy cheeks enveloping my pulsating prick. I grasped his muscled pecs and pumped my hips, furiously frotting.

His whole bristling body was dewed with perspiration now, like mine. I tongued sweat off the corded muscles of his shoulders, from his tree-trunk neck. As I pistoned his crack. Until my own raging cock bubbled precum.

I pulled back, stabbed forward, driving my beefy cap up against Clarence's pucker. He stiffened, every massive muscle on his stretched body tightening with tension.

I plowed my hood through his resisting ring and into his gripping chute — followed immediately by inches and inches of throbbing hard shaft. I didn't stop stuffing his anus until my balls pressed against his buttocks.

I felt his tremors of delight all through me, his ass muscles clamping my cock even tighter. I pumped, gripping his chest with one hand, his own turgid meat with the other, ferociously fucking the man's ass.

I churned and churned his chute, reaming his anus, slamming into his ass over and over again. Digging my fingernails into his clenched pecs and tugging on his cock in rhythm. My thighs cracked off his bruised buttocks, rocking him, cocking him, my grunts steaming into his ears, teeth biting into his neck.

Then I jerked, jolted by searing orgasm. My thrusting prick exploded in Clarence's ass, blasting him full of heated seed. As his trussed-up cock went off in my riding hand, shooting ropes of sperm out the tip. We danced together in white-hot ecstasy, he on the end of his chain, me on the end of his ass.

I was gone before Lenny got back from his bum steer. Leaving it up to Clarence to explain what had happened, if he so wanted. The big guy was still locked up on his toes, semen dripping from his ass and cock.

For me, it was simple: Clarence had been mine, Lenny had taken him away; and you don't steal from a cop and expect to get away with it.

AGONY UNCLE
By Landon Dixon

Darelle gripped my hand and looked at me, his brown eyes wide.

"There's nothing to be afraid of," I reassured the tall, thin, dark-skinned eighteen-year-old. "It's just an interview. I went through it myself when I turned eighteen."

A lot of young men had gone through it — being 'interviewed' by 'Uncle Simon,' the man who ran the main industry in town, virtually controlled the entire county. I worked at his plant now. Darelle wanted to work there.

"Y-yeah, s-sure. I g-guess so," he stammered, his hand damp in mine, shaking like the rest of his wiry body.

I kissed him on his soft, plush lips. He pressed the doorbell of the huge, stone mansion.

The door opened up almost instantly. Javier stood there, totally naked. His smooth, burnished copper body gleamed in the afternoon sun, cock dangling over his shaven sack, between his slender, shapely legs. "Come in," he said, staring at Darelle. "We've been expecting you."

Darelle and I followed Javier down the long, red-carpeted hallway, still holding hands, watching Javier's ripe, rounded buttocks deliciously clench and unclench, his thin hips swish from side to side. He led us into the enormous living room of the home, where Richard and Thomas were waiting, standing by the large stone fireplace, as stunningly naked as Javier.

Richard was short, compact, with lustrous black hair and amber, almond-shaped eyes. His body and balls were shaven smooth as the other men's, his cock rising up semi-erect between his sturdy legs. Thomas was taller, leaner, had a blank expression on his pretty, freckled face. He had curly red hair and sky-blue eyes, porcelain skin. His cock hung down, engorged more than Richard's.

"Good, he's here."

Darelle and I jumped, our hands parting.

Uncle Simon walked into the room, nude as all the others, but more than twice their ages. The silver-haired man carried a black leather bag in his right hand, like a doctor's bag. His cock was soft, but thick, his chest hairy as his balls. He appraised Darelle with his clear, grey eyes, and his red lips flickered a stern smile as he said, "Let's begin."

The three young men helped Darelle off with his clothes. He was wearing a dark blue suit, white shirt and red tie, pair of polished black shoes, anxious to make a good impression. Now, he made a better impression, as his ebony body was fully revealed, and he stood naked in the middle of the wood-paneled room.

His skin was dark and velvety as hot, humid night, long, tight muscles pronounced on his arms and legs, his humped pecs clenched, ribbed stomach rising and falling. His butt cheeks bulged out boldly, twin mounds of molasses-colored and textured flesh, and his cock jutted out proudly, aroused to almost full erection by the feel of the men's hands upon him, all the excitement and anticipation. The blue-black shaft was long and veined, perfectly mushroomed cap purple in color.

"You came prepared. Good," Uncle Simon stated. Then to the three other naked men, and me, "Position him."

I stripped off my own clothes, helped the other men lead Darelle over to the fireplace. My cock throbbed out in front of me, as we positioned Darelle up against the mantel of the fireplace. Richard and Thomas took a hand apiece and stretched out Darelle's arms, pinned the slender hands against the wooden mantel. While Javier and I crouched down and pulled Darelle's legs slightly apart, secured his feet with our own hands around his slim ankles.

He leaned forward, butt cheeks thrust out on one side, cock on the other. His body trembled in our gripping hands, skin dewed with sweat now. His breathing came in gasps.

Uncle Simon placed the black bag down on the carpet and walked up behind Darelle. He placed his two soft hands on the young man's lush buttocks, sunk his manicured fingers into the rich meat. Darelle shuddered, butt cheeks jumping in Uncle Simon's grasping hands.

The older man squeezed, plying the younger man's ample cheeks. Then he opened his fingers and let the back meat spring out into its gorgeous curved form again. He ran his fingernails over the pair, up and down, across, gently stroking, scraping Darelle's ass.

Darelle shivered, buttocks rippling. We held his hands and feet tight, his legs and arms shaking. We could all see the perspiration trickle down the sides of his body, from his clean-shaven armpits.

Uncle Simon cupped Darelle's butt cheeks, as much as he could. Then he palmed the quivering swells, up one swollen mass and down the other, both together. He warmed Darelle's buttocks, rubbing, caressing, cupping. Then suddenly biting his fingernails in, sharply.

Darelle jumped, his cheeks spasming. Uncle Simon dropped to his knees at Darelle's packed ass and bit his teeth into the young man's right butt cheek.

Darelle cried out. We struggled to hold him in place. Uncle Simon moved his head over to the other buttock, bit into that one, chewed on the thick flesh. Before splitting Darelle's cheeks open with his digging fingers and diving his tongue in between, spearing the wet, pink tip of his deft mouth-organ against Darelle's dark butthole.

Darelle shook violently, as if he'd just been jolted with electrical shock, Uncle Simon plugging his tongue into the teenager's pucker. The older man dropped his head lower, pulled Darelle's cheeks even wider apart. He licked from Darelle's balls on the other side all along his smooth crack in one damp, dragging stroke, all the way up to Darelle's tailbone.

My cock pulsated, body and face burning with heat. Like Richard's, and Thomas', and Javier's. We all longed to touch our cocks, pull on them, feed them into Darelle's luscious mouth and ass. But we did nothing, but what Uncle Simon had told us to do, holding onto Darelle. The man demanded total obedience, at work and in his home.

He licked up and down Darelle's deep bum cleavage, slow and sensuously, stroking the young man's crack with his long, budded tongue. Darelle shivered with every lick, his mouth hanging open and nostrils flared, cock vibrating, coursing like a cable with sexual electricity.

Finally, Uncle Simon took one long, last lap at Darelle's crack, and then brought his head back. He formed his tongue into a rigid pink blade, pulled Darelle's buttocks as wide open as they would go, and jabbed the sticker right into the teenager's stretched asshole.

Darelle yelped, jumping up onto his toes, stuck wet and hot inside his sensitive chute. Uncle Simon burrowed forward, sinking his tongue all the way into Darelle's anus, his cheeks pressing against Darelle's cheeks, fingers blazing white on the tremoring black skin.

It was enough to drive a drop of precum into the gaping slit of my granite cock, and I was only watching. Not feeling that wicked tongue snake and lodge up my butt. I knew what Uncle Simon was doing, though, squirming that appendage of his around inside Darelle's chute.

He pulled back to the ring, plunged in to the superheated core, fucking Darelle's ass with his tongue now. Then rimming the groaning guy, winding his tongue around and around

Darelle's starfish, nipping at pucker, eating ass. We four had a hard time controlling Darelle's arms and legs, the guy's body and buttocks trembling wildly out of control.

Uncle Simon popped his black bag open, pulled out a pink, twelve-inch, veined-shaft, bulbous-headed, silicon dong. He lubed the sex toy. Then stuffed the molded tip of the pleasure tool into Darelle's ass, slowly, steadily, unrelentingly drove the shaft home.

Darelle screamed, his buttocks clenching tight. It was the wrong thing to do, the dildo locked only halfway into his chute. Uncle Simon frowned.

Darelle twisted his head around and saw the older man's expression, fought to relax his sphincter, and succeeded. His buttocks bubbled out full again, and Uncle Simon shoved the rest of the prick into his ass, just an inch shy of total.

We all held our breath, as Uncle Simon turned, twisted the cock around inside Darelle. He pulled six inches out, plunged six inches in. Did it again and again, faster and faster, fucking Darelle's delightfully rippling bum with the tool.

"Enough pleasure," Uncle Simon announced, yanking the dildo all the way out of Darelle's ass, the bulbed tip popping out of the young man's gaping pucker. "Time for some pain. The true test of manhood."

Uncle Simon took a red leather riding crop out of his bag, stood up. He tested the flexibility of the wicked instrument, then raised it up high in his right hand, brought it whistling down across Darelle's vulnerable bare buttocks.

The crack of hard leather against taut flesh exploded like a gunshot in the house, echoed, reverberated, all through Darelle's quivering body and our clutching hands. His shriek of pain, and pleasure, followed soon after.

Another crack, another cry. Uncle Simon whipped Darelle's ass, setting the humped buttocks to violent gyration, the young man's body jumping with each and every stinging blow.

I bit my lip almost to bleeding, shuddering with the brutal butt-lashing myself, cock jumping up into the air in sympathy. Uncle Simon absolutely flogged Darelle's bum. Until ridges formed on the supple cheeks, and the heavy, heated strokes flashed dull white on the gleaming ebony background.

Uncle Simon dropped the crop and stabbed two fingers into Darelle's ass. "Suck his cock," he instructed me, "while I finger-fuck him."

It was my reward for bringing Darelle to the interview. I dove down onto all-fours and crawled around in front of Darelle, scrambled up onto my knees. There was no need to hold onto his legs anymore, his feet were planted deep in the carpet now.

His cock stuck out from his loins like a nightstick. I slipped my lips over the bloated tip, glided my mouth down the steely shaft.

Darelle whimpered, looked down at me, sweat pouring off his anguished face and onto my ecstatic one. Uncle Simon drove the young man's cock back and forth in my sucking mouth, by ramming his two digits in and out of Darelle's ass.

Uncle Simon pulled his fingers free and beckoned at Javier. I felt Darelle's cock jump forward in my mouth, almost down my throat. As Javier crowded in behind the guy and stuck his cockhead where Uncle Simon's fingers had been only moments before. I bit down on Darelle's shaft, holding the dong steady, as Javier slammed his erection into the teenager's blistered backside.

Darelle moaned, Javier buried to the balls in his butt.

I sucked cock again, bobbing my head only slightly, letting the glistening black snake pump between my lips and over my tongue in rhythm to Javier's cock pumping Darelle's ass. The guy thumped against the young man's beaten cheeks, pistoning full-length in his anus.

The pounding tempo became harder and harder, faster and faster. Javier grunted, yelled, his body shaking against Darelle's, thrusting cock spurting hot liquid orgasm against the teenager's bowels. I could almost taste it on the other side — was tasting salty precum leak out the tip of Darelle's sucked-upon cock.

Richard stepped up to the young man's backside. Then Thomas. They furiously fucked steaming chute. As I sucked black iron cock. They came, crying out, spurting their molten joy into Darelle's ass. I swallowed more precum, sucking pipe with abandon.

I wanted to suck him off totally, feel his full load hotly splash the back of my throat, fill my mouth. But I guess Darelle was just too overwhelmed by it all, shocked to sexual rigidity, cock gone numb as the rest of him by the ravaging experience.

Uncle Simon said, "Get up."

I got up.

"Fuck his cream-filled ass," he told me.

I got in behind Darelle. Semen streamed down the guy's legs, out of his weeping asshole. His butt cheeks rippled involuntarily with surface tension, skin sheened with perspiration. It was my place of honor to fuck his ass last. I oiled and gripped my dick and split Darelle's dusky cheeks, plowed into his pink chute.

It was hot, squishy, delicious. Exaltation rose up through my body like a heated tide, as I went in and in and in. Until my thighs pressed against Darelle's burning buttocks, bone embedded.

Uncle Simon grasped Darelle's cock and pumped. I grasped Darelle's waist and pumped his ass with my cock. Uncle Simon twisted the groaning guy's nipples, pulled on them, jacking dong with smooth, quick strokes.

I hammered Darelle's ass, churning his full, sucking chute. My cock surged in the spermed tunnel, shunting urgently back and forth. I couldn't make it last. Too much had gone on before.

Darelle screamed, his body jumping, Uncle Simon's sure, sensual hand tugging blast after blast of semen at last out of the lucky guy's cock. As I pile-drove in a frenzy, cracking against

Darelle's ass then jumped, myself, jetting jizz into the guy's chute, adding to the steaming loads already there, my body and brain ablaze with the all-out orgasm organized so well by Uncle Simon.

# # # # #

Needless to say, Darelle got a job at the plant, having passed the interview with flying colors. I work alongside him. The pay's good and the work is enjoyable; employment at Uncle Simon's place of business bringing much satisfaction, servitude at Uncle Simon's home even more.

DORRIEN'S DUNGEON X
By R. W. Clinger

My desk is covered with lawsuits: a dog bite case, damage to private property, slander, theft, a car accident, and ten others. My IN and OUT bins are completely full. When five more cases are wrapped up, ten arrive on my desk at Lloyd, Bradshaw & Tanner. This is the life of a defense attorney, mind you. All work and no play makes TJ Sloane (me!) a very mean little boy.

Dorrien Bradshaw enters my office: massive in size at six-three, 240 pounds of steel, chocolate brown skin that I want to lick and bite. His azure-colored eyes show kindness and concern for me. His bright-white smile is lost, which is sort of a surprise for me, since he's always chipper. He stands across from my desk in his Brooks Brothers suit, snaps a picture of me with his Droid II, shows me the pic, and rattles off, "Look at you, TJ. Take a good, hard look. Analyze yourself for a minute and tell me what you see."

I see a Jamaican man with amber-colored eyes, a fifty dollar buzz cut, luscious-red lips, 190 pounds on a five-eleven frame, and a jaw line that can rock anyone's world. I'm jockish and pretty and black and sexy as hell and …

"You need a sexual release, guy," Dorrien says. "See the wrinkles around your eyes and mouth. See the way your shoulders are slouched. You need some help."

"What kind of help?" I ask after he pulls his cell phone away from me, pocketing it.

"I'm just the guy to ask. The man who is always on top of things around here," he chortles, pushes his right hand into his front shirt pocket, which covers his massive pec and erect nipple, and pulls out a coal-black business card with white lettering. My boss tosses me the card and says, "Use this place … Something tells me you need it and will surely like it."

I pick the business card up from my desk and review its information: DUNGEON X. A city address is listed, as well as a phone number, and a Website. Hours of operation tell me: 24/7. I look up at Dorrien again and ask, "I've heard of this place before. It's a fag club for brothers, right?"

My boss nods his head, blisters with a gleaming smile, and responds, "You'll need three hundred dollars to get in the door. Show the card. Only a selective group of men get inside."

I flip the card over and see the number 435 on the back. "What's the number for?"

"The four tells the owner you're a special guest. There are only one hundred guest cards given out a month to men who are not members. You're number thirty-five."

"You a member?" I inquire, raising an eyebrow. I always thought Dorrien straight, since he has a wife and three girls.

He clears his throat with nervousness, and replies, "Let's just say I like some heavy duty action when it comes to rough sex, and Dungeon X offers that to me."

I study the business card again with interest, and confess, "It will be our little secret."

"That's a wise decision, TJ. Discreet is a noble cause. I respect discreet."

"Likewise," I reply, slip the card away, give him a professional wink, and watch him leave my office.

Two nights later, I decide life just about sucks because of all the work I do. Now, I elect to cash in my Dungeon X card at 873 West Street in the city. The place is a wall of bricks with a rust-colored steel door. There is no fluorescent DUNGEON X sign that hangs above the place. There are no windows. There are no party sounds from inside. Instead, the edifice and door look like every other building in a bad part of the city.

I move up to the door, try the steel lever, and discover it locked and immobile. I tap on the door three times like any old Joe and …

An upper part of the steel door slides open, and some sexy Nigerian's brown eyes appear. His rough voice states, "Card and cash."

I pass him the business card from Dorrien and three hundred in cash.

The Nigerian says, "Number thirty-five. Enter."

The steel door unlocks, swings inward, and I step inside Dungeon X for the very first time.

An X-shaped bar is tended by two, black quarterback-sized dudes with pulsing muscles. Both are decked out in leather-studded vests and hats. Dr. Dre blasts down from overhead speakers. The walls are black and trimmed in blood red. A number of black studs sit around the bar, hit on each other, talk, and become buzzed. Bottles of Yvonne Chaka Chaka beer are shared; I order one and slug it down. Two Kenyans are pressed together in a nearby corner; one man is on his knees, blowing his boyfriend/lover/husband/stranger.

I have a second Yvonne Chaka Chaka, take in the sites, and feel a brother dressed in leather getup roll his left palm up and along my thigh and grasp my cock and balls, which he begins to massage with tender strokes. The dungeon master is soon pulled away from me by another man, some hulking South African with a sexy scar along his right cheek. The two head to the opposite side of the bar where they meet a door marked DX. In a matter of seconds they vanish behind the door, and leave me to follow behind.

I work my way across the dark bar, find the door, pull it open, and step inside a dim hallway with florescent yellow and green stripes on a set of declining stairs. Now, I take the stairs, work my way deeper into Dungeon X, and end up in a different world at the bottom of the narrow stairwell.

A Heavy D song echoes off the coal black walls. A hallway approximately fifty feet long stretches out in front of me. Rooms to the right and left of the hallway are occupied by the sexually naughtiest black men who roam the city. At the end of the semi-illuminated hallway is a cocoa-colored stud strapped face-down on a man-sized wheel, which is attached to the wall. Each of the man's ankles and wrists are belted to the wheel with white, leather straps. The chocolate-colored man is shaped like an X on the wheel, ready for sexual use. Two black dudes in leather hoods stand behind the man, slashing his naked and tight bottom with leather straps. Yelps of excitement and sexual splendor echo down the hallway, fill my ears with desire, and cause the new pounder between my legs to throb with elation.

I make my way down the hallway. The first room on the right is approximately twelve feet deep and fourteen feet wide. The room is all cement, without windows, and smells of antiseptic. A naked blond man has a leash around his neck, which is fastened to the middle of the floor. His arms are spread wide and his wrists are buckled into chains that hang down from the cement ceiling. Three husky and naked Jamaicans with condom-covered boners stand around the blond. Each awaits his turn to bang the blond with steady and impulsive hip-thrusts, eventually getting off.

The first room on the left is a similar show. Two Puerto Rican men in their early twenties face each other. Ropes hang down from the ceiling and secure their wrists. A leather device has their swollen cocks tied together, and an iron ball on a durable linked chain hangs between them, resting on the cement floor. A Mexican man of hulking size circles the pair, holding a fourteen-inch long apple-red dildo in his right hand, which is ready for use.

The second room on the right is lined with six muscular, black men. Each is pinned to the wall with linked chains, gagged with orange balls, and their ankles are tightened in shackles. These men are approximately a foot apart and their sizes range from five-nine to six-one. All of their brown-colored cocks are upright and ready to be sucked by two titanic men with abundant muscles. Both of these men have black leather hoods pulled tightly over their heads. And both hold whips in their right hands, prepared to sting the line-up of men with euphoric and mind-numbing pleasure.

As I pass this third room and head to the next one, sounds of glory escape one of the men, joy discovered as his juicy-dark flesh is being whipped by one of the authoritative men while the other man in charge sucks the plump rod between his legs. The yelps sound uncivilized, but safe, and cause the eight-inch flag between my legs to bounce with zeal.

The second room on the left is occupied by two men. One beefy, rock-hard Amazonian is straddled in an aluminum-colored operating chair. His legs are spread wide open, positioned in stirrups. The man's arms are stiff above his head with their wrists tied together with bull rope. His chest sports erect nipples, both of which are decorated with aluminum clamps. This blindfolded man wears a studded collar, black leather boots, and nothing more. A second man inside the room is fully dressed in leather gear: mask, gloves, boots, and an X-shaped getup, which is all studded with stainless steel barbs. This dungeon master stands directly over his partner's middle and jacks his toy off by using his right hand, quick and fierce movement that draws my attention to the scene even more, and causes me to lick my lips.

The third room on the right is empty. Three sets of chains hang down from the cement ceiling. Each set is accessorized with silver wrist cuffs. Centered between the dangling cuffs are three, thirty-six-inch dildos, which protrude from the floor; pleasure instruments for a trio of men while being sexually, but consensually, used.

The last room on the left showcases a spider web harness/hammock constructed out of thick bull rope. The web hangs in the center of the room by long ropes, which dangle down from the cement ceiling. It rests approximately three feet off the floor, swinging to and fro, unused at the moment.

To my surprise, this final room is being occupied by a single man who welcomes me inside. The man is almost naked, except for the leather-studded straps around his ankles and wrists, and a black leather hood covering his face. My companion is around six-three and weighs almost 250 pounds. Azure-colored eyes welcome me with excitement, shimmering in the playroom's dim light. I study his muscular frame with zeal and hunger: plump nipples the color of medium chocolate; springs of dark curly hair between his exploding pecs; inflated abs and dented navel; narrow and curly-black treasure trail that falls into a triangular patch of black coils, upright shaft of ten inches, which is fully uncut and accessorized with plum-sized balls. He grunts at me, "Get rid of the clothes."

In doing so, X — as I call the stranger — takes a whiff of my neck. His fingers find my cotton shirt, which he removes and drops to the floor. The digits pinch both of my nipples and fall over each of my hairless abs. He huffs like a bull and nudges my head with his leather-covered one. He inhales my masculine scent a second time and whispers, "Hot smell ... I can't wait to get a whiff of your ass."

The buttons on my jeans are pealed loose. Their zipper is pulled down and X discovers no Rufskins or Unicos or 2[X]ist briefs underneath. Instead, he yanks the eight-inch shaft out of its denim cove and provides it with a handy, up and down stroke, which causes a gasp to exit my mouth; a mere beginning to valid pleasure between us.

I half-expect the stud to fall to his knees and lather my poker with his tongue. Part of me wishes he would shove my beef down the back of his throat and brush my spiral pubic hairs against his lips. I also want the man to tug on my balls, yanking down on the pair, which will inevitably send a ripple of bliss to rush throughout my body. None of these desires transpire, though. Instead, X grunts, "Get on the web."

Of course, he assists me with climbing on the rope web. The brother hoists me up, and I roll onto my back. In doing so, his tongue exits his beautiful red lips and laps at my notched, black stomach, taking his first taste of me. Now, my body is pulled to the edge of the web for his easy access, and my ass is exposed. X doesn't take a lick or sniff of the prize, though. Instead, he ties my ankles and wrists to leather straps that hang from the cement ceiling. I become X-shape on the web, ready for the stranger's use, or however he sees fit to fill his sexual needs by manipulating my body.

"Enjoy the ride," he gruffly says and begins to swing me to and fro on the web. As this process is carried out, he leans over a bit, outstretches his tongue, and licks the underside area of my boner and balls with every forward and backward motion.

On the web, I gasp for air, enlightened by his tongue-bath. Our motion is concurrent and wild and everything I have anticipated regarding this evening at Dungeon X. The lattice-like rope beneath my body makes a crrrk … crrrk … crrrk noise as I continue to swing. The stranger pushes me backward, and I fly forward, into his protrusion of tongue, plump lips, and rounded, mask-covered chin. Quick licks are applied to my knob and balls during each melodic stride, and another gasp of pleasure exits my mouth.

"Hungry for you," X grunts and stops the web from moving. Now, he holds the rope hammock still with his left palm. His right hand grabs the eight-inch dagger between my legs by its base. Within seconds, he lowers his mouth over my tool, plummeting the meat into the back of his throat, gagging himself on the erect prize.

What transpires next is nothing shocking between men in sexual action. X becomes busy with my shaft inside his mouth. I watch his mask-covered head bob up and down in a speedy manner. He moans and gags, lost under his dick-eating spell. The guy's work is thrifty and sends me into body-numbing joy.

He becomes chaotic with his mouth-job and rushes his head north and south on my shaft.

I squirm on the web and attempt to thrust my hips upward, bolting my poker inside his system, finding a sense of jubilation in doing so. I call out to the black dungeon master, "Suck it, man! ... Make me shoot my load!"

He grumbles something indecipherable, obviously enjoying his task. The man continues to bob his head on my limb, fulfilling his own desire.

Honestly, I want to reach between my legs and place my palms on the back of the stranger's head, just so he can be rough with me. The straps that secure my wrists prevent me from doing so. Instead, I utter idiosyncrasies on the web, trapped on the ropes and under his naughty care.

Once he completes his mouth-to-shaft action, he pulls away from me and ends up in one of the room's corners. An orange ball-gag is found and slipped over my head. X mumbles, "Eat this," tightening the device at the rear of my head. Once this is accomplished, he shares, "Thatta boy." Following this pony show, he finds aluminum clips and pinches them over my nipples. He gives the clips a tug, offering tantalizing pain for me. Now, he smacks my clean-shaven abs once ... twice ... three times until I let out a murmur of hurt. He says down to me on the rope web, "You like that and know it."

I do like it ... and him ... whoever he is. Feeling delirious under the sexy brute's care, I become flushed, semi-unconscious, but still into the man's sexual gig. Animal-like grunts and growls escape the corners of my mouth.

X decides to shut me up by pulling on my balls. One tug turns into three tugs, which only catapults into more bliss. He blasts down at me, "Growl all you like, brother ... You're not going anywhere."

The rod between my legs bounces with enlightenment. I raise my hips with chaotic lust as a vibration of pure gratification circulates through my middle. Everything about this moment on the web is enriched with fantastical indulgence. Dorrien's Dungeon X is exactly what I need to deflate by, due to my fast-paced and brain-beating position at Lloyd, Bradshaw & Tanner.

The master is on his knees with his face buried in my bottom. His hands are strapped to the edge of the web, and he yanks my rear to and fro, lathering the area around my tight, black hole with his protruding tongue. The deviant man laps at my flesh, his face still concealed from me. His slippery tongue rapidly exits the leather mask, laps at my sweaty flesh, flies back inside, becomes concealed, and exits again. Slurps and greedy grumbles of contentment escape his mouth as his tongue-tour on my ass continues.

Eventually, the rim-job on my bottom is finished, and he decides to pop the tip of his wet digit into my man-cave, sliding it into my middle as far as it will go, keeping residence here for three … five … seven seconds, until he finally decides to pull the pink sliver out of my rump and continue this process for the next ten minutes.

As he eats my tunnel, becoming hypnotized by my skin and juices, he growls with satisfaction. More licks, laps, and protrusions occur to my TJ-center. His tongue plummets into my behind and pulls out a number of times. I yelp with elation; an obscure rash of sounds is only heard. Again and again my man-cavern is teased by his slick appendage as it slips inside and exits numerous times.

Minutes pass before he pulls away from me and finds a twelve-inch rubber dildo and applies it to my taut rear. The dildo is studded with inflated nubs, which will surely offer more pleasure. Before sliding the tip of the device inside my rear, X runs it along one of my cheeks, the other cheek, and my chin. He whispers down to me, "You want to eat this with your ass. I'm sure you do."

The plastic tool rolls down and along my corded neck, over my right, clipped nipple, and bounces along the cut abs that line my stomach. The dildo discovers my navel, teasing its dented structure, and falls southward, where it temporarily stops next to my pumped flag. "I'm doing it, guy," the black beast rattles off and lowers the dildo to the opening of my rump. "Get ready."

Before the dildo enters my epicenter, he lubes eleven inches of its plastic. Now, he presses the tip of the twelve inches against my bottom and warns, "Brace yourself."

One inch of the lust-torch enters my man-tomb and breaks me open; I gasp from its girth, edgy because of immediate pain. Two inches cram inside me, which causes me to gurgle under the stranger's touch. Three inches spread my ass apart even more, which is assisted by four ... five ... and six more inches. I howl behind the ball-gag, lost and bemused because of X's handy work. He slides seven inches of the tool inside my rump and playfully laughs down at me, knowing I have discovered both splendor and angst, all at the same time. Eight inches just about causes me to lose oxygen. Nine inches of the dildo compressed into my sliver of manness shifts arcs of bewilderment throughout my entire system. Ten inches force my eyelids to flutter sporadically. Eleven inches of his faux dick punches against my intestines, kidneys, and the bottom of my lungs. All eleven inches pull quickly out of my ass, slide back inside, and pull out yet again, action that transpires for the next ...

How long am I delirious on the rope hammock as he uses the rigid dildo inside my narrow rump? Why is the cement room spinning in circles, feeling unstoppable? How much of the sex toy's use can I handle until I begin to bleed? How many bubbles of pre-ooze leaks out of my hose and decorates my navel because of X's game?

I think: Drowning. Suffocation. Man-lust. X's sexual exploits. Under his tough touch. Just relax. Enjoy the ride. Free yourself. This is why I'm here. Explore this wild and crazy life of the queer underworld. Take all of this black man's horny fury ... just the way he wants to give it to me. Let him bang me until I cannot be banged again.

Relentlessly, the fake cock slides into my fissure, releases, and is pushed in again. Numbness finds me. My breath is lost. I begin to hallucinate and feel as if I will pass out. How I keep conscious is beyond my comprehension.

Eventually, minutes compiled upon minutes, the twelve-inch dildo is finally released from my constricted bottom and set aside. "Enough," X says above me. "I have other plans for you, guy."

My swollen shaft is pulled toward him, released, and snapped against my torso. My seducer accomplishes this a second time ... three times ... four times, and laughs down at me, pleased to drive me into a state of sexual no return. Now, the chain connected to my balls is tugged on. Now, the clamps on my nipples are squeezed. Now, my dildo-used asshole is spanked three times. Now, my abs are slapped. Now, our worlds are fully combined.

What transpires next is nothing out of the ordinary, of course. I assume many men before me have swung to and fro in this knotted web, having had someone like X use their flesh and man-goods in the same manner that the hooded black man currently uses mine. Nothing about today is unusual and ...

"It's time for my pole, brother ... I think you're ready for it," he coaches down to me, blue-eyed and smiling, mostly concealed by the leather mask that he still sports. "Ready or not, here it comes," he adds, and pushes his condom-covered stick forward.

His junk just about splits me into two equal parts. Five inches of his post enters me ... seven inches ... all ten inches, and causes my rump to sting with masculine delight. I wriggle beneath him because of his rough motion. The brother is far too occupied at the moment to respond in a cordial manner, though. Instead, he rushes his weight into me, pulls out, plunges his shaft down to its hairy base, and holds the wood still within my narrow and tight man-gorge, teasing me to his fullest potential.

A grunt and hearty growl escape the corners of my mouth as he uses my canal as a dick-harbor. X chuckles above me, reaches for my eight-inch stick between my legs, and gives it a stroke up and down. Half of me believes he is going to finish me off, allowing me to finally explode my built-up load, but he doesn't. Instead, he releases my dong and continues his ass-banging with my tight rectum.

The rope web careens me to and fro as the underground god bumps into my bottom, pulls away, and bumps into me again and again and again. Our motion becomes frantic but enjoyable. Both of us delightfully moan with complete satisfaction. Our middles smack together with ease, fall apart, and smack together yet another time. The motion between us is sloppy but concurrent. We glide forward and backward at opposite times but at the same velocity. Both of us growl with extraordinary dungeon-bliss, caught up in our nasty, underground black act between naked and lustful men.

Fuck me, I think. Fuck me hard ... and harder. Don't stop. Drive your dick into me. Use me. Abuse me. Please me ... Fuck me harder, man. I want it and need it, and you know I want it and need it. Don't hold back. Please me ... Tease me, motherfucker.

Sweat flies off the dungeon master's massive chest and stings my abs. The perspiration bubbles, sizzles my skin, and eventually evaporates. Hip-thrusts ensue against my opening, fall away, and ensue again. X's breathing intensifies, and he grits his teeth. The man's black brow becomes furrowed, and he explodes with: "Ready to shoot, brother."

I mumble under the ball-gag: Spray your load, X. But what spills out of me is nothing less than a gurgle. Rushed sounds ... lost.

As if X hears me, he yanks his goods out of my backside, removes the condom, which he immediately tosses to the cement floor, and begins to stroke himself off with his right paw. His left paw is also busy; it quickly leashes against my timber and starts to move up and down in a spirited manner. Speedily, he strokes both of us off at the same time. The synchronized motion with his black paws is intense, wild, and most alluring. No-name man becomes a maniac with his fists, bolting his palms in a north and south motion that is unending and deliberate.

As my mind spins on the web, semi-comatose, breathless, and feeling whipped, X informs between my legs, "Exploding, brother!" Within seconds his white shoot flies out of his stick and spirals against my torso. The spew clings to my clipped nipples, lined torso, and fills my pitted navel. Huffs and puffs exit the beast at the edge of the web. Whimpers and rumbles and grouses of passion escape his mouth. In doing so, two more arcs of guy-splash is bucked out of his hose and splats against my chained balls, eventually dripping to the cement floor.

Shivers of erotic splendor cascade throughout my center, stinging my every muscle. I choke on the ball-gag, come to after almost passing out, and feel an untouched release between my legs. A wash of ooze shoots out of my poker and flies against my chin and neck, lathering my pores. I attempt to buck my hips upward, but am already spent, empty of my dungeon goo. Now, I lay limp on the web, dazed and confused, with my cock already growing soft.

The ball-gag is released from my mouth. While X pants, post-sexed and pleasured, he removes the chain from my balls. When the clamps are finally unhinged from my nipples, I find the courage to ask, "Who are you? What is your name?"

X stands over me, motionless with his stinging-blue eyes locked on my molten brown ones. He huffs at me, grins wildly, and gruffly whispers, "Do you really want to know who I am?"

"I do … Tell me. Show yourself."

The black leather hood is removed from his head and …

"Dorrien Bradshaw," I gasp, shocked to see my boss standing above me with his hands on his hips and his massive chest heaving for breath. "It's you."

The lawyer grins from ear to ear, happy to come forward and unmask himself. He says, "Hello, number thirty-five. Glad you could make it to Dungeon X this evening," and he moves overtop me, connecting his firm and muscular chest to my sticky one, and ends up biting my lower lip with lust, a brisk motion that I find a total turn-on, welcoming me to his underground club for the most naughtiest men, and beginning a new and rather tasteless, but enjoyed, relationship with him.

SAFE WORD: BALLBUSTING
By R. W. Clinger

PART 1 — D&S 101

I pull my attention away from editing a summertime BBQ cookbook for my employer, Stayman Press. My curious stare scans my boyfriend of three years again. Truth is I'm hard as a rock between my legs for the guy, totally into his dark chocolate skin. Theodore McGregor Favous stands at six-two, weighs 220 pounds, sports emerald green eyes, a sweet crew cut, goatee, and has a hairy torso of sculpted muscle. The twenty-seven-year-old arrives at our apartment with a box in his arms, which he places on the sofa.

Curiosity always kills me and I ask, "What's in the box, Theo?"

"Stay away from the box, Dardin. It's none of your business," he jokes, since everything in his life just happens to be my business.

He always calls me by my last name, refusing to call me by my first name, Matteau. And sometimes, he calls me Babe, Guy, or Chocolate Morsel, whatever he's in the mood to label me with.

My man observes me next to the sofa, taking in my editing good looks, maybe ready to hump me like he usually does after his nine-hour shift of playing nurse at First Presbyterian Hospital on Roshner Street: five-eleven, crystal blue eyes, 190 pounds, coconut cream skin, twenty-nine years old, chiseled like a jock, no fat, and America's Queer Top Model stuff.

Sweet looking.

A black truffle ready to be eaten — all me.

I scan the New York City apartment again, just to tease him, making him believe I don't give a flying shit about him, of course. My eyes shift to the secondhand Belgium sofa, faux Tiffany lights, cedar end tables, and reproduced Steve Walker paintings that hang on the walls. Again, my eyes take in the Greenwich Village tenant, scan him up and down, lick my lips with hunger, and prattle, "I want to know what's in the box, man."

Of course, I peak into the box and gasp with excitement. Bondage toys stare back at me! The box is filled with colorful dildos, stainless steel cuffs, mouth-gags, two iron balls on chains, leather straps, hoods, whips, black leather gloves, cock clamps, cock rings, and male chastity belts.

I pull a nipple clamp out of the box and say, "Where did you get all the sex goodies?"

"Craigslist. A guy is moving from New York City to San Francisco. I answered his ad."

"Used goods. Even better." I take a whiff of the box and smell a stranger's urine and semen, loving the mixed aroma. I place the nipple clamp back into the box and pull out a pair of cuffs. "Theo, I know nothing about bondage and dungeon stuff."

He admits at my side, "We're going to learn together."

"I can hardly wait," I say, and drool over the box of toys.

He pulls out a fourteen-inch navy blue dildo from the box, waves the toy in front of me, and says, "The fucker is almost as big as your dick."

"I'm bigger," I lie, teasing him.

"We can prove it. Drop your jeans and let's find out."

I pull the plastic cock away from him, shove the tip of it into my mouth, quickly release it, smack my lips together, and reply, "Why don't you shut the fuck up and shove it into my ass already?"

He laughs at me and begins to punch my right shoulder with some rough play, knowing it's exactly what I want. I jab him in the chest with a full-throttled punch, knocking him to the floor. Immediately, I snatch a pair of stainless steel cuffs out of his happy box of toys and slap them over his wrists at his stomach.

Theo smiles on the floor and instructs, "Do my ankles, too, bitch."

I listen, rip off his tight, ab-lined T-shirt, and drop it to the floor.

"Fuck you!" exits his beautiful mouth, which causes me to pull a bright orange ball-gag out of the box, swing it to and fro in front of him, and warn, "If you don't shut the fuck up, you'll wear this."

He wiggles on the floor, obviously enjoying his capture, and our rough game of man-lust. My partner rolls over and tries to crawl away from me, but I step on his back, pin him to the apartment's Berber, and rattle off behind him, "Theo, you can't get away from me."

Honestly, I'm bone-hard between my legs, into our sex-gig. Juice actually leaks out of my nine-inch man-hose and decorates my Unico boxer-briefs under Diesel jeans.

Theo and I have always talked about some dungeon bondage shared between us. Both of us have always been interested in some D&S role playing, want to be tied up, and partake in other naughty leather games. This evening is a class of D&S 101 for us. New dungeon guys trying out the rough stuff for the first time. Mutual tie-me-up-and-tease-me antics that will inevitably cause us both pleasure.

I whip my boyfriend a number of times with a leather strap from out of our happy box: on his back; against his ass; over a shoulder; along his neck ...

Submissive Theo screams in pleasure and pain at the top of his mannish voice, into our game, loving the blasts with the strap, being my playmate, my pet, and making me glow as his master.

"Oh my Christ!" fills our apartment. My boyfriend/lover/roommate/toy screams at the top of his lungs. "Fuck you, Dardin!"

His reaction to my rough play keeps a solid nine-inch shaft built between my inner thighs. Bubbles of man-spurt leaks out of its head, coating cotton. A ripple of glee rushes throughout my body and warms me with sin as blast after blast with the strap plays holy terror with my black man's skin.

Theo's yelps are grainy and rough. At one point, I think he sobs from bliss-filled rage, into our combination. Tears drip out of his emerald green eyes and roll down and over his cheeks. More yelps fill the apartment, again and again and again and ...

The apartment's doorbell chimes and Twilia Favous, Theo's mother, hollers in the hallway, "Boys! ... What's going on in there? ... Baby Theo, are you hurt?"

As Twilia uses her fist on the door, continuing to scream with concern, I drop the leather strap to the floor and kick it under the couch; we don't find it for a month.

Theo utters with complete horror, "Shit, Dardin ... Mother has a key. Get me out of these cuffs."

More Twilia bangs ensue on the apartment's front door. Theo's mother yells through the wood, "Theo! ... Baby! ... I'm coming in!"

Just as Theo is about to yell to his mother not to enter apartment J-1, a key is heard in the lock, which twists and tumbles the brass levers behind the faux gold knob and ...

"Jesus, Mary, and JoJo," Theo numbly chants on his knees, still cuffed and partially naked on the Berber.

"Crap," falls out of my lips and my eyes grow wide. The guy-wood between my legs promptly deflates as my steady stare takes in the door and Twilia Favous's sudden entrance.

The apartment's front door swings open, and here stands my lover's mother: 330 pounds of black blubber in a banana-colored sundress, straw hat, three chins, swollen ankles, and whore-red lipstick on her flabby lips. Mother Twilia holds a lime green purse with long straps in her right hand and an entry key to the apartment in her left hand; both items fall to the hallway tile because of what she sees in her son's apartment.

What Twilia Favous sees:

Her baby boy kneels on the living room floor with stainless steel cuffs around his ankles and wrists. Theodore is bare-chested with firm nipples, and sports a denim-covered man-mound between his legs. His shredded T-shirt is strewn on the floor. The box of naughty XXX toys sits in the center of the sofa's pillows. I'm quite sure she sees all of the sexual gadgets inside: ball-gags, nipple clamps, dildos, duct tape, barbed-wire, chastity cock-belt, block of wax, leather whips, a leather hood, numerous belts, chains, and other devices of fun.

She crosses herself and cries out to Theo, "Baby, what has Dardin done to you? ... My poor baby."

What Matteau Dardin (me!) has done to Twilia's sexy son is play dungeon master in apartment J-1, and toy with the model man while her baby is cuffed, flogged, and begs to be ... fucked. What I want to accomplish with my roommate's nakedness is pornographically dick-hardening between two homosexual men, and sexual acts that Bible-Thumper Twilia Favous has never witnessed in all her fifty-eight years. What I wish for is to ...

Before Theo or I can utter a single phrase or sentence to defend our D&S behavior, Twilia immediately finds her Verizon cellular within the folds of her purse and exclaims, "Baby, I'm calling 911. We can both put this criminal behind bars." As expected, she points directly at me, posing judgment based on our dungeon play.

What transpires during the next few minutes is rather embarrassing and comical: as I uncuff my submissive lover, he yells at Twilia not to call the police; Twilia questions her son about his current position on the floor, his mangled T-shirt, and the box of XXX goodies on the sofa; Theo's dark skin turns a shade of auburn red as he confesses our naughty time together to his mother; Twilia becomes confused, as expected; Theo clarifies that we were having sex, sharing a little roughhousing between naked buddies; Twilia grabs her heart with her right palm and gasps with shock; she drops her cell to the hallway and its screen shatters; I laugh out loud because of the excitement; Twilia finds her composure and says something to God; she snatches up her broken phone and purse; the woman quickly bolts down the hallway, vanishing from the D&S scene.

Of course, Theo calls out for his mother. Half of the call is with heavy laughter; the other half is filled with concern. When I eventually snag the chocolate morsel within my arms and squeeze him against my skin, he stops yelling for his mother.

Now, coming to terms with the unexpected Twilia encounter, I hold her son next to me and say, "It's over. Let it go, Theo. Give your mother some time to digest what she now knows about us. There's no reason to panic. She'll come around."

Eventually, I convince him of other things, too: stripping out of his clothes, getting down on his hands and knees again, letting me cuff and whip him, letting me fuck him, and begging me to shoot my load against his face, precisely how he wants to be ooze-garnished with my sticky cargo.

"Keep your nose out of my box."

"Fuck you."

Theo gives my right shoulder a playful shove and says, "Fuck you back."

"Bring it on."

And we collide, kiss as boyfriends, completely caught up in each other and our rough games.

PART 2 – DUNGEON J-1

Two days later in what Theo and I call Dungeon J-1 opposed to our apartment, he melts a block of wax in an aluminum bowl with a BurnzOmatic. I sit next to him at our coffee table and read a D&S manual regarding sexual acts with heated wax. I say,

"The book says you can use the wax on my inner thighs, navel, abs, armpits, pecs, nipples, cock, and balls."

Theo stirs the hot wax with a wooden spatula from the kitchen. The wax is a caramel hue, lighter than my sexy skin, and Theo's. Just looking at its molten fabric causes my joint to bob between my legs with excitement.

"Are you ready for me yet?" I question.

"Get undressed, and don't worry about it."

I stand by the sofa and strip out of my clothes: Unico boxer-briefs and Pistol Pete jeans. In doing so, I ask, "Is the safe word the same?"

"Ball busting?"

"That be it."

Theo raises the spatula from the aluminum bowl and a long string of caramel wax hangs down from its wood. Now, he stirs the concoction and says, "I think we're ready now."

"Music to my ears," I reply, and supply my black junk with a healthy tug.

He stands from the sofa and strips out of his clothes: Nike running shorts and a tight tee that defines his swollen pecs and abs; no underwear. The guy is already firm between his legs: ten inches of muscled staff rises to our intimate occasion.

I reach out and snap two fingertips off his thumper's head. The fleshly instrument bounces once … twice … three times, and drips out a bubble of warm goo, which falls to the floor.

Theo now finds a wool blanket and sprawls it over the living room floor in front of the Sony television. He's a little anal and spreads all of its corners out flat, looks at me, and asks, "Do you think it's going to be too itchy for us to fuck around on?"

"What's a few scruffs and scratches on our skin. Bring it on, pal. I think I'm ready for it."

Satisfied with my answer, he lies down on the wool blanket, spreads his legs, looks up at me, and admits, "I forgot to light the candles."

"Don't panic. I'm on it." I spend the next two minutes lighting candles in the apartment, adding a dungeon-like and ominous feel to our intimate evening. When I return to my roommate's side, his cock stands at full mast, ready for whatever is about to happen between us.

I bring the moment into full motion by kneeling over his black and hairy chest. Now, I rub the tip of my tongue along both of his nipples, grasp the upright tool between his firm legs, give it a few consecutive strokes, tug on his balls, and eventually lick every ab on his sculpted torso. My lips fall to the dark-colored poker between his legs and collapse over its mass. I take half of the ten inches into my throat, bob my head up and down, give it plenty of suction, pull away, and smack my lips together with inebriated happiness. When this is complete, I wipe the back of my right hand across my mouth, smile down at his black beauty, and ask, "You ready for the wax?"

"Ready as I will ever be," he replies with hunger in his eyes for our connection and naughty gig.

What follows between us is nothing less than heaven and hell mixing, and a male-cocktail of pleasure with pain. The aluminum bowl of wax sits on the wool blanket to Theo's right. I scoop a string of hot wax out with the wooden spatula, hold it over his right nipple, drizzle some against the pointed blackness, and wait a few seconds for it to cool.

My boyfriend hisses beneath my touch, surprised by the heated discomfort. His chocolaty hue seems to exit his face. Anguish settles into his eyes, and then a smile forms on his face as he discovers a sense of ultimate euphoria.

"I'm removing it now," I warn him, knowing that his nipple is going to sting with excruciating pain, and that I might take off some skin from his pec with the hardening wax. "It will be a quick and precise yank. Enjoy the agony, guy. I know I will."

One pull with two fingertips is all it takes to remove the wax from his nipple. What transpires is a girlish whimper from my big and black lover. A tear falls out of the corner of his right eye and becomes lost on the wool blanket. Satisfied with our consensual play, he giggles, and instructs, "More please. Don't stop."

Dungeon J-1 becomes our recreational area of man-fun. I drip wax on his abs and pull it off, searing his skin. More drops of hot wax fall against his navel, cools, and is ripped off with a hearty tug. I decorate his armpits, remove black hair with quick pulls, and cause the nurse beneath me to howl with agonizing niceness. Now, I coat his right ball with some hot wax, tell him not to move, allow the liquid to become a solid mass in a matter of seconds, and rip it off.

Theo cries, which is no surprise for either of us. His teeth click together because of the discomfort, but his cock stays firm between his legs, sexually into our two-man show, desiring more. He instructs, "Put some on my cock ... Do it ... I can't wait any longer. I want to feel the pain, brother."

Masculine and horrendous screams surface from Dungeon J-1 because of the wax-sport we play together. Vulgar howling echoes off the walls and ceiling. As more wax is applied to Theo's shaft, and ripped off with aggressive speed, he bellows on the wool blanket, under my touch and care, and relishes our combined D&S amusement.

I slap him to keep him quiet: across his face; against his left temple; along his right thigh; over his mounded pecs; against his swinging balls and his tower-like cock. My slaps are wild and brisk and cause the man to only scream louder, at the top of his lungs at some moments, but always keeping an enchanted and spirited look of delight on his model-like face, loving our time spent together.

Not once does my partner use the safe word. Ball busting is never whispered, chanted, or cried out. We practice our lust-recreation with mutual emotions and unlimited bliss, completely into each other, and our wax-task.

After forty minutes of screams in Dungeon J-1, some asshole neighbor in the apartment building calls the city police, and Officer Maxim Cogg arrives at our front door. I tell Theo not to move and that I will handle the cop.

"Do you want to cover me up?"

"Fuck no. It's nobody's business what we like to do together."

I move up to the apartment's front door, unlock the three brass locks, crack the door open, and peep into the hallway. What I see is rather sexually enlightening. Cogg is a beautiful, richly dark-colored officer of the law in a too-tight and navy blue uniform. He stands at approximately five-eight, weighs 165 pounds, is completely bald, sports almost-violet-colored eyes, and wears a revolver at his right hip. Because the guy is so sexy hot, I pull the door open the entire way, and let him into the apartment, welcoming the black stud to witness our flesh-waxing pastime.

Of course, he sees a naked Theo on the wool blanket, the lighted candles, the aluminum bowl of warm wax, and our spine-tingling naughties at hand. Cogg clears his throat, rubs a finger across the tip of his nose with caution, and simply asks, "Gentleman, have you been screaming?"

I nod my head in a careless, but honest manner, and admit, "My boyfriend has."

Theo waves from his blanket and says, "Sorry about that, officer. We're kind of enjoying this evening together … if you know what I mean."

Cogg fully comprehends how two dark-skinned men in apartment J-1 are sharing this evening. He nods his head, checks out my boyfriend's still-erect knob between his legs, licks his lips, and says, "Can the two of you please keep it down a little?"

Is he talking about the steeping rod between Theo's legs, or our antics? I'm not really sure. Whatever he speaks of, Theo and I both agree to his request, and apologize for the noise.

Before Officer Cogg leaves us alone to finish our night of sexual pleasure with the heated wax, he says, "You two guys have fun. Just try to keep it down."

I nod my head.

Theo waves again and responds, "Will do."

Cogg finds the courage to raise his right hand to my chin, brushes two fingertips against my flesh, and winks at me.

Truth is, I don't know what really happens. Before I can respond with my own wink, the patrolman is gone, wiggling his ass goodbye, trotting away, and defending our city of crime.

Following the man's short visit, I lock the apartment door again, turn to Theo on the wool blanket, and ask, "Ready for more wax on your cock, babe?"

He laughs at me, and the visit from the hot cop. Theo replies, "I'm always ready for you. Let's continue."

We do. But this time he screams with a pillow over his face, semi-suffocating as I apply hot wax to his ten inches of meat, and quickly rip it off with delight.

PART 3 – CAGED!

The spare bedroom's size is eight-by-ten. Very little light enters the room because it has no windows. Theo decides that it's the perfect place for a cage, which he purchases at an antique barn outside the city. He has the cage delivered to the apartment by three husky, queer friends that we know from a bar called Dungeon X.

The cage is approximately four feet long, three feet high, and constructed of welded steel bars. Its shape is that of a human on his knees. The rear opens up, a certain naked somebody can crawl inside, and the rear closes and locks. Once the fellow is inside, positioned on his hands and knees, protected by lateral, steel bars, he cannot move, which allows him to become a toy/pet for those around him inside the spare bedroom, an extension of Dungeon J-1.

# # # # #

Officer Maxim Cogg finds his way back to our apartment approximately a week after our wax scene and loud commentary. He's dressed in civilian clothes this time: tight tee, jeans, leather shoes. Theo offers him a strong drink, which he accepts.

For the next hour, we get to know Cogg: no children, no wife, no husband, no boyfriend, loves his freedom, a very selfish young man, parents dead, close to his sister, graduate of the New York Police Academy, college degree in criminal justice, and lives in Greenwich Village. The three of us discuss D&S, which Cogg enjoys and practices; a regular at the exclusive club Dungeon X. What transpires is nothing shocking: Cogg wants in on some naughties with us.

Theo adores Cogg, finding the man dreamy; I can see it in his eyes. He says to Cogg, "We have a new cage that Dardin and I haven't used yet. Are you interested?"

Cogg's almost-violet-colored eyes light up with intense fire, an obvious sign that he is interested in partaking in the fun with our new cage. "Let me see it," exits his beautiful mouth.

We show Cogg the cage; he circles it like an animal. The cutest smile forms on his face, and his eyes spin with excitement.

"What do you think?" Theo says, standing next to me as if protecting me from the sexy cop.

Cogg looks up from the cage, wildly grins with pleasure, nods his head, and asks, "Are you guys in the mood to try it out right now?"

I look at Theo. He looks at me. We both smile with utter joy, and say at the same time, "Hell yeah."

My boyfriend and I undress Cogg together. We rip his T-shirt off and drop it to the hardwood floor. His leather shoes are pulled off and tossed aside. Cogg's jeans are unbuttoned, yanked down to his ankles, and he eventually steps out of them.

What is hidden under the man's civilian clothes is rather stunning: molten hazelnut pecs of steel, hairless abs that look like a ladder, dented navel, V-shape of freshly shaven man-hair above his six inches of uncut and limp cock. Cogg's thighs are bulky with muscle. Once he is naked, he tells us to undress, which we do. In doing so, he strokes his uncut shaft up and down a few times, and grows his spike into eight full inches.

Now, on his own initiative, Cogg slides his small but muscled frame into the cage, demands that we lock it behind him, and asks, "What's the safe word, guys?"

"Ball busting," I reply, already hard between my legs, ready to use my shaft on the cop's body, and spray him down with my load.

"Great word. Nice," Cogg says on his hands and knees, our subject of interest/pet/toy.

What transpires in this extended room of Dungeon J-1 are events that one might view in an XXX film. Theo, unclothed and rock hard between his legs, decides to take a piss on Cogg's back. Cogg, to my utter surprise, loves it. He laughs in a hearty manner, enjoying my partner's play.

I get in on the fun, find some piss in my nine-inch shaft, and spray the cop down with some golden showers. Urine drips down and over Cogg's sides, tight ass, and bulky thighs. The liquid drips down from his balls, into the cage.

Following our piss-fest, Cogg begs for a cock up his tight and hairless ass. I find a ribbed, twelve-inch plastic dildo from our collection of toys and shove it into his mouth to shut him the fuck up. To my utter surprise, the cop takes ten of the plastic inches down the back of his narrow throat, gagging on the instrument, obeying his hunger for the tool … and whatever else is about to happen to him while he is secured in the cage.

Cogg begs us to use our cocks inside his fit body. He tells Theo to climb behind him and to push my boyfriend's beef into his ass. He instructs me to shove my nine-inch slammer inside his mouth and puncture his narrow throat with quick cock-jabs.

We listen to his selfish demands. Theo's ten inches of spike takes harbor in the cop's rear. His condom-covered stick carries out some hasty movement on the black officer of the law in the cage, thrifty with the spike's to and fro work. I shove my nine inches of protein tube into the caged cop's mouth, cause him to choke, and carry out some heavy duty forward and backward friction.

Together, Theo and I build up a synchronized motion. We gun our dicks forward, release them from Cogg's taut holes, punch the tools forward again, pull back, and carry this action out for the next eight … eleven … thirteen minutes. Sweat flies off of our bodies and splats against the police officer's skin and the cage's steel bars. Growls and grunts fill the room by all three of us, laborious with our action. Cogg takes our blasting with such zeal, captivated by his time in the cage, lost under our touch, a prisoner in Dungeon J-1, just the way Theo and I want him to be.

Our subject has tears in his eyes from his pleasure. Saliva drips from his mouth and falls to the cage's steel bottom plate.

I bang his face repeatedly and strongly, shifting my weight to and fro, sending us both into a tailspin of male delight.

Theo is a monster in motion behind Cogg. With his palms planted on Cogg's hips, he bangs the cop's ass with all his might. Ten inches of his meaty slab punctures the officer's bottom, pulls out, and punctures it yet again and again and again. Theo calls Cogg the naughtiest names, labels he would certainly never mention in front of Twilia's presence.

Our trio of fun with the cage continues for the next twenty minutes. The action is zealous and lively. Each of us learn our duties and carry them out well. All three of us are fully into our game, delighted and on fire and ...

Cogg lets out a sequence of excited and guttural murmurs and comes on his own, without his eight-inch stick between his legs needing to be licked or jacked. The cop is so turned on by our cage-antics that he creams without even being touched. String after string of white ooze leaks out of his black poker and decorates the space between his knees, splashing the cage's steel bottom with his festive sap.

It's too much to watch during our fuck-fest in the spare bedroom. Seeing Cogg come on his own only sends ripples of excitement through my lover's body, and my own. This prompts the two of us to quickly pull our flags out of the black man and jack our rods up and down with right fists. We now stare at each other in an intoxicated manner of boyfriend lust, hypnotized and perplexed.

Of course, it only takes approximately four jacks each before spew releases from our duo of joints and starts to fly into the cage. Theo and I come at the same time, as usual. Thick, white man-sap splatters against the cop's pretty face, used ass, and supine back. Streams of the goo roll down and over Cogg's beautiful cheeks and rounded ass, glazing his skin in the cage. Jet after jet of the ooze bedazzles our new D&S friend — just the way he wants to be bedazzled.

Within seconds after our chest-heaving and dick-throttling explosions, the fire alarm in the apartment blares. Some asshole tenant (probably the same one who called the city police on Theo and me during our wax-fest) probably fell asleep in bed with a cigarette, catching his bedroom on fire.

All three of us smell smoke. Fire engines are heard in the distant part of the city. A sense of panic settles into the spare bedroom and Cogg immediately yells, "Ball busting! ... Ball busting!"

As Theo unlocks the cage and frees Cogg, I grab three towels from the bathroom, one for each of us. When I return from my cotton quest, Cogg is surprisingly already out of the cage. He winks at me, reaches for a Pottery Barn towel, and says, "Thanks, man."

Hurriedly, we clean Cogg off with the towels, dress as if we are late for dates, throw on jeans and T-shirts with superhuman speed, laugh like boys, and eventually exit apartment J-1, rushing to safety on the city sidewalk below.

Safe at last, Cogg settles between us. We stare up at the apartment building and see thick, black spirals of smoke exiting one of the apartment windows. I'm guessing it's J-3, which is next door to our apartment. Now, we witness the NYFD on the scene, who take care of the fire, which isn't a fire at all, according to what we learn. The truth behind the smoke is simple: Henrey Mason, a seventy-six year old buzzard in apartment J-5, left a pot on his stove for a considerable amount of time, which inevitably burned his beanies and wienies. Minimal damage is done to his apartment; all tenants are allowed in the building after an hour, including Henrey, who will surely need to scrub down his walls and apply a new coat of paint to his own dungeon.

PART 4 – DUNGEON DILEMMA

Some five days after the accidental fire in apartment J-5, Theo leaves me hanging in the spare bedroom from the ceiling for well over two hours. I have a red ball-gag in my mouth and sport leather bands around my wrists, which are connected to chains that hang down from the ceiling. My ankles are strapped together with thin, plastic straps. Theo has my cock and balls in a black leather sheath, which is stretched tight and connected to a stainless steel chain that is attached to the bedroom's floor. I'm positioned approximately four feet away from the cage, hanging perpendicular to its mass.

Theo calls me a naughty man, whips me with a fluorescent yellow plastic stick, informs me I have been a very bad boy, and applies stinging welts to my bottom. Now, disgusted with me, he tells me to think about how naughty I am, and how shameful I should feel.

In truth, he lets me hang in the spare bedroom while he goes grocery shopping and runs some errands. And while hanging here in our additional room of Dungeon J-1 I feel weak, abused, somewhat tortured, but crave every minute of it.

Approximately ninety minutes later, Cogg arrives in his cop uniform and finds me in the apartment, hanging from the ceiling in the spare bedroom. He circles me, strips out of his clothes, tugs on my nipples, and laughs. He says something demeaning like: "Motherfucker should stay up there all day," which is music to my ears. Cogg spanks my ass with a bare hand, pulls a few strands of black hair out of my left armpit, and continues to circle me.

What transpires is something rather exciting during our unlimited D&S play. Cogg decides to keep his officer of the law boots on, dresses in an X-shape, black leather getup, and decides to flog my bottom with a leather strap.

Pain skies throughout my system with his every blast. Arcs of primal anguish burn within my core. Welts are applied to my chest, thighs, shoulders, and back. Cogg is brutal with my skin, and loves his dominant position as a dungeon master while I hang from the ceiling.

I'm bitten and beaten with utter delight. The police officer spanks my bottom with joy. He slaps my rippled stomach, licks each of my curved abs, taunts my rear with his protruding tongue, and applies more welts to my splayed back. Name after hideous name fills my ears. Cogg's labels are humiliating and daunting, precise, and desired. Again, he pinches my nipples, twisting both with essential pain. Again, he licks and laps at my bottom. Again, strands of hair are pulled out of my left armpit. Again, he bites my back with his opened and vampiric mouth. Again, Cogg obeys his every wish to use and abuse my skin for his sexual needs, pleasuring the both of us, fully.

He pisses on me. Cogg stands in front of me with his legs parted. He holds his limp cock in his right hand, stares directly at my hanging torso, now into my eyes, and prattles, "You want some golden showers, guy?"

I do. Bring it on. I mumble my approval behind the ball-gag and nod my head ever so slightly.

Cogg shares a shitty grin with me of lunacy. His eyes mix with mine and ...

A stream of golden urine arcs out of his meat and splashes against my chest. The liquid rolls down and over my abs, into the leather contraption that secures my balls and cock, and drips to the floor. A flood of sorts occurs. More piss is applied to my torso, inner thighs, and feet. The officer of the law goes wild on my hanging body, emptying his system of his yellow liquid.

Cogg now has other things in mind to abuse my skin for both of our fantasies. He retrieves a condom inside the bedroom, applies the plastic to his upright and hard eight inches, finds a chair to stand on behind me, and ...

Two of the cop's inches enter my bottom. Three inches begin to pulverize my center. Four and five inches massage my insides as he grasps my black hips with his sturdy palms. He jacks his weight into me, pulls out, and into me again. Six inches cause my world to spin and spin and spin. Seven inches of his throbber pulverize my middle. Eight final and wanted inches split me into what feels like two halves, and pivot my dangling world into euphoria.

Pumping motion after motion ensues inside my bottom. Cogg blasts his weight forward, pushes away, and bashes into me yet again. His hunger for my body is limitless and passionate as he pulverizes my flesh.

My body is like butchered meat in a locker for his use, dangling from the ceiling. A to and fro motion occurs between us. My stretched body swings forward and backward as the cop continues his banging adventure on my deliciously tight rump.

Bites are applied to my shoulders, spine, and right arm. Cogg's vampire-like teeth sink into my skin and almost draw blood. As his banging ensues, my eyes light up with obsessed pain. The police officer's movements become tyrannical behind me, an ass-breaking act that sends me into a cyclone of pulverized joy.

"Fuck you!" he hollers at me, nailing my rump with his weight. Again, his teeth sink into my left shoulder, almost breaking its skin.

My entire body aches from hanging. A desired numbness settles throughout my every limb. I gasp for air as Cogg bangs my rump with all of his weight. Hump after insidious hump continues. I hear the man grunt and groan behind me, swinging my body to and fro, fucking me without even pivoting his middle forward and backward.

At one point during our connection, his teeth buried into my right shoulder, his left palm pressed into my ribs, his eight-inch rock jammed into my bottom, he reaches around my core, removes the cock restraint, then finds the upright slab of meat between my legs. Cogg wraps his right palm around the tool and begins to stroke it up and down: with passion, quickly, undaunted. His stroking continues for the next two ... five ... eight minutes, until I can't keep my load contained, until I murmur unclear nuances of desirable sounds in front of him.

I come rather suddenly by his handy friction. Jizz twirls out of my joint and decorates the bedroom. Strings of the goo fly against the steel cage. I shake in front of the cop, empty my system, and groan behind the ball-gag as bliss between men is discovered yet again.

Officer Cogg is not finished with me as of yet. Once I blow my load inside the spare bedroom, he yanks his bolt out of my rump, jumps off the chair. Here, he charges around me and stands in front of me, approximately three feet away. The cop cocks his legs apart and begins to man-handle his meat with both fists. Sweat flies off of his torso and garnishes my feet.

Heaving breath escapes his beefy lips. The guy cranks and cranks his steel, groaning and grunting, and sweats profusely, everywhere. Hip-jolts occur as his fists rush up and down on his device. More groans and grunts are heard. More sweat is flung off his hairless body and decorates my feet.

Cogg eventually comes. Goo is bucked out of his stem and twirls against my perspiration-covered abs, concave navel, and cock-stem. A stream of the sticky stuff glazes my balls and thighs. The man is like an endless vat of cream, shooting volumes of cop-ooze out of his spike.

What transpires next is rather shocking for me, and for Cogg, of course. As he finishes his sap-spraying extravaganza, the metal eyehooks that hang from the ceiling and keep me suspended let loose. Both pull free from the ceiling and cause me to drop to the floor. Pain rushes into my right shoulder as I land on the floating wooden boards that make up the spare bedroom's floor. A humph sound escapes my throat. My body falls in a fetal position. A flood of unprepared for pain skies through my right side and …

I begin to laugh behind the ball-gag, sit up, and realize that I'm perfectly fine. Cogg the cop laughs with me, right at my side. He kneels over my body, the tip of his cream-covered cock touching my left kneecap. The man strokes my hair in an endearing manner, removes the ball-gag from my mouth, and asks me, "Are you alright?"

I reply with a laugh, "That wasn't in the program."

"It wasn't, was it?" The man now releases my ankles from their captivity and begins on my wrists.

I sit in a pile of ceiling debris, look up, and see a hole above me the diameter of a two-person table.

Cogg asks, "Anything broken?"

I shake my head and reply, "All's good."

"That could have been ugly. You could have really been hurt."

I sit with his sweat and man-cream on my body. My shoulders and the top of my head are covered in ceiling dust. Here, I continue to laugh, happy to be in Cogg's company.

# # # # #

Theo returns from his errands and finds Cogg and me in the spare bedroom. He stands over us with surprise and asks, "What the hell happened in here?" An adorable smile forms on his face, which I always like to see; something that sort of melts me.

"A little accident happened," I reply, sharing my own smile.

My lover looks up at the ceiling and admits, "That's definitely some damage."

Cogg laughs.

I laugh.

Theo laughs.

We spend the next hour cleaning up the room. Cogg knows a construction guy who can fix the ceiling, one of his personal friends; Theo and I agree to hire him.

Following clean-up, I take a shower. Both men decide to join me, and water sports are carried out with much guy-laughter for the next hour.

PART 5 — TWO-HEADED MONSTER

Maxim Cogg spends a lot of time at our apartment. He decides to stay a few nights, sleeping between us. His buddy, Cavanaugh Daily, repairs the dungeon room's ceiling at no charge; a favor he owes Cogg.

Theo has a new side-gig, outside of his nursing. He sells naughty products to all of his queer buddies: ball-gags, cock rings, Fleshjacks, a variety of lubes, butt plugs and clamps, dildos, faux vibrating asses, whips, chains, nipple suckers, and an unlimited catalogue of seedy toys for dungeon masters.

Theo decides to make Friday evenings official dungeon nights inside the apartment. I agree. Cogg agrees. And my partner loves it that we are so easy to get along with.

# # # # #

"We need a new toy to try out," I tell Theo over breakfast one morning.

Cogg joins us for strawberry cream cheese-filled French toast and admits, "I'm sure you have something new in your box of man-toys to share with us, Theo."

A smile surfaces on my lover's face: wide, brimming, simply adorable. He responds, "A two-headed monster. It's a dildo that's two inches wide and fourteen inches on either side. It screws into the floor and comes with ankle and wrist cuffs, and collars that are leashed together by a heavy duty chain."

Bald and charming Cogg has a line of cream cheese on his right cheek, which looks like guy-load. I wipe it away as he asks, "So we are basically pinned to the floor and can't move because we will be leashed together, right?"

"Exactly," Theo confirms. "I expect it to be my big seller in the next few months. The price is rather cheap."

"I'm cheap," Cogg admits and winks at us.

"We know," I respond, falling for the guy, enjoying his cop company. "That's why we like you. You have no limits."

# # # # #

I really don't know who Theo's dungeon toys supplier is, but honestly, I really don't care. I'm just kind of thrilled he brings home the two-headed monster for us to try out.

Cogg is on vacation from his cop job for the next three days; his trip to Philadelphia to hook-up with a dungeon master somehow gets canceled. So the guy decides to stay at our place for the next few days, enjoying our company. He holds the two-headed contraption in his hands and beams with a smile. "I love it, guys. This rocks. I can't wait to have one of these plastic heads up my ass."

Theo witnesses the wood already growing in Cogg's white, Rufskin shorts. He removes the new toy from our sexy guest and informs, "Tonight Dungeon J-1 is open for business. For now, we put the toy away ... and bring it out later to use."

This night, inside Dungeon J-1, Cogg and I decide to take on the two-headed monster dildo.

Theo becomes the dungeon master, dressing in a black leather hood and matching wrist and ankle bands, all of which are studded.

It is determined the safe word stays the same: ball busting.

The two-headed monster is screwed into the spare bedroom's floor, next to the cage, which hasn't been used in a week; shame on us. Cogg slips a black leather-studded collar around his neck and I do the same. Our necks are now connected by a stainless steel chain, which stretches between us. Both of our ankles and wrists are cuffed.

Theo decides to use orange-colored ball-gags in our mouths, decorating us. Now ready to abuse us the way we want to be abused, of course, he stands over us with a plastic, fluorescent yellow rod and says behind his hood, "Let the game begin, fuckers."

In dungeon master mode, Theo growls down at us to back into our dildos. Cogg carries out this act first, stretching his petite ass with the two-inch wide piece of plastic. Grunts and murmurs escape the cop as he backs into the lubed dildo, sliding seven of its fourteen inches into his bottom with skill, whimpering from the pain.

It's my turn to accomplish the same action. Theo decides to strike my back three times with the plastic rod and call me a sinister name like jizz-eater. The hits are brutal, powerful, and sting like mad. Yelps escape my mouth because of his hits and from backing into the two-headed dildo, which roughly separates my rump and punctures my center.

Cogg lets out another moan, consuming all fourteen inches of the plastic dildo inside his bottom. He sniffles on his end of the new toy, swears, and growls like a wild animal.

The first two inches of the plastic pick breaks me open with unbelievable pain. I cringe with anguish on my end of the device. The next two inches pulverize my bottom with zeal. Pleasure is found, and more is welcomed. Five ... six ... and seven inches cram into my center as I fall onto the plastic stick even more, breaking my system open for its handy use and offering of bliss. Eight ... nine ... ten inches of Theo's upcoming best-selling toy is sucked into my rear as I slide backward, which causes me to feel dizzy and somewhat unconscious. Twelve ... thirteen ... and all fourteen inches of the manmade dick securely locks inside my epicenter, puncturing my organs, and causes me to smile with masculine euphoria.

Cogg howls on his end of the fake cock while moving to and fro. In doing so, he pulls my neck backwards, choking me. Of course, elation is discovered from his movement: suffocation, pressure added to the stem between my legs, untamable lust. Cogg is greedy with his motion on the bogus shaft. He glides east and west in a hyper manner, getting himself off. Hollow screams attempt to exit his mouth, but the ball-gag is in the way.

Pain is desired in the game of bondage, Theo always says. He stands over me with his yellow plastic rod and strikes my black back, shoulders, and arms. The guy is brutal with his swings, and almost cuts my skin open.

I gag, thrust backward, move forward, scream behind the orange ball in my mouth, and pleasure myself on the two-headed monster between Cogg and me. My motion is concurrent and prosaic, which soon turns into a wild to and fro action that causes tingles of elation to spin throughout my core.

The events that transpire within the next few minutes are rather mind-blowing:

Cogg and I shift east and west. Both of us choke each other because of the tight collars attached around our necks. Grunts and groans echo within Dungeon J-1.

Theo continues to strike us with his yellow, plastic rod. He calls us the most vicious and humiliating names that Cogg and I desire. Theo also climbs on his knees and bites at our asses. Sometimes he pulls our cocks down with his busy fists, teasing us to come.

Cogg literally screams behind his ball-gag as elation is discovered. His ass-thrusting on the dildo becomes erratic and aggressive. More screams escape the sides of his open mouth. Stick-welts continue to slap against his back and ass.

I become dazed and confused on the plastic stick that connects Cogg's ass with mine. The ankle and wrist cuffs prevent me from freedom. Lust is discovered to the fullest. I harbor zeal because of Cogg's satisfaction, my ass ramming into the dildo that separates us, and Theo's dungeon master spell with his slicing-through-the-air hits with the plastic rod.

Cogg is the first to blow his load. Theo stands over the cop, bends over, reaches between the man's legs with his right hand and milks the eight-inch joint with north and south friction.

The officer of the law moans with deep satisfaction. A gasp is heard as Theo continues to spank the man's back with the yellow, plastic rod. Cogg continues to shift his weight on the two-headed monster between us, obviously enjoying his ride.

"Come, motherfucker!" my partner yells down at our sexy, third wheel, tugging on his manly utter, willing the cop to blow his load. Another brisk snap is heard as Cogg is struck again with the yellow stick, which stings the man's back, welting it hard.

Cogg comes. How can he not? A long and passionate sound escapes his gagged mouth. Although I can't see him behind me, I imagine strings of creamy white shit leaking out of his hose and garnishing the boarded floor.

As expected, I am next to fire my man-cargo onto the floor boards, emptying my shaft with amorous joy. Like Theo's handy time with the cop, he takes a hearty interest in my own log. Nine inches of solid shaft desires his right hand to rock my world, so I can spray guy-goo all over the spare bedroom's floor.

My lover/boyfriend/master/addiction beats me with his long, yellow play-stick. Theo adds welts to my sides, shoulders, the back of my neck, and both ass cheeks. His wallops are unyielding and offer much pain that I crave. I swear, I begin to bleed from my back, become hypnotized and mesmerized and …

"Shoot your cream!" he yells above me, falls to his knees, and uses the yellow stick on my erection, swishing it back and forth, adding enlightening stings to its skin.

I gasp in pain with the gag in my mouth. My dick rocks with hurt, but is excited at the same time. In truth, after many stick-slaps to my cock with Theo's plastic tool, I feel an orgasm surface between my legs. Swirls of jubilation ski throughout my torso, ass, and head. These spirals of satisfaction send my system into a full-fledged shoot-fest, and I explode gunk all over the floor, pooling my spunk on the wood, becoming spent in a matter of seconds, windblown and exhausted.

Theo is last to come. He faces me as I continue to rock back and forth on the two-headed monster that is secured to the floor. My dungeon lover stands in front of me and cranks his ten-inch pole with both fists. His palms rush up and down on his shaft and grumbles of glee escape his mouth. The nurse thrusts his hips forward, backward, and forward again. Perspiration swings off of his body and splashes against my face and back. More hip-thrusts ensue for three … five … seven minutes. My extroverted partner jostles his beef with speedy motion. A cackle escapes his mouth, informing me that the master of Dungeon J-1 is about to burst his load. Theo now grumbles, "Firing," and shoots out a flow of man-sap from his hose, dousing my back, shoulders, and ass. More of the goop explodes out of his stiff dong and flies onto Cogg's dildo-inhabited ass and over his back. The dungeon master drains his post, emptying it with skill, also becoming spent, just like Cogg and me.

AFTERWARD — SPENT

Maxim Cogg permanently moves into the apartment. The hot cop becomes our chocolate lover, thrilled to be a part of our lives. He constantly brings man-on-man toys home for our use, which we break-in on Friday nights while playing in Dungeon J-1.

Theo continues to be the dungeon master, fulfilling Cogg's desires to the fullest, and my sexual expectations. He decides to invest some of his earned money into a future dungeon bar called Crave A Slave in Greenwich Village. Theo plans to work there when he's not at First Presby playing nurse. Theo wants Cogg and me to go in on the bar-gig and be co-owners, which we accept.

I fall in love with both men, equally. Our threesome dungeon games continue for the next decade. Together, we run Crave A Slave and make some money, which we all invest in stocks. We also carry out some heavy duty dungeon games at our bar, and in our apartment. This is our happy ever after, the life of three men who adore each other, share relationships together and … fulfill each other's fantasies.

Life is good for us.

No, life is great.

VENICE UNABRIDGED
By Derrick Della Giorgia

Sometimes you don't feel life unless it's over. When life was over for Luanne after her divorce, she moved to Venice. When I found my man in bed with my boss, I went to visit Luanne. I guess it's like with batteries, some are rechargeable. In the right place, at the right time, inspiration kicks you in the ass re-establishing order in the tangle of steel habits, abusive remarks and forgotten happiness gemmating in your stomach. And it is a bright morning again.

When we crossed the first canal, I looked at the stagnant placid water underneath us trying to understand which direction it ran. Luanne was wearing a pair of orange leather sandals that grew on her calves with the same elegance with which the bridges wrapped the different sections of the floating city. Her muscular legs couldn't take the break.

"Come on, I want you to meet the Venetian waiting for you." Her smile was free of that web of sufferance I'd seen on her face in San Francisco when I kissed her goodbye.

"Who would that be?" I asked in an attempt of showing interest for her effort. "I told you, I just wanna spend some quality time with you. It's been a long year since our last wine!" Our friendship was shamelessly based on our common passion for wine. One would pick the place, the other the bottle of wine. Together, we'd tried 167 whites and 67 reds — she wasn't very fond of flavonoids.

"Take a deep breath, now." This new turgid woman in front of me took hold of my heavy luggage and parked it by the door of what looked like a hole in the wall. No sign, no tables, no indication of what the hairy arrogant but polite man behind the bar was there to serve.

"Cool." It was all I could conjure up.

"*Buongiorno!* Two *spritz*, please." Luanne dove into the crowded scene around a bottle of *Prosecco spento*, a special kind of local sparkling white wine that added to an orange liquor and some tonic produced the funny drinks she came back with. She looked taller in Venice, shedding layers of light as she made her way through the Italians having their *aperitivo*. She wasn't the Luanne I remembered, she wasn't the Luanne that had just divorced, the Luanne that had nothing left. Her batteries had obviously been recharged. Only this time, it was something nobody could take away from her.

"What's this?"

"Shut up and drink. You don't know what the fuck you are talking about." Those were the last words that made sense that day. She was ready to pass on the secret she'd learned.

Luanne had been living for the past year in a palace on the Canal Grande, probably the most photographed stream of water on the planet in that handkerchief of land where the most languages were spoken at any given moment. My surprise, the birthday gift I had flown fifteen hours for, was hidden in her bathroom together with all the Casanova secrets of the palace the name of which I was not supposed to use freely. To my jetlagged disbelief, a short sturdy door opened in the wall between the toilet and the sink I'd just used. A room in a room. A secret room. Except it wasn't a room. In front of me, a cold humid cave called my name with more insistence every second that passed. My eyes slowly adjusted to the dim lights, and by the time I reached the center of the hall, the metal scream of a key announced me; Luanne had locked me in there.

I thought it was funny. Taken by tiredness, I took off my shoes and jumped on the old hard mattress that was the only piece of decoration not attached to any wall. Finally, I realized where I was.

A Corinthian column divided the bookshelves behind me, mixing strangely with the rest of the architecture. A massive stone staircase climbed up to the feet of another locked door; dusty heavy curtains hung lifelessly only inches away from the remaining walls. Many pictures, most likely the signature of a professional photographer, completed the scene. What in other circumstances I would have judged surreal, didn't even bother my attention, leaving me with the vision of the intricate ceilings above me. The worn-out ivory medallion sculpted above me, circled a deep crack that conveyed the extension in time of that palace, a feeling mostly unknown to somebody that has never left the United States. The temperature I'd liked coming from the heat of the Venetian canals, started to penetrate my bones. In turn, my train of thoughts concentrated on my near future. What had Luanne planned? What was I doing there? I certainly wasn't the Casanova type!

"Luanne?" I tried to give a name to the noises that followed my introspective reflections. One after the other, coming from opposite directions, the locking and unlocking of an infinite number of keys accompanied the crescent sensation of uneasiness in my head. "Luanne?"

The short bulky door in front of me moved inward, the curtains swelled with more humid air coming from even more hidden rooms and a black Goliah appeared at the feet of the bed. The man was easily double my size in every dimension, carrying an artillery case and the set of keys that'd granted him access to the secret room. Without a word, he locked us in.

Two more revelations exploded in my mind before I uttered my first words of despair. He was completely naked, except for a strap of black patent leather that protected his balls from the mass of his quads. And he officiously and laboriously ignored my presence. Bruce — "My name is Bruce" was all he said to me before leaving two hours after his arrival, — positioned his instruments on the floor and started searching through the multitude of objects while clearing up his throat like an infuriated four-footed beast.

"WHO — ARE — YOU?" I spelled out, inspecting the room for a possible escape. My heart went from zero to galloping under my tongue, transforming respiration in an exercise for survival. I stood up on the mattress, but I didn't even reach his neck. Before I could jump away from him, I was literally hanging from his hands. Bruce tore my clothes into pieces starting from the Burberry T-shirt I'd just purchased for my Italian trip and left me on my knees begging for pardon. At that point, it was clear he was my birthday gift — which I wholeheartedly did not want. I tried to figure out what had gone through Luanne's mind when she'd hired the beast. Was she spying me now? Recording the happening? I looked down in painful resignation and noticed what awaited me. While I was putting things together to understand how the nightmare could be ended, Bruce had grown a majestic hard-on. The object getting closer to my face was the length of my forearm, the thickness of my thigh.

He clamped my hands behind my neck with a spring and some wire, and pulled my curly short hair until my lips landed on his wet foreskin. There was no way I could take that thing into my mouth. Its surface pressed against my mouth, my nose and part of my chin. When I managed to reach the base of its head, I was already gagging. The air impregnated with his sex passed fast through my nostrils, while my tongue fought for room in vain against the uncontrollable force. He wanted me to take more. Unsatisfied, he groaned and attempted a rhythmic movement in and out of my *buccal* orifice.

My spit already tasted like cum when he released me to throw me on the bed belly down. My spasmodic coughing covered every other noise, and I was left unaware of what he was doing until he started whipping me with a short little broom that had metal balls attached to the end of its bristles. He focused on my ass. The pain that fifteen hours of sitting on the plane had caused, disappeared all of a sudden leaving room for the burning fire he spread with his repetitive hits.

"Stop, please!" My voice must have not been very credible, because he increased the dose and the speed. The room commenced to fade. The pain was definitely still there, but strangely I started to detach from the Venetian ceilings, Luanne, the canals, — in fact the whole planet, — and enjoy my special treat. With my hands behind my neck and my ass in the air, I felt like a victim of a sacrifice — ready to satisfy the big black god on top of me. My fantasy was still forming in my head when I noticed on the square of floor I was able to see from that humiliating position, a bunch of pictures depicting Bruce in the unthinkable act of fucking what looked like a dwarf underneath his gigantic body. Fear invaded me. I wanted to go back outside in the sunlight, and climb the bridges of Venice among the gondolas that until then had not awaken my curiosity. Away from that dungeon of torture. "My body will tear to pieces if you fuck me!"

Bruce bent down again into the black box, preparing his next act while his left hand kept my body pinned to the mattress. I felt the redness on my butt cheeks slowly dissipate under the rough skin of his palm, and at the same time my erection reached its highest peak. My only concern was whether my ass was anatomically adapt to receive the beast's appendage. At the thought, I contracted my ring in fear.

"Please, don't hurt me!" Sadly, I realized that I wasn't even sure he understood English. His body language left no doubts that he was following a sort of ritual and nothing I could say or do would ever be significant enough to interrupt him, or make him slightly deviate from the master plan.

Then, it started. He localized my entrance with index and middle fingers and dug inside me at first very gently, as if that procedure served him only to get an idea of the kind of resistance he would encounter later. I quickly freed my mind of all the terrorizing thoughts about that monstrous intercourse. If he was going to fuck me, I'd better not fight it. His two fingers became three and brought in the depth of my canal handfuls of lube, which Bruce was scooping up from his collection of instruments of torture. I liked the feeling. He was good after all! But things changed fast. Dildos replaced fingers and in no time a metal ring was inserted into my excited but still unprepared hole. He made sure it was secured and initiated to unscrew the part of the device that was still in his hands — I deducted from the screeching and clicking originating between my trembling thighs. The ring grew bigger inside my anal muscle with every turn, dilating my hole to what felt like a parturition tunnel.

"Stop! STOP!" He was going to fuck me! "I don't want to!" Insensitive to my prayers, he squeezed my cock making sure not to miss any drop of precum. A groan, his only comment. After he swallowed it all, he stood up and made calculations on whether I was ready to welcome his tool. He pushed his hips closer and closer to me with precision movements he knew very well, and finally removed the metal forceps letting my insides adjust to his third leg. It took me a good couple of minutes before I was able to breathe in again. The beast made me cum at the second hip thrust; an abundant and continuous stream of American cum found its nest in the creases of the Venetian sheets ruffled under my weak knees. He pushed again. And again. Slowly advancing. My whole body depended on him, on his kindness, on his power, on the methodical and masterful curves drawn inside me.

"Fuck me!" I heard myself screaming, wanting more, as if there really is a point where we give up on our ideas about measures and capacities, and just ride our instincts which tell us, in a flux of energy connecting ass and heart, that "IT IS GOOD."

I came two more times, and later I went back to the bridges with Luanne.

PASSION PARTY PURGATORY
By Logan Zachary

"Welcome to the basement passion party," Charles said, as he moved back and let me step off the last stair. "While our ladies are learning about lubes and lingerie, whips and chains and all those things that excite us ..." He motioned with his big, black hand and welcomed me into his finished basement.

I looked around the brightly decorated room, but something wasn't right. I knew I wasn't the first guy here, but no one else sat on the couch or the easy chairs.

Where were the other guys?

"I have cold beer at the bar and ..." his voice trailed off. "Is there a problem?" He stepped behind the bar and opened up the refrigerator. He pulled out a cold Bud and cracked it open.

On the bar were two huge suction cups attached to leather cuffs, a whip, a butt plug, and a ball gag. I picked up one cuff and turned it over. "What are these?" I hooked the Velcro pieces together and then ripped it open.

"Debbie must've forgotten these things down here." He handed me the beer bottle and moved over next to me.

I heard a low pitched grunt from a tri-fold screen behind the bar. I took a sip and turned toward the noise.

Charles picked up the cuffs and wrapped one around the wrist that held my beer bottle, and then quickly applied the other one.

"What are you doing?" I asked.

"I just wanted to see if these handcuffs were big and strong enough for your wrists?" Charles' bald head gleamed in the track lighting, his deep chocolate skin, shiny and smooth.

I twisted my wrist and looked at the cuffs from different angles. I set down my beer bottle and pulled on the Velcro. "Do you think these things could hold me?"

The grunting noise sounded again, more urgent this time.

Charles grabbed my wrists and pulled.

I slammed into the bar, but he continued to pull me further, so my body dragged up and across the bar.

He slapped the suction cups down on the bar's surface, letting my feet dangle off the ground.

I pulled on the cuffs, but the Velcro held tight, just as the suction cups did. I kicked harder, but my feet were unable to find purchase on anything for traction.

Someone kicked the tri-fold screen. The panels rocked back and forth and fell over. Blake Connelly with a ball gag in his mouth stared at me wide eyed. He was suspended from the ceiling by his wrists, but his legs were swinging free. He groaned again and tried to warn me with his eyes.

Charles moved behind me and slipped the ball gag into my mouth. His fingers buckled the device into place.

What the …

Charles undid one wrist cuff, rolled me onto my back and re-secured my arm again. He suctioned both of my ankles to the bar, so I was held spread eagle. He clapped his hands and said, "Hail, hail, the gangbang's all here." He traced a finger down my chest to my fly and ran it up and down.

I felt an unwelcome erection start in my jeans.

"Quick response time. I like that." Charles left me and moved down the hallway that was blocked by another screen. He folded it out of the way, and revealed Jeremy's body in a sling that swung from the ceiling's rafters. He caressed the underside of Jeremy's breaded face and checked the fit of his ball gag.

Jeremy rocked his body back and forth, trying to escape, only to make the sling spin around and around. He closed his eyes. I knew Jeremy hated spin and puke rides at the fair. His compact body struggled to no avail from the leather straps that held him in place.

Charles removed the last screen to show a body bag that hung from the wall like a garment bag. A man's form was easily seen in the black plastic. The air was removed, and the man looked shrink-wrapped like a piece of meat at the deli. His husky male form looked familiar. Chris? He was supposed to be here, too.

Charles unzipped his track suit to reveal a black leather harness with silver studs. It criss-crossed his heart and highlighted his caramel colored skin. He untied his drawstring and pulled down his running pants. Leather chaps with a spike studded jockstrap clad his lower half. His huge bulge stood proudly out in front of him. He turned his back to me and a muscular ass flexed as he bent over to pick up his pants. His deep crease displayed a pink pucker that was perfect, tight, round and smooth.

I felt my cock swell as he turned to face me.

Charles looked down at my groin, slapped his ass, and smiled. "I can see you're enjoying this, too. Nice. I had hoped that there would be some fun tonight." He walked to the wall and rubbed Chris' bulge like a Genie's lamp.

Chris' low hanging balls seemed to rise up in the black latex bag and his cock swelled.

Charles rubbed faster and harder, and the shrunk wrapped body squirmed like a worm. His cock swelled and a small bubble formed at its tip. "That was easy, and over way too fast." He licked his hand. "Ennie, Meenie, Miney, Mo, who's the next one to blow?" His finger pointed at Blake.

Blake's eyes widened, and he shook his head.

Charles walked to the bar I lay across, putting me between him and Blake. Charles reached over and started to unbutton my shirt. "Blake needs some special attention." As his hands opened my shirt to my pants, he pulled the tails out. The cotton slid over my hard cock. He combed through the hair on my chest. "Blake, are you hairy or smooth? Do you shave? Are your balls hairy or …?"

Blake struggled to free his hands. He kicked his feet and swung back and forth.

Charles stopped massaging me and moved over to Blake. He opened his shirt and revealed a smooth chest, a little beer belly, but still a fine body. "So soft," Charles said. He started to unbuckle his belt, and Blake bucked harder. The belt opened and flopped around as Charles unbuttoned his pants and slowly unzipped his fly.

Blake's thrashing made his pants slide down his legs. A shoe fell off and one pant leg. He wore white briefs that bulged.

Charles stepped on the loose pant leg and traced a finger along his waistband. He pulled the fabric down slowly, until a line of thick, brown hair appeared. The thick bulge grew. A wet spot appeared on the white cotton.

"You have a beautiful bush." He pulled the briefs open and looked in. "Furry balls, too." He snapped the undies back into place. He pulled the other shoe and pant leg the rest of the way off. "I'll have to fix that …" he let the words hang in the air.

I strained to see what he had as he pulled out an aerosol can and sprayed a handful of foam into it. With his free hand he pulled off Blake's briefs and tossed them aside. Then he lathered up his pubes and balls with the cream.

"This should feel warm on your junk." He washed the extra foam off his hand and picked up a straight edge razor. "You'll have to stay really still, I wouldn't want to slip and cut anything off that I shouldn't …"

Shaving had never been my thing and to have razor stubble down there, scared me, I wished I could cross my legs.

"Bald Blake that has a nice ring to it." Charles picked up a washcloth and brought the blade down to his thick bush. Scrap, scrap, scrap and the thick hair was gone. "That was the easy part. You do want children, don't you?" He pressed the razor under his balls.

Blake nodded, slow and controlled.

"Nice, then I'll be careful." One hand stretched the ball sac as the other one removed the cream and the hair. With each stroke, Blake's cock grew bigger and bigger, standing straight up. "Thanks for getting that out of the way. It's a massive piece of meat to have dangling." He wiped the blade on the cloth and quickly finished.

I let out the breath I had been holding.

Charles took a warm, wet washcloth and cleaned Blake's balls. He kissed the huge mushroom head and smiled at his work. "Bald is beautiful, baby." He came to the bar and looked down at me. He ran his hand through my hair. "You would take a long, long time." His finger traced my cock as he said long, long.

But before I could respond, he ducked under the bar and pulled out a metal pipe with a glass ball on one end and an electric plug on the other. He plugged it in between my legs and looked down at my package. "You're going to have to wait your turn." He flipped a switch and the ball lit up with streaks of blue and pink electricity inside. As he brought it to his cheek, a lightning bolt formed inside and struck him. "Ahh," he moaned.

Blake bucked his restraints. His legs frantically kicking as his newly, smooth pink balls swung back and forth. His raging hard-on pooled a pearl of precum at the tip.

"Water and electricity, such a wonderful combination."

Charles brought the electric wand to Blake's nipples. An electrical storm raged in the glass ball and focused on his tender spot. The nipple rose up hard and erect to a sharp point, the electricity tingled and stimulated the tender tissue.

Blake's cock jumped as Charles circled the pink nub. He moaned.

I wasn't sure if it was pain or pleasure. He rolled his head back.

Charles moved to the other side and repeated his teasing. "Where else can I stimulate you that is tender and sensitive, like a newly shaved face?" A brilliant smile emerged from his full lips.

Blake panicked. He kicked and thrashed.

Charles adjusted the intensity and as Blake spun, his ass came into view. Charles touched a fleshy cheek.

Blake's whole body stiffened and stopped fighting.

"I'm glad you see my point." He brought the wand down to his studded jock and sparks flew everywhere. "I love the smell of electrolysis in the evening." He spun Blake's still form around and adjusted the output. He brought the ball under his erection and between his legs. His pink smooth balls dangled. The wand glowed blue and then pink as electricity shot around the globe. Charles made contact with the left nut that hung lower. A bolt of lightning zapped his ball as spidery electric legs grabbed for Blake's nut sack.

Blake's pelvis pushed forward as more precum poured out of his dick.

Charles moved to the other testicle and watched as they jumped and bounced off the glass globe. "Dance my pretties, dance." An evil gleam came into his eyes and he traced the wand between the balls and slowly traced along his cock.

Blake's dick rose up and slapped his firm belly, only to fall back down to be shocked and driven back up again.

Charles drew it down to the wet tip and held it there. He watched as Blake's cock super-balled from the wand to his belly button. Wet splats sounded as the precum coated along his treasure trail. Charles twisted the shaft of the wand and a glass probe fell out of the bottom and hung in the air. It was six inches long, slender and glowed red. "Red is for the rectum." Charles picked up the probe and brought it behind Blake.

"No, no," Blake tried to say as he shook his head.

Charles slowly guided the glowing tube between his fleshy butt cheeks. As soon as it made contact with the skin, Blake closed his eyes. Charles grinned. "This won't take long."

I watched in amazed horror as the tube disappeared into Blake's ass. A red glow came from behind him as his dick continued its arc.

Blake clenched his teeth into the ball gag and his legs spread and rose. The end of his cock exploded. Thick, white cum flowed out of him. Part of the first burst landed on my hairy chest, glistening in the light.

Charles moved the wand down to the smooth balls and milked out more cream. Wave after wave of screaming orgasms flowed through Blake's body and poured out of his cock. A puddle of semen formed below his dangling feet.

"Shocking I know, but oh so electric." Charles removed the probe and wand from Blake's body.

Blake's whole body drooped, hung spent from his wrists. His cock stood straight out and still dripped cum.

Charles walked over to me and wiped the blob of cum off my chest with a finger. He brought it to his mouth and tasted it. "Salty, sweet. Wanna try?" He offered his finger to me.

I shook my head.

"Delicious, you'll find out what you're missing." Charles cleaned his finger and then went to rub my fly. "Still hard. Good boy, don't let that bad boy go down, or you'll pay, with blood, sweat and tears, and I'm not talking the music group. I'll be right back; there was one more before you." He pointed at Jeremy.

Jeremy freaked. He bucked in the sling and made it spin faster.

"Round and round you go, where you stop, only I know ..." Charles picked up a black doctor's bag and set it on Jeremy's belly. "I love these pants with the snaps. They're easy on and off in a snap." He pulled hard, and the snaps opened like a line from a machine gun. He held them in his hand and Jeremy swung bare ass in the sling. "I'm glad you forgot your underwear, makes my job so much easier." He stroked up one of Jeremy's bound legs. His dark brown complexion and black hair showed a gym body to perfection.

His cock lay over his belly as his balls dropped down between his legs.

"Your wife beater is toast." He pulled out a metal device and squeezed the handles together. They opened like a pair of scissors, but instead of a blade it had a duck bill. Charles used the side of the bill and cut the sheer cotton. A burly hairy chest emerged on such a compact, tight body. "To shave or not to shave, that is the question."

Jeremy pulled harder on his restraints.

Charles clamped the duck bill closed and stepped between his legs. He slid the cold metal up Jeremy's leg and stopped at his crotch. "Your low hangers are hanging. Not talking?" He picked them up and set them on his cock. He guided the metal between his cheeks and pressed. "This will open you up."

Jeremy tensed as the metal touched his hole.

Charles poured lube onto the end. "Breathe deep." He slid the device in. "Let's see what's inside." He grasped the handles, and the duck bill opened. "Oh, so tight, relax." He shot more lube inside the opening and squeezed harder.

I could see a dark opening, wet, warm, and welcoming.

Charles must have read my thoughts. "What can we insert into that hole?" He opened and closed the duck bill, as he grabbed his jock's pouch. He set the device down.

Jeremy screamed with his ball gag in his mouth.

Charles opened the doctor's bag. "You're all sweaty. Are you running a fever?" He pulled out a plastic tube with balls along its shaft. The balls grew larger the closer they were to the handle. The small bead at the end slipped into Jeremy easily. One by one they disappeared into him, halfway in, his cock flopped up and down. Its thick shaft deeply veined and a huge foreskin covered the tip.

I watched in amazement as the tool entered his bottom, spreading him wider and wider.

As the handle touched his taint, Jeremy closed his eyes and dropped his head back.

Charles grabbed Jeremy's cock and started to stroke it as he pulled the toy out of his ass, and slowly pushed it in. As he worked his cock, Charles increased his speed on the anal intruder. "Do you need something bigger? I have a few more things that we can try." He pulled the balls out and set the wet toy on the floor. He dug into the doctor's bag and pulled out a pink plastic fist. He looked at it and showed it to Jeremy, waving it at him. "Hello," and then he stopped, "oh wait, maybe it should be knock, knock." He motioned as if rapping on a door, then changed into a thrusting motion.

Jeremy shook his head.

Charles turned to me. "Do you need a hand?"

I shook my head.

"We'll see." He dropped the hand back into the bag and withdrew a huge dildo the size of my forearm, but wider. "This will make a big boy out of you." He rubbed it up and down his crease.

Jeremy withered in the sling as it followed his crack. As the blunt end found his hole, Charles twisted it, seeing if it would go in.

"Too tight I think. We'll have to start with something smaller." Charles pulled on his jock's basket and removed it. His huge cock sprang free and snaked toward Jeremy. His pulled a condom out of the secret pocket and wrapped his dick. He lubed his length and stepped between Jeremy's legs.

A "No," tried to escape around the rubber ball in Jeremy's mouth.

"Do you enjoy horror movies?"

Jeremy shook his head violently.

In his best *Hell Raiser* voice, Charles said, "I'll rip your hole apart." He opened his mouth wide and moved forward, his cock leading the way to the tight pucker. "Little pig, little pig, let me come in." He ran his fat mushroom tip up and down Jeremy's crack and teased him. "Not by the hair of my chinny, chin, chin … on your ass."

Jeremy's sphincter pulsated with each beat of his heart and seemed to swell and shrink.

"There's always time for lube." Charles applied another layer over his dick and smeared more over his hole. His finger tried to push more inside, but Jeremy's ass was tight. "This may take a while, and I have inches to go before I sleep."

Jeremy shook his head.

"Oh that's right, nipple clamps." Charles pulled a set out of what appeared thin air and leaned across Jeremy's body. He opened a clamp and applied to one nipple. "How does that feel?" He pulled on the chain and made Jeremy moan. "One more," he said, holding up the other one and quickly placed it on his pink erect nub, connecting them together. Another chain clamped onto the one crossing his chest. Charles pulled that one down and secured a cuff around Jeremy's hard cock. As he slid it up and down his shaft, it pulled on his nipples.

Jeremy's penis oozed precum down his shaft, making the strap slide easier. He closed his eyes as he warred with his body, pleasure or release? Release or pleasure? Maybe both?

Charles lubed his cock one more time and stepped between his legs. He glided his dick along the sweaty crease and found the tight opening. He worked Jeremy's cock and slowly entered his ass.

As soon as Charles' pubic bush pressed against his balls, Jeremy shot his load. Cum shot out of his dick, across his chest, and covered the nipple clamps.

Charles felt the flow of cream over his hand as he continued to jack Jeremy's dick, milking out his balls. He felt Jeremy's ass spasm over his shaft, but with only one stroke inside, he wasn't ready to come. He bucked into his prostate a few times, sending more pleasure spasms over his restrained partner.

Jeremy's body slowly relaxed and fell limp in the sling. His cock, still hard, dripped cum into his belly button. The cum slowly started to run off of his body and splatter on the floor.

Charles pulled himself out of Jeremy's tight ass and turned to face me. His dick glistened in the light and lube dripped off the tip. As he walked toward me, his cock bounced up and down, his heavy balls swinging like pendulums.

I watched as his beautiful, black body hypnotized my eyes. He was coming at me with that monster, and he hadn't cum yet. My poor virgin ass.

Charles looked down at me. He unzipped my fly and worked my pants down my hairy legs. "I've saved the best for last." He pulled my shirt open wide and combed his fingers through my hair. "What device would you enjoy?" He brought his hand down to my underwear and caressed my crotch. "Still hard. Nice. I knew you would be."

What did that mean?

Charles smiled. "Let's see what's under door number three." He peeled back my briefs, and my cock flopped out and slapped my belly. He worked my briefs down to my ankles and brought his face to my groin and inhaled deeply. "So manly, but I love it, too." He licked his lips and ran his tongue down my shaft to my hairy balls. He sucked one testicle into his mouth and rolled it around. He gently let it slip out from between his lips and licked up to my fat mushroom head. His raspy tongue entered the slit at the end and lapped out salty, sweet juices.

I turned my head and saw the butt plug sitting on the bar.

Charles noticed my gaze. "So you want to try the anal invader? I figured you to be more of a top, but to each his own. I don't judge."

He slipped the lubed plug between my legs and pressed it to my hole. He twisted it so it spread more lube around the circle. The rounded end spread the muscle. "This is a thick one, it may hurt, so relax, don't fight it."

Easy for you to say, your ass isn't the one on the line, I thought.

He pushed and pulled on the butt plug as he sucked on my cock.

Charles' mouth was hot and wet, sucking me like I've never been sucked before. He was able to take all of my nine thick inches down his throat.

The pressure grew and grew as the butt plug bore deeper into me. Just as the pain became too much to bear, Charles pulled back and sucked harder, distracting me.

Charles' saliva ran over my hairy balls and pooled on the bar. He gave one quick push, the plug popped into place, and my sphincter sealed around it. He picked up a red rubber ring and stretched it. "With this ring, I thee bed." He pulled it over my cock and guided my balls through the opening. The rubber cock ring pulled on my pubic hair, but it finally slipped into place. "This will keep you hard for a long time." He slipped a condom down my cock.

Why did he need me to ...?

Charles jumped onto the bar and lubed his ass. He threw a leg over my pelvis and guided his butt over my cock. "I want you deep inside me." He maneuvered my dick to his hole and slowly sat on me. He was tight, and he had to bounce on my dick a few times to drive it in. He lowered himself to me, and his balls rested on my abs.

My cock never felt so good. Warm, wet, and tight. He rode me slowly at first. When he pressed down, the butt plug pressed deeper into me, stimulating my prostate gland, precum oozed out and started to fill the condom.

Charles reached down into his chaps and pulled out a long piece of metal with a dip at the end. He lubed it up and brought it to the end of his cock. He inserted the bent end into his cock's opening and slipped it down his shaft.

I watched in amazement as it entered him so easily. Only a few inches of the metal stuck out of his dick.

Charles started to jack his penis as he rode my cock, harder and harder. He pulled and pushed and worked the metal sound in and out of his shaft as he jacked, stimulation inside and out. Precum poured out and dotted my hairy torso.

My pelvis started to match his, thrust for thrust. Our pace quickened as my butt clenched around the plug.

Charles' free hand massaged my chest and squeezed my pec. "Gimme some vanilla cream."

My heart rate increased as the stimulation intensified. I wasn't going to last much longer.

Charles jacked his cock, faster and faster. He threw his head back and slammed his ass down on my dick.

The butt plug hit my prostate and started an orgasm. The wave shot out of my cock and filled the tip of the condom, which pounded Charles' gland.

His ass tightened around my cock and milked me dry. His cock exploded and the metal sound shot out of the end of his cock and flew over my shoulder. Strings of cum coated my hairy chest, one splashed under my chin and ran down my neck.

I bucked my hips into his ass, forcing my cock deeper. My legs straightened, and I lifted off of the bar. Spasms of pleasure washed over me, and I exhaled so violently, the ball gag exploded out of my mouth and became a necklace. I gasped in fresh air, my tongue tasting the sweat and semen that had rained over me.

Charles collapsed on top of me, my cock still buried deep in his ass. He breathed into my ear as his tongue entered it. "You were great."

The basement smelled like a locker room, male sweat, semen, and testosterone. My body was spent and satisfied.

Charles slowly sat up, and my cock popped out of him, sending another wave of joy over me. He lifted his leg over me as if getting off a horse. He reached into the sink and came back with a wet washcloth. He washed my chest and worked down to my cock and balls. He cleaned me thoroughly.

"I can do that, if you release my hands," I offered.

"I like to finish a job I started." He wiped me dry and then released me.

I rubbed the circulation back into my arms and legs as I redressed.

Charles washed and released the other three men, and we stood in a semi-circle facing him. He smiled a toothy grin. "I hope you boys had fun tonight."

I avoided eye contact with Charles as the four of us started up the stairs.

Charles called after us, "And just so you know, Debbie sold the same toys to your women upstairs. Enjoy."

VALLEYSCARE
By Logan Zachary

"Welcome to ValleyScare, the last event of the season and your life ..." the rotting corpse cackled as we entered the Minnesota amusement park. Half of the rides were operating, but around every corner a zombie would pop up, or a chainsaw-wielding-manic would chase a passer-by.

Early in the day, the monsters were cute, but as the night came on and the younger children left, the real scares came out. Entrails spilled out of the dumpsters and garbage cans, eyeballs hung out of eye sockets, and severed hands and feet littered the midway.

The food stands menus changed to bat wings, vampire bites, mummy fingers, deep fried brains and eyeballs. The smell of grease and fried food made my stomach rumble, but some of the ghastly images revolted me. A severed hand crawled across our path.

"Cool trick. So, should we eat first or ..." I started to ask.

A gust of October wind chilled me as leaves swirled around our feet. Drew moved closer to me as a zombie in a bride's dress and veil staggered by. She looked at us, arms extended and bloody bouquet swaying from her wrist. A groom's head was clutched in her other hand by his hair. His eyes rolled in his head, and his mouth was open in a terrified scream.

Drew had wanted to go to this Halloween event. His deep blue eyes, even white smile, curly black hair, football player's body and tight end made it difficult for me to refuse him anything.

Me, not so much, but I went along. "Why not go to the haunted house first."

"You just want to get this over as quickly as possible." Drew pulled me close and hugged me from the side.

"Am I that obvious?"

"Yes." He kissed the side of my head and guided me to the front door of the Horror Hotel.

We walked past the front desk, and a bloody hand clanged the bell. A bellhop with an eye dangling out of his eye socket clicked his heels and saluted us. Floor to ceiling mirrors lined the hallway as we went deeper into terror.

A huge mirror swung free from the wall, separated us, and pushed me away from Drew. He reached for me, but the momentum knocked me off my feet. I tried to catch myself, but I fell hard and skidded across the floor. My back hit another mirror on the wall, which swung backward like an outside dog's door, which allowed my body to continue into the wall. I felt the floor slant downward, and I was on a metal slide and picked up speed. The wall passed over me and returned to its original position, plunging my world into blackness.

The slide narrowed and guided my body down a chute. Swinging doors burst open when my feet hit them, and my body landed on a metal tray. Hands grabbed my ankles and wrists. I blinked as my eyes tried to adjust from the blackness into the bright light. Four-inch leather restraints wrapped around my limbs and secured me onto the metal cart I landed on.

"Okay, scary. You got me. I'll scream, and then you can let me go."

The two big, burly, black men wore doctor's uniforms. They looked like bodybuilders with white surgical masks covering their faces and surgical caps covering their bald heads. Black rubber gloves covered their beefy forearms all the way up to their elbows. One turned his broad V-shaped back and rolled a cart over to me with a bunch of metal medical instruments on top. He picked up a pair of big scissors and stepped down to my ankle. He started to cut my jeans.

"What the fuck are you doing? Those are my new …"

A ball gag stopped any more of my protests. The taste of rubber and leather filled my mouth, as the other doctor secured it behind my head before I started to thrash around. His thick glasses covered his eyes and made him look bug eyed.

The other doctor cut up to my knee and kept going.

I felt my dick cringe as he worked up my leg, but he followed straight up and cut through my belt. The side of my pants fell open, and he moved to the other leg. As he neared my knee, I read his name tag: Dr. Pain.

The bug eyed man found a pair of scissors and zipped down my T-shirt's sleeves and then down the center of my chest. My hairy chest came into view as he pulled the remnants of my shirt away and threw it to the floor.

Dr. Pain pulled off my pants.

My cell phone started to ring as he balled up the denim and kicked them into the corner. I saw my wallet fall out of my back pocket. The phone rang again, but they ignored it. I looked up at the ceiling to see a mirror covered every inch of it. My reflection, clad only in briefs, socks, and shoes, pulled on the leather restraints.

The metal table was cold against my hairy arms and legs. I yelled into the gag, but nothing but grunts emerged from my mouth. I could see the muscles strain in my neck as I pulled harder.

Dr. Pain covered me with a hospital gown and tied it around my neck. He snapped the sleeves together to cover my upper arms and pulled the length down to cover my knees.

The other man leaned over me, and I read his name tag: Dr. Drill. He checked the restraints on my wrists and nodded. He moved down to my ankles and removed my shoes and socks. His long slender fingers were cold and skeletal. He ran one fingernail down the arch of my foot.

I thought I'd go through the roof. I hated being tickled, and my sweaty feet were extra sensitive.

He watched my response and took my other foot into his other hand and tickled.

I tensed my whole body, trying to ignore the tormenting touch.

Dr. Drill bent forward and reached behind his head and untied one set of ties on his mask. He raised it slightly to show me his tongue and licked between my toes.

I screamed and screamed against the gag. My teeth bore down on the leather strap, and I tasted blood. My molars worked on the leather, which softened but refused to cut.

Dr. Pain approached me with another leather strap and placed it across my forehead and secured my head to the table.

I couldn't lift my head up anymore, so I watched their work in the mirror.

His wet tongue worked between each toe and sucked on them one by one. After each one was washed, his tongue traced along the arch and down to the heel.

My back arched as I tried to escape.

His hand worked up my hairy leg, tickling each hair as he went, combing the fur to my knee.

Dr. Pain approached with a straight edge razor and reached under my gown. He grabbed my underwear and slashed one side.

My balls rolled out of their confinement after the freedom came.

Dr. Pain walked around the other side of the table and slashed the other side.

I felt the cotton slide out from under my ass; the cold metal awoke my cheeks.

Dr. Drill untied the strings at my neck and pulled the gown down, exposing my hairy chest. He picked up the straight edge razor and made it flash in the light. He brought it down to one of my nipples and scraped the sharp blade over my sensitive skin.

My nipple rose up to the stimulation.

He shaved the hair around the whole nipple and stroked a few times to remove any dead skin, making the pink area very tender. His wet mouth descended on it and sucked my nipple into his mouth. His teeth rolled the end back and forth, applying a little pressure, making some pain, but some pleasure, too. His tongue licked around and around.

My cock swelled to full length and tented the gown. In the mirror, the folds hid that fact, but I knew.

Dr. Pain brought my ruined underwear to my face and held them to my nose, allowing me to smell my musky ball sweat and butt. He rubbed it against my cheek and then brought it to his nose and inhaled deeply.

Dr. Drill moved to the other side of the table and shaved my other nipple. His mask was still in place over his nose, but his tongue protruded from his mouth and licked my tender spots. His lips surrounded the small mound and sucked it hard into his mouth. His teeth bit and pulled gently on the point. As he chewed, he raised a hole punch for leather and showed it to me. He squeezed the handles and made the metal click. He brought it down to the opposite nipple and pinched.

I tried to shake my head. "No, no, no!"

Dr. Pain picked up the discarded straight edge and moved down to my pelvis.

I felt the gown rise up and a cool breeze flowed over my hairy balls. My cock was still covered, but my balls were hanging out.

Dr. Pain picked up a remote control and pressed a button.

My legs started to spread as the lower half of table split and pulled them further and further apart.

I felt open and exposed.

The table stopped, and Dr. Pain stepped between my legs. He brought the blade to my taint and ran it up to the base of my balls. He teased my low hangers with the razor.

I felt my balls rise up.

Dr Pain nodded and stared to shave my testicles.

I watched as my hairy balls became smooth and pink. He ran the razor over my sensitive flesh with the skill of a surgeon. I held my breath as he worked.

Dr. Drill put the hole punch down, walked to the wall, and pulled on a hose that coiled around a metal wheel. He pulled the metal nozzle to the table and watched as Dr. Pain worked. Clumps of hair fell to the floor and over a drain in the tile. Dr. Drill tapped my ass with the rounded tip when Dr. Pain finished his task.

Dr. Pain pulled on one of my butt cheeks and quickly shaved around my hairy hole.

My pucker tightened and quivered as the sharp blade rolled over the pink opening.

Dr. Drill sprayed a cool mist of water to clean away the hair.

Water dripped off my balls and ass, swirling down the floor drain. I closed my eyes, embarrassed at the attention, only to have them fly open when the cold metal tip entered me. A stream of cold water filled me and pressure rose deep inside my bowels. More water flowed into me and suddenly a spray showered around the room as the water gushed out of my ass.

The doctors stepped out of the way and waited for the flood to stop. Dr. Drill entered me again, cleaning me out good. The cold water tingled and burned my newly shaved skin.

My cock bounced up and down under the gown, precum flowed out of the tip and soaked into the damp gown.

As Dr. Drill pulled the hose out of me, he ran it along my cock. The cold metal tingled along my engorged flesh. Condensation on the metal and sweat from my balls made it slide easy. He pulled the hose away from my erection and rolled it back on the wheel. Water dripped from the hose as it dripped from me.

Dr. Pain picked up a speculum and inserted it into the jar of lube. He pulled the trigger, and the duck bill opened and closed. He stepped between my legs, lube running down the metal.

I felt a cold pressure on my pucker, and inch by inch, the curved steel entered. As the handle touched my butt, he pressed down to open me wide.

Dr. Drill picked up a glass tube that lit up with an eerie blue light. He moved next to Dr. Pain and inserted it into me. He nodded at Dr. Pain and motioned for him to do something.

Dr. Pain left the speculum inside, stepped back and untied his drawstring on his scrubs. His pants fell to the floor and a huge black penis rose up.

I gasped as I saw the girth, even with the distance from the mirror; I couldn't believe its size.

Dr. Pain hip-bumped Dr. Drill out of the way, took the blue light and motioned for his next move.

Dr. Drill untied his drawstring and let his pants drop. His ebony uncut cock was even bigger than Dr. Pain's. He jacked his member a few times with the rubber glove. A pearl of precum swelled at the tip, and he wiped it along my leg.

Dr. Pain removed the tools from my ass, grabbed his monster, and rubbed it up and down my newly shaved crack. The fat mushroom head explored my opening and rolled over it.

The leather strap that held my head in place released, and the table slid back underneath me. My head fell back and thick fingers fumbled with the ball gag. It popped out of my mouth.

I worked my jaw a few times to relieve the tension. As my mouth opened wide, Dr. Drill drilled my tonsils. His thick, veiny cock slipped down my throat, almost gagging me. His huge black, furry balls bounced off my eyes. His foreskin held a pool of precum, which poured over my taste buds.

The masculine scent of sweat and balls filled my nose, as salty, sweetness trickled across my tongue and down my throat.

Swallowing and breathing at the same time was a trick. He pulled out of me and dropped a black ball into my mouth, forcing me to suck on it. Curly hair tickled my lips, as the other testicle rolled over my cheek.

Dr. Drill's balls covered my eyes, but he pulled out of me for a second, and I saw what was coming next. The reflection in the mirror revealed Dr. Pain, unrolling a condom on his anaconda. He lubed the length and snaked the head between my cheeks. It pressed on my hole and waited.

My butt tensed, but suddenly the gown was ripped off me, and my cock sprang up. A huge black hand grasped my engorged pink flesh and stroked. My body relaxed, and the fat dick's head popped into me. He pulled on me as he pumped inch by inch into me.

Before I could say anything, the other massive dick entered my mouth again, spit roasting me between these two muscle men. I looked like the cream filling in an Oreo cookie, and knew I'd be creaming soon.

A finger explored the slit on my cock and pushed inside, digging, searching. A cold slender metal tool played along my shaft, dripping with lube. The rounded end circled my cock's opening and slipped in, stretching my dick as it went deeper.

He jacked from the outside as it penetrated me on the inside, stimulating the inside and the outside at the same time.

My balls threatened to release then and there, but the strange sensation stopped it. The metal sound plugged me. It stopped, and I felt it roll inside me, a wetness escaped at the end. He pulled the sound out of me as he jacked my cock, and then pushed it back in. Inside and outside, orally and anally, push and pull, my body was overrun with stimulation.

Dr. Drill reached down to my tender nipples and pinched them, rolling them in between his fingers as his cock slammed into my mouth. He applied nipple clamps to each side and pulled on them and twisted.

Drool ran down my cheeks and lube dripped from my ass, as both men pistoned into me. My cock was oozing and demanding more, more, more.

I wished my hands were free to squeeze their tight asses, run my fingers over their abs and comb through their pubes. The pleasure built in my balls, and I thrust my cock into his hand as he jacked. I needed to come, shoot my load. The sound sent new sensations deep inside.

Dr. Pain thrust into me one more time, hitting my prostate with his climax. His cock swelled and contracted in my ass with each orgasm. His load filled the condom, and the heat erupted into me and out of my cock.

The metal sound shot out of my dick and straight into the air as cum burst out of me. Wave after wave of thick cream sprayed across my torso and chest.

Dr. Drill reached over and scooped up a blob and brought it to his mouth. He moaned as he thrust into me and unloaded his balls down my throat. Sweet, salty cream flowed into me and out of me.

I sucked down hard on his cock, and he screamed as another wave poured out of him. He pulled his oversensitive dick out of me with a wet pop. Another loud pop came out of my ass, as Dr. Pain's dick left. Sweat ran over my spent body and pooled on the metal table and onto the floor.

The Doctors sank to the floor, panting and clutching their spent dicks.

A few minutes later, two pairs of black hands came up and inserted a long metal key into the restraints. The leather straps released, and the blood flow returned to my hands and feet. I sat up slowly, as my head spun. WOW! What a ride.

A door burst open, and Drew walked in. He carried a paper bag. "I thought you might want a clean set of clothes ..." he started.

"You bastard," I said. My bare feet touched the wet, cold tile floor, and goo oozed between my toes. "You set me up."

A smile came across his full lips. "I did this for you. You said this was a fantasy you had, so I wanted to make your dreams come true." He took me into his arms and kissed me.

"This was a nightmare." I hugged him back, as we spun around.

"Some nightmare, you have come running down your leg and all over your chest. And from that shit eating grin on your face, you had one hell of a time. I wish I was the lucky one."

I pushed against him, and his feet slipped on the wet floor. He fell back and landed on the table I had just left. "Get him boys, "I said.

Dr. Pain and Dr. Drill slapped the leather restraints around Drew's ankles and wrists.

"What the ..." he said.

I picked up the ball gag and slipped it into his mouth. "It's time for your physical, dear." I kissed him on the forehead and walked over to the paper bag on the floor. I swung my bare ass from side to side for him to see. "And if you're good, I may even join in ..."

I lifted a gigantic black dildo and waved it at the men. "Doctors, he's all yours ..."

DUNGEON INTERVIEW
By Jay Starre

Adam drove up through the Sierra Nevada foothills on a bright October afternoon and marveled at the surprisingly bucolic landscape. The grassy slopes had gone autumn golden, one of the main reasons California was called the Golden State. Live Oaks dotted the rolling hills with their deep green while cattle and horses meandered about contentedly, most likely relieved that the worst of the summer heat had come and gone.

The young business graduate was both extremely excited and extremely nervous. Under his plaid shorts, his cock swelled into an aching boner every time he recalled his meeting the previous morning with the two executive producers of Dark Dick Productions.

Cole had done most of the talking.

"The interview tomorrow won't be any typing test. Are you willing to take it as it comes? I promise you it won't be vanilla, and once we begin you won't have any say in what happens. I'm giving you fair warning. This is not an opportunity for the timid."

Behind him his shorter business partner, Roman, sprawled in an office chair against one wall, beefy thighs wide and one hand casually cupping the bulge in his crotch. He hadn't added much to the conversation, but his huge golden eyes missed nothing. The way he looked over Adam as he'd stood there and answered Cole's blunt questions had been unnerving.

Both men were handsome as hell — and hot, too. Both were black, but they were completely different from one another. Cole was tall and lean with a narrow face, long nose, pursed mouth and a prominent dimpled chin. His head was shaved and his arched brows hovered above dark eyes. Roman was rather short but extremely husky. His broad face boasted large blunt features and those big golden eyes. His hair was buzzed short to create a dark cap that only emphasized the largeness of his head and boldness of his features. His mouth was enormous.

Adam had been nervous during that interview but confident of his abilities and certain of his willingness to perform the duties the job required. He admitted as much without hesitation. His honesty seemed to be the clincher.

"Give him the address to our studio," Roman said from his chair.

Cole stepped forward and shook Adam's hand. His palm was large and warm and his grip firm. Adam was thrilled.

The miles fell behind him quickly, and he soon passed through Sonora, a town that blended historic sites such as old mining camps and sawmills with the typical California suburban blight, and then drove higher into the foothills where pine forest, cabins and state parks began to replace the oak savanna and cattle.

He slowed as his GPS gently informed him the driveway he sought would shortly pop up on his right. A screen of forest blocked the view down the paved drive, but within a hundred yards the trees opened up as a high wall and gate loomed. He had to stop and get out to speak into an intercom before the gate was opened for him.

The building behind the walls was amazing. It was more like a chateau than any studio he'd ever seen. Several stories tall, it claimed a high peaked roof and a stone facade dotted by long narrow windows. A manicured pine forest surrounded it while sculpted shrubs lined the drive and the front steps.

Although it looked like something out of Switzerland, it did fit in with the surroundings. This high in the hills it snowed quite a bit in the winter, and Adam could just picture it nestled among a white blanket of the puffy stuff.

A voice he hadn't recognized as belonging to either of his prospective employers had crackled through the intercom, while no one came out the door to greet him. He parked beside a bright yellow Mustang and got out.

Cole had told him he needn't bring anything with him and that he should dress casually. Of course he was still determined to look his best and had chosen his wardrobe carefully. It was still quite warm that time of year, so he donned plaid designer shorts, sandals, and a snug polo shirt. His athletically slim body was displayed adequately without being vulgar.

As he mounted the stone steps that led to the front door, he had to laugh at himself for his careful planning. These guys ran a porn film company. He might have been better off showing up naked.

Just as he thought that, the big oak door opened and there to greet him was a naked man! "Welcome Adam. Thank you for being punctual. I'll escort you to the Dungeon. Masters Cole and Roman are waiting."

The man wasn't entirely naked. He wore two items, a black leather collar and a black leather jockstrap. Both were dotted with gold grommets while two big gold rings dangled from the collar, front and back, and another dangled from the bottom of the jockstrap between his bare thighs. Adam felt a chill of expectation as he fantasized those rings being attached to ropes or chains or cuffs of some sort.

The man was built somewhat like Adam himself, taller by a bit but just as slim and fit and just as white. In fact, he was a platinum blond with luminescent ivory skin. Even though he was dressed so unusually, he seemed completely at ease and even smiled pleasantly as he waved Adam in and then closed the door after him.

As he turned to lead him down the long entry hall, his firm ass-cheeks outlined by that black jockstrap naturally drew Adam's attention. His eyes widened as he noticed the single tattoo splashed across the left cheek. A curved black dick! It was erect and the fat head was spurting. Small black stars splashed across the upper cheek, representing splatters of jizz.

He recognized the image. It was the logo of Black Dick Productions.

He tore his eyes from that jiggling image and looked around. The floor beneath his feet was cream marble while the walls were dark wooden paneling. Heavy Victorian furniture lined those walls. Vases of Chinese porcelain contained flowers. It was all very decadent.

"You're on your own from here. I've been ordered not to intrude."

The smile was a little broader now, and Adam was sure he detected a glint of nasty glee in the blue eyes as the jock-strapped doorman stepped aside and waved a hand toward a set of descending stairs.

He peered down. Steps of rough stone marched downward between narrow walls of the same stone. Lamps set in the wall resembled torches with iron grates surrounding them. The beat of music wafted upward from somewhere below.

"Uh, thanks," he muttered as he began his descent.

The music grew steadily louder. It was a heavy unrushed beat that reminded him of some kind of wild animal's heartbeat. His imagination was running away with him! Truthfully, he had no idea what to expect.

An archway loomed below. The music emanated from there, with no door blocking his way beyond. His feet slowed, and he had to force himself to take a deep breath and move ahead more quickly.

He was there. He stopped and peered within, his heart beating much more rapidly than that music. What he saw had him gasping out loud.

As if on cue the music ceased.

"Remove your clothes at the entry. Then please come in, Adam."

Cole stood in the center of the large chamber. His partner, Roman, was behind him. Both men were nearly as naked as their doorman.

His hands trembled as he obeyed. He'd come all this way for an interview to become the men's private secretary. A naked private secretary, it seemed!

As he undressed, he glanced around. The room was cavernous with ceilings he couldn't quite see in the gloom above. The floor was marble, as well as the walls, all of a dark royal blue with delicate veins of crimson. Dozens more of those peculiar lamps in stanchions of iron grating either lined the marble walls or were planted atop six foot pillars of more marble.

Two large mirrors on either side of the room faced each other with Cole and Roman between them. Two immense flat-screen television monitors were set on the back wall. Both were playing scenes from what were obviously porn movies.

All this was daunting enough, but there was more. Cole was standing, but Roman was not. He was lying face-down on some kind of strange platform, and as Adam looked more closely, he realized he was cuffed in place, both wrists and ankles!

The platform was shaped like a giant X. Roman's hands were stretched out over the upper arms of the X while his feet were clamped to the lower arms. He was spread-eagled with his large black ass stretched wide open.

Adam was so busy gawking, he at first didn't even realize he was actually naked himself by this time. His soaring hard-on alerted him to the fact, and he was suddenly embarrassed and dropped his hands to hide the offending boner.

"Come forward. Kneel at my feet, Adam. I have your collar."

"My collar?" he managed to reply in a choked voice.

"Address either Roman or myself as Master or Sir. Understood?"

Cole had a beautiful voice, not really deep but powerful and melodic. In fact, almost hypnotizing. He spoke softly yet unambiguously.

"Uhh, yes Sir," Adam mumbled as he found himself stumbling forward, his bobbing pink cock thrust out in front of him. In seconds, he was standing before the tall executive.

A gloved hand came out to settle on his naked shoulder. It pushed downward, like the voice, gently but unequivocally. Adam dropped, his knees like jelly already. He was face-to-face with Cole's crotch.

A jock-strap made out of supple black leather with red striping on the edges held a pouch of silver chain mesh that bulged with potent promise. He stared directly at that gleaming pouch and pondered what he was supposed to say or do now. Should he bury his face in that crotch? He all at once wanted to, very much.

A gloved hand settled on his head and pushed it back. He looked up to see a second gloved hand descending — holding a collar just like the one the doorman wore! His emotions were in such turmoil, he found himself staring at everything that came in sight with absolute focus. He noted how the gloves were made of that same supple black leather, and also had small red striping down the center of each finger and along the wrist.

The collar slid around his neck and snapped in place along the back. The leather felt so soft against his flesh it was almost like a second skin. But it was a collar. A collar!

He looked up into Cole's dark eyes. Above them he wore a snug black leather cap with a shortened red leather visor. Adam tore his eyes from those intimidating orbs and looked lower. A leather harness outlined his chest and shoulders, again in black with red piping. Although he was tall and lean, he was admirably muscled. The harness emphasized the smooth swell of each tit and the protruding brown nipple in its center. The leather also emphasized the broadness of his shoulders. And on each of his biceps, a broad leather band in black and red emphasized the girth of those muscles. Against all that black, his skin looked richer, a dark chocolate brown and smooth from neck to ankle.

He looked back up and noted a faint smile on Cole's plump lips. He suddenly found the nerve to speak. "What do you want me to do? I'm not sure what's going on ... Sir."

"No need for questions, Adam. Just do as I tell you. Now I'm telling you to crawl forward and kneel between Roman's legs."

One hand on his head and one on his shoulder pressed downward. He obeyed, finding himself on hands and knees and turning toward that strange X behind Cole. As he began to crawl, he became acutely aware of his nakedness. His balls hung down between his thighs, vulnerable and ludicrously on display. His cock, which had remained stiff as an iron pole, slapped against his legs as he moved. The collar felt snug — and somehow permanent.

He flushed all over. It was warm in the room, but he knew it was his own emotions that were making him so hot. To what lengths would he go to get this job? And was it all about a job anymore?

He had a lot of questions and was dying to ask Cole for the answers but had been warned not to. Best to go along and see what transpired. Go with the flow. But a moment later when he was stopped directly before Roman's parted ass-crack and faced a totally shocking sight, he wasn't exactly sure what going with the flow would entail.

The X Roman was cuffed to was held up by four chains, one attached to each of the arms at top and bottom. In the center where those arms met, it appeared the platform was hinged. At the moment, the center was higher than the ends, so Roman was sprawled over it with his ass and hips higher than his head and feet.

On hands and knees, Adam was now between the two lower arms of the X. His face was right in Roman's ass. And it was a gorgeous ass. Two massive mounds reared up from the center of that X, spread wide with Roman's ankles pulled apart and attached by leather cuffs to either leg of the platform. A leather jock-strap outlined those gigantic mounds. The leather was a deep royal blue and set off his black skin. His deep black ass-crack was right there.

It was certainly shocking to see that husky executive mostly naked and bound to a dungeon contraption. But that was not the most stunning circumstance Adam faced. No. He had to blink and look again to be sure of what he was looking at. Blinking changed nothing.

Out of Roman's puckered dark hole, a gleaming silver chain dangled down between his spread thighs! Shiny lube glistened on the smooth crack, and on the hole and the protruding chain. He had a chain shoved up his ass.

"You will remove that chain, Adam. It's destined for another hole."

Cole's melodic voice startled him out of his shocked state. He gathered his wits and moved. He wanted this damn job and wasn't about to fuck it up by being timid!

Just as he placed his hands on the dangling end of that chain, the music started up again. A booming chant punctuated by high-pitched piping sent a startled shudder through him. He accidentally yanked on the chain.

Several glistening links slithered out of Roman's puckered hole, oozing lube along with them. The big ass jerked, then wriggled and heaved. One of the links was sucked back in!

Now, Adam was totally fascinated and intent on obeying Cole's command. He pulled on the slippery chain, feeling the slight resistance of Roman's sphincter, then the slithering response as the pressure he exerted won out. Several more links appeared. Roman's mammoth butt heaved, his ass-lips gulped, and one of the links retreated back inside the dark hole.

Adam's cock twitched and a big dollop of precum oozed out to spatter on the marble tile beneath his knees. He was so enthralled, he almost forgot about the strange surroundings and the hovering black man behind him. He tugged again, rewarded by four more links sliding out.

How many were inside Roman? He had about two feet now in his hands, and a foot of that had been in there before he started pulling it out. As Roman squirmed and sucked with his asshole to retrieve one of those disgorged links, Adam tugged again. Half a dozen links oozed out, with one being sucked back in almost immediately.

The game continued while that blaring chant vibrated throughout the chamber. He pulled out half a dozen links, Roman heaved his giant butt, and one was sucked back in. He had three feet of chain in his hand, then four! Open-mouthed, his hands shaking and his cock dribbling steadily, he finally yanked out the final foot of chain. It fell to the floor in a clatter.

He was staring right at Roman's stretched hole. With ass-lips quivering, it bubbled lube.

A gloved hand settled over his head. Cole bent down to speak directly in his ear, his hot breath tickling the lobe. "Give me the chain, Adam. And eat that hole."

With a moan that couldn't be heard above the reverberating chant, he did as he was ordered. The slippery chain was placed into Cole's gloved hands while Adam placed his own hands on the floor and leaned in toward that big dark ass-crack.

Roman continued to heave his giant butt, and his asshole still convulsed, as if he was trying to get some of that chain back in it. Adam flushed from head to toe and shuddered as he stuck out his tongue and aimed it at that inviting target.

The moment the tip settled on the quivering lips, they sucked it in. It was like a clamping suction pump had gripped his tongue! He buried his face in that crack and drove his tongue as deep as he could. The hole yawned open. He twirled his tongue around inside and sucked with his lips on the slippery rim.

The lube was tasteless but the hole was definitely a man's ass. He loved it! Slurping and lapping, he again almost forgot where he was and how totally unorthodox the job interview had turned out to be.

Then he was reminded. All at once, he felt something sliding up and down along his own parted ass-crack. The chain!

While he ate his partner's ass, Cole stood behind Adam and dangled the chain along his crack, pulling it up and down directly over his pink butt-hole.

That only made him eat more deeply. Roman's hole responded by pouting outwards, gaping wide, then collapsing into a wide-open cavern. He almost felt as if he could dive down into it head-first.

Fingers hooked in the gold ring at the back of his collar and yanked his face out of that tasty black ass. He gasped for breath and looked up. Cole grinned now, seemingly satisfied with his performance. Then as if by magic, the music abruptly ceased.

In the silence he heard his own whimpering, and Cole's demands.

"Get over here. Lick my boots with your lily-white ass in the air."

There was hardly any shame in licking boots after he'd been so eager to tongue asshole, so he was quick to obey. Though once he started licking along the black leather with his head pressed down nearly on the floor, he experienced an entirely different emotion from the heady lust of eating that ass. He felt somehow subjugated, as if he was lower than low.

He didn't mind it!

And as he smacked his lips and drooled over those boots, he was also acutely aware of his bare ass in the air. He was equally aware of his vulnerable hole pouting between his jiggling ass-cheeks.

He was even more aware when that silver chain again began to slide up and down along his butt-crack.

"That's a good boy, Adam. A very good boy. But now it's time for you to experience the Iron Cross."

Was that what he called that X? And what about Roman? He refrained from asking any stupid questions as he rose from his boot-licking and again faced Cole's shimmering mesh crotch.

"Up on your feet, Boy. Time to release Master Roman."

The chain dangling between Adam's ass cheeks was pulled out and draped over one of Cole's broad shoulders. He rose to his feet and turned to face the Iron Cross where Roman was strapped face-down. A leather-clad hand cupped one Adam's ass-cheeks and gently shoved. He stumbled forward to end up at Roman's left foot. He wore leather boots similar to Cole's but they were royal blue rather than black. Dark leather cuffs were buckled around them.

That hand retained its firm grasp on his ass-cheek as he worked, pulling his crack open so that he was aware of his hole and what might be planned for it shortly. Although his fingers shook, he finished up the job quickly. A gentle shove impelled him over to the other leg of the Iron Cross and Roman's right boot.

This time he was quicker, especially as the gloved hand on his butt squeezed a little and the fingers slid closer to his crack and hole. He shivered slightly as he remembered the feel of that silver chain recently dangling along his crack, and the way it slithered out of Cole's lubed hole.

He stepped around the right leg of the Iron Cross and headed for the upper arm. He took a moment to notice more clearly the broad shape of Roman's back, packed with muscle, along with the bulging shoulders and massive arms. A leather harness crossed over that expanse of muscle, royal blue like his jockstrap. Royal blue leather arm bands encircled each giant biceps. His hands were gloved, too, again in royal blue.

As he stepped up to work on releasing the buckles of the leather cuffs that bound Roman's wrist, he looked at the man's face for the first time. Because the front of the Iron Cross was lower than the center where his beefy black butt reared up, Adam hadn't been able to really get a good look at his head or face before.

Roman hadn't spoken a word since he'd arrived in the dungeon, Adam realized. Now he knew why. He was gagged! Staring at that royal blue leather ball protruding from his huge mouth, Adam suddenly recalled what Cole had said earlier — something about the chain he pulled from Roman's ass was destined for another hole. It wouldn't be Cole's hole, so that left one other hole. And if that chain was going up his own ass, then he was safe to assume that gag was going in his mouth.

Roman was also blindfolded. A leather mask, in royal blue, covered his big eyes. Would he be blind-folded as well? His fingers were really shaking as he unbuckled that wrist then after another gentle shove on his ass, quickly circled the upper arm of the Iron Cross and moved to that final cuff. The moment it was released, the hand on his butt pulled away.

As Roman stepped down from that platform, Cole went around it to meet with him. Adam took a moment to look around the room. The large screens caught his eye. He hadn't been paying them much attention, but now he did. On the left screen a dungeon similar to the one they were in was populated by half a dozen naked men engaged in sucking, fucking and other nasty play. There were slings and benches and leather and chains in abundance. It was a dark and rough.

The other screen depicted an outdoors romp. One man was tied to a pine tree, his legs spread, and his ass stuffed with a huge dildo. The one tied up was a husky white dude while the one doing the stuffing was a slender black dude.

He shuddered as he contemplated the size of that greasy dildo and how the dude taking it up the ass was rearing back toward it. He turned away and faced his own pair of assailants. What would happen now?

Cole had removed both ball gag and blindfold. The two were kissing! Roman's huge mouth gaped wide open and Cole seemed to be shoving his tongue down his throat. Both had their gloved hands on each other's naked butts.

He tore his eyes from that sloppy scene to look around a little more. Now he noticed the cameras for the first time. One of them protruded from the marble wall between two of the glowing lamps to his left. He turned to look at the opposite wall in the same area, and there was another. He looked around the room and spotted at least one more above the arched entry. They were filming all this! And why not? They were porn producers after all.

"Raise the upper arms of the Iron Cross, Boy. Use that pulley."

Cole's deliberate voice snapped him back to attention. He had been determined to do all he could when he arrived to secure this job, and here he was. This was no time to be daydreaming or slacking off.

He spotted the pulley chain and reached out for it. As he cranked on it, Cole did the same at the other end. The hinge in the center allowed the arms to rise until they were level and Cole stopped there, nodding to Adam to do the same.

"Now get your white butt up there, Boy."

So it was time. His heart pounded in his chest. He was about to be strapped to that Iron Cross — and helpless against whatever these two big black leather masters chose to do to him! Was he brave enough to put himself in that situation?

"Yes Sir," he blurted out, answering his own question.

He sat down on the center of the Iron Cross, feeling the smooth leather against his bare flesh. A shiver coursed through his body, and he let out a little whimper before he pulled up his feet and then spread them out along the legs of the platform, then lay down and did the same with his arms. Trembling all over and breathing rapidly, he found himself staring upwards.

He stared at himself. A mirror floated above the Iron Cross, high enough to be in shadow as it hung suspended by chains from the ceiling high above. The light from all those lamps illuminated him in a bright halo, and his naked flesh created a stark contrast to the dark leather beneath him.

With both arms and legs splayed wide, he looked like some kind of sacrifice on the altar. And in that reflection, he could see his two new Masters moving in to cuff his ankles and wrists, like some leather-clad priests about to offer him up to their own depraved god or gods.

The music started up again. More chanting, high and echoing, as if a horde of priests were singing to their nasty gods in some ancient cavern before they sacrificed the chosen one.

He gazed at himself as if looking at a stranger. His athletic limbs were supple with muscle from countless hours of swimming and tennis. His waist was narrow and his belly flat and rippled. His skin was lightly tanned where his swimsuit hadn't protected it, but it was still very light when compared to the two men securing him at hands and feet. His golden hair was in disarray, plastered over his forehead where he'd been sweating copiously in the heat of his emotion. His pale blue eyes stared back at him. His face, round and somewhat angelic, looked flushed and frightened. Or perhaps just excited.

As the pair strapped down his last wrist and final ankle, and he was trapped upon the leather Iron Cross, he found himself strangely calm. What could he do now other than submit? It was a liberating thought.

Roman loomed over him. The husky porn executive hadn't spoken since his gag came out, but now he did. Leaning in over Adam's face, he smiled. His big lips were wet and juicy looking.

"How about giving me a taste of my own ass, Boy. Shove the tongue that was up my hole in my mouth before I gag you."

That huge mouth descended to cover his own. It was a cavern of sucking lust, pulling his tongue inside it and clamping over it with vacuum cheeks. He felt as if the breath was being sucked right out of him, and he snorted for air. It was the most intense kiss he'd ever experienced.

It pulled away, and the ball gag immediately replaced it. If he'd had anything to say before, now it was too late. It only took a moment for Roman to secure it behind his head with the leather straps and buckle.

That wasn't all. He had one final look at himself in the mirror above before the blindfold settled over his eyes and all went black. He felt a moment of panic before gloved hands settled over his chest and his thighs, and he once more experienced that odd calm.

He was without sight, and with that loud music he essentially had no hearing either. He was unable to see what was about to happen to him and could only guess, then only accept it when it did happen. Again, it was a liberating notion.

But then the music began to decrease in volume as those gloved hands began to roam over his naked body. The supple leather that encased them was ever-so-soft even though the fingers inside were firm and unequivocal — like Cole's voice. Those hands went up and down his thighs, his calves and even his feet and toes. The other pair roamed over his chest, tweaked his nipples lightly, then slid under his arms to stroke his pits. He squirmed at that, but quickly realized his movements were severely restricted with his hands and feet cuffed.

The chanting was a low rumble in the background when he felt the hands on his lower body slide upward, slowly passing his knees and then trailing along the insides of his upper thighs, inexorably heading toward his crotch.

With his legs splayed wide apart and secured to opposite arms of the Iron Cross, he was wide open to any assault on his cock, balls, and ass crack. There was no way to escape those fingers as they moved closer and closer to that area.

Just as they trailed up along the upper portion of his thigh and right below his balls, something else caught his attention with electrifying effect. One of his nipples was suddenly clamped tightly by some kind of tit clamp, then a second later, the other was also clamped.

His outcry was muffled by the gag in his mouth, and the sensations bombarding his sensitive nipples were amplified by a gloved hand suddenly rising up to seize the shaft of his stiff cock and squeeze.

The fingers sliding around along his upper thigh continued to tease the area around his balls while the other hand pumped his cock in a strangling grip. His nipples were on fire, and his cock ached while he was acutely aware of the fingers still down there circling both his spread ass crack and dangling nads.

The pulley above him began to clank and clatter. What was going on? He felt his head and upper body rising. The hinge at the center of the Iron Cross apparently worked in both directions.

His nipples burned and his cock throbbed as that pulley clattered and he rose higher and higher. Then it stopped, although the hand on his cock did not relent, nor the pulsing fire in his nipples.

He couldn't see what was going on, but a moment later, when the sound of another pulley began to clatter between his legs, he realized that Roman must have moved down there to work it while Cole continued the assault on his cock.

His feet began to rise. Higher and higher, exposing more and more of his ass and crack as the gloved fingers down there continued their slithering glide around the sensitive divide.

When the cranking halted, his feet were well above his head. Splayed wide, his ass-crack was now a gaping valley, totally available for the taking. He felt his asshole pulse and then pout as gloved fingers slid all around it- without actually touching it. He could see nothing, he could say nothing, but his body spoke volumes. He squirmed and flopped, his cock sticking straight up in the air as Cole continued pumping it, his chest heaving as those tit clamps electrified his poor nipples.

Then, between the fingers teasing his round ass-cheeks and deep crack, he felt that chain once more slither along it. Greased liberally, the smooth steel links rubbed up and down his crack and directly over his pouting hole. He snorted for air and jerked wildly in his chains. He wasn't even sure exactly why he struggled so much — there was no escape possible.

"Time to explore that hole, Boy. Are you ready?"

Of course he couldn't reply to Roman's question, but he could nod his head, and he did that, vigorously.

But was he ready? Those trailing gloved fingers slid toward their target and found it. He heard lube being squirted and felt slippery stuff dribbling down his open butt-crack.

Fingers shoved deep into him.

Roman's husky voice echoed in the chamber. "Sweet, Boy. Two big black fingers in your pretty pink hole. Next, the chain."

Those two gloved fingers probed and twisted. He squirmed around that gut-churning invasion while his cock was pumped and his nipples were on fire. The music increased in volume. The throbbing voices of the chanting priests seemed to match the rhythm of Cole's pumping fist and probing digits.

He began to lose himself in the sensations — in fact wallowing in them. His nipples no longer burned, but now seemed to pulse with welcome heat. His cock felt amazing. His hole pouted outward and invited in the fingers that twisted around inside it.

He felt the first link of the chain being stuffed into him. The two fingers stretched him open, one on either side of his puckered sphincter, while that slippery link was pushed between them. Another link followed.

The fingers slid out as more links slid in. He snorted and whimpered around the gag in his mouth. He couldn't get away from the mental image of his round white ass splayed wide and those two hulking black masters between his legs feeding him that silver chain.

He could feel more and more links sliding into him and wondered how much they intended on shoving up his ass. How much was in there already? He groaned around the gag in his mouth as the stuffing halted, then reared and bucked as those links were suddenly jerked back out, one by one.

His hole was a slippery slot, unable to resist that yanking withdrawal. The chain came out, inch by inch, until he felt the final one pop out and his sphincter bloom outward after it.

Fingers drove into him. He grunted and his body heaved. The fingers yanked out and that chain once more slid into his well-lubed hole. This time he was sure all five feet of it had been fed to him. He had never felt so stuffed.

As these links were slowly yanked out, he could just picture the pair of black masters smirking between his legs and enjoying his bound helplessness. That mental image only made him more willing to wallow in the moment.

Just as the final link retreated and his asshole felt deliciously empty, hands settled on his head. The leather blindfold was being unbuckled! He blinked rapidly and peered up at Roman's broad features in the glare of the lamps and television screens. With his head raised, he found himself facing Cole who stood between his spread thighs with a big grin on his face, just like he'd imagined. The gag was removed just in time for him to gasp aloud at what he saw.

Cole had released his fierce grip on Adam's cock. Instead, his hand was on his own. His mesh pouch had been removed, either by him or his partner. Out of that hole in his leather jockstrap, a foot long black dick reared upwards.

"Fuck, what a cock ... Sir," Adam blurted out.

"I'm glad you find it to your liking, Boy. But for today, this isn't the cock you're going to get," Cole informed him in his matter-of-fact tone.

Roman had already moved back to Adam's feet to stand beside his partner. His gloved hand, in royal blue, took hold of that lengthy shaft as well and both men pumped it. It wasn't thick but it was long and had a wicked curve to it, as well as a blunt mushroom knob at the end which would surely serve as a useful battering ram to open up any hole it attacked.

As Adam watched in awe, the husky black master stepped between Cole's muscular thighs and faced the bound job applicant, his expressive golden eyes staring right into his.

The look on his face said it all as he backed onto that lengthy pole. His big mouth formed a huge pouting circle and his big nostrils flared while those golden eyes got even bigger. That knob was apparently sliding deep into his well-lubed hole.

All that gorgeous black muscle tensed and rippled. The royal blue harness stretched around his massive tits and shoulders. Down at his crotch, the blue jockstrap hid his own cock, but the bulge there was considerable.

Even as his eyes zeroed in on that bulging pouch, Cole reached around with his gloved hands and unsnapped it. It fell away to reveal a dark cock that instantly reared up now that it was free from its confinement.

It was like a third arm! It wasn't nearly as long as Cole's but it was incredibly thick. The head was flared and divided by a long piss slit oozing precum. The shaft was deep black but the head was almost pink.

Adam knew where it was going.

"I'm going to use Roman's black cock to fuck your white ass, and you're going to love every fat fucking inch of it. Isn't that right, Boy?"

"Yes, Sir," Adam managed to bleat out now that he could speak. What else could he say?

Cole smirked and winked as he smacked Roman's lush black butt for emphasis and jammed his prick deeper, shoving him forward between Adam's splayed thighs at the same time.

He slam-fucked that big ass, driving his partner's hips against Adam's open thighs and forcing that thick tube of dark meat deep into his quivering slot. Again, harder. Then again, and again.

It really did feel like he was being fucked by Cole, even though it was Roman's cock in his ass. It was as if Roman was just the flesh between them, a helpless cock doing his Master's will, and Adam was even less, the hole that served the cock that served the Master.

The feel of all that dark cock gutting him was like nothing he'd ever experienced. In his emotional state of mind, it was actually easy to take all that meat. His asshole had been warmed up by the fingers and the chain, and strangely enough, being bound to the Iron Cross and helpless allowed him to completely relax the muscles of his sphincter.

Every ramming entry of that black battering ram stretched his gaping ass-lips and savagely massaged his prostate. In the best way possible. And now that he was no longer blind-folded, he managed to look into the mirrors on either side and see himself.

The clamps on his nipples stretched them downward. Weighted with round lead balls, they dangled from his smooth chest like pendulums, rocking back and forth in time to the thrusting piston of Roman's cock being rammed into his ass by Cole's pounding hips.

Sweat coated his pale body. His own cock reared up still stiff and twitching, a pink spear smeared with lube and precum. His ivory-white ass-cheeks were spread wide open, his pink hole stuffed with black cock and oozing lube.

The voices of the chanting priests in the background soared and swelled into a crescendo as he felt his entire body quiver like a strung bow. The image of himself spread wide across that Iron

Cross, feet high in the air and his ass being plowed by black cock, all at once proved too much.

"I'm coming, Sir! Oh God, I can't help myself! I'm shooting with a black cock up my ass! Oh thank you, Sir! Thank you!"

He blubbered out that stream of nasty nonsense as his cock erupted in a spray of jizz. The goo flew high in the air to land on his own chin and neck. The powerful orgasm was made more intense by the vicious pounding of his hole as Roman's enormous cock still reamed it.

Cole continued fucking them both, which only prolonged Adam's rapture. Cum continued to spurt from the head of his cock as the two black masters stood between his spread thighs and fucked him.

His head was still swimming when they pulled out. Groaning at the emptiness left behind, he watched as they both aimed their black cocks at his white ass and let loose with loads of their own.

Cum shot out to land on his balls, his crack and his rosy gaping hole. He could see it in the mirrors.

That's when he realized someone else was in the room. The doorman.

"You've passed the interview. Welcome to Black Dick Productions. Daniel here will provide you with your proof of employment, so to speak!"

Cole and Roman laughed out loud as they slapped Adam's cum-dripping ass with their gloved hands and moved aside.

Adam understood Cole's announcement when he recognized what the doorman had in his hands. A tray with tattooing tools! There was no doubt about it. He was about to be tattooed with that black dick logo.

His two new employers, and Masters, remained in the dungeon while Daniel worked. Adam remained shackled and spread-eagled during the entire operation. The thrumming of the electric needle and the pricking pain it elicited only made his clamped nipples ache even more, especially since either Cole or

Roman tugged on them every once in a while just to send shockwaves of painful pleasure up and down his body.

His hole pursed and dribbled, then strained against the thrust of a trio of gloved fingers probing it every so often. He lost track of time and didn't know how long the tattooing took, but it seemed endless.

When it was finally complete, he could see the result in the mirrors. His white left ass-cheek now boasted a black dick spurting stars!

"Now you are a member of the team. Welcome aboard, Adam."

Cole's words were emphasized by a resounding smack on the ass-cheek without the tattoo. Then to Adam's gawking and grunting surprise, the dark prick rearing from his jock-strap was thrust deep into the new employee's drooling asshole.

He was fucked again, and fucked good. Then it was Roman's turn.

As he took that enormous black cock deep into his ass, he stared up into Cole's dark eyes as the Master who had just fucked him stood beside his chest and slowly tortured his nipples by tugging on the clamps still attached.

He blurted out the first thing that came to mind. "Am I getting overtime?"

Cole and Roman burst into laughter.

"You bet. And a raise already, too!"

"Thank you, Sir! Ohhhhh ... yes! Thank you, Sir!"

STEAMY GEORGIA NIGHT
By Jay Starre

"It's hot as hell tonight! Doesn't this damn state ever cool down?"

Dean always grew bitchy when he was nervous. Bobby got fidgety. He was pacing around the pick-up truck while his partner lounged on the open tailgate and complained.

"It's Georgia. It's the South, and it's summer. What the hell did you expect? Take off your shirt if you're hot."

Bobby already had and wore only his shorts and sandals, displaying the lean physique so carefully honed in the gym. At twenty-two he was young enough to believe a hot body was the ticket to getting what he wanted. It worked for him more often than not.

Dean rolled his eyes but then followed his buddy's advice. He wore shorts, too, but instead of sandals, he sported hiking boots. He pulled off his tank top and tossed it in a ball onto the truck deck behind him. Dean joined Bobby in the gym regularly but wasn't as keen and the differences in their efforts were obvious in the results. He was well-built but had a layer of padding over his muscles from a diet of burgers, chips and pop, along with those less-than-eager workouts.

"Headlights! It must be Johnny."

"Let's hope so. If it's someone else, pretend we're drinking like we planned."

They had a case of beer prominently displayed on the tail gate beside Dean along with two open bottles. Each of them grabbed one and held it as if they had been drinking. It was just pretense, as neither drank nor used any of the drugs they pedaled when making a deal.

The headlights washed over them and the surrounding woods. The dirt road was isolated, and the little clearing they parked in was at least a mile from the main road. No one was likely to find them there at midnight, other than Johnny. He was their buyer.

The headlights approached slowly, rising and falling as the vehicle traveled over the road's bumpy surface. Finally, it halted just in front of them with those lights illuminating them in a garish glow.

They could make out the shape of another pick-up, which was a good sign. Johnny had told them he'd be driving a Chevy truck. The lights remained on as the engine was turned off, and the driver's door opened. In the glare, they couldn't see into the cab, but as only one person emerged, they assumed there was only one occupant. They were wrong.

"Hey dudes, it's Johnny here. How ya'll doin' tonight?"

"Hot and sweaty. We got what you ordered though, man. Some good shit, too," Dean answered for the both of them. He wasn't one to waste time. It was usually up to Bobby to be the sociable one.

"Want a beer, Johnny? They aren't cold, but they're wet, man," Bobby said as he came forward and shook hands with the Georgia boy.

They had been dealing with each other for over a year. Sometimes Johnny came up to Boston, and sometimes, like now, the pair of northerners came down to Georgia to deliver. So far it all had worked out for both sides.

Until now.

"Sure, but I know how impatient Dean is. Get out the stuff and let's make the exchange. I got the cash for ya'll."

Johnny's hand was very sweaty, and his voice was a little high, but he was smiling as usual, and his rush to get the deal done was typical. Bobby felt a tingle of alarm in his balls, where he most of his emotions stemmed from, but let it pass.

"Fucking right on. Let's do it and cut the bullshit," Dean agreed as he jumped up onto the truck deck and stepped up to the locked metal box that occupied the front two feet of it. It took only a moment to remove the padlock and open it. Buried in the bottom under stinky grease-stained rags and an assortment of tools were the packaged drugs.

He returned to the tail gate and hopped down to the grass. With a wink, he handed the package over. Johnny reached into his back pocket, pulled out an envelope, and handed it to Dean.

As Dean began to count, Bobby looked around. They had a pair of bright flashlights propped up on the sides of the deck but hadn't turned them on yet. He was about to suggest Johnny turn off his headlights and they use the flashlights instead when he heard a voice snap out at them from behind him.

"Don't move. Raise your arms, Boys, and hold 'em high. You are under arrest."

The dreaded words no drug dealer ever wanted to hear!

Pivoting toward that voice, Bobby spotted an enormous figure approaching in the glaring beam of those headlights. Behind him the passenger door of the truck stood wide open. Johnny had obviously ratted them out!

For an instant, he thought of running. But that figure was almost on top of him, and even in the blinding glare, it was clear he cradled a rifle in his arms.

"No sense in getting a load of buckshot in the ass, so don't even think of running into those damn woods, Boy. Both of you, put your hands on the tailgate and spread your legs."

The voice was deep and chilling, even with the lazy drawl of a southern accent. Shaking from head to toe, Bobby obeyed.

"Sorry, Boys. It was either me or you," Johnny whined as he stepped back to allow the cop to move in behind the pair.

Dean hadn't said anything yet, which was totally unlike him. When he was nervous, or scared out of his wits like now, he usually spit out a stream of nonsense. Bobby glanced at him and saw how big his blue eyes were. He was shaking as much as Bobby and biting his lip. He knew his buddy well and was certain he was about to burst into some kind of wild plea for mercy.

"Shut the hell up, Johnny, and hold the shotgun on them while I cuff and search them. Get those legs spread, Boys! Now, and I mean fucking right now!"

It happened so quickly neither of them had time to catch their breath. The cop reached over Dean and seized both his hands, whipped them around behind his back and cuffed them, shoving down on his neck with an elbow at the same time so that his face was planted on the tailgate.

A moment later, Bobby felt the huge bulk of the man move in behind him. His uniform pressed into his naked back and his giant hands grabbed his own and yanked them backwards then cuffed them. His head was forced down, and his face pressed against the tailgate. Boots kicked his sandals wide apart.

Big hands quickly ran over his naked back then down to his butt where they groped intimately in search of more drugs — or concealed weapons. Bobby shivered as he felt those massive hands on him, especially when they dug into his ass-crack and then up under his spread legs to grope his cock and balls.

He hadn't been able to see the officer's face in the glare. But when he reached over him to grab his hands, he noticed the cop was wearing a short-sleeved shirt. Bobby was able to get a look at the powerful forearms and the big paws. They were black. The officer was black.

Those black hands were rough as they groped him through his shorts, but they weren't as quick as they could have been. They clearly lingered, especially as they dug into his ass-crack. The hands were still there when the officer's deep drawl startled him with a frightening warning.

"I believe the situation calls for closer inspection. I am going to pull down your shorts, Boy. Don't move!"

The lingering hands moved lightning-fast. They were around his waist and tearing open the buttons on his fly then yanking down on both shorts and underwear in a split second. His shorts were tangled in his sandals briefly before the officer tore them off and tossed them up onto the deck of the pick-up. He was naked!

Breathless and shaking, Bobby felt warm Georgia air wafting up between his quivering butt-cheeks and around his dangling balls and cock. But there wasn't much time to think about that. Those massive black hands were groping him again. One hand probed between his compact ass globes while the other ran over his balls and cock.

His cock betrayed him. It began to stiffen immediately, regardless of how frightened he was. That's when his partner betrayed him, too.

"Look Officer, we'll do whatever you want if you'll let us go! My buddy here has one fine ass, as you can tell, and he can suck dick like a champ! I'm sure he'd be willing to oblige you."

Bobby's mouth dropped open. The asshole! What he said was true, Bobby had a sweet ass and sucked cock better than most, but so did Dean. The fucker had a nice round butt, and he slurped down dick with his plump lips like there was no tomorrow.

Before Bobby could blurt out anything in his defense, Dean blabbered on. "Sorry, Bobby, better you than me! Besides you might like it."

Fingers were roaming up and down his crack and a blunt thumb was rubbing against the rim of his snug asshole. He was shaking and fuming, but again before he could say anything, it was the officer who spoke in his ear.

"I am not a nice man. You are not going to just 'like it.' Understand? You are going to fucking love it, or at least pretend you love it, if you know what's good for you and your friend."

Bobby was stunned. Did that mean the cop was going to let them go? And did that mean those big black hands were going to do whatever they wanted to him? And what about the officer's cock? What did he have planned for it?

As if reading his victim's mind, the Georgia cop whipped it out, just like that. Unzipping and releasing it, the huge snake reared up to slap between Bobby's white butt-cheeks. He couldn't see it with his face down against the tail gate, but he sure as hell could feel it.

The thing throbbed against his flesh with heated rigidity. He could feel the enormous length lying against his crack, from his balls up to his waist. It had to be at least a goddamn foot long!

Facing Dean, he could see his buddy's blue eyes grow even bigger. He was looking back at Bobby's bare ass, and obviously getting a good look at that monster cop cock. "Holy shit, Bobby! Either you are gonna really like it — or I don't know what to say!"

"Sheriff Washington, are we gonna go ahead with the plan then? Ya'll want me to fetch the gear?"

Johnny's whine would have been irritating enough if Bobby wasn't already frightened to death, fuming mad at both his partner and the Georgia informer, and seething with a nervous sexual excitement he could hardly contain. It seemed like the pair, Sheriff Washington and Johnny had something planned.

And it involved that big black cock and Bobby's bare white butt.

"Of course we're going with the plan. Now get that fat ass of yours in gear. Give me the goddamn shotgun first."

The Sheriff stepped back, and the big cock moved away from his ass. Bobby breathed a sigh of relief, even though the reprieve was temporary. Something told him the officer would be true to his word, and he would have to put out or end up in a jail cell — for years maybe!

"If you think you're getting off easy, Boy, think again," he said to Dean as he casually cradled the shotgun in one arm and used the other hand to reach around the bent-over drug dealer's waist. Just like he'd done to Bobby, he tore open Dean's fly

Down came his shorts and skivvies. The officer yanked them off over his boots and tossed them up beside his partner's. He stood back slightly and then laughed. Bobby gasped as he felt the barrel of the shotgun suddenly slide up and down in the deep valley of his ass-crack.

"Just because you gave up your buddy doesn't mean you'll be getting a free ticket out of here tonight. No, Boy, you are going to help us use your partner here, you are going to hold him down and watch, and you are going to help feed him this black cock of mine, and more."

While the officer drawled out those words, he pulled the shotgun barrel out of Bobby's butt and shoved it between the plumper cheeks of Dean's round can. The blue-eyed drug dealer let out a little yelp and then blabbered out his response.

"Sure, Sheriff! Whatever you say, Sir! I'll be real helpful. I know what Bobby likes, and I can make sure he gives you whatever you want! Isn't that right, Bobby?"

He stared into Bobby's eyes, his words of betrayal hanging in the air. What did he expect him to say to that? Was there anything he could do except go along? Dean was actually doing the right thing. Whine, beg, go along with whatever the Sheriff wanted. His buddy was not stupid, even if he was a coward.

He nodded, but didn't trust himself to speak out loud.

"Well, well, boys. Bobby Mason and Dean Homer, looks like we're going to have us a gay old time tonight in the woods. I love a steamy Georgia night and a sweet piece of white boy to idle the evening away with. Now get up on the deck, boys! Crawl to the front with your faces down on the deck. Then Bobby, I want you on your knees facing me. Dean, you'll be standing behind him. Don't waste my time. Snap to it, goddamnit!"

The shotgun barrel pulled out of Dean's ass, and a big black hand snapped out to whack that round white butt, then quickly moved to smack Bobby's solid one. With their hands cuffed behind them, it wasn't easy to obey. But the pair did their best by scrambling to climb up onto the truck deck, raising one knee at a time to heave themselves onto the tailgate, then crawl forward into the back.

It was humiliating, crawling like that with their bare asses in the air and their hands cuffed behind them. That was certainly the Sheriff's intention. He guffawed loudly as he stepped up onto the truck deck to join them, joined by his lackey Johnny a moment later with arms full of gear.

"Take off their cuffs and shackle the skinny one to the posts, like I showed you this morning, Johnny. You two don't make any stupid moves; just cooperate, and you won't end up in jail. Understand?"

"Yes, Sir!" Dean bleated out instantly.

Bobby rolled his golden brown eyes. Dean sure was getting into it, and quickly. He realized he better do the same or worse might happen to them. "Yes, Sir," he piped up.

"Nice. You Boys just might work out in the long run. We'll see how you perform tonight."

Work out in the long run? What the hell did he have in store for them beyond tonight? Bobby had no time to fret over that one as Johnny moved in on him and whispered in his ear as he removed his cuffs. "I hate to do this to ya'll, but what choice did I have? If ya'll do as ya'll are told, ya'll won't have nothin' to worry about in the end. Just don't argue with the Sheriff."

Bobby could hardly be mad at Johnny. The kid was even younger than him at only twenty, and he could see how the hulk of a Sheriff had easily intimidated him. The one he was mad at was Dean, although he knew that was stupid.

Being mad helped him though. He was less afraid.

The crickets and frogs in the woods seemed to raise their voices in a demanding chorus in the daunting silence that followed as Sheriff Washington stood near the tailgate with his shotgun in his arms and watched while Johnny positioned the pair on the truck deck.

After removing their cuffs, he'd tossed out a thick blanket over the hard metal of the deck before he spread Bobby over it on his back. Then he fastened a pair of padded leather cuffs to each wrist, spread them wide and secured the silver chains attached to them to the posts in the front corners of the truck walls. The hapless drug dealer gritted his teeth and bit back a groan as he once more found himself cuffed and helpless.

It got worse. Johnny had more shackles and chains, which he immediately attached to each of Bobby's ankles. He pulled each ankle back and attached it to one of his wrists. He was spread-eagled with his ass in the air. Wide open.

He briefly struggled against the bonds and felt his body tense uncomfortably then realized that wasn't going to work. Exhaling deeply, he settled into the shackles. Once he did that, he was more comfortable than he thought possible. The cuffs supported his legs and arms and the padded shackles caused no pain to his wrists and ankles.

But that comfortable relaxation lasted only a moment. Of course he found himself staring up at the hovering Sheriff, a dark shadow back-lit by the glaring headlights. His cock was still out and Bobby could see it rearing up from his crotch. His asshole was totally exposed to the glowering cop and that big cock of his.

He clenched his nervous slot and groaned out loud. What would happen next?

The pair of heavy-duty flashlights they'd brought suddenly came on. Positioned by Johnny on either side of the tool box in front of the spread-eagled Bobby, they illuminated the three of them, Bobby spread-eagled on his back, Dean standing nervously just in front of him with his bare calves against the tool box, and the hulk of a Sheriff hovering over them.

They were hardly three of a kind. Bobby was lean and muscular with a buzz-cut of ink-black hair, golden brown eyes and a narrow face with a dimpled, prominent chin. Dean was thicker and shorter with shaggy blond hair, those bright blue eyes and a plump almost cherubic face. The Sheriff was physically menacing, both tall and broad, but had surprisingly soft features. His large dark eyes were wide-set, his nose broad and his mouth full and lips wet. He was smiling, white teeth in straight rows and the tip of a plump tongue just showing.

For an instant, perhaps fooled by that engaging expression, Bobby believed it was all a joke and the Sheriff intended on calling it off and letting them go with a warning.

"Looks like I've got some fine ass and mouth to work over tonight. Let's get started."

So much for calling it off! A moment later, still smiling, the Sheriff stepped in close enough to lay his pipe of a cock down in Bobby's open crack. The giant meat pulsed against his sensitive flesh, like some kind of writhing black snake about to burrow its way up his innards. Bobby let out a groan and shuddered all over.

"We won't be needing this shotgun, Johnny, but keep it handy. Get naked and come on over here and help. It's going to take all three of us to fill this Boy up."

Bobby shuddered again and moaned. What the hell did this big black Sheriff have in mind for him? And what could he do about it? Shut up and put out, that was about it.

His two fellow drug dealers apparently suffered no qualms about sacrificing him as they quickly followed Sheriff Washington's nasty orders. Before he knew it, both Dean and Johnny were busy playing with his butt, spreading it wider while rubbing the Sheriff's massive prick as it continued to pulse in the valley of his crack with a seething heat.

Those hands all over his ass had him squirming but what happened next had him thrashing.

"Before we grease him up, let's get him nice and wet with our tongues, Boys. Let's eat him out."

Down came that dark smiling face, replacing the huge cock with a broad tongue. On his back, Bobby stared up at the trio surrounding him, illuminated in the garish light of truck headlights and the twin beams of powerful flashlights. All three faces pressed into his spread ass.

Sheriff Washington didn't waste any time. His tongue dove right into the pink slot in the center of that divide. He tickled it with the tip of his tongue and then probed, then tickled it some more before clamping his lips over it and starting to suck voraciously.

"Oh my god. Oh fuck. Oh hell," Bobby mumbled as those big lips and fat tongue took control of his hole.

But that was only the half of it. Both Johnny and Dean were busy licking all over his butt with their own tongues. They actually looked a little alike. Both had shaggy mops of hair, Dean blond and Johnny sandy-brown, and they both had plump faces and round mouths. Those mouths were busy licking ass before they met in the middle and began to kiss.

Bobby wallowed in the slurping tongue-bath, still frightened and angry, but finding himself surrendering to the excitement of it all. If he tried not to think about jail and all that shit, and merely gave in to the wet and warm attack on his ass and hole, he would be able to enjoy it!

Then that tongue managed to probe its way past his sphincter and begin burrowing its way up his fuck-chute. As that fat appendage dug around inside him, he felt himself melting around it. The steamy night seemed even hotter, and as sweat broke out from every pour of his body, he felt the same happening to the three attacking him.

Their tongues and lips were wet with spit, their faces coated in sweat, their hands, too, and their bare chests and thighs slick and slippery against his own. The Sheriff alone remained clothed, although his huge cock reared bare and glorious from his unzipped fly.

He reared from his feast with a smack of his big lips and drawled out more commands. "You too eat some of this fine ass before we get to the next step."

He wrapped one big black hand around the back of Dean's neck and forced his face against Bobby's spit-gobbed hole. His pal was quick to start licking and sucking on the gooey orifice. Bobby writhed in his chains and heaved up into that mouth as he watched the Sheriff latch his other hand onto Johnny's neck and pull him into a sloppy kiss. Drool dribbled from their mouths onto Bobby's pale ass.

Sheriff Washington made them change places, yanking Dean's face out of Bobby's ass and replacing it with Johnny's as he clamped his plump lips over the blond drug dealer's. Johnny had the luck to eat out an ass already well-primed by the two preceding him. The hole oozed spit and gaped open as he attacked it with his pointed tongue to stroke and tickle it.

Four stiff cocks jutted from four crotches as the wild ass attack continued. Washington himself finished the feast off with a final clamp of his lips over the violated hole. He sucked it nearly inside out before he pulled out and rose to his feet.

"Now that we got this Boy all wet and sloppy, time to feed him some good old Georgia cop cock."

Bobby stared up at the looming cock he was speaking of, gasping as he contemplated its girth and length. He had never taken a cock up his ass that size before. It pressed down into his crack, and he shuddered as the heat of it seemed to burn his sensitive flesh.

"Lick it before you grease it up, Boys."

They obeyed eagerly. Bobby had to wonder if they were just happy it wasn't going to be their tight assholes getting boned by that giant rod, or if they were trying to make the big Sheriff happy, or it they really wanted to get that black meat in their mouths.

Dean ended up getting the first real mouthful of it as the Sheriff's grip on the back of his neck held him in place and he drove deep. The blond gurgled and snorted as more than half of the dark tube drilled past his pink lips.

The cock was yanked out and shoved into Johnny's mouth. They were still kneeling on either side of Bobby's ass with their faces down in his crack as Washington took turns face-fucking them. Between feeding it to the pair, he rubbed the gooey shaft all over Bobby's crack and spit-dripping butt-lips. Then he crammed it back into their mouths one after the other.

Bobby stared up at the Sheriff's face, fascinated by the soft look of it, the way he smiled so easily and even chuckled now and then. He found himself wanting to trust the man, wanting to please him, wanting to be on his good side, rather than being the criminal he intended on punishing.

But then he looked at the mammoth cock sliding in and out of his gurgling friends' pursed lips, and thought of how the smiling cop intended on ramming it up his ass, whether he liked it or not, and found himself once more terrified of the massively-built Sheriff.

The brutal truth, he had them by the balls! He could still arrest them and toss them in jail if it suited his purposes. And for the moment, Bobby was in shackles and helpless to do anything except obey his every whim, no matter how degraded and nasty.

"Get the grease, Johnny."

Bobby moaned out loud. It was time! His hole pouted and dripped against the tube of that fat black flesh where it lay on his crack and Dean sucked on it. Whether he wanted that cock up his ass or not, his hole seemed eager enough for it.

The shaggy-haired Georgia boy was quick to obey their dark master. He reached over to his bag beside them and pulled out a tube of Love-Lube. He was actually grinning as he aimed it at that giant cock and squeezed.

A thick stream of clear goo landed on the dark snake just as Dean pulled off with a smack of his pretty lips. Johnny continued to squirt the goo all over that cock as the pair rubbed it in with their hands. It was Dean who massaged the slippery stuff over Bobby's balls and stiff cock, too, while Johnny continued to smear it over the length of the Sheriff's giant cock.

"Sweet, Boys. Now get some of that over the head and that hole."

He pulled his cock back enough so that the knob settled between Bobby's well-eaten ass-lips. He could see it there, a flared crown that looked like some kind of dark magic mushroom. It was gigantic!

Washington continued to smile down at him as his pair of helpers rubbed the slippery lube all over his cock-head and into Bobby's hole at the same time. Slippery fingers rubbed his ass-lips and dipped between them as he gasped and squirmed. One finger, then two, then even three probed his hole while they rubbed the flared knob that pressed against his ass entrance.

With all that attention, his hole was fortunately primed for it when it came. Dean was the one to push the head into him, turning his big blue eyes downward and staring into Bobby's golden orbs as he gauged his pal's reaction.

"How's that feel, Bobby? It's fucking huge I know, but I bet you like it," he said.

"Don't be a smart-ass, Dean Homer. In fact, stand up, and you, too, Johnny, so I can finger your fat asses while I fuck your skinny buddy."

Of course they didn't really have fat asses, nor was Bobby skinny, but whatever the Sheriff said, they weren't about to contradict. The pair stood up, huddled close against Bobby's bent-back thighs, their hands still down in his ass-crack as the Sheriff reached into the gooey mess and coated his huge black fingers with slippery lube.

Bobby gasped. He shuddered as the flared knob strained his ass-lips while Dean pushed it against them and slowly between. He did enjoy a glimmer of bitter satisfaction at the look of startled shock on Dean's face as that big black hand probed his plump ass and a pair of greased fingers cork-screwed up into his snug hole.

Johnny grunted as the same thing happened to him, but both were smart enough not to let those dark fingers violating their tender holes deter them from the task at hand. They were supposed to feed that huge black snake to their shackled pal. They did it with a vengeance.

The flange of that giant knob hovered just against the rim of Bobby's hole, stretching it mercilessly. Shiny lube glistened in the glaring light. Both drug dealers used their fingers to push at it. The lips quivered wildly, then caved in. The black head slid between them to disappear within the pink hole.

"Ohhhhhhhh ... what are you doing to me?"

Bobby's moan grew louder as the pair used their fingers to push more of the black snake into his ass. And louder as an inch of the fat shank followed the blunt crown.

"What are we doing to you, boy?" Sheriff Washington replied, staring down into Bobby's golden eyes. "We are stuffing you with black cock, and once that's done, you will be totally changed. No longer will you be a low-life drug peddler. You will be my personal servant. You will belong to Sheriff Washington, asshole, balls, cock, heart and soul."

Bobby had no idea what he meant by that. His servant? Belong to him? He grunted as his two partners pushed even more hot cock into his churning gut. The giant knob pressed its way deeper while the thick shaft stretched open his tender lips as it slithered slowly beyond them. He was totally focused on the aching sensations in his hole, and those dark eyes boring into his from above, until he realized his two buddies were experiencing some deep gut-probing, too.

"How many fucking fingers you got up my ass, Sheriff?" Dean blurted out.

"That was only two, boy. How does three feel?"

"Uggghhhh! Yes Sir! Whatever you want Sir! We're your boys, Sir!"

Bobby tore his eyes from the Sheriff's and looked at his buddy's round white ass hovering above him to the left. A massive black hand was buried between the smooth cheeks. He could imagine those three greased fingers digging around in poor Dean's hole, and had to smile for the first time. Served him right.

His attention returned to his own violated hole as more of that black snake eased deeper into his gut. Where was that head now? It had slid past his tender prostate and was burrowing somewhere high up inside. It felt fucking amazing. He realized it was time to stop being a little pussy and man up.

"Fuck yeah, Sir! Give me that big black cock! Stuff my ass with it! I'm all yours!"

Speaking the words out loud seemed to make them come true. With a loud slurp, his asshole expanded and pushed outward to gulp in another several inches of fat black shaft. Johnny and Dean, both grunting from the three black fingers pawing at their own guts, took advantage of the yielding sphincter to shove even more cock inside it.

"That's it, Boy! You know who your Sheriff is now, don't you? Take that black anaconda all the way up your hungry hole. You know what's good for you, don't you? For the first time in your life, you know what you have to do, don't you? Don't you?"

Bobby wasn't entirely sure what the hell the Sheriff was talking about, but he knew what he had to say, and do. "Yes, Sir! I know what I have to do! I gotta take all that fucking black cock up my greedy fucking asshole!"

Amazing even himself, he relaxed his anal muscles and heaved upwards, his ankles and wrists clattering against their shackles. His efforts, combined with the eager co-operation of his two partners, forced that massive black cock all the home, right to the plump black nads.

"Hell yeah, Boy. You have my cock balls-deep. Now you're on the right track. After we fuck that ass good, we'll talk about what you have to do next."

The steamy night got even steamier. Now that the Sheriff had his cock buried to the hilt, he no longer needed Dean and Johnny's help. He ordered them to kiss each other while they jerked each other's stiff cocks over Bobby's plugged ass. One of his hands remained in each of their round butts and probed deep while he lay into Bobby's upended ass with his massive prick.

It was a good thing Bobby had mustered up the will power to relax his asshole because the Sheriff quickly usurped his authority by fucking it with a relentless savagery. With his fingers rooting deep in the other two drug dealer's poor holes, he thrust downwards into Bobby's lubed slot with his massive cock.

All he could do was groan and squirm and take it as his pink hole oozed lube around the black pole driving down into it. The Sheriff obviously enjoyed what he was doing, shoving deep, pulling out until the flared head hovered right at the sphincter, and teasing it briefly before plunging home. Over and over and over. He knew how to master a hole, undoubtedly.

At the same time, between satisfied grunts, he laid out the new ground rules for his trio of fuck-boys.

"Now, like Johnny here, the two of you will no longer serve your drug dealer pimps, but serve your new pimp, me. You will go back to Boston, and you will continue dealing with those scum, but you will do everything under my personal supervision."

His black cock rammed deep into Bobby's gut. His fingers twisted and thrust up Dean and Johnny's gooey holes. The toads in the ponds hidden in the woods croaked out their encouragement.

"You will return here to me for further instructions once a month. And of course, you will serve my big black cock at that time and whenever I deem it necessary. Understood? Understood?"

His cock drove home with a squishing certainty to emphasize his words. His fingers plunged far up Dean and Johnny's holes.

Following a chorus of squeals, all three young drug dealers shouted out their answers.

"Yes, Sir!"

"Whatever ya'll say, Sir!"

"Fuck yeah, Bobby and I are your men, Sir!"

With hot cock throbbing in his battered gut, Bobby realized what he was promising. Unlike Dean, who jumped on the band wagon as soon as he heard the music playing, the young drug dealer thought ahead to all the ramifications of what this big sheriff demanded of them.

"Are you prepared to be my little snitches, boys? Are you?"

Punctuating that demand with action, Sheriff Washington rammed his black cock balls-deep into Bobby's churning gut and thrust his dark fingers far up Dean and Johnny's well-lubed holes.

The three squealed and squirmed as they shouted out their enthusiastic promises. Bobby, on his back with his wrists and ankles shackled and huge cock buried in his ass, understood completely his new situation. He would be a snitch, under the Sheriff's grinding black knuckle and his to command. It would be dangerous, the dudes they dealt with were hardly nice guys, but dealing drugs was dangerous, too.

And there was a definite bonus involved. That huge cock throbbed inside him, stuffing him to the max. He couldn't deny it. He loved it.

"Time to seal those promises with a juicy load! Here it comes!"

The Sheriff yanked his cock out of Bobby's hole and sprayed. A gusher of jizz erupted from the dark head. It flew in an arc upwards, then descended to land on Bobby's face. He snorted in the stench of raw cum while being quick to lap up what fell on his lips and chin.

Both Dean and Johnny joined in with flying loads of their own. The Sheriff's fingers up their asses had prodded their prostates while they had jerked each other off over Bobby's upended ass. Their cum splattered it in a gooey mess.

"Boys, do your pal a favor and help him come, too."

They understood. Even as they were still dripping, they each crammed a pair of fingers up Bobby's well-stretched hole and grabbed his stiff dick to pump it at the same time. The pink slot gaped wide due to the girth of that black cock recently pummeling it. All four fingers slipped in easily.

With hands on his cock and up his ass, the taste of cum on his tongue, and the intense gaze of the Sheriff bearing down on him, Bobby surrendered to his own orgasm. Flopping in his shackles, moaning and grunting, he sprayed his own belly and chest with a juicy load.

The stink of sweat and cum was rife in the Georgia night as Bobby was finally released and the trio were allowed to dress under the watchful eye of the Sheriff.

"Get your white asses back to Boston and do as I've told you. You'll be back here in a month with details of all your contacts. Understood?"

Dean piped up with his usual nonsense. "Yes, Sir! And does that mean we'll be getting some more of that black cock of yours? Bobby sure did love it, Sir, and he'll be eager to serve you again, I'm sure!"

The big sheriff laughed out loud. Bobby, mad again at Dean for throwing him under the bus, was mollified by the black officer's casual response.

"Hell yeah. This big black snake of mine can't get enough white boy ass. Next time, though, I believe it will be your turn to give it up. Agreed?"

Dean's blond head bobbed as he agreed enthusiastically, although Bobby noted the way his blue eyes got big and he cringed slightly. He knew his pal well. Dean would do as he was told if he had to, but would try to get out of doing any of the hard work. So be it.

Rubbing his ass and walking a little unsteadily, he had to admit he wouldn't feel too bad if he was the one to get fucked next time again. The memory of that thick hot meat drilling deep into his butt tunnel was still very fresh. It had been pretty fucking amazing.

As they climbed back into their truck, Bobby turned and looked back at the Sheriff. He was watching, a big smile on his face. He nodded and winked.

Bobby couldn't help himself. He kind of liked the cop. And he couldn't say that about any of the drug dealers he knew.

"What a wild night, Bobby, huh? And now we gotta snitch for the big black bastard. Oh well, at least we aren't going to jail! You liked that fat cock up your ass, didn't you? I could tell! I'm sure I can work my charm on the Sheriff next time and get him to fuck you instead of me. How's that sound?"

Bobby let his buddy ramble on as he stared out the window at the Georgia woods passing by. But he had to smile. It looked as if it might all work out in the end.

MUTTS
By Diesel King

My new boy, Bubba, nearly pissed in his pants when he got up from the table to look out the window. As he looked outside onto the back property, I thought it was as good of a time as any to remind his flaky white ass that he just put down his sloppy John Hancock on my contract. He balked. Rambling on and on about some foolish nonsense that it wasn't legally binding. I let him know right then and there that I didn't give a shit what the law said out there. As far as I was concerned, my two hundred and forty-nine acres of prime North Cackalacky real estate was sovereign land that was ruled and dictated by me. I also thought it was good time to remind him of the unflattering pictures I had of his sweet-looking face dolled up so pretty under a red wig with his pouty lips wrapped around my mighty anaconda. That I had a few more pictures of him in a leather muzzle hanging by a suspended metal bar by fist mitts and stirrups showing off his swollen cunt hungry for some more pipe. My favorite of them all was these pictures I had of him farting out a bubbly wad of cum from his gaping hole with a ton of soupy white slime pooled on the floor beneath his sling.

All digitized and ready to be sent through electronic mail to his young wife and other snobby family members with the looming threat of them being sent out to the local newspaper for further embarrassment.

The scenario always plays out the same from this point, even with the blackmail hanging over their heads. They look outside and see the well-trained dogs. The fear of God is ignited in them. They get frantic and scared and they try to run, thinking of ways to outmaneuver me. They think that because I'm a short fucker that they can subdue me. They think because I'm such a big guy that I don't have agility on my side. And then when I react with lightening speed to tackle their ass to the ground, they want to act surprised and get offended and start to scream their fucking heads off, hoping that somewhere someone out there in the world might hear their pitiful cries.

Back in the day, when I was a ruthless motherfucker, it was nothing for me to hold them down, rip off their pants, and rape their sorry asses raw. No lube, no nothing. And if they weren't already thoroughly ruined by that humiliation, then I would put my big boot to their bellybutton and take that long post-nutt piss across their face and body and let them stew in it for about a week or so. They start feeling pretty dirty inside, pretty fucked up after a full week of not being able to bathe. They even take to tonguing a patch of skin just to feel an ounce of cleanliness. They get weaker and weaker with each passing minute, coupled that with the thoughts of having their sweet cherry busted wide open by the biggest dick this side of Interstate 40 in the most gruesome way to keep them company. Their initial anger over everything that happened quickly subsides to full submission needing desperately to find some kind of worthy validation in this world. So what better man to do that for them than the one that broke them down in the first place?

That was back in the day, of course, when I was most horny and it was urgent for me to establish my black dominance quickly in these racist woods. Nowadays, I try to impress my pieces with my quick whip in tying their flailing limbs in elaborate knots that is as beautifully sinister as it is worldwide artistically admired.

Bubba was no different, as I tackled his ass to the ground, tied his hands behind his back to his legs bent and crossed. He was still shirtless from our sex earlier, but I made the terrible mistake of letting him slip back into his standard-issued camo pants, which meant that after tying him up so elegantly I had to whip out my bowie knife to cut through them and his cheap jockstrap just to get him back naked. He shivered at the coolness of the wide blade against his alabaster skin, and started to bawl those crocodile tears. I had to laugh at his pathetic ass when he followed through on peeing on himself, begging and pleading for me not to hurt him. I got tired of his mouth and slapped some duct tape over it for effect.

I walked away to let him ponder over my next move.

When I came back, I came back in full leather regalia with a few things in my hand. Bubba seemed in awe of my big Wesco boss boots, my dry leather chaps, and studded pouch that were all tongue-cleaned to like-new perfection by my last boy. My gear didn't end there, as I also sported my custom-made studded full body harness with matching wrist cuffs that I got made down in Charlotte.

I came up behind him, so he didn't see me fitting him for his locking collar. He fought, but not nearly as hard as I would have expected out of an army man like him. He well made up for his lack of it when I took some thick lube nearby and smeared it generously over his poor puckered hole. I finger-fucked it a bit to see if it had that tight snap back that I expected out of a recently deflowered twenty-two year old. Bubba didn't seem to disappoint, even after having his hole reamed by this thick twelve-inch donkey dick. But I got him good when I swiftly stuffed his tight butt hole with that black butt plug. It looked so damn funny with its dog tail end hooking up like that. Even funnier after I slapped that canine-face muzzle on him and cut his wrists free to slip on his rubber puppy paws. His bare feet were still bound as I debated if I should spare his knees with any pads. As I weighed my options, I went ahead and locked his cock and balls to a chained leash. And before I even thought to consider what to do with his lower extremities again, I had already cut his ankles free and was dragging the poor sap across my wooden deck into the heavily shaded element.

He resisted me like most of my new pets. I don't seem to take it personally like I used to, though. I had to mature to the place where I had to accept that it was just the fear of the unknown getting to them. So I don't yank their chains and scramble their delicate eggs anymore. I don't have the fucking patience to listen them yelp and regroup anymore after such a painful jolt. I know now that as long as I get them to the top of the stairs without hurting them, I'm good. It's like something magical happen when I get them down that first step. I don't know if it is them knowing that they are not alone with so many other dogs to play with or they're so overwrought with fear that they realized that they need a master trainer like me to navigate them through the ins and outs of this tough terrain.

I led Bubba out onto the grassy lawn, where I spiked his chain in the middle of the yard between four other rubber pawed mutts angered and watchful of his new presence.

Including Bubba, I owned twenty-nine naked dogs. With one free of my hand and four others chained to the old trees around him, I had two lapping up water from the doggie dishes, one eating out of a bowl, seven fenced in the doggie suites, eight running around the large shed out back intense with dog fighting training, and six more dogs free to roam about the large property with the extra added bonus of any of them being able to mount any of the other dogs that were free of their tails or muzzles.

I had all kinds of dogs on my property, from genuine virgins to total bareback sluts, barely legal to as old as dirt, incredibly smooth to abominably hairy, with just about all of them being white.

At the time, the twenty-nine dogs on the property were all male. I tried hard to keep the number well under fifty whenever possible. Next to finding willing strays that wanted a place to call home, the numbers only spiked that high whenever I kept the dogs in mixed company. I hardly ever did that anymore after so many of the female dogs, or bitches, kept on getting pregos by some anonymous breeder. It wasn't so much as them getting knocked up that was the problem as it was them coming back hoping to track down the father to hold them responsible. The way those bitches got passed around, it could've been a number of men, not excluding me and many legion of trained guests or even some of the dogs that were free to get at them while they were in heat. And given as many mutts as those bitches probably took on my land, there weren't that many shows on television that did that many free DNA tests.

Though, to be fair and reasonable, over the course of sixteen years that I've had the place, I had close to about sixty-five hundred dogs trample across my property. As I said before, a number of them were strays, others faithful weekenders, with a healthy mix of the curious and those seeking a simple do-the-fuck-as-you-told-life in between. With maintenance and upkeep and the need to feed and house my dogs, the expenses have always been astronomical. Yet, I've always managed to make a hefty profit the way some of those mutts throw their money at my feet as if I'm some great cult leader bound to lead them to the promise land. I like to think so. But that wasn't to say that I hadn't been forced to cut my losses a time or two to maintain, putting a few of my dogs down. Not by euthanizing them, of course. That would be inhumane. What I do however is sell them off to some shifty-eyed trucker looking for man's best friend to join him on his travels or auctioned them off at basement bargains to some needy master. And those that weren't gotten by these means forced me to throw them in the back of my sports utility vehicle to take them some remote place never to find their way back again.

I would like to say that I got it like that, king of the heap with having so many dogs. Sure, I got a big black uncut dick that those white bitches and boys drool over every chance they get. Even though I own and dominate my piece of land like an emperor to his empire, I'm far from a true prize to the outside world.

I am neither handsome nor charmed. I am blacker than black, shorter than short, gruffer than gruff. I have a big flat nose and a hard rounded belly made for the ages. Big full juicy lips and yellow bulging bug eyes where the white is suppose to be. Next to my big dick, I have a wide chest and blocky arms that I'm quite proud of, something that built up well after tussling with all these dogs after all these years.

I could fit in well as a common thug on the streets of some big city up north, if I was corporately trained and raised as a pariah in the black upper crust of rural western Virginia.

Enough about me though, I got Bubba just the same, and with the gray clouds rolling in fast and his ass giving me no time to set up a temporary doghouse for him, he had to brave the element, come rain, thunder, or lightning.

He's army, I reminded myself. He's a tough mutt.

I walked over to one of the doggie suites nearby and took a dog out. I forgot what I named this particular mutt, so I don't call him by name. He tried to go for my studded codpiece, so I grab his ball leash, tugged, and walked him under my deck and ordered him to lick my boots clean.

I took my stance near the bottom of the stairwell leading up to the deck while he did this as I looked out at my many other dogs throughout the property. Because I still had on my leather gear and its incredible smell started to get to me with a lapping dog nibbling at my boots, I started to feel immediately that kind of way again.

"Dino! Bunky!" I bellowed out into the pouring rain.

I startled the dog at my feet, but he was trained well enough not to lose his stride.

"Bunky! Dino!" I bellowed out again.

I knew that those mutts hadn't gone far. The collars around each of the dog's necks prevents them from doing so, as each caller came equipped with a tracking device and a metal strip that prevented them from getting outside of the electric fence. I felt that fifteen acres was wide enough of a span for the privilege few to explore a slice of the majestic property, and enough of an ear range to come running whenever I called them back in.

"Come here, boys!"

Dino popped out first behind the dog fighting shed. He looked around the corner of the house where I was and came running. Dino was an Irish thoroughbred with dull reddish brown hair. He always amazed me with the swiftness he moved on all fours, almost like he was naturally born that way the way his muscles bulged and flexed as he panted at my feet.

Bunky popped up from afar down near the creek. Instead of always running, he sort of hand these enormous leaps forward that I would think would hurt his knees and shins. If it did, the good boy never let on. Bunky was a German-Scottish mix breed that was both big and particularly hairy around the forearms with meaty tits that craved attention and a loveable rounded belly made for keg-guzzling, as he, too, eventually made his way at my feet.

"Take this bootlicker out yonder and have some fun with him, won't you, boy," I barked down at Dino, who pawed the leash and tugged the bootlicking mutt by the balls off into the rain. "And don't forget to put him back in his cage after you're done with him."

Dino wasted no time running out to one of the oil dispensers scattered about the property and immediately mounted the howling dog just as the wind was picking up.

"Come with me, boy," I winked at Bunky, moving over to the adjacent basement door.

I tried not to show any favoritism toward any of my pets, but if I had to, my attention would most definitely go to the oversized dog. Not only hands down as my favorite pet currently on my property but also amongst one of my favorite pets of all-time.

With his full gruffly beard and big ball of a build, even I would've never guessed that much when he showed up at my place about five years ago.

Bunky was one of those strays that heard about my place from one of my sell-offs he met while out on the road. My dog sold Bunky on my utopia and he came springing at full speed from the Midwestern ranch where he hailed. Bunky unquestionably made his mark on me when he showed up on my doorstep, butt-naked with a collar fitted around his thick neck and his clothes neatly folded in a pile next to him. I wasn't sure if I was impressed or if I wanted to burst out laughing. Either way, I simply refused to fuck the old bastard after he thoroughly treated me to a few outstanding blowjobs. At the time, I lacked a serious appreciation for a mature dog, making a mockery of them at every step as I equated youth with beauty and being blessed with a tight ass. So I put him through the ropes of transforming from man into beast without a tail or a muzzle, and took him outside where I had twenty or so free dogs roaming the property at the time. I gave him a few simple instructions, and before long the mutt had a line of dogs growing from his ass. I left him be, giving it no second thought. When I looked outside of my bedroom window the next day, Bunky was still there where I left him white-knuckling it on his hands and knees taking dog dick with some dried crud speckled across his beard.

"He ain't moved?" I asked my then-midnight overseer as I made way out into the yard.

"Not once, boss!" The overseer beamed in sheer amazement. "Not even to flinch or to scratch or to give his arms and legs a break from that stationary position."

I should've known that the mutt was special back then. But with a yard full of virgins and wet bitches that needed be plucked, I still didn't bother too much with an old fart like him. Not even to clean him up. And when some of my regular guests started to take pity on the cute mutt, they decided to clean him up to use him and abuse him. I was floored when the waves of guests passed right by their favored usuals just to get to Bunky. My sex room was siphoned off for weekends on end with special reservation just to have Bunky in their presence. I got high-dollar offers in the tens of thousands range from men and women alike to rent out the ol' boy or to buy him from out under me. Still, I wasn't convinced that he was anywhere near special, but smart enough to be leery of selling him off after he handed himself off so willingly to me. My outlook soon changed when I came across Bunky lying back in a sling with some tit clamps on. He was doing the usual suck and fuck on both ends. But what made it somewhat special was the earnestness in everything he was doing. While he sucked one oral top off furiously, he reached back and started twisting the nipples of the top egging him on to drain his filthy load in his mouth. As for the top that was straight fucking him, he was doing everything in his power internally and externally to get him off. All this while bathing in arches of golden piss, never once thinking of losing his stride in any of his tasks. An even prouder moment for me came when I saw him splayed out on the heavy worktable getting double-fucked in the rear. He was sucking off one of my guests while giving two more thorough hand jobs. It wasn't like he was insatiable or anything, as it was that he knew that he had this job to do, and he knew he had to do amazingly well to ever do it again. And when I finally gave in to having the butch blob to myself, it was like his sweet mouth was made just for me. Everything I leveled against the fuck after that was both his pleasure and mine. There was no other way to explain it.

"You need to take a leak, boy?" I asked, entering my cinderblock dungeon room.

Bunky shook his head and whimpered.

"Then you know what to do then, boy." I said confidently.

Bunky seemed at a loss for a moment, not knowing what to do since there was so many things that he knew that I liked to do to him in that dungeon. So I made it crystal clear once I removed one of my boots for him. He looked at me with a smile in his eyes and cautiously fixed his way between the parallel bars and placed his forearms on the metal rack before them.

I took off my other boot and put both in front of his downward face. I let him look at them, giving him the wordless command not to touch them in any form. I went back to the back of the room to retrieve enough rope from a huge spool to execute what I wanted to do. When I returned with the rope with another bowie knife to Bunky, he proved to be obedient in keeping his hands and his tongue in his mouth and away from my boots. However, his nose was quite busy in inhaling the foot funk that escaped its leather confinement.

"Good boy," I patted the big mutt on the head with.

I squatted, taking part of the rope and tying both of his meaty forearms to the metal rack beneath. After I had got him immobile from that end, I reached over behind me and scored his mouth with a ball gag. He waited with great reserve as I tied his ankles to the parallel bars giving him enough room to spread his legs wide enough to accommodate me. Once I felt that he was good, I checked the parallel bars he was in between and tied a rope high above his back to link the two. I took another piece of rope and tied it in the middle of that rope with more than a plenty left to spare, squishing the top of my smelly boot and tying it to his face in a sea of elaborate knots across his big head.

"Mutts like you like sniffing smelly things." I laughed, swatting Bunky fat ass with my hand.

I kept on hitting him there until I saw his skin turn red, and even then I didn't stop until heard him sniffing between his bouts of whimpering.

"Sniff good, doggy, sniff good." I mouthed encouragingly with my hand taking a harder stance against his fleshy derriere.

I spanked Bunky for the longest time. His ass was fire-engine red by the time my hand got tired of slapping it, developing newer calluses in the process. And after I felt like Bunky was taking in my boot funk like it was the natural air he normally breathed, I rubbed my dick on the top of his crack and eased my way into it.

Bunky was a big boy with a fluff of meatiness that only seemed to solidify his masculinity. It was because of that extra meat that he had such a deep crack that even with nearly twelve inches of dick sprouting from my crotch, it was nearly impossible to give him every inch. But with so much dick to spare, it only left out three or so inches after I got all that I could inside of him. Of course, looking at him with my big boss boots attached to his face, I was in no rush to do that.

"Oh, shit! Oh, yeah ... shit!" I groaned, feeling the warm asshole swallow up the best inches of my dick. "This is what I'm talking about!"

Even through the ball gag in his mouth, I could hear Bunky howl into the smelly boot. That seemed to really turn me on. Not the howling itself, but knowing that the only way he could take air was inhaling what sweated from the bottom of my feet.

I seemed to go crazy at the thought and decided to hold my dick right there inside of the mutt. Holding it there, sniffing my boot and having me inside of him, only made the white dog go crazy, bucking back and rearing up his ass ready for me to fuck him. As an owner of so many dogs, I don't often like to be told what to do by one of my mutts, but this was an exception as I began to fuck him, ramming my dick into him as deep as I could.

"Oh, damn. Open up that hole for me, Bunky." I said after some time, feeling like the more I pounded his hole the flatter his ass got. The more I felt this way, the more I plowed into him relentlessly, extracting the real grunts and groans out of him through my boot.

"Just inhale, you no good mutt, just inhale that funky shit," I barked.

The more I went at that hole the more Bunky showed me how hungry he was for me to be inside of him. He wanted me, and I gave him me to the point that I had his knees buckling underneath me.

"Damn," I groaned, holding his big ass up for the continuous fuck. "You got that kind of ass that makes me want to paint your filthy walls white."

So I pounded and pounded some more, a good ways from exploding when it just proved too much for the boot-sniffer. He started yelping and weeping and the next thing I know he lifted up his leg and creamed down his thigh, only to be followed by a little bit of piss.

"Bad doggy," I grunted and chuckled after I learned what had just happened.

But that didn't deter me. I just kept right on fucking him for about a good fifty minutes longer with him letting me know at every stroke that it was his pleasure to serve me like this, taking care of his owner this way, stroking my dick with his ass as if he was still going hard for his very first nutt.

"I'm going to paint your walls, mutt. I'm going to paint your fucking walls!"

My load poured inside of his guts. It just kept pouring and pouring and pouring until everything inside of me kicked out.

I took a deep breath and looked at Bunky with my boot tied to his face and thought he was the prettiest dog that I had ever groomed.

But my attention soon waned as I pulled out of him and moved toward the door underneath the deck and looked out at one of my many dogs hungry for a sniff of my other boot.

THE ESCAPE AT CHATEAU MOREGO
By Diesel King

The Great Count of Morego stood silently over the forlorn body, still gracious in admiring its firm stocky muscles as the unique but handsome being slept soundlessly at the Count's sizeable feet.

The Count and his many guardsmen laid the hairless creatures with the large glowing white wings in the middle of the garden, under the moonlit stars. The Count desired a chance of scenery for the human-like creature he had christened Angelwings, an unusual being that he had under lock and key for several months that he kept hidden in a secluded chamber not far from the dungeon of the sprawling manor. The Count believed, with the festivities going on over in the nearby rolling hills that the gray ambiguous skin covering the beast was more becoming of the night.

It was where the Count came across Angelwings for the very first time, at night, and in that particular garden. The Count was on his way to make good use of the young farmhands who double as lowly hustlers after the harvest moon in the nearby local villages. As the Count was leaving the chateau, his eye caught a shimmering flash of light dance down from the heavens above. The Count was anxious to ignore such a spectacle. His dark nature was throbbing at full staff, with the knowledge that somewhere out there in the nearby villages was an untouched peasant lad awaiting the nightly thrust of his doleful spear and viscid semen. He was very much undeterred until, from his angle, in the front, he saw that the dash of light was moving toward the back of his manor.

The Count was concerned about his home but not enough to change his plans, as he sent his servants to check the interior of the chateau for fire or any other indicators of a meteorite (meteor showers were prevalent in the area). As the Count waited to hear word back from the house, he snuck off into the courtyard of the midnight garden where he went to retrieve a boxed kit he kept in a bench for the nights he went out to seek the hustlers.

The Count was fortunate to come across the box, and in the nearby distance was Angelwings, naked, sprawled out on the ground, mildly disoriented.

The Count, though a tall heavy black man with a thick manicured goatee framing his supple lips, stood cautiously over the enormous being trying his hardest to reconcile its human-like features against his large spanning wings cropping out of his back and dull gray skin.

Oddly enough, not knowing whether the creature was a human in disguise or some kind of celestial being, the Count was nevertheless pleased with his universal looks. He sensed that the feelings were quite mutual, with a look of pure lust burning red in the creature's black eyes. Yet, the Count was unsure if he should indulge his perverse fantasies with Angelwings as he feared that Angelwings might cause harm to him if the being were to reject him or his advances.

"Count," the Count heard a voice called from the front of the manor. "Count!"

The Count, a usually calm and calculated man, suddenly became flustered, not knowing if moving the creature on his own might or might not be a wise move.

"There you are Count." Dukor, a stout oatmeal-colored youthful-looking manservant appeared naked out of the chateau in a hurry toward his Count and the garden. "Morrow," the head house servant, "has been looking all over for you. The manor is clear. Your chariot awaits you.

"Damn, the chariot," the Count barked angrily at the only man he had ever truly trusted, knowing exactly what needed to be done in a secretive short period of time as the Count bent over to help the creature upright. "I need you to help me get this inside."

Dukor, absolutely stumped in figuring out what "it" was, obliged by helping the Count lead the docile being into a room off the stairwell before descending totaling into the dark unexplored dungeon. It was there that the Count and Dukor suspended the body of Angelwings in cuffs for both men to admire his flesh and strength.

"He's quite exotic yet traditionally good-looking." Dukor commented, with a fine mat of thick hair coving the front of his flat belly and spreading across his square chest.

"I agree ... that is why it will be your job to stay in here and get him prepared while I am gone."

"Gone where?" Dukor asked in an attempt to stop himself from getting the words out, knowing full well that he was in no position to question the count of the manor.

"That, my boy, is none of your concern where I'm heading off to." The Count offered offended.

At that late of hour, Dukor already knew that his beloved count was primed to go into the village and satisfy his sexual appetite.

An insatiable need that Dukor often felt he felt short of sating.

Dukor with his pork sword dangling long and soft between his leonine thighs was more than a domestic servant to the Count. His roles included trusted confidant and submissive sex slave, being used at any given whim, without refusal, to pacify any perverse act the Count felt the need to inflict on him.

"Too bad for you," Dukor offered to Angelwings after the Count retreated into the village. "After the Count has had his way with the man-whores that litter the back alleys, he will return refreshed and ready to reignite his fire at your expense."

Dukor spent several minutes studying Angelwings intensely, as a whole, as the being hung off the wall. But Dukor soon found that he had to stop short of drooling over the spitting cobra lazily nestled between his legs.

Without thinking, Dukor reached over for it, grabbing hold to it as if it as his own, slowly stroking it until it was hard and pointing straight forward.

"Feeling nice?" Dukor asked to the mounting backdrop of the elated whimpers coming from the captive.

Dukor descended onto his knees and onto the stone floor, holding the long heated dick to his puckered lips. He stuck out his tongue, coating and massaging the fat mushroom head with tender swabs of saliva, eventually swallowing the large monster whole. It would have been a feat for anybody, but Dukor had long learned the secret of relaxing his tongue and opening his throat to yield to the hefty dick.

Dukor was impressed.

Not only of himself, but at the beast that could hold out longer than the Count usually could, and that Angelwings dare tasted like the salty flesh of his Count.

Dukor began to suck even more furiously, closing his throat at certain places, hoping that Angelwings would will his way to orgasm — if a creature like him could.

At last, in the mist of Angelwings growling in pleasure, Dukor felt the usual swelling of an already swollen dick in his mouth. And just as it was about to erupt, Dukor pulled his lips off of him — a luxury that the Count never granted him — and watched the powerful jets of creamy white stuff fly where it may, as Dukor listened to Angelwings pant.

"Thought I was going to drink your seed?" Dukor rose to his feet and asked with one of the smuggest looks a dastardly servant could even give. "There is a saying that it is better to have had than lost than to never have had at all. Once, you had freedom out there. Then, to your dismay, the Count found you other there, and now all you will ever know is pure hell. And as a parting gift to an even great gift you lost, I just released you of your final act of sheer pleasure.

Dukor walked over to a nearby table equipped with several small drawers. It was there, out of one of them, he pulled out an abnormally huge lifelike, two-toned black flesh colored dildo with a large helmet head and a thick skin covering otherwise deep veins running along the shaft with two-oversized orbs trapped in the loose folds of a sac. And out the other drawer, Dukor pulled out a small jar of off-white cream.

"You like?" Dukor asked, taking the stuff from the jar and smearing it onto the faux penis. "I made it from hardened gelatin and colored it to perfection using the soil and flowers from the gardens. Of course, it took me many of tries with the hardened gelatin, the coloring, and the carving to produce such a specimen."

Dukor set it on the table and walked over to the other side of the room where he gauged a small freestanding table stand against the waist of Angelwings floundering in the distance, trying to break free of the strains that were keeping him suspended.

"I take it that you know what will come next, I see. Telling me that you've had something up that gray bung of yours before?"

Dukor went about his business, taking the small table and sliding it behind Angelwings who was kicking violently to no good use. He was too far off the wall with the table directly behind him to do anything. The best he could do was bump against it from time to time, hitting it to his hurt and annoyance rather than knock it over.

"You tired yourself out, I see." Dukor sated after Angelwings subsided in flailing his lower limbs.

Dukor went back over to the table with the drawers and pulled out another jar and a cloth, covering the cloth with the jar, and came behind Angelwings, moving the freestanding table over to the side, placing it over his nose and mouth.

Being that Angelwings appeared to be hanging like a bat sleeping upright, Dukor knew better. He knew from experience that the beast and his other sense were keen and wide awake, if not heightened by the sudden droopiness of his heavy eyes and the temporary paralysis of his strong limbs.

"My Count asked me to prepare you for him … and that is exactly what I plan on doing." Dukor said, standing behind the captive with the greased dildo.

Dukor teased Angelwings with the huge thing, sliding it up and down his crack and teasing at his entrance, letting Angelwings know that insertion was only a moment away. Dukor took one hand spreading open his butt cheeks to get an exact location of his ground zero, as he began to push the slimy thing into him. Angelwings was stubborn at first, as much as a sleeping hole could be, before Dukor unyieldingly rammed the dildo into him in one vicious thrust. In spite of the sedative, Angelwings jumped and yelped while Dukor slid the table underneath him to hold the dildo in place.

"If you think this is cruel and unusual, the Count has a true sense of hell to offer."

Dukor was right. The Count came home. he worked over his newly awakened conquest. He began moving Angelwings from his suspended state to the large slab table, placing his arms in retrains next to his body and bound his poor legs and feet to two separate planks connected to the table, like fingers to a hand. The Count initiated Angelwings into his world by covering the heavenly creature from head to toe in his post-nutt piss stored from the fourth hustler he had mastered that night. The Count used some of the acrid liquid and started to rub it around the recently unplugged, still-lubed hole

Despite the dildo, his hole snapped back into a tight puckered mystery. The more the Count was able to work his hole open, the more fingers he was able to thrust into him until he had his full hand inside of him, trusting and turning it with deep sobs of exhale coming from his winged captive creature.

It was on the brink of being uncontrollable sobs when the Count offered his forearm, causing sweat to roll off man and beast as Angelwings started to breath harder and deeper with each invading inch, squeezing harder and tighter than ever before. And as the Count took the harsh role as his bully, punching in and out of his insides, Angelwings began to find a reluctant pleasure in his searing pain causing a flurry of distaste and confusion when he came again.

... and that was just the beginning.

# # # # #

Many of seasons had come and gone. The Count had meticulously molded Angelwings to subject to his perverse whims. And whenever the Count felt that Angelwings had become too comfortable in conforming to his deepest darkest desires, the Count found a way to muster many more deviant impulses.

The Count was in the throes of passion one night with Angelwings, ramming his large schlong between the whimpering lips of Angelwings' quivering butthole when their entire world was shattered. Dukor had come in, interrupting their tryst to announce that the region was under siege by the neighboring countrymen. Up until then, it had been many days since Dukor had laid eyes on Angelwings, who he had graciously befriend over the months, frequently bathing him and taking care of his own otherwise deprived carnal desires whenever the Count left the chateau for any substantial amount of time.

The Count did not act too kindly to this news. Not of the pending war of the land, but to a mere manservant interrupting him in his rhythm and stride. The Count scolded Dukor, pulling out of Angelwings to strike the manservant with his hand over and over again. It wasn't uncommon for the Count to strike

Dukor, in private or in public, but this time the Count was relentless in knocking Dukor down onto his knees.

"You stupid, stupid, degenerate!" The Count gnarled after one of his blows caused Dukor's nose to bleed. "Come here little fuck! This will teach you to interfere with your Count."

The Count then grabbed Dukor by the strains of his short cropped hair and forced his mouth onto his groin.

It was practically unbearable to hear the demonic gurgling filling the room, with Dukor gagging and choking on it, trying to breath for his dear life. For a short while after, it looked as if Dukor stopped breathing as the Count held him by the throat with both hands, offering only the sound of his dick working over his wet open mouth, fucking it until he came — finally letting go of his chokehold.

As all this was going on, Angelwings' was bound to the slab, trying to free his limbs. Though there was nothing new or peculiar about the way the Count acted, especially toward him, Angelwings was disgusted by the way it looked when he was inflicting it on someone else for the very first time. Angelwings was enraged, attempting to break out of his restraints and help his friend. And then something wonderful happened.

Instead of breaking through the restraints like he wanted, Angelwings had melted through them, still leaving the cuffs intact. He soon realized this, and got up. Rather than walking over to him, though, like he thought he could, he flew over to the Count, who had already begun his second round of assaults on Dukor.

The scuffle was brief. It appeared at first that Angelwings was overpowering the man that had violated him for many months, but was quickly subdued by his larger-than-life wings fluttering about in a relatively small room. The Count grabbed Angelwings by the cusp of his pinion and manhandled him into the stone wall. In an even quicker effort, the Count grabbed a nearby sedative and threw it into Angelwings' face, soon weakening the raging beast.

The Count, though private about his dealings in that particular room and in the nearby dungeon, called for his guardsmen to haul the sleeping creature back out into the midnight garden.

It was out there that The Great Count of Morego stood over his forlorn body, still a great admirer of his stocky muscularity that made up the winged beast he called Angelwings, with a silver sword in his hand. He couldn't live with an unruly subject. Yet, he couldn't dispose of him in the chateau because blood and death was an unbearable stench to get rid of, something of an unfortunate experience the Count knew all too well.

The Count had his sword in hand ready to dole out death when Dukor grew a conscious and interfered once more. The Count paused on his behalf, as it appeared that he was contemplating his words, before Dukor felt the wrath of the Count swinging his sword at him. He was startled that his beloved count would turn on him so easily after so many years together. Even more damning was that the guards that Dukor had befriended over the years stood by idly, like he was some sort of sworn enemy of the Count. Dukor understood that they were men of the Count, hired to defend him at all cost, but he had shared so much of his adult life with them, and the bonds that came with growing together, he thought it meant something. Especially since with him and the beast out of the way, it meant that the Count was more likely to pursue the hunky men to quench his sexual thirst.

Dukor was backed into a corner against the chateau with the guardsmen surrounding him and the Count swinging his blade at him. The Count was about to plunge for the merciless kill when Dukor saw the man he saw as his master and torturer eyes bulge out his socket, with death at his back. For it was. Angelwings had grabbed a dagger from an unbeknownst guard and stabbed the Count with it, causing him to stagger wildly before ultimately falling to the ground.

And before the guards could intervene, Angelwings grabbed Dukor and flew off toward the moon and landed in a densely wooded area on the other side of the rolling hills.

"You killed him." Dukor said trembling the moment he had both feet on the ground.

Angelwings looked down upon Dukor, fully taking in the significance in their respective heights. So while it didn't easily permit, Angelwings leaned forward and kissed Dukor. And in spite of the vertical awkwardness the kiss felt natural on both parts, with each hungry mouth wanting more of the other. Angelwings then took Dukor by his solid middle and straddled him to his waist, slowly entering into his seasoned abyss. Dukor began to groan instantly the more his moistened hole began to become more impaled on the dick, twisting roughly for his pleasure. Angelwings met his mouth, withdrawing entirely and the pushing back in. The more Dukor panted and moaned, the more Angelwings pumped into him with even greater fervor. Eventually, the sensation became too much, leaving Angelwings to buy his long-yearning seeds into the now former manservant.

Angelwings was heavily spent, waiting for the swelling inside of Dukor to subside before pulling out and helping him to the ground.

# # # # #

As Angelwings awoke groggily and heavily spent on the ground from their tryst, his eyes awoke to Dukor standing over him with a sword.

"You were sweet, but I must avenge my lover."

The Authors

A.J. DAMIAN likes writing steamy stories about hot guys. She is a part-time writer, and so far she has written three stories for STARbooks Press. Contact: armanddesigns@gmail.com.

DERRICK DELLA GIORGIA was born in Italy and currently lives between Manhattan and Rome. His work has been published in several anthologies and literary magazines. Visit him at www.derrickdellagiorgia.com.

DIESEL KING is the proud poppa of his first short story collection.

DONALD WEBB resides in Victoria, BC. He has been published in numerous gay magazines and anthologies. He is currently seeking an agent/publisher for a completed mystery novel.

Residing on English Bay in Vancouver, Canada, JAY STARRE has pumped out steamy gay fiction for dozens of anthologies and has written two gay erotic novels. Contact Jay Starre on Facebook.

LANDON DIXON's writing credits include the magazines and anthologies.

LOGAN ZACHARY (loganzachary2002@yahoo.com) is an author of mysteries, short stories, and over forty erotica stories, living in Minneapolis with his partner, Paul, and his dog, Ripley, who runs the house. www.loganzacharydicklit.com.

R. W. CLINGER writes for STARbooks Press and can be reached at kenitorico@verizon.net.

THOBY MUSGRAVE is a novice writer living in Sydney, Australia. thobymusgrave@yahoo.com.

The Editor

MARCUS ANTHONY is a writer and editor, residing in Newport News, Virginia. He has been known to wear a little leather now and again.

earing any underwear. "Excuse me," I said, having a hard time lo

linded by that bulge in his crotch, "but don't I know you?" "May

ind of t̶ bou

with Ray God

t loser? in?"

aid. "Lik s str

ce body e on

lly, he l I e

ı up to t any

istaking e sa

ı, I coul ery

ood raci ne s

ing with e in

we go o beh

vill see u in

ed?" he vent

privacy. gra

-hard. I

ck, traci t, so

ed it, ha

with my bin

bbing, I n co

he sound of unzipping filled the small space. I don't know who's

, but before I knew it, I had his rod in my hand, and mine was in

nt to do?" he asked, his tone challenging. I knew exactly, and sar